IT'S NOT WHAT YOU THINK

Clare Mackintosh is a former police officer and a bestselling crime author. Her books have sold more than three million copies, been optioned for television and translated into forty languages. She appears regularly at literary festivals and bookshop events across the UK and beyond.

Also by Clare Mackintosh

Fiction
I Let You Go
I See You
Let Me Lie
After the End
Hostage
The Last Party
A Game of Lies
Other People's Houses

Non-Fiction
A Cotswold Family Life
I Promise It Won't Always Hurt Like This

CLARE MACKINTOSH

IT'S NOT WHAT YOU THINK

HarperCollins*Publishers*

HarperCollins*Publishers* Ltd
1 London Bridge Street,
London SE1 9GF

www.harpercollins.co.uk

HarperCollins*Publishers*
Macken House, 39/40 Mayor Street Upper
Dublin 1, D01 C9W8, Ireland

First published by HarperCollins*Publishers* Ltd 2026
1

Copyright © Clare Mackintosh 2026

Clare Mackintosh asserts the moral right to be identified as the author of this work.

A catalogue record for this book is available from the British Library.

ISBN: 978-0-00-874258-4 (HB)
ISBN: 978-0-00-874259-1 (TPB)

This novel is entirely a work of fiction. The names, characters and incidents portrayed in it are the work of the author's imagination. Any resemblance to actual persons, living or dead, events or localities is entirely coincidental.

Set in Sabon LT Std by HarperCollins*Publishers* India

Printed and bound in the UK using 100% Renewable Electricity at CPI Group (UK) Ltd

All rights reserved. No part of this publication may be reproduced, stored in a retrieval system, or transmitted, in any form or by any means, electronic, mechanical, photocopying, recording or otherwise, without the prior written permission of the publishers.

Without limiting the exclusive rights of any author, contributor or the publisher of this publication, any unauthorised use of this publication to train generative artificial intelligence (AI) technologies is expressly prohibited. HarperCollins also exercise their rights under Article 4(3) of the Digital Single Market Directive 2019/790 and expressly reserve this publication from the text and data mining exception.

For everyone who tells me that
I Let You Go is your favourite book.
This one's for you.

PART ONE
NADEEKA

CHAPTER 1

The lights change from green to amber. Nadeeka hesitates for a heartbeat before pressing her foot flat against the accelerator. It's a pedestrian crossing but the pavement is empty, and ordinarily she would mutter to herself about people who press the button then don't wait for the green man, but she doesn't have the time, doesn't have the head-space to think about anything other than where she's going and what she will find when she gets there.

Ahead of her, a car edges through the lights at the precise second they switch to red, and now it's too late for her to stop even if she wanted to. She grips the steering wheel as though it's a life ring and she's drowning, then she flies through the crossing, ten miles over the speed limit.

Three seconds later there's a burst of siren; a flash of blue in her rear-view mirror.

'No, no, no, no!' Nadeeka is horrified by the prospect of being pulled over, but more so by the delay this will cause. She has to get home. It's been a whole hour since she spoke to Jamie; fifteen minutes since she finally put her finger on what had been wrong with their conversation; ten since she grabbed her car keys and left the office. Anything could have happened in that time.

The police car overtakes her and for a moment she entertains the idea that it has simply been trying to pass her, but then it slows down, forcing her to slow too, and she gives in to the inevitable and pulls over.

'Do you know why we've stopped you?' The policeman is tall and broad, his upper body filling her open window as he rests one forearm on the roof of her car. His breath mists in the cold December air. Nadeeka doesn't want to feel intimidated, but she finds herself leaning to the left, making space in front of his too-close face. Even though the policeman is in uniform – even though an actual police car is in front of her, even though his female colleague is standing next to it – Nadeeka has read too many news articles to trust what she sees.

'Could I see some ID, please?' She feels foolish asking. Rude, even. But that's what kills women, isn't it? Politeness.

The policeman gives an amused smile, but he pulls a lanyard out from beneath his ballistic vest and dangles the laminated card in front of her. She reads his name – Police Constable Dan Harrington – and nods, although she has no idea what a real police ID card looks like. Nadeeka has been lucky; in almost forty years, she has never needed the police.

PC Harrington tucks away his badge. 'Well, do you?'

It takes Nadeeka a moment to remember the question; another moment to decide what to say. Maybe PC Harrington saw her speeding but didn't see her run a red light. Is one offence worse than the other? She shakes her head mutely.

'You were doing forty in a thirty.'

'Was I? I'm so sorry.' Nadeeka glances at the clock, imagines what's happening right now at home. Her hands twitch on the steering wheel.

'And you drove through a pedestrian crossing when the light was red.'

PRAISE FOR *IT'S NOT WHAT YOU THINK*

'A standalone thriller right up there with the iconic *I Let You Go*. It's madly twisty and super pacy and so, so clever'
Lisa Jewell

'I have read a million thrillers, and written quite a few, and I always see the twists coming – but not this time. Clare Mackintosh is a solid-gold storyteller at the top of her game'
Lee Child

'Engrossing, with Mackintosh's trademark unexpected twists – a nail-biter of a thriller!'
Shari Lapena

'What a story! An extraordinarily clever plot, this was one of my favourite books of the year. An absolute triumph'
Andrea Mara

'With its sophisticated, twisting storytelling and bold, thought-provoking themes, *It's Not What You Think* is exactly what I thought it would be: another sure-fire hit for Clare Mackintosh!'
Louise Candlish

'Clare is a masterful storyteller who's at the top of her game and who loves to shift the narrative to keep us hungry for more. I was captivated – the definition of a one-sitting read'
John Marrs

'I'm a huge fan of Clare Mackintosh and right now she's top of her game. With her trademark twists, skilful plotting and her natural instinct for storytelling, Clare will always be one of my go-to reads'
Heidi Perks

'A stylish, clever and original thriller. Packed with twists, this book is so addictive it should come with a warning'
Alice Feeney

'Wow. WOW. I tore through Clare's book and hereby declare it to be her best thriller yet . . . I literally couldn't stop reading, I was so gripped'
Jill Mansell

'Packed with the author's trademark twists, an immensely readable thriller for these troubled times. I flew through it'
Sarah Hilary

It's Not What You Think

Fuck, fuck, fuck.

'In a hurry, are you?'

'Yes,' Nadeeka says. 'But that's no excuse, I realize that.' She knows instinctively that she's expected to be meek. Partly because she is in the wrong, but also because she is a woman and he is a man, and because her skin is brown and his is white.

'What's your name?'

'Nadeeka Prasanna.'

In front of the car, the female police officer is reciting Nadeeka's licence plate into her radio, frowning in a way that makes Nadeeka nervous.

'Address?'

She gives it to him, complete with her postcode.

'And the car's registered there?'

She nods. A trickle of sweat makes its way down her spine. This is absurd. Nadeeka owns her car outright, it has tax and MOT and there's no contraband in the boot, yet she feels as though she's been caught with stolen goods. PC Harrington is waiting – for someone on the other end of the radio to confirm her address, Nadeeka assumes – and when he eventually gives a curt nod, she lets out her relief in a long breath.

'Where were you off to in such a rush, then?'

Nadeeka notes the past tense and feels a clutch of fear that she might not be allowed to continue on her way. 'To my house,' she says. 'I—' And then her voice breaks, tears springing to her eyes.

'Are you okay?' It's the first time the female officer has spoken. She comes towards the car window and PC Harrington moves to one side, so now they are both looking in at her, an exhibit in a car-shaped cage.

'Not really. My partner—' She breaks off again, unable to finish.

'Is there a problem at home?' the female officer says, and Nadeeka knows what sort of problem she means, and so she shakes her head. Jamie isn't like that, thank God.

'I'm probably just overthinking it,' Nadeeka says, 'because of what's happened in the past. But I needed to see it for myself, to prove that—'

'See *what* for yourself?' PC Harrington has less patience than his female colleague.

Nadeeka bites the inside of her cheek. Beneath her cream blouse and navy blazer, her armpits are clammy.

'Alternatively,' PC Harrington says, 'we can just write you a ticket and—'

'See that my partner isn't cheating on me.' It comes out in a rush, the first time she's acknowledged it head-on.

There's a pause.

'Do you think he is?' The policewoman sounds genuinely interested. Close up, she doesn't look as intimidating, her downturned mouth the result of genetics or age, rather than grumpiness.

Tears spill over Nadeeka's lower lashes. 'I don't know.'

Her heart aches. She's been here before, and she knows it has made her untrusting. Jamie has the patience of a saint to put up with her questions and suspicions. 'I'm not your ex-husband,' he'd said gently, when he had found her looking through the jacket he'd left hanging in the hall. 'I would never, ever cheat on you.' He had turned out his own pockets for her then, in spite of her protestations, and insisted she have the passcode for his phone. 'I've got nothing to hide,' he had said. 'You can look any time you want.'

Jamie's expression had been open, and Nadeeka had detected no resentment in his voice. She'd found it impossible not to draw comparisons with Scott, who had once punched a hole through the wall when he'd found her looking at his phone. 'I was just looking up the menu for the Chinese takeaway,' Nadeeka had tried to explain. 'My phone's upstairs.' Scott hadn't listened, and the hole had stayed until earlier this year, when Jamie had quietly filled it in and repainted the wall.

It's Not What You Think

'My daughters' dad was seeing other women the whole time we were married,' Nadeeka tells the police officers now. 'He listed all his affairs when he walked out, because, apparently, hurting me once wasn't enough.'

'What a shit,' the policewoman says. 'I had one of those once. He got T-boned by a ten-tonne artic, and it couldn't have happened to a nicer guy, to be honest.' Her blonde hair is escaping the confines of its scrunchie. 'Your bloke, though: I'm sure it's not what you think. Has he ever given you any reason to suspect he's seeing someone else?'

PC Harrington looks pointedly at his watch.

Nadeeka shakes her head and then shrugs helplessly. She's come to realize her instincts aren't reliable. 'I called Jamie from work this morning,' she explains. 'I heard a woman's voice and him telling her he'd just be a minute, then he told me it was the HR director who had popped into his office.'

'Maybe it was,' the policewoman says. 'It sounds to me as though you're carrying a lot of emotional baggage from your previous relationship which might be colouring how you're viewing this one.'

'Are we therapists now?' PC Harrington says under his breath. He takes a small pad of printed tickets from a pocket on the side of his trousers and flips to a new page. He has slim fingers, with neatly filed nails.

'But when I put down the phone,' Nadeeka says, because now she can't stop, 'I couldn't shake the feeling that something was wrong. Then it hit me.'

'What?' The policewoman's eyes are round. PC Harrington balances his pad on Nadeeka's open window and begins filling out a form with small, careful block capitals.

'I heard a train in the background.' Nadeeka replays it now, in her head: the distinctive rumble that had seemed to be such a huge compromise when she and Scott had bought the house, but which now was simply background noise. 'But Jamie's office isn't anywhere near the train line,' she explains. 'Our house is. The train runs right past the end of the garden. Jamie was at home when I spoke to him, I'm sure of it.'

The policewoman's mouth drops open in vicarious outrage. 'The bastard!' She turns to PC Harrington. 'Put that away.'

'She ran a red light.'

'So would I, if my scumbag boyfriend lied to me.' She snatches the booklet from her colleague's grasp and nods to Nadeeka. 'Go on, love. Give him what for.'

Nadeeka doesn't want to give Jamie what for. She wants to be wrong. She wants to get home to an empty house. She wants to discover that the train line in the town she's lived in for twenty years does, in fact, pass close enough to Jamie's office for her to have heard it.

She sticks to the speed limit and doesn't run any more red lights, and precisely forty-five minutes after leaving work she pulls into the cul-de-sac where she and Jamie and her daughters live.

She frowns. There's a police car outside her house.

Nadeeka and Scott had been renting when Maya was born, but by the time Nish came along they had bought 10, Cedar Walk, a three-bedroomed semi with space in the garden for a trampoline and a veg patch. Technically, Scott still owns half. The financial agreement thrashed out in the divorce stipulates that the house can't be sold until both children are in secondary school, which gives Nadeeka another five years to save enough to buy Scott out. The money Jamie gives her each month to cover his share of the bills goes straight into what Nadeeka calls her 'freedom fund'.

She parks behind the police car. Bloody PC Harrington. Presumably he overruled his female colleague – because how dare a police officer show some compassion towards a woman in distress? – and broke some speed limits of his own to get here before her. Fine. Let him give her a bloody ticket for running a red light. She's got more important things to worry about.

But the uniformed officer standing by the car isn't PC Harrington, and now she sees there is blue and white tape across her open front door and her feet slow of their own accord, as though they already know what's behind it. Blood thrums in her ears, her pulse loud and insistent, and, as the police officer is telling her she can't go inside, Nadeeka shakes her head to clear the confusion. This is her house. Of course she can go inside. She lives here.

'You live here?' The officer blinks rapidly. He's young, Nadeeka realizes, barely into his twenties, with peach-fuzz cheeks and the remnants of teenage acne. She realizes, too, that he doesn't know how to deal with this turn of events, which suggests that whatever has brought the police to her door is very bad indeed.

She rips at the tape.

'Wait! You can't—'

But Nadeeka is already in the little hall where her daughters' coats will hang when their father drops them home, and where Jamie's coat is now, and even in the grip of her panic she feels the bittersweet stab of vindication. She was right. Jamie hadn't been at work when she phoned. But she can't process what this means, because there's a man in a suit standing in the doorway to the lounge, and beyond him . . . beyond him is—

'Oh, my God.' Her voice cracks.

The dating apps had been the hell Nadeeka's single friends had warned her about. A lawless wasteland of incels and perverts; of older men looking for younger models; of men with kids who wanted women 'without baggage'. Nadeeka had terrible dates with men who wouldn't take no for an answer, and she had dates where she thought she'd felt a spark, only to be ghosted the next day. For eighteen months she had diligently shaved her legs every other Saturday afternoon and curled some life into her hair, before pasting on a smile to go halves on another expensive dinner.

'Are you Ms Prasanna?' the man in the suit is saying. He's well-built, several inches taller than her, with grey flecks in his brown hair and the hint of a belly.

Nadeeka's eyes are fixed on the lounge carpet.

On her first date with Jamie, she'd laughed so hard she got a stitch. He had seemed quiet – even a little awkward – when she'd arrived at the bar, but, as the date had unfurled, so had Jamie. He had made up stories about the people around them. *See that woman with the notebook? She's a taxidermist, trying to figure out the best way to stuff a canary. That couple? He's just told her he's having an affair with their tennis coach, but she's not sad about it because – plot twist – she is, too.* He had shared these absurdities deadpan, and Nadeeka had noticed how he'd watched her to see how they landed, sensitive to whether she was having as good a time as he was. She had noticed, too, the little things. The way he'd asked the barman how his day had been, and actually listened to the answer. The way he'd moved their wine glasses to make it easier for the waitress to set down the many dishes of tapas they'd ordered. The way he hadn't once looked at his phone.

Afterwards, Jamie had walked her home and kissed her goodbye, and she had almost broken her no-sex-on-a-first-date rule. It hadn't only been the spark when their lips had touched, but the warmth spreading through her as he held her, new and yet wholly familiar. Like coming home. Nadeeka had braced herself for disappointment – Jamie had been too good to be true – but when she woke up the next day he'd already messaged her. *Is it uncool to ask if we can do that again soon?*

*

It's Not What You Think

'Jamie?' she whispers now.

'You're James Golding's partner?' The man in the suit takes a step towards her.

'Jamie . . .' she says, and this time it's barely a moan, barely even a breath.

They had deleted the dating apps together – the twenty-first-century equivalent of declaring they were 'going steady'.

'We're so lucky,' Nadeeka had said, thinking of friends still on the dating merry-go-round.

'No, not lucky.' Jamie had opened her hand; traced a finger along her heart line. 'We were always meant to be together; it just took a while to find each other.'

'Ms Prasanna.' The man in the suit has wire-framed glasses and a thick moustache which covers his top lip. 'My name is Detective Inspector Burton. We were called to a disturbance and, when we arrived, we found your partner—'

'Is he . . .' She can't finish.

'I'm so sorry,' Detective Inspector Burton says.

She can't hear what he says next, but she doesn't need to, because the answer is on the silvery grey carpet, now flooded with crimson. The answer is in the eyes staring blindly towards her.

Jamie is dead.

CHAPTER 2

Nadeeka tries to speak, but the words won't come. This can't be possible. She's hallucinating. Having a nightmare. Jamie can't be – he can't be *dead*.

'I'm so sorry.' DI Burton puts a hand on her shoulder. 'You shouldn't be seeing this.' He's steering her towards the front door, gently but firmly, and Nadeeka twists around, because surely if she looks a second time she'll see an empty room, a spotless carpet?

But he's still there. Jamie. One arm flung against the wall, blood blurring the outline of his body so it's impossible to say where his sweater finishes and the carpet begins. A sob erupts from within her and her legs buckle. The detective inspector puts one arm around her, gripping both her elbows, marching her forward. Out of the house.

'There should have been someone on the cordon,' he says, as they step on to the drive. He looks meaningfully at the uniformed police officer.

'Sorry.' The lad flushes a deep red. 'Sir,' he adds hurriedly.

It's Not What You Think

There's a bench by the front door. Nadeeka put it there so she could watch the girls when they were playing on their scooters. Cedar Walk is a cul-de-sac, the residents mostly families or downsized retirees, but Nadeeka only knows the neighbours to nod to, and she likes to keep an eye on her daughters. You never know what could happen, even in a nice neighbourhood like this one. She half-sits, half-falls on to the hard wooden seat. The front of the house doesn't get the sun, and the bench is still frosted with cold. Damp seeps into her trousers.

DI Burton sits next to her, his body turned to face her. 'I'm so sorry, both for your loss and for how you learned of it – neither of those things should have happened. I know this is a terrible shock, but I need to ask you some questions. Is that okay?'

Nadeeka nods mutely.

'When did you last see your partner alive?'

'This morning.' Nadeeka takes a gulp of air. Her body isn't behaving normally; her breathing is ragged and lumpy, and there's a buzzing in her ears like a fly against a window. 'Before I left for work. But I just spoke to him. I called him, you see, then I came home because . . .' Nadeeka stops. She doesn't want to tell the detective she thought Jamie was with another woman. She doesn't want him to think badly of Jamie, not when Jamie . . . She blinks rapidly, trying to force away the sudden, violent image of his body. The outstretched arm, the blood-soaked sweater, the *smell*.

'Deep breaths, now,' DI Burton says. 'Nice and slow.'

Like rust, she thinks. Like dirty pennies. Like the butcher's shop when the cleaver hits the block. She's hyperventilating. The buzzing in her ears is so loud now it's all she can hear, and she feels a hand on her back, pushing her forward so her head is on her knees. The uniformed officer says, *She needs an ambulance*, but DI Burton says, *She'll be fine*, and he tells Nadeeka to breathe *in then out, in then out – that's right, you're doing great*, until eventually she's doing it on her own.

She straightens. Slowly, cautiously. 'I – I'm sorry. I suddenly felt faint.'

'You're in shock,' DI Burton says. 'This is a terrible thing to happen.'

'I heard someone in the background when I was on the phone to Jamie,' Nadeeka says, now that she's able to speak again. 'Someone was in the house. A woman.' She mustn't hold anything back, even if it makes the police think badly of Jamie. 'Whoever it was would have been the last person to see Jamie alive. They might have seen who—' Nadeeka breaks off. She feels suddenly stupid. The last person to see Jamie alive wasn't a witness, was she? She was a killer.

'The voice you heard was very likely the person who attacked your partner,' DI Burton says, confirming her thoughts. 'It's very important you tell us everything you can remember about that call.'

Nadeeka heard the voice of a murderer. A chill runs through her at the thought. She should have called Jamie back after he hung up on her, rather than driving home, trying to catch him out. Maybe if she'd rung back she'd have distracted his attacker, or—

'You said the voice was female. Are you certain of that?'

'Completely certain.'

'Any discernible accent?'

'I'm not sure.' Nadeeka feels panicky. Why hadn't she taken more notice? Identifying the woman she heard is critical, and Nadeeka has nothing useful to offer the police.

'Were there any other voices?'

'No. At least, I don't think so. I only heard the woman.' Only *wanted* to hear the woman, Nadeeka thinks, remembering how quickly her mind jumped to conclusions. She wonders now if there *had* been a second voice; if the woman had been talking to someone other than Jamie. She presses her palms into the sockets of her eyes, trying to remember, but already it seems like

It's Not What You Think

a fever dream. How is it possible that two hours ago she was talking to Jamie, and now he's dead?

'What did the woman say?'

'I don't remember. I mean, I didn't hear. You know the way you're aware the television is on in the next room but you can't make out what programme's on?'

DI Burton nods.

A thought strikes Nadeeka. 'Who called the police?'

'Control room had an anonymous call in on the nines. We're working on tracing it. The caller gave your address, but unfortunately by the time we arrived . . .'

A movement from inside the house catches Nadeeka's eye. She jumps up, her heart thumping at twice the speed, because there was only Jamie in the house, and if he's moving, then he can't be dead . . .

'Forensics.' DI Burton must have seen the hope on Nadeeka's face, because he breaks the news gently. 'They'll be there for some time, I'm afraid.'

A broad-shouldered man with a shaved head comes out of the house with Jamie's laptop and mobile phone in clear plastic bags. He's wearing a paper suit with a hood, and a mask covering the lower half of his face. His feet are encased in blue plastic shoe coverings.

Nadeeka watches as Jamie's belongings are loaded into the back of a van. 'Why are they taking his computer?' At the back of her mind, something starts to grow. An ugly, painful *what if*. She searches DI Burton's face for answers. 'Do you think there's something on it? Something bad? Is that why someone killed him?' She sinks back down on to the bench.

'At this stage, we simply don't know.'

Nadeeka is reassured by the way DI Burton doesn't break eye contact. She's glad he's being straight with her, not pulling any punches; that he's honest about not having all the answers.

'But this is the only opportunity we have to secure all the

evidence,' he adds. 'If we were to realize further down the line that we needed Jamie's phone, or fingerprints from a specific part of the house, it would be too late. We have to do a thorough job now. For Jamie's sake.' DI Burton gives a brief nod to the forensics officer, who is on his way back into the house. 'We want to find the person who did this and bring them to justice.'

Tears spill over Nadeeka's eyelashes. 'I just don't understand who would do something like this.'

'Did Jamie have any enemies?'

'Enemies? He's a health and safety inspector, not a gangster.'

Nadeeka's teeth are chattering, and her words bump into each other. DI Burton takes off his jacket and drapes it around her shoulders. 'Come and sit in my car. I'll put the heating on.'

They walk towards a blue Vauxhall Corsa.

'Had Jamie fallen out with anyone recently?' There's a *beep* as the car unlocks. 'When police arrived on scene – ' DI Burton opens the passenger door for her ' – they found the front door ajar and your partner's body in the living room. The front door latches automatically, but there was no sign of forced entry, which suggests Jamie opened the door to his attacker. It's possible he knew them – maybe even expected their visit.'

Nadeeka shakes her head. 'Jamie's from Sheffield. He relocated to be with me six months ago and hasn't really got to know anyone locally yet. To be honest, he was struggling to settle. The only people he knew apart from his colleagues were ones I introduced him to, so . . .'

Her sentence tails away as it hits her. She looks around the quiet cul-de-sac in which she has always felt so safe.

If Jamie knew his killer, what if she knows them too?

CHAPTER 3

The efficient heater in DI Burton's car is drowning out the buzzing in Nadeeka's head. Her shoes crinkle a piece of paper; the sort left by mechanics after your car's been serviced. Nadeeka's own car is a Petri dish of reusable shopping bags and hair bands; snack wrappers discarded between school pick-up and gymnastics. Craft projects carried between class and home shed glitter and flakes of paint on the back seats.

DI Burton's car is spotless. There is nothing inside, not even an empty water bottle or a packet of chewing gum. He doesn't have children, Nadeeka thinks, before she remembers that he is a police officer, and so this is a police car, and the reason she's in a police car is because her boyfriend is . . .

She screws up her face, trying to block out the image of Jamie lying in a pool of blood. 'Was he stabbed?' she says, and it comes out abrupt, and too loud for the distance between them.

DI Burton isn't thrown. 'There will need to be a post-mortem to establish the precise cause of death, but yes, he was stabbed.'

Nadeeka takes a sharp inward breath but then it's trapped,

pressure in her chest building along with the buzzing in her head. She forces it out and it escapes with a sob.

'I'm so sorry,' DI Burton says again. The spine on his black notebook cracks when he opens it. It will fill up with other people's tragedies, Nadeeka thinks, but Jamie's death will always be on the first page. She imagines how the notebook will end up, scuffed and bulging with words, filed in a cabinet with dozens of others.

'How long had you been in a relationship with Jamie Golding?'

'Since February.' Nadeeka does the maths for him. 'Ten months. I know what you're thinking.'

'No judgement here.'

'My ex said it was too fast. But when you know, you know.' It's what Jamie always used to say, and Nadeeka's voice cracks on the last word. She can't tear her eyes away from her house, from the paper-suited officer carrying exhibits to his van. Two grave-faced men in black suits are walking towards the house, and the uniformed officer with the peach-fuzz cheeks lifts the blue and white tape as the men duck under it. More detectives, Nadeeka supposes. She pictures them swarming over her house, picking up her things, and she can't imagine how it will ever feel like home again.

'We'll give you a receipt for everything we need to take.' DI Burton follows her gaze. 'You'll get it all back.'

'I don't care,' she says dully.

'So you met in February,' DI Burton prompts.

'Right. Jamie was at a conference locally, and we matched.'

'Matched?'

'On a dating app.'

'I see.' DI Burton's phone is vibrating. He cancels the call without looking at it. 'And he moved in with you . . .'

'At the start of June.' Across the street, the man at No. 17 is winding Christmas lights around the tree in his front garden, and Nadeeka wonders if he's doing it simply so he can gawp at her house. 'Jamie was still in Sheffield when we met. It was a 150-mile round trip, and with me having the girls it was really hard. Jamie always came here, to save me the drive, but then in the middle of April he was made redundant.'

'He was a health and safety inspector, you said?'

'Yes, that's right. A job came up in a construction company on the edge of town about two weeks afterwards. It seemed like fate, you know?'

Nadeeka can still hear the trepidation in Jamie's voice when he'd told her. Trying but failing to be casual; the unspoken suggestion like a baton in an outstretched hand. *Their offices are about twenty minutes from you. I could get there by bus.* Jamie didn't have a car.

Nadeeka had taken the baton and run with it. *You could move in with me and the girls.*

Is it too soon?

I don't know. Is it?

It was – of course it was – but it didn't *feel* too soon. They missed each other so much during the week. They'd taken to video-calling each evening while they cooked tea, and, when Nadeeka had gone to answer the front door one time, she had come back to find Jamie testing Maya on her times tables. Nadeeka had hovered in the doorway for a minute, revelling in the easy relationship Jamie already had with her elder daughter.

Jamie had applied for the job. He didn't have to take it, they reasoned, but he should at least try for it.

He got it. And Nadeeka had sat down with the girls and said, 'You know how Jamie stays at weekends? How would you feel if he stayed in the week, too?'

There had been lots of questions.

'Will we have pizza every night?' Nish had said, with great excitement. Jamie always ordered pizza on Fridays.

Nadeeka had laughed. 'Not every night, no.'

Maya had been quieter. 'Are we supposed to call him Dad?'

'Definitely not. You have a dad already. Jamie is just Jamie.'

Maya had nodded slowly, absorbing the answer.

'And look, if you don't want him living here, that's totally fine. This is your house as well as mine.'

'No, I think it's okay,' Maya said. 'I like him.'

'Me too,' Nish said.

Nadeeka had grinned. 'Me three.'

A month later, Jamie had arrived with his clothes stuffed into laundry bags, like a student returning home at the end of term.

'I did have a suitcase,' he said, 'but the zip broke.'

They had stood on the drive, Nadeeka feeling suddenly awkward. 'Come in,' she said, and then screwed up her face. 'I don't need to say that – it's your home too now. I don't want you to feel like a guest.'

'Hey.' Jamie had put his hands either side of her face. 'Breathe. It's going to be fine. Better than fine.'

'Better than fine,' Nadeeka had echoed. She was worried about Maya and Nish, who had spent the morning closeted in Maya's room, refusing to let Nadeeka come in. Were they having second thoughts? But as Nadeeka and Jamie had turned to go inside, both laden with laundry bags, Maya and Nish had appeared at the door holding a banner. Maya's signature bubble letters, enthusiastically filled in with felt-tip pen, spelled out *Welcome home Jamie!*

Jamie had been too overwhelmed to speak. He had dropped his laundry bags and wrapped Maya and Nish in a bear hug, careful not to crush the banner.

'Did you bring pizza?' Nish had said, and they'd all laughed.

'How were things between you?' DI Burton says. 'In general, I mean? Did you have a good relationship?' Another plastic exhibit bag is leaving her house to be placed in the van, and Nadeeka wonders if the contents arrived in a laundry bag, six short months ago.

It's Not What You Think

'The best.' Nadeeka answers so quickly it sounds defensive, and she tempers it with something more truthful. 'We had a few . . . teething troubles, I suppose you'd call them.'

'Such as?'

'Jamie found the relocation hard. He had good friends in Sheffield; he played cricket there in the summer; he'd been at his company for a long time . . . Here, he only knew me.' The windows of the police car are steaming up and Nadeeka can't see her house properly, only misty shapes as people come and go through the open front door. 'How long will forensics take?'

'Quite a while, I'm afraid. Do you have somewhere you could stay tonight?'

A part of Nadeeka is relieved she will have to go somewhere else. She doesn't want to go back, doesn't know if she'll ever be able to walk into her living room without seeing Jamie lying there. 'I'll call my ex-mother-in-law. She won't mind, and the girls love staying there.'

'How long have you been divorced?'

'Three years. Scott has the girls every other weekend, and sometimes after school. If it suits him,' she adds, under her breath.

'Sounds like you get on better with your ex's mother-in-law than your ex,' DI Burton says.

'*She* didn't cheat on me.'

'I see. And how did your ex – ' DI Burton checks his notebook ' – Scott, was it?'

'Scott Hadley.'

'Thank you. How did Scott get on with Jamie?'

Nadeeka pulls her coat sleeve over her hand and wipes the condensation from the window. 'They didn't spend any time together,' she says, 'so they didn't really need to get on.'

The man at No. 17 has laid out an inflatable Santa on the lawn and is slowly pumping air into it. Nadeeka and Jamie had planned to get a tree this weekend, to decorate with the girls.

They have already made the cake, Nadeeka showing Jamie how she adds *puhul dosi* and *chow chow*; how the cinnamon and cardamom gives the fruit mixture an earthy aroma she remembers so vividly from her childhood.

DI Burton seems satisfied with Nadeeka's answer, even though it didn't really answer his question at all. Scott and Jamie hadn't spent time together because both men had made their feelings about the other absolutely clear from the outset. Putting them together would have been akin to pulling the pin on a grenade and dropping it into a box of fireworks, and so Nadeeka had worked hard to ensure the two men had as little contact with each other as possible. Of course, that hadn't stopped them sharing their respective opinions with Nadeeka. *You're far too good to have been with a cheating bastard like him*, Jamie would tell her, and his eyes would darken, as though it physically pained him to think of Nadeeka treated badly. Scott had pulled even fewer punches. *Who the fuck does the bloke think he is? Muscling his way into my girls' home? I'm telling you, Nads, if he puts a foot out of line I'll fucking kill him.*

Nadeeka watches the blurry shapes move inside her house.

How did Scott get on with Jamie?

He absolutely hated him.

CHAPTER 4

'I'll need to take a full statement from you,' DI Burton says, 'but for now, maybe it's best if you go to your mother-in-law's—'

'Ex-mother-in-law.'

'*Ex*-mother-in-law's house. Try to get some rest. What's your mobile number?' He wakes up his phone and clears a backlog of notifications.

Nadeeka recites her number, and he taps it in. A second later, her own phone rings.

'Now you have mine,' DI Burton says. 'Call me any time. As often as you need. I'll be what we call your family liaison officer. A single point of contact so you don't have to deal with lots of different people. Okay?'

Nadeeka nods, even though she's far from okay.

'Would you like me to call anyone for you? Your mother—' DI Burton stops. 'Ex-mother-in-law?'

'It's fine.' There she goes again. *Fine. Totally fine. Nothing to see here. Only my partner murdered on my living room floor.* 'I'll call her now.'

Nadeeka is too hot now, claustrophobically so, and she opens the car door and spills into the frosty air as though she's bursting through the surface of a lake. She takes out her phone and stares for a second at the missed call from an unknown number, before remembering it was DI Burton who called her. She saves it, then brings up the number for her ex-mother-in-law, one of the few people Nadeeka knows who still favours a landline.

Only then there's more movement by the front door of Nadeeka's house, and, when she looks, her hand drops to her side and the phone clatters on to the pavement. The buzzing in her ears is a thrum, is a drumbeat, is a hundred-decibel drill. She sees the grave-faced men in the black suits emerge from the house, one backwards, and she knows before she sees it what they're carrying, but even so, when she does see it . . .

'Careful now.' DI Burton's with her in an instant, his firm grip back on her elbows, one shoulder behind her, keeping her upright.

The cry that erupts from Nadeeka's open mouth doesn't sound like her. Doesn't even sound human. She moans as though she's in physical pain, as though she's the one with a knife through her stomach, the one zipped into that black bag making its way from the house to the waiting van. Not a van, she realizes now. A *private ambulance*; the euphemism for a vehicle reserved for the dead, not the dying.

'Keep breathing,' DI Burton says. 'You're doing so well, you're being so brave.' He's talking to her as though she's a child.

'Where are they taking him?' It's hard to get the words out.

'To the mortuary. You'll have an opportunity to see him there, if you want to.'

Nadeeka nods vigorously, then shakes her head just as forcefully. If she sees Jamie's body, is that how she'll always remember him? She imagines him staring at her with glassy eyes. Or will they close his eyelids? Will they put make-up on him? A sweep of blusher so he looks as though he's simply asleep? She thinks of Jamie's face, his beautiful, handsome face, and a wave of

It's Not What You Think

despair crashes over her at the realization that she'll never see it again. The secret smile as he shared a private joke with her above the kids' heads; the glint in his eyes when she emerged from the bathroom and dropped her towel. How lucky she'd been to have had a second chance at love; how cruel to now have it stolen from her.

'You don't have to decide now.' DI Burton stoops and picks up her phone. 'It doesn't look as though the screen's cracked.' He hands it to her and in a fleeting but intense rush of anger Nadeeka almost hurls it back at him. What does it matter if the screen is cracked? What does anything matter any more?

The door to the black van slams shut. Nadeeka flinches. She and DI Burton watch in silence as the van reverses into next door's driveway, then pulls away, turning right out of Cedar Walk. Nadeeka's face is wet with tears. He's gone. Jamie's gone.

'Could you let me have any next-of-kin details?' DI Burton says, after a moment.

Nadeeka tries to focus. 'His parents live in Sheffield. I have an address – I was going to send them a Christmas card. I'll message you their details.'

'Thank you. It can wait until you're at your mother-in-law's,' DI Burton says.

Nadeeka doesn't bother correcting him.

Kath Hadley has always answered the phone as though she's about to be scammed, a note of suspicion in her no-nonsense voice. 'Hello?'

'It's me . . .' Nadeeka's voice wobbles.

'What's happened?'

Nadeeka hears a familiar sound in the background. A laugh, high-pitched and overexcited, pumped on sugar and attention. 'Oh! Are the girls there?'

'Scott dropped them off for a couple of hours while he went for a run. It's only a few weeks till his race.'

Nadeeka bites back her frustration. Heaven forbid the man should look after his own kids on one of the few days he actually has them. Scott, Nadeeka came to realize during their nine-year-marriage, is an excellent father when he wants to be, but he is fundamentally selfish and will always put his own needs first.

'You know I'm always happy to spend time with the girls,' Kath says.

'Actually, that's why I'm calling.' Nadeeka swallows. 'Could we stop the night with you?'

There's a pause. 'You too? Is everything okay?'

'I'll explain later.' In half an hour, Nadeeka will be in Kath's warm kitchen. Kath will cluck over Nadeeka the same way she clucks over the girls, and Nadeeka can cry as much as she wants. For now, she needs to keep it together. 'Can I come, though?'

'Of course you can.'

Kath will assume Nadeeka and Jamie have had a row. Right now, Kath will be wondering how she can say *I told you so* without saying *I told you so*, because Kath is forthright but not unpleasant, and although she thought Nadeeka had been rushing things with Jamie, she only wants good things for the mother of her grandchildren. It's unusual, Nadeeka knows, to still hang out with your mother-in-law once you're divorced, but, as a woman once married to a serial cheater herself, Kath takes a firm line on infidelity. *Bloody fool*, Kath said, when Nadeeka told her what Scott had done. *He'll realize one day that the grass isn't always greener in someone else's bed.*

Later, when Scott had come to the same conclusion himself, Kath had tried to persuade Nadeeka to take him back, but Nadeeka had been firm, and Kath had eventually given up. Scott is now living with a Spanish woman he met in the queue for a concert, although this hasn't stopped him occasionally drunk-texting Nadeeka with declarations of love she deletes without acknowledging them.

She calls him now. His mobile rings and rings, and, just as

It's Not What You Think

Nadeeka is preparing to leave a terse voicemail message, a familiar voice answers.

'Hello?'

'Kath?'

'Oh, it's you, love. Scott left his phone here – he'd forget his head if it wasn't screwed on.'

'Right. I'll see you in a bit, then.'

'Bye, love.'

Nadeeka hangs up. Something is tugging at the corner of her mind, but it slides away before she can grab hold of it.

'Is everything all right?' DI Burton says.

'Yes. We can stay at Scott's mum's tonight.'

'Would you like me to drop you off?'

'Thank you, but I'll be fine.' Nadeeka needs to be on her own.

She feels the weight of DI Burton's scrutiny as she takes a final glance back at her house. The peach-fuzz police officer has stepped away, and perhaps, Nadeeka thinks, if she avoids looking at the blue and white tape across the door she can convince herself that everything is the same as it was this morning. But it's no good: the image of Jamie lying in his own blood is seared into her brain.

Nothing is the same.

Nothing will ever be the same again.

CHAPTER 5

Kath's house smells of baking and fresh laundry. When Maya and Nish had been toddlers and Nadeeka would pick them up from Kath's house, she would sniff their clothes and get the heady scent of lilac and lavender.

'She's washed their clothes again,' Nadeeka said to Scott one time.

'So?'

'They were only with her for a couple of hours.' Nadeeka had felt judged. Did Kath think her granddaughters were grubby? Had Nadeeka not used the right washing powder?

Scott had shrugged. 'Maybe they got muddy.'

'Did the girls make a mess?' Nadeeka had asked Kath, the next time she picked them up.

'Oh, goodness, no, love, they've been good as gold.'

'Only, their clothes were clean on this morning.' Nadeeka had lost the battle to keep her tone light. 'But maybe you don't think I'm looking after them—'

'Oh, love!' Kath had clasped her hands either side of Nadeeka's face. 'You're a brilliant mum. I just like helping you out, and I enjoy taking care of them. I used to have three boys and a husband to keep me busy, and now it's just me.' She had moved away, busying herself at the sink. 'But if you'd rather I didn't . . .'

'No, it's lovely.' Nadeeka had felt like a bitch. '*You're* lovely. Thank you for looking after us all.' Her own parents had gone back to Sri Lanka to care for her dad's parents, and Nadeeka envied her friends whose mums were on hand to support them. She was lucky to have Kath nearby.

Now, Nadeeka watches as her former mother-in-law takes a load of washing from the tumble-dryer and starts folding it. 'Can I help?'

'You just sit quietly. You're terribly pale.'

It's only the start of December but Kath's house is Christmas-ready, with tinsel draped over the clock on the wall, and a wooden nativity scene on the kitchen windowsill. On the dresser behind Kath is a large snowman with a head on springs that nods as she moves about the kitchen.

Nadeeka's phone beeps and she looks at the screen, hoping she'll see Jamie's name there; that she'll discover it's all been a terrible mistake. But it's DI Burton, thanking her for the contact details for Jamie's parents. The parents Nadeeka hasn't even met. She'll see them for the first time at his funeral, she supposes, and the thought squeezes her chest tight, because a funeral makes all this seem real. Jamie in a coffin. Jamie being carried into church, being lowered into the ground. She lets out a sob.

'Oh, love.' Kath drops her washing and puts an arm around her former daughter-in-law. The vertical lines between her brows deepen.

'I was thinking about the funeral,' Nadeeka says in a small voice.

'When do you think it will be?'

'The detective inspector said we'll have to wait for the post-mortem.'

'Of course. They can tell all sorts from the angle and depth of the knife wound, you know.' Kath watches a lot of crime dramas. 'Is the DI your FLO? Family liaison officer,' she adds, seeing Nadeeka's blank expression.

'I suppose so. I can call him any time, he said. Day or night.'

'That's right.' Kath nods sagely. 'They're on duty 24/7, are FLOs. Even sleep in the family's house sometimes.'

Nadeeka wonders if DI Burton will offer to do that. The thought of taking the girls back to a murder scene is horrific, but what other choice does she have? They can't just walk away from their home. She pictures DI Burton making himself comfortable on the sofa, and tries to imagine if it would make her feel safer.

'He said the forensics team will be finished by tomorrow,' she says, feeling as though she's reading lines from a script. How is this her life now?

'They'll be using luminol, I expect. It detects even a tiny trace of—' Kath stops abruptly. 'Sorry, love, I was forgetting myself. You know you and the girls can stay here as long as you need to.'

'Thank you. I want to keep the girls in their routine as far as possible, otherwise they'll know something's wrong, but I'm so scared of going back there.' Nadeeka picks at the skin on her bottom lip. She drops her voice to a whisper. 'I'm scared they're going to come back, Kath.'

'Maybe Scott could move back in. Just till the police have caught the perps.'

'Oh, no, I don't think—'

Nadeeka breaks off mid-protestation as Maya runs into the kitchen, skidding to an excited stop in front of the table. 'Daddy's here! I just saw his car!' She looks at Nadeeka curiously. 'Have you been crying?'

'Only a tiny bit. I'm okay.' Nadeeka forces a smile to prove it and, satisfied, Maya dashes off again.

It's Not What You Think

They haven't told Maya and Nish that Jamie is dead. *There was an accident*, was all Nadeeka had said when she arrived at Kath's. *Jamie's at the hospital*. It wasn't a lie, but it wasn't the truth; but then how can you tell a nine-year-old and a six-year-old that their mother's boyfriend has been brutally murdered a few feet from the sofa on which they curl up to watch TV?

Nadeeka listens to the commotion in the hall as Maya and Nish greet their dad as though he's been gone for weeks instead of a couple of hours. They adore Scott, and Nadeeka had harboured hopes that, one day, the girls would love Jamie too. They had been starting to, she thought, although the process hadn't been helped by whatever Scott was saying or doing on his weekends with the girls. There was always a little more backchat for a few days after they came home; a little less enthusiasm for Jamie's suggestions. Jamie had found that hard, Nadeeka knew, although he had been stoic about it. *Just give her space*, he had said one time after Maya had shouted at him and stormed upstairs to her room. *My being here is a big change for her*. Soon afterwards, Maya had snuck back down to give Jamie a picture she'd drawn of him, before running back to her room, suddenly shy. *She needs to apologize*, Nadeeka had said, but Jamie was putting the drawing on the fridge. *This* is *an apology*, he'd said.

Tears prick the back of Nadeeka's eyes at the memory, and when Scott comes into the kitchen, Nish hanging off him and Maya chattering non-stop about her day, she's crying again.

'What's up with you?' Scott's wearing a pair of black Lycra leggings, an Under Armour hoodie zipped up over his running vest. 'Dickhead not the Mr Perfect you thought he was?'

Nadeeka lets the tears fall, her face slack and her eyes unseeing as she blinks at her ex-husband. Jamie was never Mr Perfect, but then Nadeeka never claimed to be Mrs Perfect either. And maybe she and Jamie wouldn't have been forever, but shouldn't they at least have been given the chance to find out?

She drops her head, not wanting the girls to see her tears, but

Kath's already on the case. 'Girls, I think I left my glasses in my bedroom. Would you see if you can find them?'

'I'll find them!'

'No, I will, I'm the best at hide-and-seek!'

Their socked feet pound up the stairs. The buzzing in Nadeeka's ears is back, making Kath's voice sound muffled, as though she's speaking through a pillow.

'The house was broken into,' she's telling Scott. 'Jamie was attacked with a knife and he died. Nadeeka and the girls are staying here until the crime scene investigators have finished gathering evidence.'

So concise, Nadeeka thinks. She wouldn't have known where to start. She can't seem to order her thoughts; everything is swirling around as though she's in a snow globe. Was Jamie's killer the woman he was having an affair with? *Was* he even having an affair? It's disorientating to think she may never have the answers.

The kitchen falls silent. Thumps and bangs come through the ceiling as Maya and Nish rampage through Kath's room.

'Fucking hell, Nads.' There's no banter in Scott's voice now. 'I'm so sorry. That's . . . I don't know what to say.'

'It's awful,' Kath says.

'I'm really sorry.' Scott pulls out a chair and sits opposite Nadeeka. 'I know how much you liked him.'

He's trying to sound sincere, Nadeeka knows, but there's an edge to his voice. Like Kath's unspoken *I warned you about moving so fast*, Scott is holding back on what he really thinks.

She gives a tight nod. Maybe Scott's glad Jamie's dead. Maybe he considers it karma for her throwing Scott out; for moving another man into what used to be their home. He unzips his hoodie and it falls open to reveal a bright orange singlet with a perfect crease across the chest. Nadeeka wonders whether the Spanish girlfriend does his ironing, or whether he still drops his laundry round to Kath's.

It's Not What You Think

'Good run?' she says.

He shrugs. Looks away. 'It was all right. I pushed out a 15k, so I'm happy with that.'

'Where did you go?'

'The nature reserve at Castledean. There's a trail there.'

And Nadeeka pins it down, that whisper of a thought she'd had when she'd called Scott's mobile and Kath had answered. Scott *always* takes his phone when he runs. He uses an app with a motivational coach who talks him through each session and shoots him verbal high fives every few minutes. Nadeeka had given it a go once, such was Scott's enthusiasm for it, but had found it so unbearable – *You go, girl! You've got this! Way to go!* – that she had switched back to her audiobook after barely a kilometre.

'How come you didn't take your phone?' she asks him now.

Scott shrugs. 'I guess I forgot it.'

'I thought you couldn't run without the motivational coach.'

'The race rules say no headphones, because the route crosses a couple of roads, so I figured I'd better practise without it.'

'So did you forget it, or did you decide not to take it?'

'What's with the interrogation?' He's speaking loudly now – defensively – and what had begun in Nadeeka as mild curiosity is now outright suspicion.

'Or did you actually go somewhere else?' she says. 'Somewhere you shouldn't have been?'

'Now, now . . .' Kath raises her eyebrows at Nadeeka. 'You've had a terrible shock, love, but that's no reason to—'

'It doesn't matter, Mum.' Scott shakes his head, letting out a short, sharp breath as he does. He looks Nadeeka in the eyes. 'You've had a shitter of a day, Nads, so I'm going to give you the benefit of the doubt and put all *this* – ' he circles the air around her ' – down to that.' He pushes back his chair, scraping it against the floor tiles. 'I'll see you tomorrow, Mum.'

He shouts a goodbye to Maya and Nish, who race down the

stairs to catch him before he leaves. Kath walks out to the car with them, but Nadeeka sits motionless at the kitchen table, her mind in overdrive.

So Scott forgot his phone. Or he decided to try running without it. Either excuse is plausible, she supposes. But who runs a fifteen-kilometre trail without breaking a sweat, and comes home with a spotless running vest still bearing knife-sharp folds?

A liar, she thinks. That's who.

CHAPTER 6

It's still dark when Nadeeka wakes. She's disorientated, groggy from fitful sleep, and her eyes are swollen and sore. Something feels different. It takes a second, and then . . .

Her eyes snap open. This isn't her bed.

Where is she? And why does she ache all over, as though she's been hit by a car?

She isn't in hospital, she can smell lavender washing powder on the sheets tangled around her, which means she must have stayed at Kath's last night.

And then it hits her. An avalanche of scenes that crush her so hard she has to fight for breath. Driving home from work; the police car outside her house; Jamie's outstretched arm. DI Burton leading her outside. Blood. So much blood. It plays like a movie, fast-forwarded to the point at which Kath pressed pause last night, telling the girls that Mummy wasn't feeling well and needed to go to bed. 'It's not even *our* bedtime yet!' Maya had crowed, and the pair of them had fallen about in hysterics. Nish had insisted on tucking Nadeeka into bed, playing Mummy and telling her to *sleep tight, mind the bed bugs don't bite*, and Nadeeka had held it together until Kath took away her granddaughters and gently closed the door, leaving Nadeeka alone with a grief that made her feel as though she was dying too.

She lies on her back now in Kath's spare room, her eyes wide open. Tears trace the contours of her ears and dampen her neck. She feels paralysed by everything that happened yesterday and everything that needs doing today, all the people she needs to speak to. Thoughts appear in the darkness, and she grabs at them and sticks them to her to-do list, only for them to float away a second later. She needs to register Jamie's death and speak to the undertaker; cancel his mobile phone contract and notify the DVLA. Jamie's boss needs to know, and is it enough that DI Burton has notified Jamie's family, or should Nadeeka call them? She doesn't know if she's capable of talking, but it feels wrong to text. And she needs to register his death. And tell the DVLA. And cancel Jamie's phone contract and . . . she's dizzy with the weight of it all.

She throws off the covers. It must be before seven; the heating hasn't kicked in, and there's a bite to the air. She reaches for the dressing gown Kath gave her last night and pushes her feet into fluffy slippers that swim on her narrow feet as she quietly makes her way downstairs.

Five-thirty.

Nadeeka feels better with the light on. More in control. She finds her phone and pins down her to-do list properly so it can't escape again. *Notify DVLA, cancel phone contract, funeral director, work, bank, credit card.* It feels less overwhelming now, less urgent. What does it matter when Vodafone find out that Jamie has died? And as she thinks it she finds herself tapping the *call* button, staring at the smiling photo on the screen as the call goes to voicemail.

Hi, this is Jamie Golding. I can't get to the phone right now, but leave a message and I'll get back to you as soon as I can.

It's Not What You Think

Nadeeka ends the call, bent double over the kitchen table, her chest heaving with silent sobs. She calls again.

Hi, this is Jamie . . .

She will never hear his voice again. Never again hear him whisper *Goodnight, my love* as she drifts off to sleep. Never again hear him talk about their plans for the future, about places they'll visit with Maya and Nish, and the weekend breaks they'll book for when the girls are with Scott.

Hi, this is Jamie . . .

Nadeeka brings up her to-do list and deletes *cancel phone contract*.

When Kath comes downstairs, she tells Nadeeka to go back to bed, that she'll sort the girls out. Nadeeka thanks her, but the school run is an island of normality in an ocean of unknowns, and she feels almost fiercely territorial over it. Over her daughters, too, because among the midnight whisperings that had kept her tossing and turning had been the repeated fear: *what if I lose them too?*

Kath looks a little put out, but she doesn't push the issue. 'Whatever you think, love. I'll make you all a nice breakfast before you go.'

While Kath grills bacon, Nadeeka phones work, informing her line manager in a taut, clipped voice that her partner has died unexpectedly, and she won't be in for a few days.

'Oh, my God, Nadeeka.' There's a moment's silence on the line, as though Helen doesn't know what to say. 'I'm so sorry.'

Now it's Nadeeka who doesn't know what to say. *Thanks? Yes, me too?*

'That was the guy we met a couple of weeks ago, wasn't it? He seemed so lovely.'

'He was,' Nadeeka says tightly. Jamie had surprised her as she left work, standing in reception with a small but beautiful bouquet of her favourite flowers.

'He was so nice to ask about how the prep was going for the fair.' The recruitment fair at Echelon Warehousing, where Nadeeka works, is this month; her inbox is overflowing with emails from college tutors asking about start times and minibus parking, and foreign-born workers wanting information about visas. 'I said to the others afterwards: he seemed genuinely interested, which is more than my husband is!' Helen stops abruptly. 'God, Nadeeka, I'm so sorry.'

'I have to go.'

'I can't imagine how you must be—'

Nadeeka ends the call before the kindness can undo her. This is how she will survive this, she decides: by pushing the pain deep down beneath her to-do list. *DVLA, credit card, funeral director*. It has already become a mantra.

'Quick sticks!' she says, as the girls tumble out of the car. 'We don't want to be late.'

'Will Jamie still be in hospital when we get back from school?' Maya's book bag bangs against her legs as she twirls her way along the pavement.

'I'm not sure.' Nadeeka's throat is tight. *DVLA, credit card, funeral director*, she thinks. She says hello to a throng of mothers by the school gate, but the smile they return is sad, and accompanied by tilted heads that tell Nadeeka she can't pretend everything is fine.

'We're so sorry,' one of the women says. Sara, is it? Or Charlotte? Nadeeka definitely knows her name, but, when she reaches for it, it doesn't come. She hugs the girls and shoos them into class.

' . . . Maeve in year three,' Sara or Charlotte is saying. 'Her grandpa lives opposite you. Such a terrible thing to happen.'

Nadeeka thinks of the man wrapping Christmas lights around the tree in his front garden. Watching the drama unfold. Reporting back. She thinks of the whisper network that masquerades as the PTA. 'Thank you,' she says automatically. 'Excuse me, I have to . . .'

The woman calls after her. 'If there's anything we can do!'

Bring him back, Nadeeka wants to say, and by the time she gets to her car she's crying again.

When she turns into Cedar Walk, she feels a rush of blood to her head and has to slow the car. There's no police car now, no blue and white tape, just DI Burton standing by her front door, his breath misting the air. He's wearing a thick black overcoat and brown leather gloves like the driving pair Nadeeka's father used to keep in his car.

'Ms Prasanna,' DI Burton says, as she gets out of the car.

'Nadeeka is fine.' Her feet feel heavy, as reluctant to step into the house as she is.

'Nadeeka. And please, call me Colin. How are you?' The DI's face is so full of concern that Nadeeka has to look away. 'Did you manage to get any sleep?'

'A little.' Nadeeka hesitates. 'This is going to sound weird, but could you not . . .' She lets out an awkward laugh that doesn't sound like hers. 'Would you mind not being nice to me? I mean, I don't want you to be horrible, but I'm just about holding it together, and if . . .' She tails off. She sounds unhinged.

'If people are too kind, it brings your emotions to the surface,' Colin says.

'Yes, exactly that.' And then Nadeeka has to blink fast and swallow hard, because empathy is a close cousin to kindness.

'We'll stick to the facts, then.' Colin takes out the key Nadeeka left with him yesterday, opens the front door, then hands it to her. 'You can have this back; we've got everything we need for now.' His gaze is level. 'Ready?'

Nadeeka gives a tight nod. There's a strong smell in the hallway. Not yesterday's metallic tang – so familiar and yet so terrifying – but a lemony scent so sharp it pricks at Nadeeka's eyes.

'The cleaners have only just finished,' Colin says. 'The forensic team uses some potent chemicals, and it wouldn't be safe to leave them lingering on surfaces, so the crime scene clean-up firm came in early this morning. We use them a lot; they'll have done a good job.'

They have. Nadeeka's house has a spring-clean feel that, if she's honest, it hasn't had for years. The skirting boards have been wiped clean, and the chrome door handles shine as the light catches them. And in the living room . . .

Nadeeka's breath catches. She steadies herself on the doorframe. The silver-grey carpet is spotless, with neat lines like a freshly mown lawn. The furniture isn't quite as it should be – the sofa has been pushed back against the wall, and the coffee table isn't straight – but otherwise it looks exactly the way it was when Nadeeka left for work yesterday morning. As though nothing had happened. The only legacy of Jamie's murder is the pain in her chest and the detective inspector standing beside her.

'Would you prefer it if we talked in the kitchen?' Colin says, after a moment's silence.

Nadeeka nods and leads the way. Maybe she'll move the furniture around later, make it look different. The spot where Jamie died is where Maya and Nish practise headstands against the wall, Nadeeka and Jamie on the sofa holding up imaginary scorecards.

Colin declines a coffee. He snaps open his notebook. 'Major crime analysts have traced the anonymous 999 call to a phone box. There's no CCTV in the immediate area, but we've put out an appeal for dashcam footage – it's adjacent to a busy road, so we're optimistic.' He makes a swift mark on his page, ticking off item one on his agenda. 'On that note, officers carried out house-to-house enquiries in this street yesterday and identified a number of properties with door cameras. All the footage has been seized and is being reviewed.'

Tick.

It's Not What You Think

Nadeeka listens mutely as Colin lists the extensive enquiries the police have already carried out, none of which gives her the answers to the question she has carried around since arriving home yesterday, which is, why would someone want to kill Jamie?

'We don't know the answer to that yet,' Colin says. 'The circumstances lead me to believe this was a very specific attack on Jamie, not an opportunist break-in. Establishing a potential motive would be a big step towards identifying his murderer – or murderers. Do you happen to know any of the passwords Jamie used?'

'I don't know his laptop password, but the PIN for his phone is 6490.' Nadeeka thinks of Jamie's insistence that she know it; his constant reassurance that he wasn't like Scott, that he'd never cheat on her.

'That's really helpful, thank you.'

'I thought he was having an affair.' Nadeeka blurts it out.

Colin's expression shows no reaction. 'The woman you heard?'

'Not only that.' Nadeeka shifts in her seat. She knows she needs to tell the police everything, but it feels wrong to talk about Jamie like this. *Speaking ill of the dead*, Kath would call it. 'Jamie's behaviour changed over the past month or so. He started staying late at work, and, when I asked what project he had on, he just said it was nothing exciting, or changed the subject. He always looked away when he said it – that's a sign of lying, isn't it?'

'So they say. Did you suspect Jamie of cheating on you with anyone in particular?'

'I don't have a clue.' Nadeeka sighs. 'I didn't even know if my instincts were right, or if I was just being paranoid because of what my ex did.'

'I ask because . . .' And now it's Colin who looks away, seemingly uncomfortable. 'One of your neighbours told us they'd seen a woman visiting the house. At least three times, maybe more. Always when you were at work.'

Nadeeka looks at the clock on the wall and watches the second hand glide silently past the jaunty orange numbers. She swallows. 'Did they say what she looked like?'

Colin flicks backwards through his notebook. 'Dark brown, almost black hair. Slim build. Between thirty and thirty-five.' He looks up. 'Does that sound like anyone you know?'

Nadeeka thinks of Scott's Spanish girlfriend. She shakes her head. 'It could be anyone.'

'It's a little vague, certainly. And it might be nothing. A delivery driver, perhaps.'

He's trying to make her feel better. Nadeeka changes the subject.

'I know we can't have a funeral until after the post-mortem, but do I need to speak to the undertakers anyway? And I suppose I need to register Jamie's death?' She takes out her phone. 'I wrote a list. I need to notify the DVLA and cancel Jamie's credit card, and in order to register his death I need the medical certificate, is that right? And I have to call his parents and let his work know, and . . .' She starts to cry.

'I can help with some of that,' Colin says. 'That's why I'm here with you and not in the incident room with the rest of the team. Jamie's death certificate won't be issued until after the inquest, but you'll be given an interim certificate, and I'll give you a link for a service called Tell Us Once, which will cover all the government agencies, like the DVLA, as well as HMRC and the passport office.'

'Oh! I didn't think of those two.' Nadeeka stares in dismay at her list. What else might she have forgotten?

'Death was certified by the force medical examiner,' Colin says, 'and it's that document you'll need in order to register the death. But if you'd like, I can do that for you?'

Nadeeka feels a rush of relief. 'Yes, please. I can't bring myself to . . . It's so *final*, I suppose.'

It's Not What You Think

'Leave it with me.' Colin makes a note. 'Is there anything else I can do?'

Bring him back.

Nadeeka shakes her head. 'You've been very kind.'

'Not too kind, I hope?'

She laughs, the sensation already alien to her after less than twenty-four hours. 'Thank you.'

'I'll call you later.'

The house is too quiet when he's gone. Nadeeka doesn't know what to do. Where to start. How to *be*. None of this seems real. How can Jamie be dead?

A sharp ringing slices through the silence and Nadeeka claps a hand over her mouth, stifling her cry of alarm. *It's just the doorbell, Nadeeka. Your own bloody doorbell.* She's halfway to the door when she thinks that maybe this is exactly what Jamie was doing this time yesterday. The last thing he *ever* did.

Her feet begin to slow. Jamie opened the door to someone who killed him.

Nadeeka doesn't move an inch. The door is painted white, with scuff marks where Nadeeka uses her foot to close it when she has her hands full of groceries. On the doorframe, pencil marks show how the girls have grown each year.

The doorbell rings again. And then Nadeeka hears the distinctive sound of a key sliding into a lock.

Her lock.

Nadeeka's pulse is racing, but her feet are rooted to the spot. *What do I do now?* She feels outside of her body, impotently observing herself quaking with fear in her own house. Where is her phone? She'll call DI Burton – no, she'll call 999. Or should she run upstairs and hide, and—

In the event, she does none of these things, because, in the split-second it has taken her to make a decision, the door has opened.

'Oh! Hello, love.' Kath is carrying a foil-wrapped pie dish. 'I thought you must be here, what with your car being outside, but when you didn't answer I thought maybe you'd gone for a walk, and I didn't want to leave this on the doorstep, not with so many cats about.'

As she talks, she makes her way to the kitchen, and Nadeeka presses her hand to her chest to calm her racing heart. 'You scared me,' she says, when she's regained some level of control. 'I thought . . .' She shakes her head. 'Stupid of me.'

'Oh, love.' Kath puts the dish in the fridge. 'Thirty minutes, gas mark four, or whatever that is in new money.' She moves to comfort Nadeeka. 'It's understandable you're scared. We were burgled once – long time ago, before we had Scott – and I couldn't sleep for a month. Kept hearing noises and thinking someone was in the house. We had to sell up in the end.'

Nadeeka thinks that this is perhaps not the reassuring story Kath thinks it is. She doesn't want to sell her daughters' home. She just wants to feel safe here again.

'Why don't you all stay with me for a few more days?' Kath suggests.

Nadeeka shakes her head. 'Thank you, but we'll have to come back here eventually, and the longer we leave it, the harder it will be.'

'Could the police put someone outside, maybe?'

'Maybe,' Nadeeka says, unconvinced. She might not watch as many crime dramas as Kath, but she's fairly certain police budgets don't stretch to personal protection. Last month at work someone had sealed shut the warehouse doors with industrial glue, and the police had closed the case within twenty-four hours. *A prank*, they'd called it. A prank that had caused a backlog of work costing thousands of pounds . . .

'Or like I said,' Kath tries again, 'I'm sure Scott would—'

'No, thank you,' Nadeeka says firmly. 'We'll be fine.'

Maybe if she says it often enough, she'll believe it.

It's Not What You Think

*

When Kath goes, she double-locks the front door, then checks the back door and all the windows. This is how they will live now, she thinks. Barricaded into their home, ready to fend off an unknown attacker. She shivers. She thinks of all the times she's longed for peace and quiet; now she can't wait for the girls to be home, for their giggles and bickering to drown out her thoughts. She goes upstairs, averting her gaze as she passes the open door to the living room, and wanders restlessly into the girls' bedrooms; the bathroom; and, finally, the room she shared with Jamie. The T-shirt he used to sleep in is stuffed under his pillows and she takes it out and presses it to her face, inhaling the scent of him. How long will it last? Could she somehow preserve it? Along with the musky warmth of Jamie himself, there's a trace of his aftershave, sharp and fresh. Nadeeka remembers noticing it the night they first kissed, then catching a trace of it in her hair the following morning. She finds the bottle in the bathroom and dabs some behind her ears, her breath catching. His watch is on the windowsill, and she takes off her own and puts on his. It's too big for her wrist, but she likes the weight of it, likes knowing that what was once against his skin is now against hers.

On the landing, in an awkward nook useful for nothing else, is a desk in which Nadeeka used to keep birthday cards and wrapping paper, and which she cleared out when Jamie had moved in. *You don't need to do that*, he had protested, when she'd showed him. Nadeeka had insisted. *I want you to feel as though you have a space that's just for you.* Jamie had worked there occasionally, and played computer games that involved jets flying low over enemy ground. Slowly, the drawers had filled up with paperwork and who knows what else?

Now, Nadeeka sits at the desk. She puts her palms flat on the pitted oak and presses them into the wood. *Why?* she asks Jamie. *Why did someone want you dead?* She pulls out the top drawer and starts carefully sifting through the paperwork. She finds old receipts, HMRC letters, a laminated library card. As she works, she becomes less careful and more frantic, desperate for answers, for anything that will tell her what happened. The bottom drawer sticks fast and, when she kneels on the floor and yanks at it, it flies out with such force that she falls back, pulling the drawer with her. She scrambles on to her knees again, but just as she is slotting the drawer into its runners she sees something in the desk cavity, stashed in the space between the runners and the floor.

It's a framed photograph. The surround is black enamel with a silver trim, and it cost £12.99 from Next. Nadeeka knows this because she was the one who bought it. She had chosen it to showcase the photograph at which she's now looking, which is of the four of them: Nadeeka and Jamie, Maya and Nish. They're laughing, posing for a selfie on Blackpool pier, at the end of a long but brilliant day of jumping waves and eating salty chips on the beach. Nadeeka had printed out the photo and had it framed for Jamie. He had loved it and taken it into work – Nadeeka had seen it on his desk one time, when Jamie had FaceTimed her from the office. 'I like having you all with me at work,' he'd said.

Nadeeka stares at the photo. If that was true, why would he bring it home and hide it in a drawer?

CHAPTER 7

Nadeeka's mind is beginning to settle, the buzzing giving way to thoughts that are more coherent – albeit no less perplexing. It's no longer a list of admin tasks swirling about her head, but questions that are far bigger, far more important.

Why did Jamie bring home a photograph he'd professed to love?

What else had he been keeping from her?

Why had someone wanted him dead?

She processes the questions logically. Maybe Jamie only *told* her he liked the photo, and hid it here to save her feelings. Maybe his office has introduced a clear-desk policy. *Or maybe,* a voice whispers, *maybe he was having an affair and couldn't bear seeing the face of the woman he was betraying.*

Nadeeka has read every scrap of paper in Jamie's desk. She's searched the pockets in his trousers and the boxes of odds-and-ends in the bottom of the wardrobe. She has found nothing. No secret phone, no love letters.

See! part of her thinks. *You were worrying about nothing.*

But you heard a woman's voice, comes the immediate retort. *He lied to you about where he was.*

She wonders why she even cares, given what happened next, but she needs to know that her relationship with Jamie was everything she'd believed it was. She needs to tether her grief in something real and true.

Jamie had told Nadeeka he was finding the relocation harder to handle than he'd expected. She had wondered – either through intuition or paranoia – if perhaps he'd really meant he was finding *her* harder to handle. That he had made a mistake moving in with her.

'The girls are at Scott's this weekend,' she had said a couple of weeks ago. 'We could take a drive out – maybe go up to the Peak District?'

Jamie had paused for a second too long. 'Sure,' he'd said, but the smile he'd offered up hadn't reached his eyes. He hadn't asked which day they should go, or looked up restaurants the way he normally would, and when Nadeeka didn't mention it again, nor did he. The weekend had arrived, and they had stayed home, Nadeeka casting surreptitious glances at Jamie as they sat on the sofa, watching a film. As the credits had rolled, she had reached for him.

'Bedtime?' She had run her fingers suggestively across his thigh.

'Good idea. I'm exhausted.'

He had gone straight up, and by the time Nadeeka had locked up he'd been in bed, his slow, even breaths suggesting he was asleep. Or pretending to be.

This was not Nadeeka's first rodeo; she knew the signs of cheating. The emotional detachment, the waning sex life, the evasive answers to straightforward questions. Nadeeka hadn't wanted to see them in Jamie – she had wanted so badly to believe that things would be different this time – but in the weeks prior to his murder they had all been there.

She tries to pinpoint when it had been that Jamie had started

It's Not What You Think

keeping his phone in his pocket instead of leaving it on the side. Not as far back as the summer, certainly. A month, perhaps? Six weeks, at most. Late October. That must have been when it started.

Downstairs, Nadeeka directs her restlessness into moving the sofa and hoovering the already spotless floor, then goes to make a cup of tea, before discovering there's no milk in the fridge. She contemplates abandoning the idea – she didn't want it anyway – but the girls will want cereal in the morning, and maybe a breath of fresh air will do her good.

A couple of streets away from Cedar Walk is what everyone locally calls the corner shop, even though it's slap-bang in the middle of a row of buildings. Jamie had always preferred to go to one of the big supermarkets on the outskirts of town, but Nadeeka tries to shop with independents when she can. The corner shop recently fell victim to an arson attack which almost set the whole building ablaze, and she imagines they need all the support they can get.

The shattered windows at the front of the shop have been replaced now, and the façade has fresh paint, but the brickwork either side of the door is still streaked with black. As Nadeeka walks in, a bell jangles and Surinder comes out of the stock room, carrying a crate of fizzy drinks. He stops short when he sees her and, although he doesn't do the head tilt, it's obvious he knows about Jamie.

'I heard what happened.' Surinder uses the crate to prop open the stock room door. He straightens and looks at Nadeeka. 'How are you?'

Nadeeka takes a litre of milk from the fridge. 'All over the place, to be honest.' She feels suddenly exhausted, her limbs too heavy for her body. Does everyone know about Jamie? She'll have to talk to the girls tonight before they hear from someone else. God knows how: there's no chapter in the parenting manuals for how to tell your kids their mum's partner has been stabbed to death.

'This used to be a nice area,' Surinder says. 'I don't know what's going on lately.'

'Did the fire cause a lot of damage?' She wanders purposelessly around the tiny shop. Does she need anything else? Does she care?

'No stock lost, fortunately, but I had to close for three days. That's a lot of business.'

'I'm sorry.'

'People have been very kind, though,' Surinder says. 'A neighbour cooked food; a friend of ours took the boys to school. We even had money pushed through the door. It's not a bad neighbourhood, really.'

Nadeeka feels a pang of guilt at not having offered to help. She takes her milk to the till. 'Do the police know who did it?'

'Kids, probably. They found a bottle of lighter fluid dumped in the bin at the end of the street.' Surinder pushes the milk towards her. 'No charge.'

'You can't do that.' Nadeeka feels in her pockets for change she can leave on the counter.

'It's nothing.' Surinder's eyes are full of compassion. 'And please: if we can do anything to help—'

'And if *I* can help *you*!' Nadeeka cuts across him, embarrassed by the man's generosity, when all she had done in response to his own crisis was to say, *God, how terrible*, and take the girls elsewhere for their baking ingredients. 'With the boys, or . . .' She tails off. An empty offer, made too late. 'Such a terrible thing to happen to your lovely shop.'

'No one was hurt, and that is all that counts. If the phone hadn't woken me up, it might have been another story, but . . .' Surinder presses his palms together and dips his head.

'Well, thank you for the milk. You're very kind.' As Nadeeka turns to go, a thought strikes her. 'Who was calling you?'

It's Not What You Think

'I'm sorry?'

'The fire was in the early hours of the morning, right? Who was calling you at that time of night?'

'No one.' Surinder shrugs. 'A wrong number, perhaps? My guardian angel, I think. Without that call, we could all have died.'

Nadeeka thinks about this as she walks home. She wonders about the anonymous call that alerted the police to Jamie's murder. Is it possible it's connected to Surinder's arson? Could someone be setting up crimes, then calling the authorities so they can watch the chaos unfold? She'll mention it to DI Burton. He said to pass on anything she thinks of, no matter how insignificant it seems.

At home, Nadeeka puts the milk in the fridge but doesn't bother making tea. Instead, she gets changed – she's still wearing the clothes she wore to work yesterday – and gets in the car. Jamie rarely went out without Nadeeka, except to pop to the shops or to go to work. If he really had started seeing another woman, it was very possible he'd met her in the office.

ATP Construction is based on an industrial estate, between a tyre manufacturer and a cake factory which render the air between them a cloying mix of sweetness and hot rubber. Nadeeka waits in reception while a young blonde woman finishes a call. They are in the headquarters of the company, a UK-wide business putting sprawling housing developments on previously green fields.

'Sorry about that.' The receptionist has tortoiseshell glasses, pushed up by her cheeks when she smiles. 'How can I help you?'

Nadeeka's throat tightens. 'I . . . my partner works here. Jamie Golding.'

'Of course. Health and safety, right? You must be Nadia.'

'Nadeeka.'

'Sorry.'

'Could I speak to Jamie's line manager? Or to someone in HR?'

The receptionist's eyebrows rise. 'Is there a problem?'

'I just really need to speak to someone.'

'Carrie Finder's head of People and Culture, but she's on leave today . . .' The receptionist is tapping long glossy nails on her keyboard. 'But Adam Bennington's in. He's Jamie's boss's boss.'

'Great. I'd like to talk to him, please.'

The receptionist lifts the phone. 'What shall I say it's regarding?'

'Just tell him it's important.'

Adam Bennington is close to retirement age. His eyes crease with compassion as Nadeeka haltingly tells him that Jamie won't be back at work; that he died yesterday.

'I'm so sorry for your loss,' he says.

'I wondered how Jamie had been getting on at work,' Nadeeka says. 'Whether he was performing well, if he got on well with his colleagues, that sort of thing.' *Whether he was sleeping with one of them.* She digs her nails into her palms.

'Jamie had settled in very well. He was managing his workload well, and although he was quiet, he seemed to get on with every—' Adam stops suddenly. 'Nadia—'

'Nadeeka.'

'Nadeeka, I don't want to pry, but these questions . . . Had Jamie been struggling? Did he take his own life?'

'No!' It's so loud it hangs in the air for a split-second.

Adam looks mortified. 'I'm so sorry, I didn't mean to—'

'He was murdered.'

The phone on Adam's desk rings and he reaches out to silence it. His mouth has dropped open.

'It's possible the police will want to speak to you.'

Adam blinks rapidly. 'Of course. Anything to help.' He leans forward, resting his forearms on the desk. 'I can't imagine what you must be going through. Is there anything we can do to support you?'

'I'd like to collect Jamie's personal things, if that's okay?'

'Of course. I'll show you where his desk is.'

A few people look up as Adam leads Nadeeka through the large, open-plan office. There are no construction workers at this site, only the back-office departments that support them, which Nadeeka now realizes are staffed mostly by women. Had Jamie ever mentioned that? She turns her head this way and that, looking at all the women, trying to work out who Jamie would have found attractive. Is one of these women a murderer? Or could their boyfriend or husband be responsible? *Yes, that makes sense . . . The boyfriend gets suspicious and follows his girlfriend to Cedar Walk, where he finds her* in flagrante *with Jamie. There's an altercation, things get out of hand, the boyfriend pulls out a knife and—*

'Here we are.' Adam stops by a desk flanked by blue screens. 'I'll give you some privacy, but if you need me . . .' He gestures to his office.

Nadeeka stutters her thanks, forcing away the unwelcome image of her partner with another woman. She's glad of the screens that shield her from view as she sits at Jamie's desk. She takes a moment to steady herself. His pen pot is a mug they bought in Tenby; his mouse-mat a photo of the sunset above the train track at the end of their garden. Jamie's handwriting is on a notepad on one side of the desk. The whole cubicle is tidy, as though he's gone on leave, and Nadeeka thinks that's what she'll tell herself: that he's gone away for a bit. That he'll be back.

She begins searching the drawers – with more care than she'd employed at home – but there's hardly anything in them. The usual soup of pens and elastic bands in the top drawer; a cereal bar and an overripe banana in the bottom. Training guides; health and safety manuals; a hard hat with *Jamie* written in indelible marker on one side. She takes out this last and holds it in her lap, cradling it like a baby, bent over with the effort of not crying.

On the desk is an A4 navy-blue diary with *ATP Construction* embossed in gold on the cover. Still clutching the hard hat, Nadeeka opens it. It's full of meetings – online and in person – written in Jamie's untidy scrawl. As she flicks through the pages, she sees her own initials and stops, but when she looks more closely she realizes it isn't *NP* but *ND*. She turns the page to the following week, only to see the same initials there, too: *ND*. Written in the same blue ink as the rest of the entries, but smaller than Jamie's usual handwriting, and tucked into the bottom right-hand corner of the box, as though the addition had been an afterthought.

Or a secret.

The initials appear in the following week too, and the one after that. Nadeeka finds five of them in total. She takes out her phone and opens WhatsApp, opening the thread of messages between her and Jamie and scrolling back to last week, to the Friday evening marked in Jamie's diary with *ND*.

Sorry, love, I definitely have to work late tonight. Not sure what time I'll get away – eat with the girls and I'll get something later? Xxx

Nadeeka's heart thuds. She scrolls backwards through their messages, ignoring the hearts and the smiley faces and the silly photos they sent each other throughout the day.

Monday, 5.30 p.m.: *Someone's messed up and I need to stay late to fix things. Shouldn't be too late. Love you xxx*

On she scrolls, matching dates and reading the messages she had taken at face value when she'd received them.

Bloody IT system's down! Will be home around 8 xxx

Got a few things to finish up. Hopefully it won't take long xxx

The only 'ND' date that doesn't match with a text is 10th November, and she frowns. Was he home that night or—

It's Not What You Think

'Nadia?'

The receptionist's voice brings Nadeeka back to the office with a start. She snaps shut the diary and turns her phone screen-down.

'Sorry to interrupt. Adam just told me what happened, and I wanted to say how incredibly sorry I am. Jamie was a lovely man.'

'Yes. Yes, he was.' Nadeeka's throat constricts, and she tries not to cry.

'Can I get you a glass of water? Cup of tea?'

'No, thank you. You're very kind.' Nadeeka gathers Jamie's things, clutching the desk diary to her chest. 'I think I'm just going to—'

'Um . . .' The receptionist points to the yellow hard hat. 'That's actually . . . I mean, you can't . . .' She pulls an awkward face. 'It's company property, you see.'

Nadeeka blinks at the hat, at the marker pen *Jamie*. 'Right.' She hands it over, then she walks towards the exit, and all the people who had nodded politely when she'd arrived are getting out of their seats now and saying *I'm so sorry for your loss*, and *He was a great guy*, and Nadeeka can't bear it. Who is ND? And why was Jamie meeting them in secret?

Had Jamie been a great guy? She doesn't know any more.

In fact, Nadeeka's starting to think she didn't know Jamie at all.

CHAPTER 8

'And you have no idea who ND is?' DI Colin Burton is wearing the same suit and tie he was wearing yesterday, and Nadeeka wonders if it's a kind of uniform; if he's one of those men who find it easier to wear the same thing each day.

'None at all.' Nadeeka watches Colin's face as he turns the pages of Jamie's desk diary. They're sitting in a café around the corner from the police station, slotted into a booth which offers little protection from the frigid air that blasts in every time the door opens.

'The coffee here's my guilty pleasure,' Colin had explained, when he'd arrived. Nadeeka had been early, turning the laminated menu over in her hands without reading it. 'The machine at the nick's on the blink, so it's instant or nothing.' He'd smiled at the waitress. 'Americano with oat milk, please.'

'I think ND is someone Jamie was meeting,' Nadeeka says now. She stirs the latte she doesn't remember ordering.

'A woman?' Colin says it gently, watching her face for a reaction.

It's Not What You Think

She nods, her lips pressed tight. She doesn't want it to be true, but what other explanation is there? 'I'm wondering if it's someone he works with. A colleague, or even a client.'

Colin slides the diary into a transparent plastic bag and secures it with a tag. He flips open a small booklet and fills out a receipt in neat, joined-up handwriting.

'Adam Bennington is Jamie's boss,' Nadeeka says. 'He'll be able to give you a list of employees. We need to see who has the initials ND, then establish if they match the description of the woman the neighbours saw coming to the house.' Her coffee is still untouched. 'Jamie had to have a photo taken for his pass when he started, which means HR probably have everyone's picture on file. Although they don't call it Human Resources, actually . . .' Nadeeka frowns. 'People and something, the receptionist called it.'

'Sounds as though you have this all sewn up.' Colin tears off the receipt and hands it to her.

Nadeeka flushes. 'Sorry. I don't mean to tell you how to do your job.' She pushes the receipt into her pocket.

'It's fine. I imagine you feel better when you're doing something constructive?'

Nadeeka nods.

'These things are all happening, I promise, and much, much more.' Colin interlaces his fingers. He wears a slim gold wedding band, too loose for his finger. 'I know it must feel as though everything is moving frustratingly slowly, and, believe me, I wish I had a more concrete update for you, but there's a whole team working flat-out to find the person responsible for Jamie's murder.'

Tears prick at Nadeeka's eyes. 'I know. It's just that it feels like . . .' She searches for an explanation. 'Like being in a snow globe.'

The corners of Colin's mouth twitch. 'I'm not sure I follow.'

'Like someone snatched up my life and gave it a hard shake,

57

and now everything has settled in a different place, and nothing looks the same any more.'

'I see.'

'So I do want justice for Jamie, of course I do – I want to find out who killed him – but I want other answers, too. I want to know who he was seeing. I want to know . . .' Nadeeka's tears start to fall. 'I want to know why I wasn't enough for him.'

Colin passes her a napkin from the plastic dispenser on the table. It's hard and scratchy, and not remotely absorbent, but she presses it to her face gratefully.

'May I see the messages he sent you?'

Nadeeka opens WhatsApp. She leans awkwardly across the table so she can show him the relevant exchanges, trying her best to scroll quickly past the hearts and memes and – Nadeeka is mortified to now realize – the suggestiveness and innuendo.

If Colin notices the sexting, he's gentlemanly enough to ignore it. 'This is really useful.' He pulls an apologetic face. 'I know this is going to be inconvenient, but I'd like to borrow your phone and get these messages downloaded as potential evidence.'

'Can't you just take screenshots? Or I could forward them to you?' Nadeeka's hand closes automatically around her phone, the way Maya's does around the remote when it's time for bed. 'If the school needs to contact me, or—'

'If I take it now, I can have it back to you tomorrow afternoon.' Colin looks at his watch. 'Tomorrow morning, if I bribe the analysts with some decent biscuits.'

Nadeeka can let the school have her work mobile number, she supposes, and if she wants to find out the truth about Jamie she can surely cope without a phone for twenty-four hours. Somewhat reluctantly, she exchanges her phone for another slip of green paper, and dutifully writes down her passcode on Colin's copy.

'Is there anything else on your mind?' Colin seals her phone in another plastic bag.

It's Not What You Think

'I wondered whether you'd found anything out about the anonymous caller?'

'Unfortunately not. Someone has come forward to say they saw a man using the phone box around the time of the call, but we've been able to trace and eliminate that individual.'

'This might be nothing,' Nadeeka says, 'but there was an arson attack on a shop around the corner from us, and someone made an anonymous call to the occupants just as the fire took hold.' She outlines her theory, feeling faintly ridiculous as she does. He'll think she's one of those 'true crime' obsessives, creating connections and conspiracies out of thin air.

But Colin listens intently, writing down the information and pushing Nadeeka for more details. 'I'll be frank with you,' he says, when he's finished writing. 'Everything we've learned about Jamie's murder so far suggests this was personal, which means it's unlikely to be connected to the arson, but let me look on the system and see where the investigation's at.'

'Thank you.'

'As for *our* investigation . . .' Colin's expression grows serious. 'As I said, the incident room is working flat-out, but I don't want to give you false hope. The quality of your neighbours' doorcams is variable, and, although we have footage of a vehicle in Cedar Walk around the time of the murder, the registration plate isn't visible.'

'What about fingerprints? DNA?'

'Our crime scene investigators managed to lift a number of prints from your property, but there's no match on the Police National Computer, which means our man – or woman – doesn't have a criminal record.'

'But somebody must have seen something!' Nadeeka's voice rises. She thinks of Maeve's grandpa and his inflatable snowman; of the couple next door but one, who say hello on bin day. Surely someone in Cedar Walk at least *glanced* out of their window while Jamie was being attacked?

'We've taken statements from all your neighbours. Apart from the dark-haired woman who's visited the house in the past, who may or may not be connected, nobody saw anything unusual on the day of the murder.'

'A murderer can't just disappear into thin air . . .'

Colin glances across the café, to where an elderly woman is eking out a pot of tea for one. He drops his voice, perhaps in the hope that Nadeeka will do the same. 'Hopefully this diary – and the messages from your phone – will open up a line of enquiry, and we're still getting calls from the public in response to our appeal. But . . .'

His shoulders lift in the hint of a shrug, and Nadeeka feels a flash of anger. This isn't just a police investigation, these are people's lives. Jamie's life. Her life. *Their* life.

'So what? What are you saying exactly?' she demands.

Colin holds Nadeeka's gaze. There's a long pause before he answers.

'I'm saying that, right now, we have no leads.'

CHAPTER 9

Nadeeka collects the girls from school. When they get home, she installs them in the kitchen with a glass of milk and a biscuit each and tells them she has something important to talk about.

'Is Daddy going to live with us again?' Maya looks hopeful. 'He's always saying he wants to.'

Bloody hell, Scott. What happened to presenting a united front to the kids?

When Nadeeka discovered Scott had been cheating on her, she had thrown him out. He'd gone to stay with his mum for a week, and Nadeeka had told the girls that Kath had asked him for some help around the house. A week had turned into a month, and then Nadeeka and Scott had sat down with their daughters and given them the age-old explanation that they would always be a family, and would always love each other, but that Mummy and Daddy had decided they would be happier living separately.

'No,' Nadeeka says firmly. 'Daddy's very happy living with Gabriela.' She has no idea if this is true, but Scott is no longer her problem to deal with. She takes a deep breath. 'This is about Jamie.'

'Jamie's not going to live somewhere else, is he?' Nish says. 'We only just finished our castle. He said he'd bring it to school so I can show Miss Key how the drawbridge works.' Jamie and Nish's junk model Norman castle has been taking shape in the utility room for the past few weeks. What started as a Blue Peter challenge had turned into an obsession with the recycling, Nish racing to Jamie in excitement whenever she found the perfect piece of packaging for a tricky piece of fortification.

'It's an amazing castle.' Nadeeka fights to keep her voice level. 'Miss Key is going to be so impressed.'

Maya – older and more perceptive than her sister – fixes anxious eyes on Nadeeka. 'You said Jamie was in hospital. Is he really sick? Is it cancer?'

Nadeeka knows the girls will take their lead from her, so she is determined not to cry. 'There was an accident.' Beneath the table, she grips the edge of her chair, pressing her fingertips against the wood. 'Jamie died.' She swallows. 'It's very sad, but . . .'

But what? There is no but; there is nothing that could possibly mitigate the fact that Jamie has been murdered – right here, in their own home. Nadeeka presses her fingertips harder into the wood, but perhaps it doesn't matter whether she cries or not, because Maya is sobbing anyway. Tears spill over her thick dark lashes and fall, unchecked, to her lap.

Nish frowns as she processes what Nadeeka has said, then she takes her lead from Maya and bursts into tears.

'I don't believe you.' Maya shakes her head, her voice rough and angry.

'It's true. I'm so sorry.'

'Actually *forever* dead?' Nish says.

'That's the only kind of dead, stupid!' Maya snaps.

'I'm not stupid!'

It's Not What You Think

Nadeeka pulls them into her, cutting off the argument and squeezing them tight, and crying too, harder now because she isn't only crying for Jamie, and for herself, but for the second family she created after Scott had blown up the first. She's crying for her daughters, who at nine and six are having to deal with the fallout of an adult world.

They sleep together that night, the three of them spooned in Nadeeka's bed and the girls falling asleep within seconds. Nadeeka could have wriggled out and spent the evening downstairs, but she was afraid the girls would have nightmares, or that they'd wake and be frightened, so she stayed wedged between her daughters, reliving the moment she had come home from work to discover her home had become a crime scene.

I'm saying that, right now, we have no leads.

How is that possible? How can a man be murdered in broad daylight, in what is generally held to be a *nice* neighbourhood, and no one see his attacker? But then Nadeeka thinks about all the unsolved crimes she has read about – the murders and robberies and sexual assaults – and realizes it must happen all the time. Jamie is a statistic. Another unsolved crime. Detective Inspector Colin Burton and his team will continue to turn over stones until they run out, and then they will quietly push the investigation to the back of the cupboard. Because, by then, someone else will have been murdered or raped or robbed, and the police's stretched resources will need to be redirected.

Nadeeka is still thinking about this when her alarm goes off and she wakes from broken sleep that has left her more tired than eleven hours in bed should merit. What if the lack of leads means the investigation team is already becoming lacklustre? She imagines the major crime incident room where she supposes DI Burton works (the image heavily reliant on the crime dramas

Kath has recommended over the years) and pictures his team slumped in their chairs, idly checking emails or completing a crossword. Nothing to do, no leads to follow. Just days away from *we've done all we can, lads.*

Nadeeka wonders if she should keep the girls at home, give them time to absorb the traumatic hand they have all been dealt. She watches them eat their cereal, changing her mind with each spoonful they take, and finally decides they are better off at school. That they will be *safer* at school, she thinks, because, although she is trying hard to pretend that home is still the same place it was before Jamie died, that isn't at all how it feels. All night, Nadeeka had seen shadows, heard footsteps; repeatedly snatched herself from nightmares with her heart thumping and her hair plastered to her cheek.

So she navigates the school gate once more, glad of the cardboard castle which she holds like a shield against the head tilts of concern – and of gossip.

'Wow!' Miss Key's reaction is gratifyingly enthusiastic. 'What an amazing model!'

Nish beams. Her favourite teaching assistant is, as ever, in colourful dungarees peppered with animal pin badges, with two plaits that make her look young enough to be in school herself. She claps delightedly when Nish shows her how to operate the drawbridge, and touches the fortifications deferentially. 'And are these loo rolls?'

Nish nods. 'And this bit is egg boxes, smooshed up and painted green to look like grass.'

'I don't suppose we could keep it in class for a bit?' Miss Key glances at Nadeeka. 'We'd be ever so careful.'

'If that's okay with Nish,' Nadeeka says, and, since Nish looks as though she might explode with happiness, the castle stays at school. Nadeeka says a hurried goodbye as her eyes fill with tears. How ridiculous to cry over a cardboard castle! It's only that she's handing over yet another link to Jamie, albeit this one was received with more reverence than his bagged-and-tagged laptop or his yellow safety helmet.

Nadeeka thinks about the receptionist's awkwardness when she tried to take the hard hat away. Could she be ND? Before she knows what she's doing she's on her way to ATP Construction. She doesn't want to be at home, jumping at shadows, waiting for DI Burton to bring news. If Jamie was killed because of an affair he was having, then Nadeeka and her daughters have nothing to fear. No one is lying in wait to break into the house; no one is coming for Nadeeka. How ironic, she thinks, that the answer she wants least is the one that will give her the peace of mind she needs.

'Oh! Hi.'

Is it Nadeeka's imagination, or is the receptionist's greeting a little less warm today? There's the now-familiar head tilt, but is there something else in the young woman's expression?

'I don't think I got your name yesterday,' Nadeeka says.

'It's Stacie.'

'Oh.' Not ND. 'Hi, Stacie.'

'Did you want to see Mr Bennington again? Only, he's in a meeting at the moment.'

'No, I . . . I wondered if I could have a list of Jamie's colleagues.' Nadeeka makes herself smile at Stacie, as though this is a perfectly normal request. 'So I can invite them to the funeral,' she explains, having hit upon this – surely plausible – reason on her way here.

'Oh, my God, of course.' Stacie's expression softens. 'You poor thing, having all that to arrange, too. You can give me the details, if you like – I'll write down my email address – and I'll share them with the team.'

'I'd like to send them personally.' Nadeeka leaves a beat. 'It's what Jamie would have wanted.' This last is clearly impossible to argue with because Stacie taps on her keyboard and a moment later the printer beside her whirs and spits out a document.

Nadeeka itches to snatch it up herself, but she waits until Stacey hands it to her. 'Thanks.'

Sarah Thompson, Michael Edwards, Priya Kapoor, Emma Robinson, Chloe Zhang, Nicole Davis . . .

'Nicole Davis.' Nadeeka snaps her focus back to Stacie. 'Is she in today?'

'Um . . .' Stacie stands up and scans the open-plan office. 'I'm sure I saw . . . yeah, she's in. Can I ask why—'

'Which one? That desk there? Dark hair?' Nadeeka points, conscious of her voice rising, but unable to control it. Nicole Davis. ND.

'Yes, she's an account manager, but—'

Nadeeka doesn't wait to hear the rest. She makes her way through the open-plan office towards the desk on the far side which, like Jamie's, is surrounded by blue dividers. Above these screens is a gleam of mahogany hair pushed back by a pair of glasses, and as Nadeeka draws closer she sees smoky eyeliner on porcelain-pale skin; a deep red stain on full lips. And now Nicole is looking up at Nadeeka expectantly. She's in her late twenties, wearing a white blouse that is somehow at once demure and provocative, the buttons low enough to show a shadow of cleavage. Her eyes are blue, startling against her dark hair.

'Can I help you?'

'Nicole Davis?'

'That's right.'

'Nicole Davis,' Nadeeka says again, or maybe she shouts it, because the curious expression on Nicole's face is replaced with a frown.

'Who are you?'

'This is Jamie Golding's partner.' Stacie has appeared by Nadeeka's side. 'Jamie who *died*,' she clarifies, dropping her voice to a whisper as though what she's saying would cause offence if conveyed at normal office volumes.

'I'm so sorry for your loss,' Nicole says.

It's Not What You Think

Nadeeka hesitates. Now that she's here, she doesn't know what to say. She can't stop looking at Nicole, taking in her narrow waist, the lack of wedding ring, the tiny silver cuff on her left ear. Is she Jamie's type? She couldn't be more different from Nadeeka, but what does that tell her?

'Did you . . .' Nadeeka swallows. 'Did you know Jamie well?'

'Not very.' Nicole glances at Stacie and her eyebrows flick upwards in a conspiratorial *wtf?* 'He hadn't been here long, but everyone works pretty closely together, so—'

'How closely?'

Other people in the office are watching them now. Two or three have stood up to get a better view.

'I'm sorry?' Nicole gives a confused half-laugh.

'Jamie had "ND" written in his diary.' Heat floods Nadeeka's face. She puts a hand in her pocket, wanting to show Nicole the messages and the photos of the diary entries, then she remembers the police have her phone. 'Four times,' she says instead. 'Four times last month he said he was working late, and instead he was meeting ND.'

There is a long and uncomfortable pause.

'Sorry,' Nicole says, eventually, 'but what exactly has that got to do with me?'

'When did you last see Jamie?'

'I beg your pardon?'

'Jamie was murdered on Monday afternoon. Did you see him on Monday?' Nadeeka's voice rises. 'Do you know what happened to him?'

And now Nicole's on her feet, telling Nadeeka she's *got a bloody nerve*, and Nadeeka is choking on her words, tears streaming down her face. What was she thinking, coming here?

'Ms Prasanna.'

Nadeeka feels a hand on her shoulder. She turns to see Adam Bennington, Stacie hovering by his left elbow.

'She just barged in,' Stacie says.

'This must be a very upsetting time for you, Ms Prasanna—' Adam says.

'It's pretty bloody upsetting to be accused of having an affair and then murdering someone, too,' Nicole chips in, although something about the younger woman's expression makes Nadeeka think she's revelling in the drama.

'—but if you need anything else, I'd prefer it if you came through me.' Adam's smile is kind but firm.

'I'll show her out, Adam,' says a woman wearing a navy blazer, who looks vaguely officious.

'Thanks, Carrie.'

They talk over her head, the way doctors do over patients, and then Nadeeka finds herself propelled past desks, past muffled titters and low voices, and out to reception, where Carrie opens the door leading to the car park.

'Everyone at ATP Construction would like to express their condolences for your loss,' she says. 'But we will not condone the harassment of our staff.'

'But I think she knows—'

There is no trace now of the supportive smile that a moment ago had mirrored Adam Bennington's. 'If you come back here again,' Carrie says, emphasizing every word, 'I will call the police.'

And a second later Nadeeka finds herself in the car park, the door to ATP Construction firmly closed.

CHAPTER 10

Nadeeka is on hold. Every thirty seconds Vivaldi's *Four Seasons* stops mid-note and Nadeeka opens her mouth to speak, only for a recorded announcement to remind her that the police non-emergency line is experiencing an unusually high number of calls, and that she is currently number eleven in the queue.

It feels strange to be using a proper phone. Nadeeka never uses the landline; the only people who call this number are her parents and the occasional scammer offering a reduction on the Sky TV package she doesn't have. She hates not having her mobile. She hadn't realized how much she uses it, but now she finds herself reaching for it every few minutes to check her messages or look something up, or to set a reminder.

You are currently number ten in the queue, the recorded message tells her, and the terrible music starts again. Nadeeka sighs. She wishes she'd written DI Burton's number down so she could have found out how much longer he'll need to keep hold of her phone. It hadn't occurred to her to make a note of some of her contacts before dropping her phone in an evidence bag, and now she feels weirdly isolated. She doesn't even know Kath's number; she had to call Scott, whose phone number seems to be imprinted on her brain.

You are currently number nine in the queue.

Of course, if she'd taken Jamie's advice and backed up her phone regularly, everything would be in *the cloud*, wherever that is. *You can set it up to happen automatically*, he'd told her a few weeks ago, after she'd dropped her phone in the bath and was panicking about what might have been lost. *I will*, Nadeeka had promised, but then a bag of uncooked rice and the airing cupboard had got her phone working again, and she never did get around to backing it up.

You are currently number ten in the queue.

'What?' Nadeeka takes the phone from her ear and glares at the disembodied voice. 'I was number nine a second ago!'

But there's no one there to care, and as Vivaldi kicks in again Nadeeka lets out a frustrated scream. She ends the call.

For a moment, she sits motionless at the kitchen table, fighting the urge to burst into tears. Everything feels so *hard*. Even the prospect of taking out the bins is exhausting.

After Scott had moved out, Nadeeka had become a one-woman machine, taking over all the jobs that had traditionally been his, and ticking off tasks with ruthless efficiency.

'I don't know how you do it all,' Jamie had said. They'd been a few dates in by that point and were video-calling late into the evening. Nadeeka had been making the girls' lunchboxes, her phone propped up on the windowsill. She'd already done a load of washing, cleared away tea and tidied the living room while they'd been chatting.

'I'm brilliant,' Nadeeka had deadpanned.

Jamie had laughed. 'You are!'

After he'd moved in, Nadeeka had continued to be a whirlwind. She did the grocery shopping and planned the meals; took charge of household admin and organized date nights.

It's Not What You Think

'Let me help,' Jamie kept saying.

Nadeeka had insisted she was fine. 'It's all under control.'

Finally, Jamie had taken her face in his hands and locked his eyes on hers. 'I know you *can* do it all,' he'd said softly, 'but you don't *have* to. I want to help.'

'So much of it is for Nish and Maya, though,' Nadeeka had said. 'Dentist's appointments, and buying new shoes, and finding enough egg boxes for whatever craft project their class is doing next . . .'

'Then we all muck in. You, me and the girls. We're a team.'

So they had become one. And whereas Scott had always asked Nadeeka to tell him if she wanted him to do anything, then practically expected a medal for doing it, Jamie simply looked to see what needed doing and quietly did it.

Nadeeka picks up her car keys, her eyes filling with tears. Why is it that the one person she needs more than anyone else right now is the one person who can't be here?

The front desk of the police station is so high that Nadeeka has to tip back her head to speak to the man behind it, who doesn't have a name badge, only maroon epaulettes with C7449 embroidered on them.

C7449 looks for DI Burton's extension number. 'Do you know what department he's in? He's not listed under major crime, but there's a lot of musical chairs goes on upstairs – I can't keep up.' He pushes his glasses on to the top of his head and picks up the phone. Nadeeka wonders if Vivaldi's *Four Seasons* plays for internal calls as well as for external ones.

'Is there a DI Burton in the office today?' C7449 is saying. 'First name Colin.' He looks at Nadeeka for confirmation and she nods. There's a long pause. 'I've got a lady downstairs asking to speak to him. Apparently, he's taken her phone for forensics and said he'd have it back to her by yesterday.' Another long pause. 'Well, could *you* come down? Because she's got young children and she needs her phone back, and—' He stops abruptly, then replaces the receiver. 'And because it's your job,' he mutters darkly. He grins at Nadeeka. 'Someone'll be down shortly.'

Shortly turns out to be twenty minutes; *someone* a tall, slim woman in her late thirties who introduces herself as Detective Chief Inspector Lauren Caldwell, from major crime. She has caramel-streaked brown hair, held back in a loose ponytail that swings as she leads Nadeeka into a side room.

'I wanted to speak to DI Burton,' Nadeeka says, as soon as the door closes. 'My family liaison officer.'

'Do you mean Burden, perhaps?'

'Um . . . maybe?' Nadeeka flushes. As someone who works in recruitment, she prides herself on getting people's names right. 'I might have misheard him. The first few hours were such a blur.'

'Him?' DCI Caldwell smiles. 'Ah, then it's not DS Burden, because DS Burden is a woman. Don't worry, I'll find out who you need to speak to.' She swivels her chair to face the ancient-looking monitor on the side of the desk. 'We're supposedly all joined up nowadays, but sometimes the left hand doesn't know what the right hand's doing. Do you have a URN?'

'A what?' Nadeeka is close to tears again. She just wants to see Colin.

'A Unique Reference Number. It'll be four digits plus the date the incident was reported.'

The incident.

'No, I don't have a bloody reference number.' Nadeeka fights to keep her voice under control. 'What I have is a boyfriend in the mortuary, no clue who put him there, and a police force that doesn't seem to give a shit about finding out.'

There's a beat.

DCI Caldwell turns her full attention on Nadeeka. 'I'm so sorry. Both for your loss and for the way you're feeling now. What's your boyfriend's name?'

It's Not What You Think

'Jamie Golding.' Tears prick at the backs of Nadeeka's eyes.

The faintest of frowns crosses DCI Caldwell's expression. 'Jamie or James?'

'Um . . . James, I suppose, although no one ever called him that.'

'And he died on . . .'

'Monday.'

DCI Caldwell glances at her watch before typing Monday's date into the computer. Nadeeka tries to see the screen, but it's angled away from her.

'Where did this happen?' The detective chief inspector is frowning more deeply now.

'At home. Ten, Cedar Walk.' Nadeeka has a bad feeling. Has the investigation into Jamie's murder been closed already? DI Burton had admitted they had no leads, but he'd also promised that a team of detectives was working around the clock; that they were doing everything they could to—

'Ms Prasanna . . .' DCI Caldwell opens her mouth, but she can't seem to form any words. Her gaze flicks to the screen and then to her notebook, before landing once again on Nadeeka.

'What is it? What's wrong?' Nadeeka grips the edge of the table. There's something serious on that screen. Something DI Burton's been keeping from her? 'Are my daughters and I in danger?' she whispers.

'I can't find a Jamie Golding on our system,' DCI Caldwell says.

'As I said, his full name was James.'

'And there are no incidents recorded against your address.'

Nadeeka stares at her. 'This is unbelievable.' She has always supported the police, believing they do a tough job in even tougher circumstances, but this is outright incompetence. 'I want to speak to Colin Burton right now.'

'I'm afraid that's going to be a problem. There *is* no Colin Burton working here.'

Nadeeka pushes back her chair and stands. 'Which station does he work at, then?'

'No, I . . .' DCI Lauren Caldwell hesitates. 'Whoever it was who said he was DI Burton . . . wasn't a police officer.'

'I don't understand.' Nadeeka's pulse thrums in her ears. The room feels unnaturally hot and airless, and she puts a hand on the desk to steady herself.

'All unexplained deaths across the force are included in a daily briefing, but I've checked Monday's and there's no mention of your partner's name.'

'What are you saying?' It comes out in a whisper, as though the words themselves are as afraid as she is, and she sinks slowly back on to the plastic chair.

DCI Lauren Caldwell holds Nadeeka's gaze. 'I'm saying, there's no record that this murder ever happened.'

PART TWO
LAUREN

CHAPTER 11

Detective Chief Inspector Lauren Caldwell is still getting the measure of her team. She took over the major crime unit six months ago, following five years on the counter-terrorism unit and numerous lengthy discussions about whether working with one's significant other was a terrible idea.

'I know at least ten other couples who work together,' Fraser responded, after Lauren had presented him with yet another list of pros and cons. 'Getting it on with other coppers is an occupational hazard.'

'I'm an occupational hazard, am I?' Lauren had raised an eyebrow, pretending to take offence. 'Working together is one thing; the issue is how we'd cope with my being your boss.'

'If it doesn't bother me, it shouldn't bother you.'

'Will you call me *ma'am*?'

Fraser had wiggled his eyebrows lasciviously. 'Only on our days off.'

The prestige of the DCI job had been too good to turn down, so Lauren had set her reservations aside, and, six months in, she thinks it's working for them. Domestic squabbles and wedding preparations get left at home; at work, it's strictly business. Detective Chief Inspector Lauren Caldwell and Detective Sergeant Fraser Hogan.

'Does Nadeeka Prasanna have mental health issues?' Fraser says now. They're in the briefing room, Lauren's core team gathered around one end of the large oval table. Fraser has taken off his pale pink tie and his shirt is open at the neck beneath a cashmere sweater. Both had been gifts from Lauren last Christmas. Their strict separation of home life and work is helped by the fact that Fraser is really good at his job. One of the best on the team, in fact. Lauren wouldn't hesitate to haul Fraser into her office if she had to, but it would sure as hell make for an awkward atmosphere at dinner, so it's a relief he never gives her cause to.

'She's not on any medication,' Lauren says, 'and she doesn't identify as having a disability, but beyond that . . . who knows?'

'Maybe it's a wind-up?' Detective Constable Kenric Fennell is wearing a shiny purple tie that puts Lauren in mind of a chocolate wrapper. 'Some kind of bet?' The narrow lines in the hairline just above his ears are freshly shaved, which Lauren supposes is the sort of thing you have time for when you're in your early twenties and your mum still does your laundry.

Lauren shakes her head. 'We're not talking about a bunch of kids here. The impression I got from Nadeeka Prasanna was of an intelligent, educated, professional woman. Whether her partner really has been murdered or not, I think she genuinely believes he has been.'

'Or she wants us to *think* he has been.' DS Matt Draper's contribution is thrown in casually, but as the oldest detective on major crime – both in age and in service – the respect he commands is automatic.

Fraser looks at him. 'You think she killed her partner?'

'Killed him; arranged to have him killed; conspired with him to fabricate a murder that would enable him to disappear.' He counts off the options on long, slim fingers. 'Could be a life insurance job.'

'Excellent theories,' Lauren says, 'and ones we mustn't lose sight of. Kenric, can you look into the alleged victim, James Golding? Find out if he was in debt and if he had any criminal associates.'

'Will do, ma'am.'

'Bahnaz?' Lauren looks around for Detective Constable McDonnell and finds her – as ever – at the back of the group. 'There's no record of the murder on the system, but I want a more thorough dive. Pull up every job that came in during the relevant time parameters and make sure we're not missing anything because of some kind of technical glitch or recording error. Also, ask whoever was duty inspector on Monday whether we had any cross-border jobs that day. I can't see another force taking unilateral ownership of a murder without telling us, but stranger things have happened.'

'I will, ma'am, but it'll have to be tomorrow?' Bahnaz pulls an apologetic face. 'I have to pick up the kids from nursery at twelve?' Most of Bahnaz's statements finish with an unspoken question mark, as though she's unsure of what she's saying, or how it might land.

'Of course. You go.'

Lauren catches Kenric rolling his eyes as Bahnaz gets her coat, and she makes a mental note to have a word with him. Frustrating though it may be for the team to pick up the slack, Bahnaz's request for flexible working was authorized by HR and she shouldn't be made to feel shit about it.

'I can look into the cross-border stuff,' DC Sonya Marston says. 'I don't mind staying late if there's overtime on offer.' Her hair is so thick it forms a pyramid, the blunt blonde ends parallel with her shoulders.

'There is – ' Lauren holds up a hand, anticipating the inevitable reaction ' – but there are also limits, so please come to me for authorization *before* you work late.'

'Cool. The trainers my youngest wants for Christmas cost two hundred quid, if you can believe it.' Sonya sighs and her hair bobs up and down. 'To think they used to be happy with a selection box and a stocking full of tat.'

'I was lucky if I even got that,' Matt says.

'It was a piece of coal in your day, wasn't it?' Fraser grins and there's a ripple of laughter around the room. Lauren resumes the briefing before the rest of the team start chipping in.

'Nadeeka Prasanna was pulled over for running a red light around fifteen minutes before she arrived home and found the alleged crime scene.' She pauses. 'Might be a coincidence, of course.'

'Or she might have done it deliberately,' Kenric says, 'to create an alibi for herself.'

'Right. Can you track down the two officers who spoke to her and see what they made of her? If their cameras were on, I'd like to see what her body language was like.'

Kenric nods. 'Are we treating her as a sig wit?'

'Absolutely. She'll have all the support we always offer a close relative of a murder victim, but she'll remain a significant witness until there's evidence to the contrary.' Lauren checks the list in her daybook. 'Sonya, I'd like background checks on Nadeeka Prasanna, please. Is she having an affair and wanted Golding out of the way? Is she set to benefit from a life assurance policy?'

To the right of her list, Lauren has written *table decorations* and *wedding invites!!!* and the sight of them temporarily throws her. She and Fraser are getting married the day after Christmas, which had seemed such a romantic day for a wedding but has turned out to be a nightmare in terms of organization. Lauren is secretly looking forward to being able to concentrate on her still-new job without the background noise of flower arrangements and seating plans.

It's Not What You Think

Shit – *seating plans*! Lauren makes a surreptitious note in her book. Maybe she and Fraser can tackle that one this evening. Will his uncle be okay sitting at the same table as his ex-wife? They should definitely check. She adds *Fraser's uncle* to her list and underlines it, then snaps her focus back to the matter in hand.

'As I see it, we're looking at three possibilities. One: Nadeeka Prasanna is mentally unwell or a fantasist, and this murder never happened. Two: Jamie Golding is indeed either dead or missing, and Nadeeka Prasanna is behind it. Or three: it happened exactly the way she says it did.'

'Then we're not only investigating a murder without a body.' Fraser raises his eyebrows. 'We're faced with a scene that's already been forensically cleaned to remove all trace of the crime.'

Lauren nods slowly. Where do they even begin?

CHAPTER 12

'Tea or wine?' Fraser says, as they arrive home. The heating has come on and the reed diffuser on the hall table has filled the air with the scent of orange and cinnamon. Both Lauren and Fraser are tidy people – shoes in the basket by the door, keys in the drawer – and their two-bedroomed house is a haven from the horrors they so often face at work. No matter what kind of day she's had, Lauren's taut muscles begin to relax the moment they step through their front door, and she spares a thought for Nadeeka Prasanna, who is spending the night with her ex-husband's mum. Lauren isn't on speaking terms with any of her exes, let alone their mothers.

'We stayed with her on Monday night, too,' Nadeeka had volunteered, after Lauren had asked whether the family might be able to go somewhere else for a couple of days. 'Kath's got her faults, but she's calm in a crisis, you know? A good person to have around when something like this . . . something like this . . .' She'd abandoned the sentence, her forehead creasing as though she was still trying to make sense of it all.

It's Not What You Think

When something like this happens, Lauren supposes Nadeeka would have said, but when did anything like this happen? A murder, sure, but a sham criminal investigation and crime scene clean-up? It was almost too extraordinary to believe.

'I trusted him,' Nadeeka kept saying, whenever Lauren asked about 'DI Burton'. 'I – I *liked* him.'

Every now and then, Lauren could detect a note of caution in Nadeeka's expression; a wariness as Lauren questioned her. Because her trust in the police had been broken? Or because Nadeeka was hiding something? Lauren wasn't ruling anything out.

'When did you go back to the house?' she'd asked. They had still been in the stale, overly hot interview room at the police station.

For a moment, Nadeeka had looked as though she wasn't going to answer. Her lips parted and a tremor ran across them, and Lauren realized the question had triggered her; that Nadeeka was back in Cedar Walk, stepping into her house to find her partner's dead body.

'Take your time.' If Nadeeka was lying about what happened, she was a damn good actress.

'Tue—' She'd composed herself. Tried again. 'Tuesday morning.'

'By which time everything had been . . .' Lauren had opted for the gentlest word she could think of ' . . . *tidied up?*'

Nadeeka had nodded. 'It was spotless.'

'And since then, have you moved anything?'

'The sofa wasn't quite in the right position, so I put it back. I've pushed the hoover around a couple of times . . .' Nadeeka had been hesitant, as though she expected Lauren to tell her off. Lauren had tried to keep her expression neutral. It wasn't Nadeeka's fault, of course, but it meant three days of DNA being trodden in and out of the house. It meant an already impossible situation made even harder.

'You weren't to know,' Lauren had said. 'But if the scene could be kept sterile from now on, that would be helpful. I'd like our forensics team to start as soon as possible.'

'Earth to Lauren,' Fraser says now.

'Sorry. Tea, please.' She takes her bag into the kitchen, not even stopping to take off her coat. 'I need to get the investigative strategy straight; I've promised the boss a briefing note before the end of the day.'

Fraser looks pointedly at his watch. It is already gone seven. 'I guess I'm cooking, then?'

'Do you mind?' Lauren sits at the kitchen table and opens her laptop.

'Course I don't. Pasta okay?'

'Great,' she says, although she isn't really listening. 'We'll have to leave the seating plan for another time.' She props up her open daybook against a pile of flatpack wedding favour boxes.

'Shame.'

Lauren throws him an amused look. 'Don't ever take up poker, you're a terrible liar.' In an open tab on her screen is the Major Crime Investigation Manual, the detective's bible for homicides, abductions and serious sexual offences. Lauren clicks on *No Body Murders*.

'You know blokes are no good at things like seating plans and choosing flowers. You women are so much better at—'

'Don't you dare, Fraser Hogan!' Lauren holds up a warning finger, her eyes still on her laptop. 'What you're doing is called weaponized incompetence. It's like those men who are deliberately slapdash when they're doing the dishes, so the *little woman* decides it's easier to do it herself. It's *our* wedding; we both pitch in.'

'To be fair, though, women *are* generally better than blokes at domestic chores . . .'

Lauren stares at him, incredulous. 'Unless you're dusting the mantelpiece with your genitals, I fail to see how—' She sees the corners of Fraser's mouth twitch and lets the rest of her tirade fall. 'You sod.' She turns back to her laptop. 'You had me going then. I thought I was marrying my dad.'

'What a grim thought.' Fraser puts a mug of tea in front of her. 'I'll make a start on the seating plan while the spaghetti's cooking. Give me the guest list and—' He catches Lauren's expression and changes tack. 'On second thoughts, I'll get it myself.'

Lauren holds up her hands in praise. 'By Jove, I think he's got it!'

Once Fraser leaves the kitchen, Lauren drums her fingers on the pitted pine table. If only Nadeeka had come to the station earlier. If only she'd guessed something had been wrong.

'So you only ever spoke to the man purporting to be a detective inspector?' Lauren had tried to keep the judgement out of her voice. 'You never dealt with another police officer?'

'Just the one in uniform who was outside the house when I got home. After that, it was only DI Burton.'

Lauren had wanted to push it – to say *But didn't you think that was odd?* – but she had held her tongue. She had thought instead about all the people who fall for doorstep scams or distraction burglaries; who take at face value something told to them by a man in a hi-vis jacket, or carrying ID from the water company. Nadeeka had seen a marked police car, a CSI, a dedicated FLO – why would she have questioned it?

A marked police car. Lauren keeps coming back to it. Could it have been stolen? Taken perhaps from the force workshop? Old police cars are sent to auction, but not before their 'Battenberg' branding is removed; could one have been intercepted?

Lauren starts typing. They will have to start from scratch, as though the murder has only just happened. House-to-house enquiries. A full crime scene examination, as well as assessments of any secondary crime scenes, such as the café where Nadeeka met up with 'DI Burton'. Doorcam footage. ANPR. Cloud data will be key. Lauren's tea goes cold as the investigative strategy slowly takes shape.

The unusual nature of Nadeeka Prasanna's crime report has offset the usual grumbles about weekend working, and the following morning there is an almost tangible buzz in the air. The noise in the briefing room steadily builds, and at nine a.m. sharp Lauren stands by the large screen at the front of the room, puts two fingers in her mouth and lets out a piercing whistle. Over the years, various line managers have suggested to Lauren that there are more appropriate ways to bring a room to order, but Lauren has quietly ignored them. A raised, too-shrill voice would undermine her authority, and clapping her hands makes her feel as though she's about to lead primary school children into a round of 'Shine, Jesus, Shine'.

The room falls silent.

'I know some of you have had to change family plans,' Lauren says, 'so thank you for showing up today. It's appreciated.' She presses her clicker, and two photographs appear on the screen. 'This is Nadeeka Prasanna and her partner, James – known as Jamie – Golding. Prasanna alleges she arrived home on Monday to find Golding had been fatally stabbed. She claims there was police tape across her front door and a marked police car in the street, but there is no record of any officers attending from this force or neighbouring forces. Golding's employer, ATP Construction, has confirmed they have had no contact with Golding since Monday morning, when he phoned in sick.'

As she's talking, Lauren realizes there's no one here from the media team, despite her specific request that they attend. The investigation could really benefit from an appeal for information from the public – particularly in relation to tracing the vehicles used by the so-called police officers – but, with confidence in the police already at an all-time low, how do they do that without causing panic? Lauren had hoped to run through a possible strategy with the media team this morning. She intends to propose they go public with the murder but hold back the detail about bogus police officers.

She looks around the room. 'I believe someone from CSI is here?'

'That's me, ma'am.' A man leaning against the wall raises a hand. 'Tony Watkins. Has the victim's partner given us access to the house?'

'Yes. We have a set of keys.'

'Cool. In the first instance, as per your instructions, ma'am, we'll be looking to confirm the likelihood a murder took place. From what I've been told, we'll have to take the carpet up – is she okay with that?'

'She'll have to be.'

'Beyond that – ' Tony shrugs ' – the usual. Do we have elims from the family?'

'Not yet, but I'm seeing Ms Prasanna later today and will get that sorted.' Lauren looks to Fraser, who gives a brief nod, picking up the tacit request to collect an elimination fingerprint kit and DNA swabs. 'Jamie Golding is no trace PNC,' she tells Tony, 'so I'll ask Ms Prasanna for something of his we can swab.'

'A toothbrush would be ideal,' Tony says.

'No problem.' Lauren switches her attention back to the wider audience. 'I want us to think about this case as two separate, but connected, crimes. Firstly, the murder; secondly, the impersonation of police officers and staff. We don't know at this stage whether the man purporting to be "DI Burton" is responsible for Golding's death or merely for the cover-up, so let's keep an open mind on that front. Matt, I'd like you and Bahnaz to focus on the murder itself. Nadeeka Prasanna believes all doorcam footage has already been handed over, but I want thorough house-to-house enquiries, please. Find out what still exists on hard drives or in the cloud.'

DS Draper nods. 'Will do, boss.'

'Locating Golding's body is a priority. It's possible he was genuinely collected by an undertaker, so check with funeral parlours within a forty-mile radius for any white adult males brought in on Monday afternoon. Until and unless we get more intel on the direction of travel, we have nothing on which to base a search area.'

They need a registration number, Lauren thinks, for at least one of the vehicles used by the phoney cops. She's listed them in her notes: the blue Corsa driven by 'DI Burton'; the black private ambulance; the white van used by the paper-suited man Nadeeka Prasanna took to be a forensics officer; and a marked police car. How the hell had they got a marked car there?

Lauren locates DC Marston. 'Sonya, I'd like you and Kenric to focus on identifying the individuals claiming to be police. According to Nadeeka Prasanna, we're looking for the following people.' She brings up a slide with five silhouetted heads and reads out the captions as they appear. '"DI Burton": white male, early sixties. A "crime scene investigator": male, white, broad-shouldered, shaved head, indeterminate age. A third white male: mid-twenties with dark hair, wearing police uniform. Finally, two men potentially posing as undertakers.'

From somewhere in the room, there's a sharp exhalation of disbelief.

'Pretty ballsy, huh?' Lauren says. A few of the team nod, but no one smiles. There's a shift in the atmosphere, the buzz that infused the room earlier morphing into a grim determination. The sheer *arrogance* of these criminals . . . Lauren has only once dealt with something similarly audacious: the removal of a painting from a museum during opening hours, where the thieves had joked openly with security guards as they lifted it off the wall.

She clicks on to the next slide, which bears a single stock image of a mobile phone, and invites the man sitting directly to her right to take over.

'Morning, everyone.' He adjusts his jacket as he stands,

smoothing the lapels. 'For those of you I've not met, I'm Hillary Kent, head of digital forensics. We'll be looking first at any smart tech in Nadeeka Prasanna's house – wifi routers, Alexas and so on. Unless the offenders' phones were in airplane mode they're likely to have automatically searched for nearby signals, and we may be able to retrieve that data.'

'Do we have the victim's phone?' The question comes from a detective drafted in from another team. Lauren's team has swollen to four times its usual size.

'No,' Hillary says. 'The so-called "DI Burton" seized Golding's phone, laptop and iPad, and later Nadeeka Prasanna's phone.'

The door at the back of the room opens, and Amber from the media team edges in, a full twenty minutes late. She seems nervy, one hand on the door, the other clutching two mobile phones. Lauren can't read her expression, but it seems more apprehensive than apologetic. Has something happened?

'Unfortunately, Ms Prasanna only had a limited free back-up service, so we don't have full access to her messages,' Hillary is saying. 'She has nevertheless given us permission to access her account, and we have been able to retrieve some of the messages sent between her and Golding. They shared their respective locations on a few occasions, and we're using these as entry points to try to access Golding's own cloud data.' He holds up a qualifying hand. 'No guarantees, of course.'

'Thanks, Hillary.' Lauren nods again and he sits back down. 'Right, everyone, let's get moving. Briefings will be daily at eight a.m. – I hope you appreciated the lie-in today – and four p.m., and I expect a full house.' Lauren's gaze travels slowly around the room. 'If you're tied up with an enquiry, I want an email update *before* briefing. Understood?'

There's a collective *Yes, ma'am*, and the room breaks up.

Lauren goes straight to Amber. 'I asked for a representative from media to be here at nine.'

'The story's hit the papers,' Amber says.

It's explanation enough, and perhaps inevitable, Lauren supposes. ATP Construction had issued a company-wide announcement about Jamie Golding's murder; of course someone was going to talk.

'Then we need a press release out as soon as possible.' She circles a hand in the air. '*We believe there's no risk to the public at large . . . reassurance patrols in the area . . . respect the privacy of the victim's family.*' She's thinking out loud. 'Stick to the facts. The murder took place on Monday, and we're *doing everything we can to bring the perpetrators to justice.* On no account do we mention the fake police.' This is what Lauren had intended to propose anyway, but it's frustrating that they now find themselves on the back foot. In police comms, there's a fine line between responsive and defensive.

Amber holds up the larger of her two phones and taps the screen to wake it. It takes Lauren a while to tune in to what she's seeing, but, when she does, her heart sinks. This is *not* what she'd intended.

Trending in the UK. The heading is followed by a list of hashtags. #*fakepolice* #*jamiegolding* #*corruptcops* #*defundthepolice*.

'How has this happened?' Lauren says, as much to herself as to Amber.

'It only takes one person. The internet does the rest.'

Lauren's carefully thought-out media strategy has gone up in smoke. The fake police story has gone viral.

CHAPTER 13

'I haven't said anything to anyone,' Nadeeka says. They're in a cluttered kitchen belonging to Nadeeka's mother-in-law, Kath, who had promised to *leave you to it, my loves,* but has since opened the door every few minutes on the pretext of collecting laundry or finding her keys, or *are you sure I can't get you anything?* Eventually, Lauren had said to Nadeeka, 'Is there somewhere we can go where we won't be disturbed?' and Kath had sniffed loudly and made a show of going to the shops.

'Who knows that the police officers you spoke to weren't real?' Lauren says.

'Only Kath,' Nadeeka says. 'I had to explain why we couldn't stay at home. I tried saying the forensics officers had forgotten to do something, but she didn't buy it. Her ex-husband was a police officer, and she watches a lot of crime dramas.' Nadeeka is wearing a pale blue sweatshirt with over-long sleeves she has tugged over her hands. As she talks, she screws the fabric between her fingers.

'Would she have told anyone?'

'Absolutely not,' Nadeeka says, but Lauren catches the flash of doubt that follows.

'Sure about that?'

'I guess she might have told Scott . . . my ex. You'll have to ask her.'

Lauren certainly will. Because if it hasn't come from Nadeeka's ex, or his mother, or from Nadeeka herself, there are only two other options. Either there's a leak from within Lauren's team, or someone from the fake team 'DI Burton' put together has been talking. Lauren hopes it's the latter; tracing back the leak could lead them to the perpetrators. The assistant chief constable has declared Jamie Golding's murder – or, more specifically, its cover-up – a critical incident, owing to the damage it could do to public confidence. The copy-and-pasted post that broke the story now exists in so many forms, across so many different social media platforms, that it is proving impossible to find the source. The pressure on Lauren's department to solve this case swiftly feels almost physical, a tight band around her temples.

'You will question Nicole Davis, won't you?' Nadeeka says. 'From Jamie's office?'

'We're speaking to anyone who had a connection to—'

'But especially her!' Nadeeka's voice rises. It's scratchy and thin, and Lauren wonders how much sleep she got last night. There are dark half-moons under her eyes and when she blinks her lids reopen slowly, as though they'd prefer to stay closed. 'She's the only one working there with the initials ND.' Nadeeka insists. 'It has to be her Jamie was meeting, which means she might know—'

'We will speak to Nicole,' Lauren says firmly. It's not uncommon for victims' relatives to feel impotent and want to take control, but Lauren is the one directing this investigation, not Nadeeka. They only have Nadeeka's word that Jamie's desk diary even exists, let alone contains references to mysterious rendezvous with an 'ND'. Nadeeka can only recall two of the five dates she supposedly saw marked in the diary; she's only certain of those because her daughters had rehearsals on those evenings.

'I remember because one of the other mums was going to

collect them,' she'd told Lauren, as they'd sat opposite each other in the windowless interview room at the police station. 'It meant Jamie and I could spend the evening together.'

'You must have been disappointed when he said he wouldn't be home till late.' Lauren had wanted to test the water. Had Nadeeka already known about the affair? Did she kill Jamie because she was consumed with jealousy? But then why tell Lauren about ND? Why go to the police station at all?

'A bit. But mostly I was glad he was settling in at work. Making friends.' Nadeeka's voice had cracked, and she'd pressed the heels of her palms into her eyes. 'I just wanted him to be happy.'

'Jamie's line manager isn't aware of Jamie spending any time with Nicole Davis,' Lauren says now.

'Maybe they kept it secret. Maybe Nicole's married.' Tears glimmer at Nadeeka's lashes, but there's bitterness in her expression. Lauren would be bitter too. In fact, it would devastate her, she thinks, and she feels renewed empathy for Nadeeka. Lauren has never been cheated on (as far as she knows), and the thought of Fraser doing so makes her stomach tie itself into knots.

'Jamie's colleagues have referred to him as quiet,' Lauren says. '*A bit of a loner*, one said.'

'That makes him sound . . . awkward.' Nadeeka shifts in her seat. 'Like he was weird or something. *Loner* is what they call school shooters, or suicide bombers.' The tears, which have been shuddering on her lashes, finally spill down her cheeks. 'He wasn't like that. He was a good man.' She tugs at her sleeves again. The hem on one of the arms is starting to fray.

'Did Jamie know anyone at ATP Construction before he started working there?' Lauren says. 'I wondered if that's how he came across the job.'

'No, he found the job on LinkedIn. I'd been wondering whether there might be something going at my place, but the only jobs were pretty low-paid.'

'What is it you do?'

'I'm in recruitment. I work at Echelon Warehousing – we're a distributor for online retailers.'

'Picking and packing?' Lauren smiles. 'I spent a summer doing that when I was at uni. We had a right laugh. It was mostly foreign workers back then.'

'It still is, although that's been harder since Brexit. Most of the office jobs have been centralized, and there wasn't anything suitable for Jamie, so it was great when the ATP job came up.'

'Did Jamie have many friends?'

'A few. Back home.'

'Home?' Lauren leaves a deliberate pause. 'Wasn't that with you?'

Nadeeka flushes. 'Where he used to live, I mean.'

'How were things between you and Jamie?'

'Fine,' Nadeeka says, but it's automatic, and it's clear she knows it. Her eyes drop to the table. 'To begin with, they were,' she adds, a little defensively. 'Better than fine. They were great. It was like we'd known each other our whole lives.' Despite her tears, a smile tugs at her lips.

'But?' Lauren says, when it's clear Nadeeka's reluctant to continue.

'But then he started staying late at work. And as I said, I was pleased he was getting to know people, that he was settling at work, but . . .' She stares blindly out of the window. 'One of the things I loved about Jamie was the way he looked at me – really looked, as if he wanted to see right into my soul, you know?'

Lauren has to stop herself from smiling. There's a particular look Fraser gives her that makes the whole world disappear. *What look?* Fraser had said once, amused by the idea that he held such power. But Lauren hadn't been able to explain. It was simply a look. And it meant everything.

'Well, a couple of weeks ago,' Nadeeka says, 'I realized he'd stopped doing that. He'd look at me, but then his eyes would kind of slide away. As if he was hiding something. That's when

It's Not What You Think

I realized he wasn't leaving his phone lying around any more, and I started getting paranoid that he might have met someone.'

'Did you confront him?'

'I didn't want to. If he wasn't cheating on me, I didn't want to ruin everything by accusing him, and if he was . . .' Nadeeka gives a sad smile. 'It was avoidance, I guess. I just kept pushing the thought back down, trying to make it go away.'

Lauren can't imagine being in a relationship like that: doubting your partner, doubting yourself. The kitchen door opens again, and she braces herself for another interruption from Kath, back from the shops, but it's Nadeeka's children. Lauren had met them earlier; two brown-eyed girls with long hair, who shyly said hello then ran off to play. They stand half in, half out of the room, the younger one staring openly at Lauren, while her older sister does the talking. 'Mum, are you nearly finished?'

Nadeeka looks to Lauren for an answer.

'Nearly.' Lauren smiles at the girls.

'We need black leggings for the show,' the older one says.

'And socks,' adds her sister. 'And big T-shirts in bright colours.'

'That's fine,' Nadeeka says. 'We have plenty of black socks and you both have leggings, and I'm sure I can find some suitable T-shirts. We'll be back home in a couple of days . . . right?' This last is directed at Lauren, who gives a non-committal nod. She's not about to rush a crime scene for the sake of some leggings.

'But we have to take them to school on Monday because we're having a costume check!'

'All the schools in the area are coming together for this year's Christmas show,' Nadeeka explains to Lauren. 'It's a multi-faith nativity written by one of the teachers.' She turns back to the children. 'I'm sure a few days won't make a difference.'

'Mrs Edwards says everyone has to have their costumes,' the older girl says, and there's a wobble in her voice that tugs at Lauren, who is happily child-free but occasionally wonders what it would be like to be so wanted, so *needed*.

'I'll be going by the house after I leave here,' Lauren says. 'I can pick up anything you need.'

'Really?' Nadeeka hesitates. 'The girls' leggings and socks will be in their drawers, but the T-shirts I'm thinking of are either under my bed or possibly in a box in the top of the wardrobe – I was going to take them to the charity shop, but I hadn't got around to it.'

'No problem,' Lauren says, and it isn't. In fact, it's ideal: it gives her the perfect excuse to poke through Nadeeka's belongings.

Lauren's mother calls as she's pulling into Cedar Walk.

'Darling, people keep asking me what wedding gifts to buy. I do wish you'd reconsider and set up a list.'

'We don't need anything, Mum. We've been living together for years; anything we've needed, we've bought.'

'How about an air fryer?'

'Can I call you back? I'm in the middle of a murder investigation.' Lauren parks outside Nadeeka's house, where a white CSI van is parked on the driveway.

'You always say that, darling, it's starting to sound like an excuse.'

'Mum, I work on a murder squad.'

There's no police tape across Nadeeka's front door, but a uniformed officer stands guard, his fingers curled into fists for warmth.

'While I've got you,' Lauren's mum says, 'have you done the sugared almonds?'

Lauren thinks of the untouched boxes on her kitchen table. 'Yes.'

'Excellent. That's one less thing we have to worry about.'

We? Lauren thinks. Her mother's primary contribution to the wedding has been to insist on complicated plans she has then left to her daughter to execute. Lauren is beginning to wish she'd given in to Fraser's suggestion that they elope. 'I'll call you later, Mum.' She ends the call.

As she gets out of the car, she realizes she's being watched. A man, grey-haired, and coatless despite the cold, is standing on the pavement on the opposite side of the road. He walks towards her.

It's Not What You Think

'Can I help you?' He's wearing slippers. A neighbour, then, Lauren thinks.

She lifts up the ID card hanging on the lanyard around her neck. 'Detective Chief Inspector Lauren Caldwell. Major crime.'

'Is that right?' The man takes hold of the card to inspect it and the lanyard tugs Lauren uncomfortably close. He points at the photo. 'That doesn't look like you.'

'It was taken a while ago.'

The man is still scrutinizing Lauren's picture. 'Detective Inspector, you say?'

'Detective *Chief* Inspector. And you are?'

'Someone with enough smarts to check people are who they say they are.' He drops the lanyard, seemingly satisfied, and Lauren takes a step back. 'Stanley Hall. No. 17.' He jerks his head towards Nadeeka's house. 'Shocking, what happened.'

'Did you know Mr Golding?'

'That's his name, is it? We said hello a few times, but he wasn't very forthcoming. I got the impression he was one of those *introverts*. Wasn't the least bit interested in the council newsletter I took over for him, despite my having circled a particularly important section on hedge maintenance.'

Lauren thinks she'd probably become an introvert if she lived opposite Stanley. 'Were you at home on Monday afternoon?' she asks him.

'I was indeed. I was putting up the Christmas decorations. My granddaughter Maeve was coming over and I wanted to surprise her.'

'When did you become aware something was going on at No. 10?'

'Not until the *police* arrived.' Stanley puts giant air quotes around the word. 'I saw the blue and white tape across the front door, so I went across. To see if I could help,' he adds.

'Of course.'

'He didn't want to know, of course. The *detective*. Which makes sense now we know he was a wrong 'un, but at the time? I was fuming, I can tell you. Almost made a complaint then and there.'

If only he had, Lauren thinks. 'Can you describe him?'

'Caucasian – that's what you say, isn't it?'

'White?'

'That's right. And in his late fifties maybe, or sixties – I'd say at least ten or fifteen years younger than me, and I'm seventy-five.'

'Build?'

'Broad shoulders, but not muscly. Not fat, either. Just solid. He had a tie on, I remember that because most people seem to dress down nowadays, even in office jobs. That ex of hers . . .' he nods to Nadeeka's house again. 'The girls' dad. I've never seen him out of gym clothes, and he's supposedly an IT manager.'

Lauren tunes out.

'Her new chap was always suited and booted; it was quite the sight seeing them squaring up to each other.'

'I'm sorry—' Lauren refocuses. 'Squaring up to each other?'

'A few weeks ago. No idea what it was about, but they had a proper shouting match. Right here in the street. Then the ex landed a punch, and the new chap brought his fist up but thought better of it. It was all over in a matter of minutes.'

'Would you be happy to give us a statement?'

'About them fighting?'

'And about what you saw on Monday. I'll send a colleague over, if that's all right?'

'That would be fine.'

The crime scene investigation officers are working in Nadeeka's living room, with the forensic lead, Hannah Foster, directing proceedings. The carpets have been ripped up and a section of skirting board taken off the wall. On the underlay, and soaked into the base of the exposed wall, is a large rust-coloured stain.

'If you ever stab someone . . .' Hannah joins Lauren in the hallway ' . . . keep your victim away from the walls. It's almost impossible to get blood out from under skirting boards, no matter how much bleach you slosh about.'

'Top tip. What's your verdict?'

'I know there was some suggestion this might have been cooked up by the pair of them so Golding could disappear, but the extent of the blood loss suggests little or no chance of life.' Hannah's mask catches on her hair as she pulls it off. 'This isn't a MisPer investigation; it's murder.'

Lauren finds Fraser upstairs, looking through the wardrobe in the master bedroom.

'She didn't give the poor bloke much room.' He pushes back the sliding doors to reveal a rack of women's clothes beside the handful of hangers holding jackets and shirts.

'Maybe the dresses are his.'

'Don't come at me with your wokery, Lauren soon-to-be-Hogan.'

'Soon to be Caldwell-Hogan, actually. Anyway, some guys just don't have much stuff. My brother's been in his place for three years and it still looks like he just moved in.'

'Golding had hardly anything. These clothes, another drawerful over there, and the desk on the landing. Are we even sure he existed?'

'He existed all right; the neighbour just told me he had a stack-up with Nadeeka's ex. Can you run a PNC check on him? His name's Scott Hadley.' Lauren moves a stool across to the wardrobe to look on the top shelf, where Nadeeka had thought the charity shop donations might be.

'Sure. I'm heading back to the nick now anyway. CSI have Golding's toothbrush and they'll fast-track the submission so we can see if his DNA's a match for any unidentified bodies.'

'Make sure it goes to Interpol too,' Lauren calls after him, her voice muffled by the wardrobe.

She finds the T-shirts, but nothing else of interest. She doesn't know what she's looking for really, but even just being here in

Nadeeka's house helps her get a handle on what kind of woman she is; what kind of relationship she had with Jamie. The place is clean, but the house is short on storage and there are baskets everywhere, overflowing with toys and shoes. Hanging on the walls are dozens of photos of Maya and Nish at different ages, and several of the girls with Jamie. On Nadeeka's nightstand is a novel and a notebook. Lauren takes a peek – she is definitely overstepping the limits of Nadeeka's permission now – but it's just lists. Things to do, groceries to buy, meals to cook. Maybe Jamie helped out, but Nadeeka definitely carried the mental load.

Lauren wonders if she's just lucky – she and Fraser have always split the chores fifty-fifty – or whether this imbalance is something that happens when a couple have children. She thinks about Bahnaz dashing off to collect her little ones, and wonders whether Bahnaz's partner ever does the same.

In the top drawer of the nightstand, Lauren finds hand cream, lip salve, a selection of hairbands, and a bundle of cards and letters secured with an elastic band. She looks through them. There are sweet notes from the kids; birthday cards from *Appa and Amma*. Nadeeka's parents, perhaps? Grandparents? A card from Jamie reads, *Six months today! Love you always and forever x*.

At the back of the drawer, tightly creased, as though it had once been screwed in a ball, is a letter. Lauren recognizes the handwriting from Jamie's card.

I'm so sorry, Nadeeka. Please believe me, I never meant to hurt you. I love you, but I think it's best if I move out. J x

Lauren sits on the edge of the bed. When had Jamie written this note, and why hadn't Nadeeka mentioned it to her? She's now spent several hours with Nadeeka and she doesn't doubt that Nadeeka loved Jamie. But it's clear, too, that she'd been terrified of losing him.

Lauren reads the note again. So Jamie had been planning to leave Nadeeka.

How far might Nadeeka have gone to stop him?

CHAPTER 14

Nicole Davis, an account manager at ATP Construction, is fidgeting with a stack of silver bracelets on her slim wrist.

'I've never been interviewed by the police before.' She laughs nervously. She has the most perfect eye make-up Lauren's ever seen – a vibrant glimmer of green shadow above thick cat's-eye flicks – and Lauren wonders if she should book someone to do her wedding make-up. She'd been planning to do it herself, but she's never been able to master eyeliner; one side is always higher than the other.

'This isn't really an interview,' Fraser says, his voice reassuring.

'We just want to ask a few questions,' Lauren adds. 'Nothing to worry about.'

'And I'm right here.' Carrie Finder is head of 'People and Culture', a title Lauren knows will have Fraser inwardly rolling his eyes. 'This is just an informal chat, isn't it, DCI Caldwell?'

Carrie is wearing a navy blazer over a patterned dress, her feet encased in white trainers with a platform sole. She has a jittery energy which makes her jump up every few minutes to close a window, or turn up the heating, or check whether anyone needs a glass of water. Lauren would have preferred to interview Nicole on her own, but Carrie had insisted on HR being present. 'Unless Nicole's under arrest, of course?' She'd given a nervous laugh which showed too many teeth.

'Nicole,' Lauren says now, 'can you tell me what your relationship to Jamie Golding was?'

'I didn't have a relationship with him!' Nicole's jangling bracelets match her outrage.

'I meant were you colleagues?' Lauren says. 'Friends?'

'Oh. Just colleagues. I maybe spoke to him in the kitchen a few times, but that's it.'

'We're a very friendly company,' Carrie says. 'We put on a summer barbecue, and the five-a-side football's been very popular.' On their way to Carrie's office, Lauren had spotted various posters advertising staff socials. A book club. A 'knit and natter'. A coach trip to see *Hamilton*. It all sounded quite nice. Fraser might scoff at 'People and Culture', but the police could do with a few tips from Carrie Finder.

'Did you ever see Jamie outside work?' Fraser asks.

'No.' Nicole shakes her head. 'Look, I feel sorry for Jamie's partner – I can't imagine what she's going through – but it's not okay for her to come in here chucking accusations around, let alone bringing the police in.'

'Absolutely,' Carrie says.

Lauren turns to look at Carrie, who immediately colours. She turns back to Nicole. 'Do you mind me asking whether you're in a relationship?'

'I do mind, as it happens. But I'm not.'

Lauren can't help but notice the way Nicole looks at Fraser as she says this. His face is impassive, but she'll tease him about it later. Fraser's undeniably good-looking, and Lauren is used to the glances he gets from other women. Even Carrie had flushed slightly when Fraser introduced himself.

It's Not What You Think

'Could you tell me what you were doing on these dates?' Lauren hands Nicole a piece of paper, on which are written the two 'ND' dates of which Nadeeka had been certain.

Nicole looks at the list, then she gets out her phone and opens her calendar. 'I was in Tenerife on the first one,' she says a moment later. 'I would have been at work on the second, more's the pity.'

'What about after work?'

'It was a Monday, so I'd have been in the gym with my mate. Ask her, if you want.'

Twenty years in the job has made Lauren a pretty good judge of character. Nicole Davis didn't have anything to do with Jamie's death. The woman's face bears no suggestion of unrequited love, or grief, or even of guilt; only irritation at having been targeted first by Nadeeka and then by the police. If Jamie had been planning on leaving Nadeeka, it wasn't for Nicole.

Lauren glances at Fraser, who gives a barely perceptible nod. Agreed. 'You've been very helpful, thank you.'

Carrie sees Nicole out. 'Would you like to speak to anyone else?'

'Not right now, but could you let me have a copy of Jamie's HR file?' Lauren says. 'I understand his partner has already given permission.'

'No problem.' Carrie crosses the room to her desk, jiggling her mouse to wake the screen. 'I can let you have his onboarding, risk assessments, training records . . .' She talks to herself as the printer whirs into action. 'No disciplinaries, no performance reviews, no complaints . . .'

'He sounds like a model employee,' Lauren says.

'The good die young, isn't that what they say?' Carrie gives another awkward laugh.

Lauren doesn't pass comment. In her experience, there's no such thing as good or bad. Everyone exists on a spectrum, and a single trigger can propel them from one side to the other.

'Mr Bennington mentioned you'd be able to give us access

to Jamie's files,' she says. 'I understand they're all stored on a central hard drive.'

'That's right.' Carrie moves her mouse again, a series of rapid clicks bringing up a folder entitled *Jamie Golding*. 'Permissions vary according to role; Jamie would have been able to see the project managers' files, for example, but not, say, anything in procurement, or legal.' She stands back and allows Lauren to take a look.

Golding's files are contained within a number of folders, each bearing the title of what Lauren assumes are construction projects. *Cairnwood Heights*, *Langford Science & Innovation Campus*, *Ridgeway Vale Housing Development*. Within each of these she finds a number of files with names like *Construction_Method_Statement.docx*, *Hazardous_Materials_Register.xlsx*, and *Accessibility_Audit.pdf*. Lauren opens and closes each one methodically, in case Golding had been using the file names as cover for something more personal.

Lauren is about to close a folder entitled *Redburn Point* when she notices the italicized text in the right-hand corner. *Last modified*. She glances at Fraser. 'Something in this folder was changed on Tuesday – the day after Golding was murdered.'

'We manage a lot of construction sites,' Carrie says. 'It's possible someone needed to access Jamie's files.'

'That's what's puzzling me,' Lauren says. 'There *are* no files.' She shows them the empty folder. 'If a file was deleted, would it be on the central hard drive?'

Carrie shakes her head. 'It would go into the recycling bin on the computer of whoever deleted it.'

'Who has access to Jamie's folders?' Fraser says.

'Only one person.' Carrie hesitates. 'The boss.'

'So do you reckon Adam Bennington is our man?' Fraser says, as they walk back to the car. 'He doesn't match the description of any of our fake police officers.'

It's Not What You Think

'Doesn't mean he's not involved.'

With Adam apparently out of the office all day, Lauren and Fraser had waited at ATP Construction with an increasingly uncomfortable Carrie until someone from digital forensics could come out to look at Adam's computer. 'I'm not sure you should be doing this without Adam's—' Carrie had started, but Lauren had shown her the warrant Bahnaz had sent through and she'd fallen silent. They had left the forensics officer to it, and Lauren's intrigued to discover what he will uncover.

'It certainly looks that way.' She unlocks the car. 'Can you find out when Jamie Golding's Hinge profile was last active? It's how he and Nadeeka met, and I'm wondering if he ever swiped right – or is it left? – on anyone with the initials ND.'

'It's right.'

Lauren raises an eyebrow and Fraser laughs.

'What? Don't tell me you never used the apps?'

'I prefer to meet my men the old-fashioned way.'

'On the phone, right?'

Now it's Lauren's turn to smile. 'Right.'

She'd been a detective inspector on the counter-terrorism unit when she first spoke to Fraser, who had called the office after a uniform officer had discovered several bags of fertilizer in a sixth-floor flat.

'What makes you think it's suspicious?' Lauren had said.

'Fourteen years in the army,' Fraser replied, without missing a beat. He had a low, quietly authoritative voice and an accent Lauren couldn't place. When the call had ended, she'd found herself disappointed. Six months later, at a leaving do for one of her sergeants, she'd heard it again, from the man standing next to her at the bar.

'Vodka and Coke, please.'

Lauren hadn't been able to recall his name. 'Fourteen years in the army?' she'd said instead.

Fraser had turned to look at her with astonishment. 'You can get that from one drinks order? If you're not a DC, your skills are going to waste.'

'I'm a DI, actually.' She'd held his gaze, a smile playing across her lips.

She had gone home with him, despite her previously strict rule about not dating anyone in the job. And now they're getting married. Despite the lists of arrangements they have yet to make, Lauren gets a tiny dart of excitement as she thinks about her wedding day; about becoming Mrs Caldwell-Hogan.

Her phone pings with a text from the detective superintendent. *Look at BBC News.* She opens the app. There have been pockets of unrest in Maidstone and a hundred miles away in Aylesbury. The accompanying photos show protestors carrying banners with DEFUND THE POLICE and NO TRUST, NO MANDATE. *We're paying taxes for the police to let the criminals clean up their own murder scenes*, a man is quoted as saying. *It's time for radical reform. If you think the same, we urge you to take to the streets and show your support.*

Fuck. Lauren puts the phone in her pocket. Could Adam Bennington be behind Jamie Golding's murder? If they solve this case quickly, they could still turn the narrative around.

And if they don't?

Things could get out of control. Fast.

Back at the station, she finds a USB stick on her desk containing the downloaded footage she requested from the officers who stopped Nadeeka for running a red light. She slots it into her laptop and presses play.

The body-worn camera is on the female officer; Lauren catches a glimpse of manicured nails as a hand adjusts her radio. The police constable is standing at the front of Nadeeka's car, reading out the licence plate, and although Lauren sees Nadeeka in the driver's seat she can't make out her expression. Did Nadeeka engineer this stop-check? Did she spot the police car and deliberately speed up, knowing they would pull her over and that, later, she'd be able to say she was nowhere near the crime scene?

But then why go there at all?

Maybe she wanted to mess with the scene. Deposit evidence on the body to . . . what? Frame someone else? Cover her back in case Jamie's body was found?

Lauren lets the back-and-forth play out in her head, testing out theories to see what feels right. She runs the footage on until the female officer joins her colleague beside the car, and Lauren can finally see Nadeeka's face up close.

'Is there a problem at home?' the female officer asks her.

Nadeeka is nodding. 'But I needed to see it for myself . . .'

Lauren watches intently. Nadeeka keeps shifting her gaze: looking first at the officers, then beyond them, then down into the car. She looks uncomfortable, nervous.

'What a shit,' the female officer says. Lauren winces. Bit unprofessional, but when you're trying to build a rapport it's easy to go too far. She's done it herself.

'I had one of those once,' the commentary continues. 'He got T-boned by a ten-tonne artic, and it couldn't have happened to a nicer guy, to be honest.'

Okay. Definitely oversharing now. Lauren brings up a second screen on her laptop and looks up the officer's details. Eleven years in the job. Should know better. On the video, Nadeeka is giving the same story she later told Lauren about hearing a train and realizing Jamie was at home. If it's a lie, it's at least a consistent one.

'The bastard!' the female officer says, swiftly followed by 'Go on, love. Give him what for!' and Lauren tips her head up and lets out her frustration in a long, slow breath. When – if – her team gets someone in the dock for Jamie Golding's murder, how is that going to look? A warranted officer inciting the victim's partner to have it out with him? The defence are going to have a field day.

Lauren writes an email to the officer's inspector. She can't not, especially given current views on police professionalism. 'Bloody idiot,' she mutters.

'You okay, boss?' It's Matt Draper, standing in Lauren's doorway with a printout and what looks distinctly like optimism.

'Give me criminals over police officers any day,' Lauren says. 'What have you got?'

'There are only four houses in the close with cameras and only two of those provide a view that extends to the street itself. In both cases, our DI Burton asked the owners for access to the cloud system so he could download the footage himself, then deleted the original data.'

'Can the manufacturers retrieve it?'

'We're working on it. But in the meantime . . .' Matt holds up the sheet of paper and walks towards Lauren's desk. 'The woman at No. 6 has a Tesla which has something called "Sentry Mode". It's basically continuously recording.'

Lauren's pulse picks up. 'And?'

'We've got the reg plate of DI Burton's blue Corsa.' Matt hands the printout to Lauren. 'It's a rental. I've asked for a full lift and forensics are standing by.'

Lauren looks at the registration number. 'Nice work.' She imagines 'DI Burton' handing back the keys at the rental desk, walking away confident he'd covered his tracks.

We're coming for you, she thinks. *It's just a matter of time.*

CHAPTER 15

There had been three files in the Redburn Point folder on Jamie Golding's hard drive. These have been retrieved from the trash folder on Adam Bennington's computer, after he had deleted them last Tuesday afternoon, immediately after Nadeeka's visit to ATP Construction.

'Which was presumably when you learned Jamie was dead?' Lauren says. She leans back in her chair. She and Fraser are sitting opposite Adam in a small, windowless interview room.

'That's right.' Adam isn't – yet – under arrest. Lauren could have used one of the statement rooms near the front desk, but she finds people like Adam respond remarkably well to the foetid air and echoing shouts of a custody suite, doing everything in their power to get out as quickly as possible.

'And your first instinct on hearing this news was to have a little tidy-up of Jamie's files?' Lauren raises an eyebrow.

'No, I – I thought I should see if there was anything pressing I'd need to reallocate.' Sweat beads on Adam's forehead, despite the air-conditioning that rattles through ancient pipes into the stale room.

Lauren lets silence fill the space between them. Beside her, Fraser scribbles a note and tilts it towards her. *Absolute bollocks*, Lauren reads, and she nods gravely, as though his contribution were extraordinarily insightful.

Adam looks nervously at Fraser's notebook, which was precisely the intent. He swallows. 'I might have deleted the files by accident.'

'You might have?' Lauren says.

'I did. I deleted them by accident. It's easily done.'

'Absolutely.' Fraser stretches his fingers over an invisible keyboard. 'Control-A-delete. Could happen to anyone.'

Adam narrows his eyes, but is wise enough not to rise to the sarcasm.

'The thing is, I've had a look at those files, and they're rather interesting.' Lauren smiles. 'Redburn Point is a housing development, right? And it's being built on the site of a reclaimed quarry.'

'Yes. It was a brownfield site. It's been empty for decades.'

'What exactly was Jamie's role in relation to Redburn Point?' Fraser asks.

'He carried out site inspections, ensured safety compliance, that sort of thing.'

Lauren opens her laptop and brings up the sections she's highlighted. 'Jamie carried out a risk assessment of Redburn Point last month, in which he identified hazardous working conditions.' She looks up. 'Were you aware of this?'

'We had a conversation about it, yes,' Adam says carefully.

'Jamie's report raises concerns over the integrity of the ground.' Lauren reads from Jamie's report. ' . . . including *visible cracking in the soil, minor displacement of scaffolding, and irregular shifts in the ground level.*'

'Health and safety officers can go overboard—'

'*Given the potential for ground instability and the unknown nature of the underlying soil conditions, I recommend immediate suspension of all site work in the affected area until a full geotechnical survey can be conducted to assess the extent of the issue.*' Lauren stops. 'Sounds expensive.'

'It was a recommendation, that's all.'

'One you didn't want to follow?' Fraser says.

'The site had been the subject of numerous surveys prior to planning permission being granted. I disagreed with Jamie's findings.'

'So you deleted the files.' Lauren holds Adam's gaze as she draws out the words. 'Where were you last Monday morning?' she says briskly, startling Adam with the sudden change of pace.

'I was out of the office. I had a client meeting.'

'Did your client meeting take you anywhere near Jamie's home address?'

'No.' Adam's face creases. 'Look, okay, I deleted the files. Closing the site for another survey would cost us a hundred grand or more, and there's nothing wrong with the ground – Jamie was out of line putting that in his risk assessment.'

'How convenient, then,' Lauren says, 'that he's no longer around to raise objections.'

'If you're suggesting I killed him—'

'I'd like the details of the client you met last Monday morning, plus the precise route you took to get there.' Lauren snaps her laptop shut. 'In the meantime, Mr Bennington, I suggest you take another look at that site survey. I'm sure you'd hate to find yourself at the wrong end of a lawsuit.'

The airless interview room has given Lauren a headache. She stuffs her coat into her backpack and hands it to Fraser with her laptop to take in the car. 'I'm going to run home,' she tells him. 'Clear my head. Do you think you could swing by Foxleigh Manor and check everything's okay?' Just over a week ago, the event manager at Lauren and Fraser's beautiful eighteenth-century wedding venue had discovered she had inadvertently double-booked the day.

'Will do,' Fraser says. He had been her hero that day: dropping everything to go to Foxleigh, and refusing to leave until they honoured their booking, the deposit for which had been paid long before the other couple's.

'I think I'll need to literally see their bookings diary before I can trust them.' Lauren screws up her face. 'Imagine if all our guests turn up and it's a different couple saying their vows.'

'Relax.' Fraser puts his hands on either side of her shoulders and squeezes. 'I'll have her write the entry in indelible ink.'

'Or in blood,' Lauren suggests, giving a lopsided grin.

'Also, I've lined up the Civic Centre as a back-up venue. Which we won't need,' he adds quickly, before Lauren can spiral. 'I'm just covering all bases.'

'I feel like your years of army logistics are finally paying off.' She grins. 'Off you go, then. I'll race you home.'

The ten-kilometre route home is exactly what Lauren needs. She weaves through the busy streets, running through a cloud of her own breath as it mists before her, working her way through the investigation to date. Everything they have so far suggests that Jamie Golding's murder was targeted, possibly even premeditated.

Adam Bennington is the first suspect they've identified with a clear motive. Had Golding threatened to be more vocal about the risks he'd identified at Redburn Point? Could that be why he'd called in sick? If so, Bennington might have gone to Cedar Walk to have it out with him, and taken things too far.

Lauren jogs on the spot as she waits for the lights to change at a pedestrian crossing. But Adam Bennington didn't strike her as a man plugged into the sorts of criminal networks that have the resources to pull off a clear-up stunt like this one. Uniformed officers, marked cars, forensic cleaning . . . these were the hallmarks of organized crime.

It's Not What You Think

Drugs, then? Nadeeka claims Golding had no history of drug-taking, but some of the most prolific dealers Lauren has dealt with were similarly clean. *Filthy stuff,* one self-confessed coke dealer told her once. *Wouldn't touch it with a bargepole.*

How about money? Laundering; gambling; counterfeiting? Lauren brainstorms as she runs, making a mental note to chase Kenric for an update on Golding's credit rating and insurance policies. When she last checked HOLMES – the computer system on which all investigative actions are logged – there were several outstanding enquiries, and Lauren wants them all ticked off tomorrow.

Fortunately for Lauren, her team are as hungry for a result as she is, and there's an almost physical energy in the briefing room when she arrives at eight the following morning. Her phone – on silent for the meeting – flashes, and Lauren glances at the screen in case it's urgent, but it's only her mother. She lets the call go to voicemail and focuses on Matt's update on the blue Corsa.

'The rental was paid for with a cloned credit card,' he says. 'Bahnaz is working with the fraud team to identify when and where the cloning took place, but it's unlikely we'll get a useful lead from that – you know how that one goes.'

'I want to know what other transactions have been made with the same card,' Lauren says. 'We know they cleaned up after themselves meticulously; did they buy bleach, cleaning cloths?' She looks at Kenric, who makes a note. 'Maybe they bought burner phones. Ask financial investigations to build up a picture.'

'Yes, boss,' Matt says. 'We've also got a photocopied driver's licence in the same name as the credit card, which is a confirmed forgery. There's CCTV on the forecourt, but not in the office where the keys are handed over.'

'Are the cars valeted between hires?' Lauren asks.

'Unfortunately, yes.'

'I rented a car at the airport when I went to Ibiza last summer,'

Kenric says. 'Found an actual hot dog in the glovebox.' There are snorts of laughter from around the room.

'In addition to the physical forensic examination,' Matt says, 'digital forensics are working on the telematics.' He looks at Lauren. 'Okay if I pass over to AJ? He'll explain it better than I will.'

'Go for it.' AJ Carter, digital forensic investigator, looks impossibly young, like a sixth-former on work experience, but Lauren has worked with him before. She knows how good he is.

AJ clears his throat. 'We use a software system called Berla to extract data from a vehicle's infotainment system. Speed logs, gear-shifts, even door-opens. If we can compile enough data, we can attempt to overlay it on a street map, in order to establish a direction of travel.'

Lauren's phone is flashing again – *Mum mobile* – and she cancels the call, her focus back on AJ. She often wonders if the general public have any idea just how much of a trail they leave behind. There's a long-held principle of forensics that 'every contact leaves a trace', and Lauren thinks the maxim holds even more truth in today's digital world. It is virtually impossible to cover your tracks completely.

'In the meantime, whoever hired the car plugged their phone into the charging port,' AJ says. 'We've been able to extract the IMEI number and have confirmed the phone was a pay-as-you-go – almost certainly a burner. The number's been fed into the intelligence system.'

'Excellent work, thank you.' Lauren turns to the wider team. 'Who's on ANPR?' Sonya Marston puts her arm in the air. 'Let's get a convoy analysis done,' Lauren says. 'See if we can identify any of the other vehicles we know were involved.'

'Yes, boss.'

Convoy analysis is a time-consuming task, but if ever an investigation warranted the budget, it's this one. The goal is to identify vehicles travelling in the same direction at the same time, based not only on their routes but on the gaps between them.

It's Not What You Think

'Kenric...' She looks around the room for DC Fennell. 'What have you found out about Jamie Golding?'

'No previous convictions, no stop-checks, no driving convictions.' Kenric swivels a pen through the fingers of his right hand as he speaks. 'No CCJs or civil cases. No kids, no previous marriages. No known criminal associates.' He looks up. 'Basically, no tea.'

'Any other updates?' Lauren's phone is flashing again. Why doesn't her mum just leave a voicemail? Or send a text?

'You asked me to check with stores to see if any uniform's been reported lost or stolen?' Bahnaz says. 'They haven't had anything recently.'

'That means nothing,' Kenric says. He looks around. 'Oh, come on: no one's going to cough to losing a helmet when they know they'll get a bollocking for it. They'll put in a request for a new one and say the old one got blood on it and had to be binned.'

'Sounds like someone's speaking from experience,' Fraser says. Kenric holds up his hands, overplaying his innocence.

'Then I want to know which officers have exceeded their kit allocation in the last two years,' Lauren says. 'And check online auctions for police uniform. Vinted, eBay, Facebook Marketplace.' She looks around for a free officer, and lands on a young PC, seconded from uniform. 'Nadeeka Prasanna met DI Burton at the Copper Kettle on Stratton Street. They don't have CCTV, but the surrounding buildings might have, and it's possible the staff might remember something. Are you happy to take that?'

The PC nods eagerly. 'Yes, ma'am.'

Lauren's mother is calling again. Has something terrible happened? Lauren's dad's not been well, and she's been so busy she hasn't had a chance to visit. She looks at the clock. 'We'll leave it there for now. Any questions, I'll be in my office.'

Lauren calls her mum back the second she leaves the room. 'Sorry, I was in a meeting. What's up? Is it Dad?'

'Have you sent the shot list to the photographer yet? Because I want to add Angela to the group shot with the cousins. She's having a difficult year, and I think she'd like to be included.'

Lauren stops walking. 'Is that it?'

'She'll be in the Important Women shot anyway, so this is just an extra—'

'No, I mean, is that all you wanted to talk to me about? I just closed down a briefing early, Mum – I thought it was something important!'

'It's your wedding day, Lauren; it's the most important day of your life.'

'Right – of *my* life! Not bloody Angela's!'

'Don't you dare shout at me!' Lauren's mum's voice cracks. 'I keep trying to help with the wedding preparations and all you do is throw it back in my face. Your brother's made it perfectly clear he's not interested in getting married, and now you're denying me—'

'Oh, for God's sake, Mum, I'm not denying any—'

But the line has gone dead. Lauren takes her phone from her ear and looks at the screen, weighing up the need to make peace with her mother against the pressure of a murder enquiry currently making headlines across the country.

'Hey.' Fraser comes up behind her, touching her gently on her waist. 'You okay?'

'Mum,' she says. It's all the explanation needed.

'She loves you. She's excited for the wedding.'

'She's got a funny way of showing it.' Lauren presses her palms against her closed eyes, fighting the sudden urge to cry. 'There's so much to do, Fraser. The seating plan, and those bloody sugared almonds, plus I've got to get bridesmaid gifts . . .'

'Says who?'

'It's just what you do.'

'Look at me.' Fraser moves to face her. 'Yasmin and Lucy won't give a shit about bridesmaid gifts. They're there to support you. The only bit of this wedding that matters is the bit where we say *I do*. Right?'

'Right.' Lauren takes a deep breath, centring herself. 'You're right.'

'I always am.' Fraser grins. 'Now, can I take anything off your plate in relation to this job?'

Lauren shakes her head. 'Thanks, but compared to a wedding?' She flashes him a smile. 'Murder's a doddle.'

In her office, Lauren starts to work her way through her inbox. She deletes a couple of dozen emails, flags a dozen more to deal with later, and sifts through the ones marked as urgent.

Matt puts a tentative head around her door. 'Am I interrupting?'

Lauren spins her chair towards the door. 'What have you got?'

'Financial investigations have got more on that cloned card.' He walks towards her desk. 'It was also used to make a payment of £4,500 to a company called Safeguard Solutions.'

'Are they a security firm?'

'Safeguard Solutions is a cleaning firm specializing in biohazard disposal.' Matt delivers the news with a 'mic drop' grin. 'They've got a website and everything.'

Lauren's mouth falls open. She spins her chair back to her desk and Googles Safeguard Solutions. She's been following the hypothesis that whoever murdered Jamie was also the person who cleaned up the scene; she has tasked officers with checking local stores to see if anyone had purchased large quantities of bleach; with looking through recycling bins near the scene for empty containers. Never once had Lauren imagined the criminals would have used a bona fide company.

Safeguard Solutions. Specialist technicians providing hoarder house clearance, crime scene cleaning and trauma decontamination across the UK.

A broad smile stretches across Lauren's face. Now they're getting somewhere.

CHAPTER 16

Gary Fisher, the one-man band behind Safeguard Solutions, is surprisingly jolly for a man who spends his days cleaning up hazardous chemicals and bodily fluids. 'Blood is my speciality,' he says, beaming at Lauren. 'That's why I'm trying to get into crime scene clean-up. I do a lot of work for the council, but it's mostly hoarders, or people who died of old age three months ago and someone's only just noticed.' Gary is wearing jogging bottoms and a matching hooded top; more PE teacher than hazardous waste cleaner, Lauren thinks.

'How did you hear about the job in Cedar Walk?' she asks.

'I got a phone call off someone from your control room. At least, that's what he told me. *Control room sergeant*, he said.' Gary holds up his hands, reinforcing his innocence. 'He asked if I could be at the property in the next hour. Well, I was supposed to be clearing a squat for the council, but I said yes, of course I could. I've been trying to get on the police rota for years.'

'What were you asked to do?'

'Get the bloodstain out of the carpet – it needs to look good as new, he said – then deep-clean the whole property.' He roots in his pocket and pulls out a phone. 'I mean, look at the state of this.'

'You've got photos?' Lauren leans forward to take the phone.

'I get difficult clients sometimes. They claim something's been damaged, or that I've not done a good enough job.' He points at the screen. 'Swipe, and you'll see how I left it. Like a show home, it was.'

But it isn't the show home shots Lauren's interested in; it's the *before* photo, with its deep slash of blood across the carpet. There's a small table on its side – upturned in a struggle? – and what look like footprints around the edges of the bloodstain. Lauren wonders if it will be possible to enhance them, perhaps see the pattern left by the sole.

'May I email these to myself, please?' She fights the urge to smile. They have a crime scene photo! Okay, so it's not the careful, cover-all-angles shots CSI would have given her, but it's a damn sight more than they had at the start of this murder investigation.

'Go ahead. Could you put in a good word for me going on the rota? I do a better job than any of the big companies you use that are all agency staff. I'm systematic, see – I don't miss bits like they do.'

More's the pity, Lauren thinks. The one time they could have done with a slapdash job. 'What do you do with your cleaning cloths and PPE when you're finished?'

'It's all incinerated. Has to be, or I lose my licence. I bag everything up, then every Tuesday afternoon it gets collected and—'

'Every Tuesday?'

'It used to be Fridays too, but business has been a bit slow lately, so I dropped back to once a week. The council deal with their own disposals, so it's just—'

'Tuesday as in today?' Lauren cuts across him. 'Are you telling me the cleaning cloths from Cedar Walk are still here?'

'They're bagged up in the basement.'

Lauren feels a surge of energy. Thank God for Gary Fisher's declining business.

*

She arrives back at the station with the crime scene photograph, Gary Fisher's elimination DNA and fingerprints, and two bags of potential evidence.

'Can you book this lot into property and send the submissions to CSI?' Lauren asks Fraser. 'They should already have the list of officers and staff who entered the property, as well as elims from Nadeeka, Jamie and the kids. If there's any other DNA on those rags, we're game on.'

'Sure.' Fraser looks at his watch. 'Uber Eats tonight? I can't see either of us getting off till at least eight.'

'Sounds good.' They lock eyes for a second, a no-touch micro-hug that gives Lauren the boost she needs to go back to her office and update the detective superintendent. Tensions locally are still high, and every other news update seems to be about another anti-police protest. This morning, Lauren had woken to the headline *Increase in assault against police down to lack of trust, says councillor*. She had swiped it away and thought instead of the advice she always gives the younger officers she mentors.

Focus on what you can control.

Lauren can't solve what has now become a national crisis; she can only do her damnedest to solve this murder, and hope that goes some way to restoring public confidence in the police. And, for the first time since she learned about Jamie Golding's murder, she thinks that might be possible. As well as the evidence they've seized from Gary Fisher, waiting in Lauren's inbox is a still image of the 'police officer' who had been standing outside Nadeeka's house when she arrived home last Monday. Lauren reads the accompanying email from Hillary Kent in digital forensics – *Managed to retrieve hard drive data from the doorbell cam at No. 14. Still working on the others* – then opens the image.

The man looks to be in his early twenties. He's white, with dark hair and no visible tattoos. He's wearing police uniform: black trousers and boots, a black fleece with the collar turned up, and a flat cap with the glint of a badge above the peak. The image is too indistinct to make out the detail of the badge, or to read the numbers on his epaulettes. The overall impression is, Lauren has to concede, convincing. She sends the image to Intelligence to circulate internally and across other forces. Going public with it would give them a greater chance of identifying the man, but that's a decision above Lauren's pay grade. In the current climate, people will be inclined to take justice into their own hands; a misidentification could be catastrophic.

Next, she sends the image to Nadeeka. *Can you confirm this is one of the men you saw?*

Her response is immediate. *Yes! That's the one DI Burton told off for letting me into the house. Do you know who he is?*

Lauren hits the call button. 'Not yet,' she says, when Nadeeka answers. 'But we're working on it. How are you?'

'Not great, to be honest. I'm trying to hold it together for the girls, but . . .' Nadeeka's voice trembles. 'I miss him so much. Maya keeps asking why he died, and it's all I can think about too. Why did this happen? Who did this to us?'

'We're going to find the person responsible for this, Nadeeka.' Lauren almost adds *I promise*, but she never promises what's out of her control.

'Kath wants Scott to move in with me and the girls.'

'Your ex?'

'I don't want him to, but I can't settle, and it's making Maya and Nish anxious. Nish wet the bed for the first time in ages, and Maya's having night terrors.' Nadeeka lets out a long, shaky breath. 'Could you maybe get a patrol car to drive by a couple of times in the evening? In case someone's watching the house?'

'I'll see what I can do.' Once again, Lauren can't promise anything. 'Have you seen anyone hanging around?'

'No . . . it's just a feeling.' Nadeeka hesitates. 'I keep thinking how they took all his stuff – his laptop, his phone – like they wanted to make sure they didn't leave a trace of him. And then DI Burton took my phone for the same reason. But what if he thinks

I've still got something? I came back to work today and I'm going to leave my laptop here – I'm too scared to keep it at home. Jamie never used it, but DI Burton doesn't know that, does he?'

Every time Nadeeka says 'DI Burton', it sets Lauren's teeth on edge. There is no 'DI Burton', just a bastard using police ID to get away with murder. Literally.

'That's a good idea. And maybe your ex-mother-in-law has a point about the girls' dad moving back in for a bit: you might feel safer with another adult in the house.'

'Maybe.' Nadeeka sounds doubtful, reminding Lauren that they have yet to speak to Scott Hadley about his stack-up with Golding.

'Would you like the crime prevention team to come round and take a look at your home security?'

'Oh, yes, please.'

'Consider it done.' Lauren ends the call. She's just adding a note to her ever-increasing list of actions when Bahnaz gives a tentative knock on Lauren's open door.

'Boss, do you have a sec?'

'Sure.'

'I looked on eBay, like you said.' Bahnaz steps into the office and pushes the door closed. 'There's so much police uniform on there, it's unbelievable. I narrowed it to down to our force, and . . .' She hesitates. 'I think you should see this.' She shows Lauren her phone, on which is an eBay page with half a dozen listings. 'The same seller listed a hi-vis jacket with the force badge on, but mostly he sells generic police shirts, trousers . . . the occasional utility belt.' Bahnaz opens a different tab on her phone. 'He sells other stuff too, so I did a reverse image search on some kids' clothes he was selling, and . . .' She shows Lauren a Facebook page. 'I know him, boss. It's Tom Chandler. He's on team three.'

The profile photo shows a grinning man wearing sunglasses, his arm around a pretty blonde woman next to him on a sun lounger. Sitting on the sand in front of them are two children, perhaps ten and twelve.

'Leave it with me.' Lauren checks the time. 'You coming to briefing?'

'Yes, I just didn't want to bring this up in front of everyone.' Bahnaz looks uncomfortable. 'Tom's a nice guy; I'm sure he's not involved in—'

'As I said,' Lauren says firmly, 'leave it with me.'

At afternoon briefing, Lauren brings the team up to speed in relation to Gary Fisher but doesn't mention Bahnaz's eBay findings. She shares the photograph of the 'uniformed PC' and pins a printout of the still image to the large board at the front of the room. Their first suspect. The other figures are question marks, captioned only with their aliases – *DI Colin Burton*; *forensics officer*; *private ambulance driver* – and Nadeeka's description of them.

Although their suspects remain unnamed, the board is beginning to fill up. They have the registration number of DI Burton's blue Corsa, and in the past hour they've been able to add a potential part index for the private ambulance, after one of Nadeeka's neighbours remembered seeing a black van with the same initials as her daughter.

'I've asked for a VODS check,' Sonya tells Lauren. It's a promising lead. A vehicle online descriptive search will produce a list of all the UK's black vans with the same letters in the registration number. 'I'll start with vans registered in a twenty-mile radius,' Sonya says, 'then I'll work my way out.'

'AJ.' Lauren turns to him. 'I understand you've been able to retrieve significant data from the victim's phone?'

'From his cloud account.' AJ clears his throat. 'We don't have his phone.'

Lauren lets the pedantry go.

'Okay if I screenshare?' He gets to his feet, bringing his laptop to the front of the room. 'We've been able to recover a number of incoming messages received in the weeks before the murder, one of which is very interesting indeed.' There's a pause as AJ connects his laptop, and a message appears on the large screen on the wall, along with a phone number. There's a collective murmur as everyone takes it in.

You're fucking dead.

'How quickly can you trace that number?' Lauren says.

'We don't need to – we had it in the system already.' AJ clicks his mouse and the screen flicks to the next slide. 'Scott Hadley. No previous convictions, but a caution for affray and several intel reports relating to recreational drug use and football disorder.'

'That's Nadeeka's ex-husband,' Lauren says, and the murmur around her grows so loud she has to hold up a hand to bring the room back to order. 'He told Nadeeka he was out for a run at the time of the murder, but we have yet to speak to him.'

'Most of the other messages are from Nadeeka Prasanna,' AJ says, 'or work-related.' He clicks his mouse and the screen shows another message.

Nice work. The boss appreciates you working out of hours to get the project signed off. You've proved yourself to be a real team player.

'Carrie Finder?' AJ turns it into a question.

'Head of HR,' Lauren explains. 'Are there any other messages from Hadley?'

'No, but there are these . . .' AJ clicks once more. 'They were sent to Jamie Golding's phone via a web-based messaging system accessed through a VPN.'

Lauren stares at the messages, each accompanied by the date it was received.

broken tide ember
silent echo breeze
foggy spiral dusk
whispering cobalt ash
crimson shadow glass

'I'm getting PTSD flashbacks to GCSE poetry.' Kenric grimaces. Sonya laughs. 'Like you did GCSE poetry!'

Kenric adopts a whimsical expression. '*I wandered, lonely as a—*'

It's Not What You Think

'Can we focus on the matter in hand, please?' Lauren snaps.

'Is it some kind of code?' Matt looks around the room. 'Like, the first letter of each word spells out a location . . .' He trails off, perhaps realizing his theory doesn't work, but it gives Lauren an idea.

'Could it be what3words? That identifies locations, right? The words are usually separated by full stops, but if someone wanted to be less obvious they might leave them out.'

'I've got the app.' Fraser takes out his phone. 'Foggy dot spiral dot dusk.' He types it in.

The entire room seems to hold its breath.

'Nope.' Fraser shakes his head. 'The closest is a foggy spiral duck, somewhere in Cornwall.'

'Silent echo breeze doesn't work either, boss,' Matt says, looking up from his own phone.

'Ember tide broken!' Bahnaz cries. Everyone turns to look at her.

'Other way around,' Fraser says. 'It's broken tide—'

'They're backwards.' Bahnaz uses two fingers to navigate the map on her screen. 'Ember tide broken is a British Legion Club.'

Lauren turns to Fraser. 'What's the next one? Breeze echo silent?' She waits impatiently for him to type it in.

'A village hall.'

'Dusk spiral foggy looks like a local pub,' Matt says. 'The Lord Admiral, on Princes Street.'

The fourth code is a boutique cinema, and the fifth another pub – the King's Arms. Lauren looks at her laptop to find the two 'ND' dates Nadeeka is sure about, then checks them against the dates on the screen.

A perfect match.

'The locations must be where Jamie met ND,' Sonya says.

'Maybe.' Lauren is more circumspect. She's never had an affair, but sending locations in code, via a secure website? It seems a little over the top. And who meets their lover in a village hall? There's something more going on here than a plain old affair.

And whatever it was . . . it got Jamie Golding killed.

CHAPTER 17

PC Tom Chandler looks significantly less relaxed than in his Facebook profile picture. He sits in Lauren's office, forearms heavy on his knees, fingers twisting around each other.

'Money's been really tight,' he says, his eyes fixed on the floor. 'Karen got Long Covid and had to stop work, and we had to take out a couple of credit cards just to pay the bills.'

'Have you spoken to anyone about this?' Lauren says. 'HR? Your skipper?'

Tom shakes his head. 'I'm on top of it.'

'Stealing equipment from work is hardly—'

'I don't steal!' Tom snaps his gaze on to Lauren. 'It's spare kit, stuff I don't need—'

'It's not yours to sell, Tom!' Lauren's voice has risen, and she takes a steadying breath. 'It's not only an abuse of taxpayers' money; you've got absolutely no idea who you're selling to, or how they plan to use the kit.'

'Some people are collectors, or they want it for fancy dress.

It's Not What You Think

One bloke was an extra. You know, in TV and films. Said he got more parts if he could bring his own uniform.'

'And what about the ones who don't tell you? The ones planning to pass themselves off as coppers?' Lauren blows out her cheeks. 'I mean, for God's sake, Tom, have you seen the news recently? The *Daily Mail* would jump all over this one.'

'Please don't stick me on, ma'am. I'm begging you.' His voice cracks. 'We're already behind on the mortgage. If I lose my job, we'll lose the house.'

Lauren doesn't respond. She's been through Tom's eBay transactions and she's almost a hundred per cent certain nothing matches the uniform worn by the man Nadeeka saw in Cedar Walk; nevertheless, what Tom has been doing is a disciplinary offence. In the current climate, it's undoubtedly a job-loser.

'I want every listing for police items deleted and the property in my office by tomorrow morning.'

'Yes, ma'am.'

She looks at him for a second, then jerks her head towards the door. 'Get back to work.'

'Are you going to stick me on?' He's fighting tears, Lauren realizes.

'I haven't decided yet.'

But she has. She just hopes she won't live to regret it.

'You all right?' Fraser glances at her before turning back to the road. They're on their way to speak to Scott Hadley, who is steadily climbing higher up Lauren's list of potential suspects.

'I spoke to the lad who's been selling kit online. Tom Chandler.'

'Did you stick him on?'

Lauren doesn't answer right away. She feels Fraser's gaze on her; can sense his surprise when he realizes she's gone against the party line.

'Everyone makes bad choices sometimes,' she says eventually. 'It's just that not everyone gets caught.'

'That's very reasonable of you.' Fraser slows, held behind a line of traffic waiting to turn right. 'I'd have stuck him on.'

'Lucky for Tom Chandler you failed your inspector's exam, then.'

'I'll have you know that was a strategic fail. All part of the big plan.'

'What plan would that be?'

Fraser grins. 'The plan for my high-flying wife to keep me in the manner to which I'd like to become accustomed.' They follow the satnav directions into a narrow street, where Fraser slows the car and points to a terraced house with a blue door. 'We're here.'

In the bay window to the right of the front path they see a man sitting at a desk, partially obscured by two huge screens. He looks up at them and frowns, but gets to his feet.

'Probably thinks we're Jehovah's Witnesses,' Fraser says, as he rings the bell.

Lauren has her ID waiting. 'Scott Hadley?'

'Who wants to know?' Scott's wearing jogging bottoms and a tightly fitted top that shows the flex of his arm muscles. A Gymshark gilet is zipped up to his neck.

'Detective Chief Inspector Caldwell, major crime. This is my colleague, Detective Sergeant Hogan. Can we come in?'

There's a pause, then Scott opens the door wider. He shows them into his office, which as well as the desk in the window contains a sofa, a wall-mounted television and an impressive gallery of framed awards.

Fraser nods to the certificates. 'What is it you do?'

'I work in IT, but my passion's in the wellness industry. I help a lot of ladies, actually.' He hands Lauren a flyer with a beaming woman on one side and a dizzying array of powders and supplements on the other.

'NutriQuest?' Lauren looks up. 'Isn't that a pyramid scheme?'

Scott gives her a patronizing smile. 'There's a lot of misinformation about multi-level marketing. Our products help people feel and look better, it's as simple as that.' He sits on the edge of his desk and folds his arms. 'Now, what can I help you with?'

'I believe you've been informed of the circumstances surrounding the death of your ex-wife's partner, Jamie Golding?' Lauren says. 'We'd like to ask you a few questions about it.'

'I don't know anything about it, sorry.' Scott picks up a paperweight from his desk; a glass sphere with a swirl of blue bubbles trapped inside.

'Then this won't take long, will it?' Lauren sits on the sofa and takes out a notebook. Fraser's still reading the certificates on the wall, which she imagines are worth about as much as the paper on which they're printed. 'Tell me, how did you get on with Jamie?'

'What's Nads been saying?'

'If you could answer the question, please, Mr Hadley.'

'Did she tell you I had something to do with him dying?' Scott passes the paperweight from one hand to the other. 'Because I wasn't anywhere near him.'

'Where were you?'

'Training.' He holds the paperweight still, studying it intently as though he's never seen it before. 'I'm doing an ultra in a few weeks.'

'I see you've done a couple of Ironmans.' Fraser points to a rack on the wall, from which at least twenty medals are hanging. 'I did Tenby a few years ago – almost killed me.' He gives a rueful laugh and Lauren mentally applauds his acting skills. She'd been at the finish line when Fraser had crossed the line with a time that put him second in his age category, his former army training having powered him through the brutal course.

'A lot of it's in your nutrition, of course.' Scott pats the pile of flyers on his desk. 'I swear by our VitaFuel Pro. I can give you a couple of samples, if you like?'

'Nice one, thanks. Was Jamie much of a runner?'

Seamless, Lauren thinks. God, Fraser's good.

Scott snorts. 'Bloke couldn't run a bath. I don't know what

Nads saw in him. Obvious what he saw in her, of course. Free house, ready-made family . . .'

There's bitterness in his voice and Lauren feels a dart of sympathy, in spite of Scott's manner. It must be tough seeing your kids with another man.

'You weren't a fan, then?' Fraser says.

'Hated the bloke.' Scott gives an exaggerated, overly defensive sigh. 'There you go: I couldn't stand him. Doesn't mean I killed him.'

'It's funny, though,' Lauren says, 'because that's almost exactly what your text to him said. *You're fucking dead*, wasn't it?'

There's a beat, Scott's face registering the information that what he'd assumed had been private is now in the hands of the police. Then he shrugs. 'The bloke was pissing me off.'

'So you threatened to kill him?' Lauren says.

'That wasn't a threat!'

'And now he really is dead.' She holds Scott's gaze. 'You can see how it looks.'

'I didn't kill him!'

'Right . . . you couldn't have, could you?' Lauren says. Scott stares at her. 'You were out running,' she reminds him.

'Yeah.' He looks at the paperweight again.

He's lying.

'Where did you go?' Fraser's being all matey again.

'Castledean nature reserve.'

'Oh, yeah, that's a nice trail. You on Strava?' Fraser puts on a terrible American accent and shoots his index fingers in Scott's direction. '*If it's not on Strava, it didn't happen*, right?'

'Right.' Scott laughs, but there's a nervous edge to it now.

'So you track your runs on your phone?' Lauren says.

'Yeah.'

'Including the Castledean one?' She holds out her hand. 'Can I take a look?'

Scott blinks. 'Actually, I think I left my phone at Mum's that time.'

Lauren exchanges a slow and deliberate glance with Fraser,

It's Not What You Think

letting Scott sweat before she continues. 'That's strange for someone so meticulous about their training, isn't it?'

'I used my watch,' Scott says suddenly.

Lauren stands. 'Show me.'

'What?'

'Show me the entry.'

'I don't have to,' Scott says, but he doesn't sound too sure.

'No, you don't have to.' Lauren sighs. 'We can arrest you and take you down to the station, then send your watch off to be analysed. It'll take a few weeks, and you'll be on police bail all that time, but then eventually we'll see that you were at Castledean nature reserve at the time of Jamie Golding's murder, and you'll be a free man again.'

Scott looks up at the ceiling, then lets out a long breath. 'I didn't go for a run.'

Lauren keeps her expression neutral. 'Why did you lie?'

'Because . . .' He crosses to the door and pushes it shut. 'I was at someone's house.' He lowers his voice. 'I'm sort of . . . seeing someone.'

'Nadeeka mentioned a Spanish woman?' Lauren says.

'That's Gabriela. My . . . er . . . girlfriend. This is her house. The girl I went to see is called Dani.' He flashes Lauren a defensive look. 'It's complicated.'

'It always is.' Lauren turns to a fresh page in her notebook. 'I'd like the name, address and telephone number of the woman you're seeing, please.'

'Gabriela and I haven't been getting on for—'

'Name. Address. Phone number.' Lauren cuts him off. 'I'm not here to judge your private life, Mr Hadley.' Although I bloody well will, she thinks.

'Men,' Lauren says darkly, as they drive away. She dials the number Scott had reluctantly handed over for Dani.

'Not all men,' Fraser says mildly.

'Present company excep—' Lauren cuts herself off as a woman answers the phone.

In the three-minute conversation that follows, Lauren ascertains two things. One, that Dani didn't know Scott already had a girlfriend; and, two, that the pair of them had indeed been together at the time of the murder.

'She said they were shagging,' Lauren says, after the call has ended. 'Do you reckon that falls under cross-training?'

'If it does, I'm signing up for an ultra.'

'Oi!' Lauren bashes his thigh.

'She might be covering for him.'

'After finding out he's living with another woman?' Lauren shakes her head. 'Doubt it. Men!' she says again, deliberately this time, throwing Fraser a sidelong glance to see if he'll rise to the bait.

He doesn't.

'Not all men, obviously,' Lauren adds, because she likes to be balanced, even in jest, and because the majority of men in her life are good ones. Unfortunately the job has made her cynical, and she approaches life now with a cautiousness – almost a suspicion – that she never had before she joined.

They're heading back into the city centre and, as the traffic slows to a crawl, Lauren sees a street sign up ahead. 'Take the second left,' she tells Fraser. 'Princes Street is where the Lord Admiral pub is.'

'Ah, date night . . .'

'I can't see the Lord Admiral making it into my top ten romantic destinations,' Lauren says, taking in the boarded-up shops and the graffiti-laden walls around them.

The pub itself butts up to a residential house with walls pockmarked by stubbed-out cigarettes, and a pint glass planted in its barren window box. The pub isn't open, but a narrow alleyway takes Lauren and Fraser to a small courtyard at the back of the building. On the opposite side of the yard is a door into what might once have been a coach house or stables.

It's Not What You Think

'Hello?' Lauren tries the back door of the pub. It opens and she calls again. 'Anyone there?'

'We're closed,' comes a voice. A few seconds later a man appears, wiping his hands on a tea towel. He opens his mouth – perhaps to ask what the hell they're doing, walking into his pub – but closes it when he sees Lauren's warrant card. He eyes them warily. 'I had an inspection last week.'

'We're not from licensing.' Lauren drops her lanyard. 'We're investigating a murder. Do you have any CCTV?'

The landlord shakes his head. 'It puts off the punters.'

Fraser holds up his phone, which shows a photo of Jamie Golding. 'Do you recognize this man?'

'Never seen him before,' the man replies, so automatically that Lauren imagines she could show him pictures of his own mother and she'd get the same answer.

'We believe he might have been here a couple of weeks before he was killed,' Lauren says. 'We're trying to establish who he was meeting.'

'We don't take bookings unless it's for food.' The landlord tucks the corner of the tea towel into his belt. It's badly stained and Lauren feels slightly queasy at the thought of the Lord Admiral's menu.

'I'd appreciate your checking,' Lauren says. 'The name's Jamie Golding, and it was November 17th.'

The landlord makes to go, then immediately turns back. 'The 17th, you say? We were closed. Private function out the back.' He nods to the building across the courtyard.

'You're sure?' Fraser says.

'Hundred per cent. They wanted drinks and pork baps, and my barmaid was sick, so I had to close the bar.'

'What was the booking?' Lauren turns towards the function room, which is dingy and dated. She imagines telling her mother that she and Fraser are holding their reception here instead of at Foxleigh Manor, and the thought reminds her she needs to confirm numbers with the caterer. Maybe they *should* move to the

Lord Admiral. Eighty pork baps would be a damn sight cheaper than goat's cheese tartlets and salmon done three ways.

'It was for a meeting,' the landlord says. 'The Freemasons. Name on the booking was the Beacon Lodge. All very cloak-and-dagger, isn't it?' He looks at Fraser as he says this.

'I wouldn't know.'

'Trouser legs up, secret handshakes, all that crap? I thought you coppers were all masons.'

'Not this one,' Fraser says.

'Mind if I take a look?' Lauren's already walking across the courtyard. Had Jamie been a Freemason? Nadeeka hadn't mentioned it, but perhaps he hadn't told her. Could joining a Masonic Lodge have been the secret Nadeeka was convinced Jamie had been keeping from her?

'Funny bunch.' The landlord takes a key from his pocket and opens the door. 'They had one of their lads fetch all the drinks – wouldn't let me so much as carry a tray. I wasn't fussed. More fool them, paying me to sit on my arse in an empty bar.'

Lauren looks around the function room, where around fifty mis-matched wooden chairs are laid out in rows. 'How did they pay?'

'Cash.'

Lauren's phone rings. If that's my bloody mother . . . she thinks. But it's Bahnaz.

'Boss, I'm at the British Legion. The night Jamie was here, they were closed for a private function.'

'Freemasons?'

'How did you know?'

'Same at the Lord Admiral.'

'Kenric says they booked the King's Arms too. There's a function room out the back, apparently. Matt's checking out the cinema now.'

'Can you do some digging into the Freemasons?' Lauren takes her phone into the courtyard, away from the curious ears of the landlord. 'Find out how many local lodges there are and start making calls. I want to know if Golding was a member.'

It's Not What You Think

After Lauren ends the call, she stands for a moment in the courtyard, her breath misting the cold air. A few days ago, they didn't have a single lead. They didn't even have a crime scene. Now Lauren's head is overflowing with threads she can't seem to bring together. Adam Bennington. Scott Hadley. The masons. Could the Freemasons be responsible for an orchestrated cover-up to protect a member's crimes? It all feels fantastical, like something from a Dan Brown thriller.

She hears Fraser's footsteps behind her and turns around.

'Are you all right?'

'Better now I'm outside.' Lauren stretches her neck from side to side. 'That room was giving me the heebie-jeebies.'

'No windows.'

'It wasn't that, it just felt . . .' She shivers. 'It felt like something bad had gone down there.' Lauren sees Fraser's mouth twitch. 'Oh, sod off. Just because you don't believe in intuition doesn't mean it doesn't exist.'

'The landlord said the room's been used a couple of times since the 17th. I've had a look around and the place looks surprisingly clean, but let's see what forensics say.'

Lauren calls CSI as they're walking back to the car.

'Speak of the devil!' Tony Watkins says. 'Your ears must have been burning. We put Golding's name into the system with a comparison request against any unidentified bodies, but no joy so far. He's not languishing in any mortuary, I'm afraid.'

Lauren wonders if this will be one of those murders where the victim's body is never found; where the perpetrators dumped it at sea or chopped it into pieces and fed it to pigs. Poor Jamie, she thinks. Poor Nadeeka. Grief comes tenfold without the closure a body brings.

'We also ran a comparison against outstanding crimes,' Tony says. 'A few weeks ago, there was an arson at a convenience store a few streets away from Cedar Walk. Uniform found a discarded bottle of lighter fuel nearby, and this is where it gets interesting.' Tony pauses. 'The prints on it belong to Jamie Golding.'

CHAPTER 18

'That's not possible.' Nadeeka looks at Lauren, then at Fraser, as though he might offer a different explanation. 'There must be some mistake.' They're sitting in her living room at Cedar Walk, the uncarpeted floor a stark reminder of Jamie's murder. Nadeeka has covered the dark stain on the floor with a rug from upstairs, the edge folded up against the wall where the skirting board used to be.

'Without taking fingerprints directly from Jamie, we can't be conclusive,' Lauren says, 'but the fingerprints on the bottle of lighter fuel match the ones we took from Jamie's glasses case.'

'But it was me who told Jamie about the arson. He was as shocked as I was.' Nadeeka's face screws up in confusion. 'None of this makes sense. If his fingerprints are on the lighter fluid, they must have got there by accident. Maybe he picked it up to throw it away – that's the kind of man he was. He hated seeing rubbish chucked on the ground.'

'Fire investigation have confirmed the lighter fluid is the same type used to start the fire at the convenience store,' Lauren says quietly.

It's Not What You Think

A pale line forms around Nadeeka's lips, as she presses them tightly together. Lauren glances at Fraser.

'Nadeeka... the owners are Pakistani. Did Jamie ever express any racist views?'

'Racist?' Nadeeka's eyes widen.

'Any concerns over people he perceived to be foreigners?' Fraser says. 'Strong views about immigration perhaps?'

'No! Jamie wasn't like that.' She shakes her head as though trying to dislodge the very idea. 'I mean, I'm Sri Lankan – it was literally in my dating profile when he matched with me. Even if he hadn't seen it before he swiped, my profile pic was right there.'

'What do you know about his previous dating history?' Fraser says.

'You mean had he had a Sri Lankan before?' Nadeeka's tone is deliberately harsh.

'Some men intentionally target women who come from...' Fraser hesitates, and Lauren knows he's trying to find a politically correct term '... specific groups,' he finishes.

Lauren backs him up. 'Unfortunately we do sometimes encounter men who use dating sites as a way to meet people from certain backgrounds, or with particular characteristics – disabilities, for example – and their intentions aren't always honourable.' Lauren thinks of the cases she's been involved with over the years: mercifully few, but memorable for all the wrong reasons. The guy with a fetish for asphyxiating overweight women; the homophobic trucker who sought out his victims on Grindr. Could Jamie have deliberately targeted Nadeeka? Got close to her in order to hurt her? If so, losing his own life could well have saved hers.

'Jamie *loved* me,' Nadeeka says, so fervently that Lauren wonders whether she's trying to convince them or herself.

'The photograph Jamie brought home from work...' Lauren treads carefully, knowing how fragile Nadeeka is right now. 'Could it be that Jamie didn't want his colleagues to see it?'

Nadeeka's jaw tightens. She's trying not to cry, her face working against itself.

Neither Lauren nor Fraser fills the silence.

'You think he was ashamed of me?' Nadeeka says eventually. 'Of my skin colour? Of Maya and Nish?' Her voice rises. 'You think he was embarrassed to be in a photograph with us?' A single tear runs down her cheek.

'I don't know,' Lauren says. 'I'm trying to figure out if taking home that photo has anything to do with the arson.'

'I couldn't help but notice that Jamie didn't have a lot of possessions,' Fraser says. 'A few clothes and books, but not much else, right? No furniture?'

'He sold most of his stuff. Said there was no point hiring a van and trying to fit it all into an already furnished house. *Who needs two sets of saucepans?* That's what he said.'

'I suppose I'm just wondering...' Fraser hesitates '...whether Jamie felt the arrangement might only be temporary.'

'Arrangement?' Nadeeka stares at him. She shakes her head over and over, seemingly unable to find the words to respond. Lauren puts a hand out to comfort her, but Nadeeka pulls her own away. 'How dare you? Do you not think this is hard enough for me already? Every second of every day I'm questioning whether Jamie was having an affair – what he was up to behind my back that got him killed. And now you're telling me he never intended to stay? That all the plans we made for the future were some kind of sick joke?'

'I'm so sorry to upset you,' Lauren says. 'Believe me, we want to know the truth as much as you do.' As soon as she says it, she wants to take it back – there can be no one more desperate for the truth than the woman in front of her – but, just as she's bracing herself for more defensiveness, there's a sudden change in Nadeeka's expression. Her jaw slackens; her brows tighten. Lauren stiffens. 'What is it?'

There's a long pause.

It's Not What You Think

'He changed my name,' Nadeeka whispers.

'He what?'

'When I went to ATP Construction, the woman on reception called me Nadia. I thought it was a mistake, but then Jamie's boss called me Nadia too, and so did another colleague. Nadia, not Nadeeka.'

'Perhaps they misheard him?' Fraser suggests.

Nadeeka's voice becomes even smaller. 'He wanted to make me sound white.'

'We don't know that for sure.' Lauren wants to reassure her, but she can't think of a plausible alternative to offer. *Nadia*. One colleague might be mistaken, but three?

'There's more.' Nadeeka presses the back of her hand to her mouth, stays that way for a few seconds, before taking a long, steadying breath. 'Jamie suggested we take the girls to Lapland to see Santa – he'd found some special deal – but it would have meant them missing their Christmas show, so I said no.' She looks at Lauren. 'I know that sounds ridiculous – who wouldn't want to go to Lapland, right? – but I didn't want the girls to miss out, and anyway, I couldn't have got away from work.'

Lauren waits, unsure where this is going.

'I said to Jamie that with the girls being half-Sri Lankan and half-British, I was really happy about the school doing a multi-faith version of the nativity. Well, Jamie got really funny about it.'

'Funny?' Lauren says.

'He threw out a load of reasons why this Lapland trip was a once-in-a-lifetime thing. But when I looked online, we could have booked at that price for any time. We had a row about it, and in the end we didn't book at all.' Nadeeka looks at Lauren. 'But when I dropped the girls at school the next day, Nish's teacher came up to me and said she was so sorry the girls wouldn't be in the show. Jamie had emailed her and said we'd be away.'

'After you and he had agreed not to book Lapland?'

Nadeeka nods. 'I couldn't work out why he didn't want

them to do the nativity.' She starts crying again. 'But it's because they're bringing in other religions, isn't it? He didn't like it.'

'We don't know that,' Lauren says again, but it's all stacking up. The photograph, the anglicized name, the arson attack against the Pakistani shopkeeper, the reluctance to support a multi-faith nativity.

'I can't believe I've been so blind.' Nadeeka stares at Lauren blankly. 'Do you know what he said when I told him about a recruitment drive I'm doing at work?'

Lauren shakes her head.

'He told me not to focus on the foreign-born workers.' Nadeeka flinches as though the memory is causing her physical pain. 'Afterwards he backtracked, saying he'd meant people might give us grief over it, but it was so . . . odd. God, I feel sick.' She wraps her arms around herself, leaning forward on to her knees. 'Knowing I was lying next to someone who was only pretending to be in love with me; knowing I let him spend time with my kids when all the time he was having such vile, despicable thoughts.'

Lauren can't imagine how that must feel. But then, she can't imagine Nadeeka not at least suspecting that Jamie wasn't all he appeared. Had she really not seen the red flags?

'Did Jamie ever break up with you?' she asks, thinking of the note she found in Nadeeka's nightstand. 'Or threaten to? I'm just trying to get a handle on his behaviour while you were together.' She has a photo of the note on her phone, but she's reluctant to let Nadeeka know the full extent of her snooping. It's important Nadeeka feels she can trust Lauren and Fraser.

'No, but . . .' Nadeeka starts to cry again. 'He almost did. He wrote me a letter saying he was leaving me – he wasn't even going to do it face-to-face! I found it in the bin.'

That explains the screwed-up paper, Lauren thinks. 'What did he say when you asked him about it?'

Nadeeka doesn't answer.

'You did speak to him about it?'

It's Not What You Think

She shakes her head slowly. 'I thought if I brought it up, it might bring up all sorts of other things too; that he'd decide he really was going to leave. So I just pretended I hadn't seen it.'

'You must have been devastated. Angry, even?' Lauren watches Nadeeka carefully.

'Devastated, yes. But no, not angry – why would I be angry? I was scared of losing him.'

'But he stayed?' Fraser says.

'Yes. And he would have left, wouldn't he, if he was seeing someone else?' Nadeeka looks at them hopefully. 'I mean, the fact that he stayed – that counts for something, right?'

'It sounds as though there was a lot going on in Jamie's head before he died,' Lauren says carefully.

'I'd been worrying about him for a few weeks. He didn't seem happy, and whenever I asked what was wrong, he just said he was finding things hard.'

'What things?'

'That's what I asked. But he just kept saying "things". I was worried that meant "us", but then I thought maybe he was having some kind of mental health breakdown. I even asked him to see the GP, though he never did.' Her face crumples. 'Maybe if he had, he might still be here.'

'Did you ever ask Jamie outright if he was seeing someone else?' Fraser is blunter than Lauren would have been, but she'd been about to ask Nadeeka the same question. Why hadn't the pair of them just *talked* to each other? All this second-guessing, all the secrets . . . Lauren couldn't be doing with it. When she wants to know how Fraser's feeling or what he's up to, she asks him. Relationships aren't rocket science.

'I asked if he still felt the same about me, and he said yes.' Nadeeka inhales sharply, then bites on her top lip, steadying herself. 'He said he loved me more than he'd ever loved anyone in the world, and then he said he was sorry.'

'Sorry?' Fraser says. 'What for?'

'That's all he said. *I'm so sorry.* For making me worry, I thought, but now . . .' She stops, and the pain she's experiencing is almost tangible.

Lauren puts a hand on Nadeeka's arm. What a nightmare to live through. If Jamie really did target her specifically as part of a sick game or fetish, the man was a monster. How must it feel for Nadeeka to realize that? To know she exposed her kids to it?

'We should get more of an insight if we're able to fully access Jamie's cloud accounts,' Fraser says. 'Find out what websites he was visiting, the accounts he was following on social media. See who he was in contact with. We need to try to get inside his head.'

They do, thinks Lauren, although she doesn't relish the prospect. The more they learn about Jamie Golding, the less she wants to know.

After Lauren and Fraser leave Cedar Walk, they make their way towards *breeze.echo.silent,* the what3words location of the village hall referenced in the messages retrieved from Jamie's phone. Bahnaz had left the office immediately after yesterday's briefing to collect her children from the childminder, but she hadn't stopped work; an update had been waiting in Lauren's inbox this morning. *Beacon Lodge doesn't exist*, Bahnaz had written. *I spoke to the Grand Lodge Official, who said each chapter meets in their own lodge – they don't use external venues. Whatever group Jamie was involved in, it wasn't the Freemasons.*

'They definitely told me they were Freemasons.' Susan Belter is chair of Neaton village hall committee. She looks up from the leather-bound appointment diary in her hand. 'I wrote it down. There was a flood at their lodge, apparently, so they needed to meet somewhere else.'

'How many of them were there?' Fraser's voice echoes in the empty hall.

'I wouldn't know, I'm afraid. They booked by phone, and

It's Not What You Think

I gave them the code for the key safe. I have to say, they left it absolutely spotless.'

Of course they did, thinks Lauren, who isn't holding out any hope of useful forensics from any of the venues they've uncovered. 'How did they pay?'

'We always ask for cash. They left the money in the teapot, as we'd agreed.'

'Do you still have it?' Whoever handled it might have worn gloves, Lauren knows, but it's worth a shot. If they could find just a single speck of DNA . . .

'Oh, gosh, no. I paid it into the bank the very next morning.'

Lauren exchanges a glance with Fraser, who is running a finger over a windowsill like an aunt checking for dust. Just their luck: criminals who clean up after themselves, and ultra-organized civilians.

'I like to keep on top of things,' Susan says. 'I bank the cash, shred the card details, that sort of thing.'

'Card details?' Lauren snaps her gaze back to Susan. 'You said you always ask for cash.'

'We do, but if someone were to damage the sound system, or break the freezer, it would cost hundreds.' Susan straightens the blind on the window next to her. 'So I take a card number, reassure them it's just as security – payment won't be taken on the card – and then, if all's well, I destroy the details.'

'Will the bits of paper still be in your shredder?' Even as Lauren asks, she knows it's a hopeless line of enquiry. What are they going to do: piece together every possible combination of numbers until they get a credit card number which may or may not be connected to Jamie's murder? She's all for leaving no stone unturned, but there are limits . . .

'No, I put them in the compost. But if you need the details, wouldn't it be easier to look at the village hall bank account?'

'But you don't take payment by card,' Lauren says, 'so . . .'

'The bank takes a holding charge. A pound, I think it is.

Then they refund it straight away. To ensure the card is valid, I suppose.' While Susan's been talking, she's been looking at her phone, and now she shows Lauren her banking app. 'Here it is.'

There it is. One pound out and one back in, against the last four digits of a debit card number.

Lauren writes them down. 'It's really important we trace the owner of this card. Would you be willing to give authorization for your bank to share details with our financial investigation unit?'

They might find out it's another cloned or stolen card, but what if it's not? What if the person who booked the hall gave his own card details, because he believed Susan Belter wouldn't actually be using it?

'Of course, if it will help. I'm sorry I can't give you a description of him.'

Fraser's phone rings and he moves away to answer it.

'We keep talking about installing cameras,' Susan says, 'but there are always so many other demands on our budget.'

'Where?' Fraser says, and Lauren turns to look at him. He's listening intently, his face taut. Alert.

'What's happened?' she mouths, but he shakes his head, his eyes flicking to Susan in explanation. He speaks to the person on the other end of the line – 'We're on our way' – then he ends the call.

Susan is still talking. 'The chap from the Freemasons said it wasn't a problem, our not having CCTV.'

I bet he did, Lauren thinks, as she follows Fraser towards the exit. 'Thanks for your time, Mrs Belter.' She wonders how many village halls and pubs have been scoped out by this group Jamie was involved in, and how many have been ruled out because they were overlooked or had cameras, or didn't take cash.

'Who was that?' she asks Fraser, once they're safely out of earshot.

'Bahnaz.' Fraser strides towards the car. 'They've found Jamie Golding's body.'

CHAPTER 19

It had been a dog-walker who'd found him. Isn't it always? Lauren thinks, as she changes into the stout boots she keeps in the boot of her car for just such occasions. She glances at Fraser's brogues. 'Those are going to get wrecked.'

'You'll have to give me a piggy-back across the muddy bits.'

'And put my back out before the wedding?' Lauren shuts the car boot and zips up her jacket. They're parked next to a large wooded area, behind two marked police cars and a white CSI van. There is a public car park three miles away on the far side of the forest, but the body has been found closer to this side, where vehicular access is barred by padlocked gates. That hasn't deterred ramblers, who have worn paths to the sides of the gates and into the dark, dense woodland.

Lauren and Fraser walk past a sign saying *Private – no trespassing*.

'Presumably the woman who found the body can't read,' Fraser says.

'All the locals ignore them.'

Lauren had spoken on the phone to the dog-walker, an over-excited woman with two lurchers barking incessantly in the background. 'The private bit is much nicer,' she'd told Lauren. 'Fewer people and not so many dog-poo bags hung on trees. Why do people do that, do you think?'

Fraser shakes his head as Lauren recounts this. 'Imagine if we all ignored the rules. It would be anarchy.'

'Oh, give over, she's not starting fires or dumping old tyres.' A twig snaps with a crack beneath Lauren's foot. 'She's walking her dogs. Apparently they jump up and people don't like it.'

'See? Anarchy.' He grins, but Lauren knows he means it. Fraser is only a few years older than her, but he has distinctly boomer-like views on the world. She often thinks it's a good job they decided against having children – Fraser would probably have them doing press-ups in the back yard every morning, on the grounds that it never did him any harm . . . She snorts.

'What?'

'Nothing.' A glimpse of white can be seen through the trees. 'There they are.'

Bodies are disposed of in many different ways. Throughout Lauren's career she has been unfortunate enough to encounter human remains in suitcases, wrapped in black bags, rolled into carpets and stuffed into bins. Jamie Golding's body is neatly zipped inside a body bag.

'Schoolboy error on their part,' says Tony Watkins, the lead CSI. He's wearing a forensic suit, his words muffled by a mask. 'I wonder if they had to get rid of him in a hurry, or if they were simply arrogant enough to think he wouldn't be found.'

Lauren crouches beside the partially uncovered shallow grave, where strong black plastic pokes through the dirt and debris at either end. 'Their fuck-up is our gain.' If this is the bag in which Golding was taken from Nadeeka's house, it's the next best thing to having the original crime scene to examine.

'The dogs started digging there.' Tony points to a scrabble of earth at one end. 'The owner called them off when she saw the zip on the bag.'

At the opposite end of the trench an area of earth has been more systematically scraped away from a section of body bag, dirt discolouring the silver metal zip that bisects it. A neat slit has been cut in the plastic to avoid contaminating the zip.

Fraser moves forward, leaning over the grave to take a look.

'What are you, a probationer?' Tony points to a plastic box a couple of metres away. 'Masks are over there.'

'Sorry.' Fraser moves away instantly. 'What a find, though. Thank God for rule-breaking dog-owners, I suppose.'

'Yes, this is a huge step forward.' Lauren takes the mask Fraser hands her. Suitably protected, they crowd around the grave again and Tony pulls apart the plastic.

Jamie Golding is still recognizable from the photographs Nadeeka sent to Lauren, but his bloated face has turned a mottled red. Lauren is breathing through her mouth but nevertheless the gassy, rotten-fruit smell of death hits the back of her throat, and she swallows hard.

'We've filmed and photographed the grave,' Tony says, 'and taken measurements. I understand you've got a dog coming?'

Lauren nods. 'After this amount of time I'm not hopeful, but it would be great to get a direction of travel and establish where they parked the van.'

The day before yesterday, they had established that someone from the fake police team had seized CCTV footage from a petrol station on the outskirts of town, indicating that at least one of the outstanding vehicles had stopped there. The back-up, however, had not been deleted. 'The lad on the tills at the time told the detective the system records over itself every twenty-four hours,' the manager had explained to Kenric. 'But it's every twenty-eight days.' He'd inserted a USB stick into the back of the computer. 'Do you want me to download it for you?' The driver of the black Mercedes had covered his face – as had the 'detective' who later seized the CCTV footage – but the van's registration could clearly be seen. Lauren's exhilaration had swiftly evaporated when the numberplates had been traced to a Kia Picanto stolen some two hundred miles away. The whole investigation felt as though they were taking two steps forward, one step back. Progress was being made, but far too slowly for Lauren's liking.

'It feels like they're laughing at us,' she says to Fraser now, as they make their way back to the car. 'The whole job is so brazen; I wouldn't be surprised to find out they've been hiding in plain sight all along.'

'What do you mean?' Fraser narrowly misses getting smacked in the face by a low branch. He holds it to one side for Lauren to pass unscathed.

'Do you remember that search for the missing girl last year? The guy who kept giving us updates on where they'd looked? And all the time she was in his shed.' Lauren grimaces. 'I reckon we've already looked into the eyes of whoever killed Jamie Golding.'

'Nadeeka?'

'No, I think she's on the level, and besides, I don't see how she could have pulled off the cover-up.' Lauren steps over a fallen log. 'And Adam Bennington, who might have had the contacts to do it, has provided a rock-solid alibi for the time of the murder: CCTV from his client's offices. If he was involved in Golding's murder, it was from a distance. Which leaves us with Scott Hadley.'

'Who also has an alibi,' Fraser reminds her.

'I didn't trust him, though, did you?'

'I'm a copper. I don't trust anyone.'

Lauren laughs. 'Not even me?'

'Except you.' Fraser takes her hand. 'I hereby promise to love, honour and trust you, in . . .' he looks at his watch, squinting to read the tiny date ' . . . precisely seventeen days' from now.'

It's Not What You Think

'Seventeen?' Lauren looks at him in horror. 'We have to get those sodding wedding favours done tonight.'

It's gone ten-thirty before all ninety-eight pieces of card have been folded into boxes, filled with sugared almonds and stacked in a plastic tub.

Lauren opens her laptop. 'I just have a few emails to reply to.'

'If you start working now, you'll end up sitting down here till three in the morning.'

'Fair point.' She shuts the laptop and puts it under her arm. 'I'll do them in bed.'

Fraser locks the back door. 'That's not exactly the point I was making.' He turns off the lights in the kitchen and goes into the living room to do the same there.

By the time he gets upstairs, Lauren is in her pyjamas, lost to the glow of her screen. As he gets into bed, she minimizes the email she'd been reading about an officer's sickness record. If Fraser notices, he doesn't say anything. Lauren doesn't like keeping things from him – they've always been straight with each other – but such is the nature of their working relationship.

'Major crime are going to have a shock when we're in Mauritius.' Fraser presses his lips against her bare shoulder, then moves back to his side of the bed. 'Three weeks of everyone having to pick up their own shit.'

Lauren opens another email. 'Matt's a steady pair of hands and Rudi Macloskey will be overseeing from CID. They'll be fine. Anyway, they can always get hold of me if they really need me.'

'You are not answering emails on our honeymoon! It was bad enough last year, when you took that call in the middle of our champagne tasting.'

'It was the chief constable—'

'Who is obviously far more important than a private vineyard tour organized by your adoring fiancé.' Fraser's tone is casual, but Lauren cringes. She had spent forty-five minutes of their two-hour tour on the phone to the chief, going over the details of something that, with hindsight, could have waited until her return to work the following week.

'I'll put my out-of-office on,' Lauren promises, knowing full well that won't stop her checking her inbox. 'Oh, excellent!'

'What?'

'The body bag has a serial number. We should be able to trace it to the manufacturers and from there find out who bought that specific bag.' Lauren starts making a list of actions. 'I wonder if private individuals can buy body bags, or only hospitals, funeral homes and so on?'

'I guess the mortuary would know,' Fraser says. He gets out of bed.

Lauren looks up in surprise. 'Where are you going?'

'To make you a camomile tea.'

'You, Fraser Hogan, are the perfect fiancé.'

'I'm only doing it so I can go to sleep without feeling guilty.'

Lauren turns back to her screen, not bothering to hide her smile. 'I know.'

CHAPTER 20

Lauren and Fraser arrive at work to find a 'Congratulations!' banner suspended from the ceiling tiles.

'Surprise!' Bahnaz pulls the string on a party popper. Nothing happens. 'Oh, crap. It's left over from my thirtieth – it must have got damp.' She looks around. 'Who's got the confetti?'

'What's going on?' Lauren mentally adds *confetti* to the list of things she still needs to do for the wedding. Not paper – she vaguely remembers the vicar saying it wasn't allowed – so . . . petals? Rice? Uncooked, presumably. She has a sudden image of dollops of basmati flying across the cobbles.

'It's your wedding shower!' Sonya is waving a clipboard. 'No excuses, boss; this is the express version. Matt, the prosecco?'

'It's no wonder you're single,' Matt grumbles, but he produces two glasses of fizz in plastic tumblers.

Lauren laughs. 'It's eight o'clock in the—'

'It's Nosecco,' Sonya stage-whispers, before raising her voice theatrically. 'And now . . . ladies and gentlemen . . . oh, and Kenric—'

'Oi!'

'We proudly present the Caldwell-Hogan Mr-and-Mrs Quiz!' There's a burst of applause, during which Lauren finds herself escorted to a stool, Fraser perching on a second stool on the opposite side of the makeshift stage. He has somehow acquired an oversized badge reading *Groom*, and now Bahnaz appears with a clip-on veil for Lauren.

'Oh, God, really?' Lauren makes a face.

'Go on, boss, it's a laugh!'

She gives in, and Sonya takes up position between her and Fraser, brandishing the clipboard like a weapon. 'Fraser, you're up first. What is Lauren's favourite colour?'

'Green,' Fraser says, without hesitation. Lauren makes herself smile. Briefing starts in fifteen minutes, and she still needs to speak to forensics about—

'Boss?' Sonya spins to face Lauren. 'Fraser's fave colour?'

'Oh! Um . . . yellow.' She looks at Fraser, who looks as though he's finding the whole experience as awkward as she is.

'Yellow?' Fraser laughs. 'Since when?'

'No answers till the end!' Sonya says. 'Now, name a food she can't stand.'

Fraser grins. 'Mushrooms. Next question!'

'Boss?'

Lauren tries to think. 'Pineapple on pizza?'

And so it goes on. Favourite film, worst habit, first film you saw together. Who said 'I love you' first, where was your first date, what was his first pet called . . .

'That's my banking security question,' Fraser says. 'You can't ask that!'

Lauren calls a halt after fifteen minutes, partly because there's work to be done and partly because she sees that the next question on Sonya's clipboard is *At what age did they lose their virginity?* – which is definitely a boundary she isn't prepared to cross.

It's Not What You Think

'Scores on the door!' Sonia motions to the rest of the team to drum their feet on the floor, creating such a noise Lauren is certain it'll bring the rest of the station running to see what's going on. 'Fraser, out of twenty-four questions you got . . . twenty-two right! Nice one!' She turns to Lauren. 'Boss, you got . . .' She looks around the room, drawing out the dramatic pause. 'Three.'

The others laugh and Lauren takes it in good spirit. She gets down from her stool and gives in to the shouts of *Give him a kiss, then, boss!*

'What *is* your favourite colour?' she asks, as Fraser gives her a squeeze.

'Red.'

Lauren pulls away, affronted. 'You never wear red!'

'Who said anything about wearing it?'

Matt claps Fraser on the back. He winks at Lauren. 'Good of you to let him win, boss.'

'Bring on the stag party!' Kenric holds his glass aloft, prompting more cheers from the male members of the team. 'I'm thinking paintballing, then pub crawl. Fancy dress, obviously.' He looks at Fraser. 'I reckon you'd rock a Snow White outfit. There's a fancy-dress shop near me does the Seven Dwarves outfits, and we could—'

'Fancy-dress shops!' Lauren snaps her fingers, turning to Kenric. 'Check which ones have realistic police uniforms and see if any of it was hired out immediately before the murder.'

A polite cough comes from the doorway, where a man in a pinstriped suit is watching them with mild curiosity. 'I'm looking for DCI Caldwell.'

'That would be me,' Lauren says.

'Detective Inspector Jules Stratman.' He walks towards her. 'We've not met, but I took over from you—'

'—on the counter-terrorism unit – of course!' Lauren snatches off her veil, mortified at being caught messing about.

'I hope I'm not interrupting?' He takes in the glasses of fizz and the scattered confetti.

'A brief moment of levity.' Lauren gives a businesslike smile. 'How are you settling in? The new Prevent package looks pretty robust.'

'There are still a few teething problems, but we'll get there.' Jules gives a self-assured shrug. 'We're having to redirect a lot of resources into domestic extremism.'

'That's worrying.' Sonya is chucking plastic glasses into a black bin bag. 'As if we didn't have enough to worry about from other countries.'

'That's why I'm here, actually,' Jules leans against the edge of a desk. 'You made an enquiry with the financial investigation unit about a card used to secure a booking at a village hall?' He doesn't wait for confirmation. 'The same card is flagged on our intelligence system as being linked to a white supremacy organization currently taking root in the UK.'

From the corner of Lauren's eye, she sees Kenric swiping at the *Congratulations!* banner with a ruler. She frowns at him, and he leaves it hanging drunkenly from one side. She thinks about Golding's prints on the bottle of lighter fluid used to set fire to the convenience store, and a sense of foreboding builds inside her.

'Neo-Nazis, you mean?' Matt asks. Slowly, the team has moved closer, and now they're all grouped around Lauren.

'Not exactly,' Jules frowns. 'There are overlaps, but the group's ideology is more rooted in cultural and religious nationalism. Their stated aims are . . .' he makes air-quotes with his fingers ' . . . "the preservation of British values"—'

'Racist-speak for *if you're not white you don't belong here,*' Kenric says drily.

'—"and the protection of British children",' Jules finishes.

Sonya grimaces. 'Just hearing this sort of shit makes me want to bleach my eyeballs. Protection from what? Learning about other languages and cultures? Protection from growing into tolerant, inclusive adults who aren't bigoted arseholes? Poor Nadeeka, discovering Jamie wasn't the person she thought he was.'

'He might genuinely have loved her,' Matt says.

'You know more about that particular relationship than I do,' Jules says, 'but for what it's worth, their latest leaflet refers to immigrants as *cockroaches*.'

'Nadeeka isn't an immigrant.' Matt looks around. 'She's – what – third generation? Second at least.'

'That's a little too nuanced for white supremacists,' Lauren says, exchanging a glance with Jules.

'Right, but Jamie's own views might have been nuanced. Even within an extremist organization, there have to be people who are more extreme than others.' Matt shrugs. 'Nadeeka's statement says the two of them never talked about current affairs.'

'Very wise,' Fraser says, bringing a smile to Lauren's lips. Not long after they'd got together they'd also realized that it was best to implement a 'no politics' rule.

'What's this organization called?' Lauren has been trying to think of all the far-right organizations she came across during her time on counter-terrorism – Blood and Honour, Combat 18, the English Defence League, the National Front.

But it won't be one of those, she realizes suddenly. Because even before Jules answers, Lauren knows what letter it will begin with.

'They're called New Dawn,' he says.

ND.

There's a beat as everyone processes what this means.

Jamie Golding wasn't meeting a woman. He was meeting a movement.

Foreboding pools in Lauren's stomach. It's clear now that Jamie's intentions were at the very least disingenuous, and very likely predatory. But did those intentions die with Jamie? Or is Nadeeka still a target?

PART THREE
NADEEKA

CHAPTER 21

Nadeeka's first thought is that someone has died. Lauren looks so serious, and although she flashes a smile at Kath, who came over to put the girls to bed, it's gone in an instant, leaving behind the sombre expression of someone about to impart terrible news.

'This is Detective Inspector Jules Stratman.' Lauren introduces the grave-faced man accompanying her. 'He's from the counter-terrorism unit.'

Nadeeka feels more resigned than afraid. The worst has already happened, after all. The girls are asleep upstairs and Kath – despite Nadeeka's protestations – is ironing school uniform. The people who matter are within these four walls, safe and sound.

'Can we sit down?' Lauren asks.

In the living room, samples of carpet make mismatched stepping-stones between the door and the sofa. Nadeeka can't decide which one to order. *Just pick one*, Kath had said. *There's hardly any difference between them.* But the simplest decisions have become monumental. At work, her colleagues are quietly picking up the slack while Nadeeka takes an hour to figure out if they should have stickers or name tags for the upcoming job fair. And all the time, in the back of her mind, she's thinking about Jamie. About how much she misses him. About whether there's another explanation for why he took home the photo of her; why he hadn't told his colleagues her real name.

'There's been a development,' Lauren says. A hiss of steam from the iron fills the pause that follows. 'Intelligence suggests Jamie was involved with an organization called New Dawn.' She stops again, perhaps for Nadeeka to say something, but the name means nothing to her. Lauren carries on. 'They're a far-right extremist movement gaining ground in the UK.'

Nadeeka laughs. She doesn't mean to – it isn't funny – but it erupts from her before she can stop it. 'That's ridiculous. Jamie wouldn't have gone near something like—' *New Dawn*, she thinks. *ND. Surely not?*

'There are chapters in most major towns and cities in the UK,' DI Stratman says. 'They meet in various locations – village halls, pubs – and often make out they're from more reputable organizations, such as the Freemasons.'

'Did Jamie ever mention joining the masons, Nadeeka?' Lauren asks.

'No, I—' Nadeeka suddenly remembers how Lauren introduced DI Stratman. *From the counter-terrorism unit.* Terrorism! Nadeeka laughs again, but it's tighter this time. Bordering on hysterical. 'This doesn't make sense. Jamie wasn't a terrorist!'

'My ex-husband was a mason.' Kath presses the tip of the iron into the corner of a sleeve. 'They do a lot of good work for charity.'

'Did Jamie ever mention any of these places to you?' Lauren's looking at her phone, her eyes flicking to Nadeeka as she rattles off a list. 'The Lord Admiral, the King's Arms, the British Legion? How about Neaton village hall?'

'No. None of them. You've got this wrong – Jamie wouldn't

have gone near anything like that. Maybe he *was* in the masons. People are always talking rubbish about Freemasons, aren't they?' Nadeeka looks to Kath for confirmation. 'Satanic rituals, the Illuminati, the occult . . .' She turns to Lauren. 'Could this supposed far-right group be another conspiracy theory?'

Pity briefly shows on Lauren's face. 'The counter-terrorism unit has been monitoring New Dawn for some time.' Her voice is calm but firm. 'They're very real, Nadeeka, and we're very certain that Jamie was involved.'

Nadeeka shakes her head. 'If Jamie was involved, they can't be as bad as you—'

'They instruct all their members to read *Mein Kampf*.' DI Stratman cuts in. 'They've claimed responsibility for several low-level attacks, and we have reason to believe their level of violence is escalating. With respect, Ms Prasanna, this is not a Dan Brown novel.'

'So . . . what?' Nadeeka gives a harsh laugh. 'Last week he was a murder victim and now he's a terrorist?'

'Jamie is still a victim,' Lauren says, 'and we're working hard to identify his killers, but we're also keen to find out as much as we can about New Dawn's activities, so if there's anything you can remember—'

Nadeeka's face is wet, and she realizes she's crying. She had so short a time with Jamie from which to form memories, and the police are slowly destroying it, twisting everything she thought she knew about their relationship.

'Did your partner have a lock-up?' DI Stratman asks. 'Somewhere he kept his belongings, perhaps?'

'No, I told you, he didn't have much stuff.'

'We've been able to build up a picture of Jamie's movements based on where he used his debit card,' Lauren says, 'but it would be helpful to have more detail. We wondered if he had a smartwatch, a Fitbit – anything like that?'

Nadeeka has lost everything of Jamie's. First to DI Burton and then to Lauren. The few possessions he had have been bagged and tagged and taken away in police cars. When she walks around her house now, it is as though he never existed. 'No,' she says shortly, and she pulls her sleeve over Jamie's watch.

'Nadeeka . . .' Lauren hesitates. 'We don't know to what extent New Dawn were aware of Jamie's relationship with you. We've not found anything that suggests there's a risk to you, but—'

'A risk?' There's a sharp burst of steam from the iron. Kath sets it down. 'You think Nadeeka could be targeted by these people?'

'We'd like to fit a panic alarm, if that's okay with you,' Lauren says.

A tight knot forms in Nadeeka's chest. They really believe this, she thinks. She nods. 'Okay.'

'And then what?' Kath scoffs. 'You lot rock up three days later? That's what happened that time I had my shed broken into.'

'Calls from the alarms go straight through to control room.' Lauren addresses her answer to Nadeeka. 'They're treated as emergencies – you'll have a car here within minutes.'

'Can't you put Nadeeka and the girls in a safe house?' Kath says. 'That's what they do on telly.'

'Unfortunately, this isn't television.' DI Stratman doesn't bother to hide his irritation. 'As it stands, we consider the risk to you and your family to be low. The alarm is a precaution, although if you notice anything at all suspicious it's imperative you tell us.'

Kath abandons the ironing and comes to sit on the arm of the sofa next to Nadeeka. 'Love, I know how you feel about Scott moving in, but—'

'I don't need—' Nadeeka tries, but when Kath gets going there's no stopping her.

'Those girls are the only grandkids I have.' She strokes

It's Not What You Think

Nadeeka's hair, and her tone softens. 'And you're the only daughter I have. I'd feel happier if Scott was here, just for a few days.'

Nadeeka exhales. Kath won't stop until she gets her way. 'Fine.'

'Good girl.'

'Only for a few days, though.'

'I'll ring him now.' Kath stands and starts patting her pockets for her phone. 'It's good timing, really – he and Gabriela have had a bust-up, so he was at mine last night.'

'The alarm will be fitted tomorrow morning,' Lauren says. She lets out a small sigh and her eyes crinkle in concern. 'I'm sorry, Nadeeka. I know this wasn't what you wanted to hear.'

'Not exactly,' Nadeeka says tightly.

When she shows them out, she can hear Kath on the phone to Scott, and she stands for a moment with her back to the locked front door, going over what Lauren and DI Stratman said, trying to make it fit.

But it doesn't.

Maybe it fits with the facts, but there has to be a place for instinct, surely, even in the face of whatever this 'intelligence' is that the police have. Intelligence isn't evidence, is it? Taking a photograph home from the office isn't evidence. Jamie's colleagues calling her Nadia isn't evidence. Jamie going to New Dawn meetings isn't evidence. It is, Nadeeka thinks (thanks to the many crime dramas she has watched at Kath's behest), what might be considered by a court as *circumstantial.*

Nadeeka *knew* Jamie. She knew their relationship – she *felt* it in her heart, in her soul – and she knows the police are wrong.

She just has to prove it.

CHAPTER 22

Jamie's parents live on the outskirts of Sheffield in a house with winter jasmine around the front porch and a brass knocker glinting from the centre of a wreath of holly and red velvet ribbons. Nadeeka rings the bell, and as the cheery *bing bong!* rings out, her stomach hollows with grief. She and Jamie were going to come here after Christmas. They would have dropped the girls at Scott's and driven up together, Nadeeka nervous but excited to meet Jamie's parents. She'd bought a tin of shortbread for Penny and a bottle of Glenmorangie for Frank. Nadeeka had imagined helping Penny in the kitchen while Jamie caught up with his dad; Penny sharing stories from Jamie's childhood.

She hears footsteps. A shadow fills the frosted glass at the side of the door and Nadeeka's breath catches.

It wasn't meant to be like this.

'You found us all right, then?' It's Frank. Managing a smile, even though his eyes don't quite catch up. He looks just like his photos: round and ruddy, with whiskery sideburns and a bald head.

'Your directions were perfect.' Nadeeka doesn't know what

to say. Frank hesitates, then he steps back and gestures for her to come in. She follows him down a narrow hall and into a lounge with pale green walls, where Penny is sitting on a cream sofa. She jumps up, and before Nadeeka can find the right words she has enveloped Nadeeka in a tight embrace.

'My boy,' Penny whispers, her voice cracking, and Nadeeka can't answer; all she can do is cling to the only other woman who loved Jamie as much as she did. She thinks again about how they'd planned to visit at Christmas, and how she'd imagined conspiring with Penny to find the perfect birthday gift for Jamie. *You know how he always claims he doesn't want anything*, she would have said, and they would have rolled their eyes good-naturedly at this unmaterialistic man of theirs.

Nadeeka pulls herself gently away, and Penny exhales, short and sharp. She holds Nadeeka's hands and gives them both a little shake. 'Onwards!' she says. A suburban battle cry of grief. 'That's what he would have wanted.' She has the same colouring as Jamie – the same scattering of freckles across her cheekbones – and recognizing it gives Nadeeka a sudden pain in her chest, like indigestion.

'Is there any news on when the funeral will be?' Frank speaks brusquely, like a man afraid he might cry. Nadeeka wishes she and Jamie had come to see his parents sooner, that she wasn't a stranger to them. She wonders if Frank has cried for his son yet, or if he's keeping it bottled inside.

'The police can't release the body until after the inquest,' Nadeeka says, as gently as she can.

At Penny's invitation, Nadeeka sits on the cream sofa, and she's about to tell them what Lauren said yesterday when she sees the silver frame on the coffee table. She puts a hand to her mouth.

Penny follows her gaze. 'Such a lovely photo. I was delighted when Jamie sent it. Maya and Nish look so much like you, don't they?' It's the picture of the four of them: Nadeeka, Jamie and the girls on Blackpool pier. Penny looks at it fondly. 'You know, he said you three were the best thing to ever happen to him.'

Nadeeka starts crying then. Slowly, she tells Penny and Frank everything that's happened, from the moment she met DI Burton to when Lauren and DI Stratman dropped the bombshell that they believed Jamie was a far-right extremist.

'I've never heard such nonsense in my life!' Frank puts down his coffee cup with such force the contents slosh on to the table. 'Who was that pretty girl he was seeing at university?' He clicks his fingers in the air, staring at Penny as though the answer is written on her forehead. 'The Indian one.'

'You're thinking of Effia,' Penny says, 'and she was Ghanaian.' She gives Nadeeka an apologetic look. 'The point my husband is rather clumsily making is that Jamie didn't have a racist bone in his body.'

'One of the police's theories is that Jamie targeted me in order to pass information to New Dawn,' Nadeeka says, 'but I just don't believe it.'

'Of course you don't,' Penny says briskly, 'because it isn't true. I knew my son, and I could tell when he was truly happy. And he was happy with you, darling girl.'

Nadeeka's heart tightens.

'Wasn't he, Frank?'

'Well, he moved halfway across the country, didn't he?'

'The police said maybe he never planned to stay,' Nadeeka says numbly. 'That moving in with so few possessions suggested a lack of commitment. I told them Jamie didn't have much, but—'

'Didn't have much!' Frank chortles. 'Come with me.' He beckons his finger and Nadeeka follows him through the house, Penny close behind them. The smell of furniture polish drifts from a wooden dresser in the kitchen, the open shelves displaying gilt-edged tureens from a dinner service kept for best.

The utility room is as tidy as the rest of the house. Frank pushes open a door and flicks a light switch, then stands back to let Nadeeka see.

Beyond the door is an integrated double garage full to the

rafters with furniture. There's a sofa and two double beds; hanging rails with clothes encased in plastic wrap; boxes marked *Kitchen glassware – very fragile!* Nadeeka spots a pile of boxes next to a vast shelving unit, and tips her head to see what's written on the side of them. *Paperbacks*, reads the first label. *Authors A to C.*

Nadeeka feels a rush of blood to her head. 'Is this all Jamie's?' She wants to touch it. She wants to open all the boxes and gorge on their contents. She wants to wear his clothes and read his books and feel – for a short time at least – that he's still with her.

'When he split up with Katie and they sold the house . . .' Penny pauses and Nadeeka nods for her to continue; she and Jamie had swapped back stories soon after they met. 'He moved into a rental near work, but it was fully furnished, so we offered him our garage for storage.'

Nadeeka's heart sank. Jamie had told her he'd sold everything. 'I guess the police were right,' she says bitterly. 'Jamie wasn't planning on sticking around long enough to need his own things.'

'Oh, no, no, darling girl!' Penny puts an arm around Nadeeka. 'Quite the opposite. He didn't want to upset your daughters by bringing in new furniture. *It's a big enough change for them to have me move in*, he told me. *Everything else needs to stay the same.*'

'But why didn't he say that to me? He told me he'd sold it all,' Nadeeka says, staring at the boxes in the garage.

'And what would you have done if he'd told you the truth?' Penny raises a teasing brow.

Nadeeka gives a half-laugh. 'I'd have insisted he bring some of his furniture.'

'Well, then.' She squeezes Nadeeka's hand. 'You and the girls were more important to him than any of this.' Penny walks towards a hanging rail and pulls back the dust sheet covering it. A dozen hangers hold a couple of smart jackets, a walking coat, a few pairs of trousers. Penny puts her hand on a chocolate-brown bomber jacket and a tremor of emotion crosses her face. 'He's had this for years.' She laughs, tears shining in her eyes. 'I always thought it was horrible.'

Nadeeka moves to put an arm around Penny. 'I've been wearing one of his coats,' she says. 'The police seized everything else, but I'd worn his coat to work and left it in the car that day. I must look ridiculous in it, but it's comforting, you know?'

Penny nods. 'I come in here sometimes, just to be close to him.'

Hanging next to the bomber jacket is a knitted jumper. Nothing special: a round-neck tweedy mix of heathery blues and greens. Nadeeka touches it. 'He wore this on one of our first video calls. I remember looking at it and thinking how *safe* it was, and how *safe* was exactly what I was looking for.'

'Take it.' Penny slips it off the hanger.

'Oh, no, I couldn't—'

'Please. Take whatever you want. It's important he . . .' Penny falters. She swallows hard. 'Important he lives on. For all of us.'

Sadness twists in Nadeeka's throat. 'Thank you,' she whispers. She loops the sweater around her shoulders. As she does, the woollen fibres release the faintest trace of Jamie's aftershave, and Nadeeka knows right away that she'll never wear this jumper. She will keep it in a box; she will try to preserve the memory of him for as long as it will last. It's all she has left.

Beside the clothes rail is an open box of books. Nadeeka crouches beside it. She looks at Penny. 'May I?'

'Of course.'

Nadeeka takes out a stack of paperbacks. *The Exchange*, by John Grisham; *Trust*, by Hernan Diaz; *Open Water*, by Caleb Azumah Nelson.

'He always did love reading,' Penny says. 'And don't think he was missing out by not having his books at your house – I know he was using the library, because he was there when I called him one time.'

Nadeeka remembers the library card she found in the desk on the landing. She'd thought nothing of it at the time, but it occurs to her now that she'd never seen Jamie bring a library book home. The book on Jamie's nightstand had been one from Nadeeka's own eclectic shelves. He'd never even mentioned using the library.

It's Not What You Think

Could Jamie have been looking at newspaper archives or local history records? Had he uncovered something that had put him in danger? Meeting Jamie's parents has reinforced Nadeeka's belief that the police are mistaken about Jamie's involvement with the far right, but she still has nothing concrete with which to convince them.

How do you prove something *didn't* happen?

How do you prove who someone really was?

Penny sends Nadeeka home with another fierce embrace and a packet of butterscotch for the girls, and Frank claps her on the back and tells her to drive carefully. 'Drop us a text to let us know you're home safe,' he says gruffly, and Nadeeka bites the inside of her cheek before their kindness undoes her.

'And . . .' Penny hesitates. 'If you wanted to meet for coffee some time? Only if . . . I mean, I'm sure you're very busy—'

'I'd love that.' Nadeeka hugs her again. From the corner of her eye, she sees Frank cuff away a tear.

On the long drive home, Nadeeka goes over all the conflicting information. Jamie loved her, but had been behaving oddly before he died. He'd been happy for his parents to have a photograph of Nadeeka and the girls, yet hadn't wanted it displayed at work. He'd attended the meetings of a white supremacy group, yet his parents were adamant he'd never held racist views.

She stops at the library on her way home. Maya and Nish love it here, and they often pop in on a Saturday to choose more books or try out the 3-D printer.

The woman on the desk smiles as she approaches. 'How can I help you?' Her name badge reads *Josephine Capstick*.

'My partner recently died,' Nadeeka says, 'and I'm not sure if he has any overdue library books.' Her voice sounds unnaturally formal, as though Jamie's death is nothing but an administrative inconvenience.

'I'm so sorry to hear that. Let me check for you.' Josephine takes Jamie's name and hums under her breath as she taps her keyboard. 'Hmm . . . it looks like he's never checked any books out, actually; just reserved them to read here.'

'Would you be able to tell me what he reserved?'

'Just a sec . . .' There's more humming, and then the printer whirs and spits out a sheet of paper with a list of around twenty titles.

Nadeeka hadn't known what to expect from Jamie's reading list. More of what she saw at his parents' house perhaps: thrillers, literary fiction, a few biographies.

But the book at the top of the list is *Mein Kampf*.

They instruct their members to read Mein Kampf, DI Stratman had said. A leaden feeling solidifies at the pit of Nadeeka's stomach. She was so sure the police had been wrong, but now . . .

'Pretty serious stuff,' Josephine says, with a smile Nadeeka doesn't return. If the librarian had any idea just *how* serious this is . . .

They Were White and They Were Slaves.

The International Jew.

The Turner Diaries.

White Identity: Racial Consciousness in the 21st Century.

'Open University, is it?' Josephine says, and for a second Nadeeka thinks that maybe that's it; that Jamie was secretly studying at the library, and the police's New Dawn theory is nothing but a horrible mix-up. And yet . . . she doesn't know all the books on the list, but they are all of a type. This is the reading list of someone obsessed with issues of race, of leadership, of identity. The reading list, Nadeeka thinks despairingly, of a white supremacist.

'Did he access anything online?' she asks Josephine, remembering her earlier thought about archives. 'You have computers people can use, right?'

'Oh, yes, and he did – his log-in details are here.' The librarian taps the side of her computer, and Nadeeka's fingers itch to turn the screen around.

It's Not What You Think

'Can you see what he looked at?'
'Yes, but it's a breach of data protection, we're not allowed to—'
'For God's sake!'
Josephine frowns.

Nadeeka bites her lip. 'Sorry.' She forces a smile. 'He said he was doing something special for me for Christmas, you see. Said he couldn't organize it from home in case adverts started popping up on my phone – you know how spooky they are nowadays. I just . . .' Her voice cracks. 'I just can't bear the thought that I'll never know.' Nadeeka's eyes fill with genuine tears. It feels so unfair that she never got to spend Christmas with Jamie. She'd been so busy with work and the girls' nativity costumes, and picking up bits and pieces for their stockings, that she'd only recently turned her attention to Jamie's present. *What would you like?* she'd asked him. *I want to get you something you'll love.* Jamie had pulled her close. *I already have it*, he'd said.

Across the library counter, Josephine's expression softens. 'You poor thing.' She glances around, then makes a few swift keystrokes and scrutinizes her screen. 'He didn't access any of our online records . . . let me check his search history.'

Nadeeka holds her breath. She doesn't know what she's looking for, but she knows there's something missing from the pieces of the puzzle she has right now. The picture Penny and Frank had painted was of a tolerant, compassionate man – the same tolerant, compassionate man Nadeeka had fallen in love with. The books packed in boxes at their house were a far cry from the terrifying list of titles he'd requested from the library yet never brought home. Surely one man couldn't become a completely different one in the space of a few short weeks?

But even as she thinks this, she remembers the sudden claims to be working late; Jamie's reluctance to spend time with her. The tense silences that had replaced his usual relaxed and gentle conversation.

'I can't see anything about Christmas presents, I'm afraid.'

Josephine's finger scrolls on her mouse, eyes scanning her screen. She turns it around to show Nadeeka.

The most recent search term reads *Why multi-culturalism doesn't work.*

Nadeeka grips the edge of the counter. She reels, a sudden wave of nausea bringing bile to the back of her throat as she reads on.

How the woke agenda is destroying Western values.

Examples of how the media is controlled by liberals.

Articles on white supremacy.

They could almost be essay titles, Nadeeka thinks. *Open University, is it?* Except that scattered among them are several searches that are far from academic.

How to conceal your identity.

What police unit deals with domestic extremism?

What sentence does arson carry?

Nadeeka can hardly bear to read them. She can no longer kid herself that this is all a mistake; that Jamie wasn't involved in the far right. But she can't bring herself to believe Lauren's theory that Jamie had always held such abhorrent views and had simply been hiding them. Nadeeka isn't stupid. She's built a career in recruitment – she *knows* people. She knew Jamie.

So when did he change?

And what changed him?

She makes herself keep reading, caught off-guard by the mundane searches that appear in Jamie's history, the contrast making his fevered research seem even more horrifying. *Cinema listings this Saturday. Weather today. How do you make people like you?*

Nadeeka stops. *How do you make people like you?* It sends a dart of pain through her heart, the way it does when Maya falls out with her best friend – a regular occurrence – or that time Nish was the only one in the class not to be invited to Sam's party.

You'll soon settle and make friends, Nadeeka had told Jamie when he moved in. He'd claimed not to be worried about it, and Nadeeka had wanted to believe him, but deep down she'd

It's Not What You Think

known he was lonely. That having a partner was very different from having a best mate around the corner; people to play cricket with at weekends. She had pushed the thought away because she hadn't wanted it to be true.

In the corridor outside Nadeeka's office at Echelon Warehousing is an A3 poster bearing the word **PREVENT** in heavy bold type, followed by *SPOT THE SIGNS*. Beneath it is a list of behaviours. *Displaying mood swings, procuring extremist reading material, keeping secrets or lying to friends and family.* Someone had come to deliver training to the recruitment and HR team, educating them on what to look out for should any of their staff become a target for extremists.

Recruiters frequently target young Muslim men, the trainer had said, and they had plenty of those at Echelon. *They look for anyone who seems disenfranchised or isolated; someone whose vulnerabilities they can exploit. Someone they can groom.*

Nadeeka remembered being surprised. She had only ever thought of grooming in the context of young girls being targeted by sleazy older men. But as she'd listened to the rest of the session she'd considered the brief stint she'd done as a head-hunter, and thought how recruitment was recruitment, whatever business you're in. Establish what your target wants, then tailor your offer accordingly. Flexible working? A pay rise? Or the feeling that you *belong*. That you *matter*.

In the library, Nadeeka stares at Jamie's search history. He'd been new to the area; had no friends, no connections. He was coming to terms with a new job, a new identity as step-parent. Jamie had been far from what Nadeeka would consider vulnerable, but so are the disenfranchised youth targeted by Islamic extremists; the women sucked into pyramid schemes; the middle-aged men swept up in conspiracies.

How do you make people like you?

A chill runs down Nadeeka's spine.

Had Jamie been radicalized?

CHAPTER 23

It's strange having Scott in the house. Nadeeka had forgotten how much space he takes up, how much noise he makes. He has music on constantly, leaving it playing in whatever room he has recently vacated, and has now commandeered Nadeeka's breakfast bar as an office, setting up a tripod to film content for his 'side-hustle'.

'Success comes from the five to nine, not the nine to five,' he tells Nadeeka, when she comes downstairs at half-past seven on Monday morning. She ignores him and puts the kettle on. Had he been this much of a knob when they were married?

'How was the sofa?' she asks. Nish would have happily given up her room – any excuse for a sleepover with her big sister – but having Scott upstairs feels too intrusive, too permanent. This is strictly a practical arrangement.

'I've slept on worse.'

'Yes, how *are* things with Gabriela?' Nadeeka says, stress making her uncharacteristically bitchy.

'Miaow!' Scott takes a slurp of some green concoction. 'We're on a break, actually, thanks to the police poking their nose in.'

It's Not What You Think

Nadeeka would never give Scott the satisfaction of telling him, but there is some comfort in being aligned on their views of the police. Lauren might make out they want to find Jamie's murderer, but the change in their focus is obvious: in the police's eyes, Jamie is as much a suspect as a victim.

Nadeeka has dropped the girls at school and is on her way to work when she notices a black car behind her. She's not sure how long it's been there, but it keeps a steady distance, dropping back at junctions, just far enough that Nadeeka can't make out who's driving it. She thinks of what Lauren said – *We don't know to what extent New Dawn were aware of Jamie's relationship with you* – and takes the next left turn without indicating. The black car takes the turn too.

It's suddenly too hot in Nadeeka's car and she turns on the air-con, blasting herself with icy air. She takes a right, and then another left, and now she's back on the main road and the black car is there too, and there is zero reason for it to have made that detour if it isn't following her.

If you notice anything at all suspicious it's imperative you tell us, DI Stratman had said, and so, with one eye on the road, Nadeeka dials Lauren's number.

'I'm being followed,' she says, as soon as Lauren answers.

'Where are you?'

'Ring road.' Panic snatches the words short. 'A black car. BMW.'

'Can you get the licence plate?'

Nadeeka looks in her rear-view mirror. Her back windscreen is smeared, and the car has dropped back again, making it hard to read the letters. *Is that a K or an H?* She reads out the licence plate as best she can, remembering too late that it will be back to front. She slows, realizing she's almost at her exit, and the BMW slows too. The vast depots of Echelon Warehousing can be seen from the ring road, the company so huge it has its own signposted exit. Nadeeka takes it now, and, as she does, the BMW picks up speed and disappears into the ether. 'It's gone,' she tells Lauren. Her heart thuds against her ribcage. 'I've just got to work.'

'I'll run a check on the BMW. Try not to worry.'

Easier said than done, Nadeeka thinks. Why would someone follow her? Maybe they know she went to see Jamie's parents; is there something of his they think she has? Or were they following to see if she was going to the police again?

Last night, Nadeeka read everything she could find online about radicalization. *Withdrawing from friends and family, being evasive about movements, expressing unusually extreme views.* She thinks about Jamie's reluctance for Maya and Nish to join the school's multi-faith production; about how cagey he was in the weeks before he died. *Radicalization often stems from a desire to reclaim authority or identity*, Nadeeka read, on a government website. Was that where it had come from? Had Nadeeka been too overbearing, too controlling? Had she not left enough space in their new life for Jamie to feel needed?

The questions are still spiralling as she walks down the long corridor next to the warehouse that leads to her office. On the other side of the glass, a hundred pickers-and-packers move between the racked shelving and the waiting boxes. One of her newer recruits, Stefan, is wrapping a board game in recycled paper. He looks up as she passes, but when she waves he looks away. Nadeeka frowns. She hopes he's settling in okay; the huge warehouse can be overwhelming for new starters.

He's not the only one behaving oddly.

'The paper ran a piece on the job fair,' Helen says, when Nadeeka reaches their shared office.

'That's great . . . isn't it?' Nadeeka is confused by Helen's guarded tone. 'I sent over the press release, but you never know what they . . .' She tails off as she sees the newspaper on her desk. 'Oh, shit.'

It's Not What You Think

'Exactly,' Helen says grimly.

Nadeeka's press release had been titled *Echelon Warehousing opens its doors: job fair offers career opportunities for all.* The news headline reads *Local Jobs For Local People!* Nadeeka's eyes travel over the copy. There is scant mention of what the job fair will entail; instead, the journalist has used Nadeeka's release as a hook for an 'in-depth' article on local unemployment. *Local man Robbie Bowers has been out of work for nine months*, reads a box-out featuring a photograph of a dejected-looking white man, *despite applying for multiple suitable jobs*. Next to it is a second case study. *Bulgarian-born Stefan Petrov received a 'golden handshake' on his first day at Echelon Warehousing.*

Nadeeka's mouth drops. 'A golden handshake? It's a twenty-quid voucher!'

'Hopefully we'll still get a decent turnout for the fair,' Helen says. 'But it's not exactly the publicity we were after.'

Nadeeka folds the newspaper. 'I need to speak to Stefan.'

She finds him in the break area, nursing a cup of coffee and scrolling through his phone. He looks up when she approaches, his expression cautious.

'Hey,' she says, pulling out the chair opposite him. 'Did you see the article?'

Stefan snorts. 'Hard to miss.' He turns his phone to show her the comments section of the online article. 'Apparently I have personally stolen about twenty jobs.'

'I'm so sorry. It's complete rubbish.'

'I know this. You know this. But a lot of people do not want to know this.' He shrugs, taking a sip of his coffee.

'Stefan . . .' Nadeeka hesitates. 'What do you know about white supremacy groups?'

He raises an eyebrow. 'It is not exactly my thing.'

'Have you heard of an organization called New Dawn?'

Stefan gives a slow nod. 'They fucked over a mate of mine.'

'Do you know anything about them?'

'Nothing, really. Why do you want to know?'

'I . . .' Nadeeka falters. 'I'm worried about what they're doing. Their influence in the area.'

Stefan nods again. 'You are right to be worried. There is a lot of anger under the surface around here. It would not take a lot for it to boil over.'

'So how do I find out more about them? How they operate, how they recruit?'

'You don't. Not looking like that.' Stefan shrugs. 'And nor do I. You wish for insider information on a group like New Dawn, you need a white guy.'

It's a throwaway comment, but, as Stefan goes back to work, Nadeeka stays in the break room, thinking about what he's said. If she's going to prove to the police that Jamie was a victim of radicalization, she needs to know more about the people who recruited him, and Stefan's right: the person asking questions needs to look like a prospective member of New Dawn.

Nadeeka knows exactly who to ask.

CHAPTER 24

'No fucking way.' Scott stands in the entrance to the kitchen, his thumbs looped into his pockets and his elbows touching the doorframe. Despite the cold, he's in a T-shirt, the sleeves taut around his biceps.

'I just need you to ask around. Show an interest and see if anyone picks up on it.'

'You want me to be *bait*?' Scott leans against the doorframe. 'Forget it, Nads. You're playing a dangerous game and you're not dragging me into it.'

'The police say Jamie was part of New Dawn, but I think he was forced into it. I need to prove that he was brainwashed.'

Scott laughs. 'You have to have a brain to be—' He catches Nadeeka's expression and stops abruptly. 'Look, I'll ask around, all right? But I'm not pretending to be a fucking fascist – those people are scum.'

'Thanks.' She calls after him as he turns to leave. 'Actually, there's one other thing.'

'I moved back as your security, not your skivvy.'

'Would you be able to get any data from this?' Nadeeka holds out Jamie's watch.

'Like what – the exact time the bloke crawled out of the Stone Age?' Scott turns it over in his hands. 'This thing's got about as much processing power as a toaster.'

'Jamie wasn't interested in gadgets.'

'Clearly.'

'Look, can you help me, or not?' Nadeeka is losing her patience.

'Well, if you're going to be like that . . .' Scott tosses the watch on to the table. 'It makes no difference to me if the police think he was Benito Mussolini, so why should I put myself out to—'

'Because I loved him!' Her voice breaks and she holds on to the back of a chair for support. Tears that have been held back for too long fall unchecked down her cheeks. 'And because he loved Maya and Nish like they were his own kids. You might not want to hear that, but it's true, and you should have been glad they were loved, instead of trying to take away the best thing to happen to us in years!'

She goes to snatch up the watch, but Scott gets there first, and their hands collide. They stare at each other, then, slowly, Nadeeka takes back her hand.

'StrideKeepers are pretty basic watches,' Scott says. 'And this one's an early model. No Bluetooth, no wifi.' He scrutinizes it. 'People use them for step count really, nothing more.'

'But will it show you *where* those steps were taken?'

'If it's got GPS.'

'So will you try?' She holds Scott's gaze, not wanting to beg, but at the same time desperate for him to say yes. She doesn't want to hand the watch to the police and have them find more damning evidence against Jamie. She wants to find the truth, and she no longer trusts that Lauren wants that too.

Scott nods. 'I'll try.'

CHAPTER 25

Nadeeka looks out of the window of the unmarked police car in which Lauren is driving them to the mortuary. She is sitting in the back like a child – or like a suspect, she supposes – because the front passenger seat is occupied by Detective Sergeant Fraser Hogan. He'd offered her the choice, but Nadeeka is half his size, and it seemed wrong to ask him to fold himself into the back.

Occasionally, Lauren says something to Fraser in a low murmur. At first, Nadeeka strains to hear – anxious not to miss anything relevant to Jamie's case – but the snippets she catches are about seating plans and salmon. They're getting married, she realizes, as they draw near to the hospital. She envies the ease they have; envies the time they get to spend together. She feels a spark of anger that she and Jamie were given so little.

'Here we are,' Lauren says, as they pull in.

It has taken Nadeeka several days to summon the courage to see Jamie's body. She has been warned about the decomposition that has taken place, and the discoloration of his skin. Lauren has explained about the viewing room, and that she will be right outside if Nadeeka feels faint or wants to leave; that Nadeeka mustn't feel under any pressure to see Jamie. No one will judge her.

But Nadeeka does want to see him. Not least because she still feels as though she's living a nightmare, the sands shifting under her feet with every step. She trusted DI Burton and he turned out not to exist; she trusted Lauren and her team, and now they have turned on Jamie. In the small hours when Nadeeka lies awake, a tiny flicker of hope whispers *Maybe Jamie is still alive. Maybe the police have the wrong man.* She knows this is absurd – that the police have Jamie's DNA – but she knows, too, that until she sees him with her own eyes she will not believe it.

The mortuary is grey and stark with clean lines and even cleaner floors. A young man in green scrubs leads them through a series of doors, a waft of disinfectant accompanying them through each one.

'Would you like something to drink first?' Fraser asks. 'Tea, coffee? I think there's a machine.'

Nadeeka shakes her head. 'I just want to see him.'

They show her to a small room with a window covered with brown curtains. Nadeeka's breath catches. When Lauren pulls those curtains back, it won't be the outside world they see, it will be Jamie. Her Jamie.

Lauren takes hold of the fabric. 'Ready?'

No, Nadeeka thinks. 'Yes,' she says.

And the curtains open.

The first time Nadeeka met Jamie, she thought how much more handsome he was in real life than in the photos he'd posted on Hinge. When he talked, his whole face became animated, and she'd thought *I could look at this face forever*.

Tears roll down her cheeks as she looks at him now. It *is* Jamie, of course – she had been foolish even to hope there had been a mistake – but the man lying on the other side of the glass is unrecognizable as *her* Jamie. No longer animated. No longer *there*, she thinks. She turns away.

'You can stay longer,' Lauren says, when she leaves the viewing room. 'Take as much time as—'

'I'm done.' Nadeeka can't look at her. She feels suddenly resentful of Lauren, with her upcoming wedding and plans for the future. 'I'd like to go home, please.'

'We've been looking at Jamie's financial transactions in the weeks before he died,' Lauren says, as they pull out of the hospital. 'There's a cash withdrawal of three hundred pounds – any idea what it was for?'

'How would I know?' In the back seat, Nadeeka flushes slightly at her own rudeness. She can't help it; she has an overwhelming desire to scream at someone, to release the pent-up tension inside her.

'It doesn't look as though he used cash much, which is why it stood out.' Fraser twists in his seat to look at her. 'Groups like New Dawn rely heavily on private donations.'

'Jamie wouldn't fund terrorist activities,' Nadeeka says firmly, although her heart sinks as she acknowledges yet another red flag from what she's learned about radicalization. *Unusual financial transactions.*

'We have to explore all possibilities.'

'When did he take the cash out?' Nadeeka waits while Fraser checks the date of the withdrawal, then makes a show of contemplating it. 'Right . . . that would have been for me. I had to get the boiler serviced, and the girls needed new shoes. Jamie offered to help.'

Fraser leaves a beat. 'Okay. That's helpful.'

Nadeeka keeps a steady gaze on the passing traffic. She keeps thinking of Jamie's parents – of Penny's brave smile and Frank's stiff upper lip – and how it would destroy them to be told their son had donated to the far right.

'There are a few other transactions we're struggling to trace,' Fraser says, 'including one from a company in China. Did Jamie have any packages delivered from overseas?'

'I don't think so.' They had joked about Jamie's shopping habit. *Have you been influenced again?* Nadeeka would say, when another package arrived.

'Intelligence suggests New Dawn have access to weapons, possibly explosives.' Lauren looks in the rear-view mirror, searching for eye contact.

Nadeeka looks away. 'He didn't get much post.'

They drive the rest of the way home in silence, Nadeeka thinking not of *all* the packages Jamie used to receive, but of one in particular. A small, square box with Chinese lettering on the label. *What's this?* she had said, bringing it into the kitchen. *Just some supplements I saw advertised on Facebook*, Jamie had said, taking the parcel. *Probably a load of rubbish.* He had put it away without opening it.

Nadeeka had never seen him taking any supplements.

When she gets home, Nadeeka crouches on the floor of the garage and sifts through the recycling. Card and paper are collected fortnightly along with glass and plastic, but boxes get stuffed into larger boxes and thrown in the garage until one of them has time to go to the tip. She pulls out the packaging for a pair of trainers, a replacement shower hose, the coffee capsules she orders online. The square box with Chinese writing isn't there. Maybe Jamie squashed it in with the card, she thinks, or maybe . . .

Nadeeka jumps to her feet.

She knows exactly where the box will be.

CHAPTER 26

Nish glares at Nadeeka as she eats her tea, pushing peas around her plate in a silent protest. On the table next to her is her precious cardboard castle.

'But it's part of the display!' she had wailed, after Nadeeka had told Miss Key she needed to take the castle home.

'Couldn't we keep it until the end of term?' Miss Key's plaits had bounced against the buckles of her dungarees. 'It's only a couple of weeks.'

'The girls' grandmother is desperate to see it. She's going away.' The lie had made Nadeeka redden.

'Where's Grandma going?' Maya had demanded. 'Is she going on holiday? Can we go?'

Nadeeka had become increasingly flustered as she navigated the girls' questions, eventually snapping that she just wanted to *take the bloody castle home!* Maya's and Nish's mouths had rounded in shock, and the bubbly Miss Key had looked personally wounded. She had picked up the castle from the centre of a display on 'Norman times' and handed it wordlessly to Nadeeka.

It is another three hours before Nadeeka can look properly at the castle. Scott has gone out for a run – taking his phone with him, Nadeeka notes – and the girls are in bed, so Nadeeka closes the kitchen door and sits at the table. She eyes the castle from several angles, trying to identify which bit of the structure might have been made from the small square box, but Jamie and Nish have covered the joins in paper tape, and the grey paint flows seamlessly from castle wall to bastion to palisade. There is only one way to discover what's underneath. Nadeeka takes a deep breath, then she rips the castle apart.

The square box originated from a company called Dragon Eye Technology in Shenzhen. There's still bubble wrap inside, and when Nadeeka pulls it out, a sheet of crumpled paper comes too. She smooths it out.

ShadowTek X9 Quick Start Guide, she reads. *Press and hold the red button for three seconds until the indicator light flashes. The device is now recording.*

The kitchen door opens and Nadeeka jumps up, hiding the instructions behind her back.

'Snapped the lace on my—' Scott stares at the ruined castle. 'What the fuck happened to Nish's model?' He takes in Nadeeka's guilty expression. 'Wait – did *you* do that?'

'Tell me this isn't what I think it is.' Nadeeka thrusts the piece of paper at him.

'You're losing the plot, Nads. What *is* this?'

'That's what I want to know. Jamie bought it about a week before he died.'

'These are instructions for a covert recording device.' Scott's mouth falls open. 'That bastard bugged the house!'

'He wouldn't do—'

'For God's sake, Nads!' Scott takes a few steps towards her. 'Wake up! The police have evidence that Jamie was part of New

It's Not What You Think

Dawn. He targeted you, and this bug proves it. He was recording you, Nads! Gathering information for them.'

The hairs on the back of Nadeeka's neck stand on end. She shakes her head, *no, no, no* . . .

Scott drops his voice, his eyes flicking to the corners of the room. 'What we need to find out is whether they're still listening.'

CHAPTER 27

They have searched everywhere. They have stood on chairs and looked in the light fittings; run their hands along the tops of cupboards and doorframes. They have felt down the seams of the curtains and in the linings of cushions. They have found nothing.

'It's a black disc,' Scott had said, having looked up the recording device online, 'about two centimetres diameter.'

'It could be anywhere,' Nadeeka says now, sitting down heavily on the stairs. She has just searched her bedroom, feeling nauseous at the thought of a microphone recording everything she and Jamie had said – and done. She thinks of all the conversations she'd thought were private, and imagines them replayed for an audience. What had New Dawn wanted from her?

'Where did you and Jamie talk the most?' Scott says. He's flushed with the exertion of clambering on to furniture, his eyes shining with determination. He looks, Nadeeka thinks bitterly, almost as though he's enjoying this. She doesn't reply, simply points to the lounge. She's paralysed by the thought that people might be listening to her right now. Nadeeka thinks of all the evenings she lay on the sofa, her feet in Jamie's lap, telling him about her day. Her eyes widen as she thinks of something.

'What?' Scott says.

She shakes her head mutely. Doesn't want to say it out loud. She's thinking about the job fair at work; about Stefan and the vitriol from people who consider his job beneath them yet still don't want him to have it. She's thinking about the black BMW that followed her to work. Is that why New Dawn chose her? Because she works for a company that employs large numbers of foreign-born workers?

'Do you still take work calls in the car?' Scott says, as though he can read her thoughts. 'Maybe he bugged the car.' He snatches up her keys from the bowl on the hall table and opens the front door, letting in a blast of cold air. He *is* enjoying this, Nadeeka thinks. Her ex-husband is one of those men who revel in the role of protector; she always had the impression it irked him that she didn't need him more.

She tries to remember when she'd had the idea for the job fair – when she would have talked to Jamie about it. She gets out her phone and scrolls back through her calendar, and it takes her breath away to think that she was blithely making hair appointments and holding meetings with no idea her life was about to implode.

Nadeeka stops scrolling as the memory of Lauren's interrogations intersects with the dates in front of her. Jamie withdrew three hundred pounds in cash. Had he been radicalized to the extent that he would have given New Dawn money? She stares at her calendar and racks her brain to remember what was happening around the same time. The girls had an after-school rehearsal for the nativity, and Nadeeka had worked from home on the Monday because the boiler man had come – that part of her lie to Lauren had been true.

Nadeeka opens Facebook. She isn't one for status updates, but she often posts photos – a pretty sunset; the girls enjoying a hot chocolate after school – in the knowledge that Facebook will surprise her with these moments in years to come. When she scrolls back, she doesn't find any photographs, just a post shared from the local paper's feed. *Police are appealing for witnesses following a fire at Shop Express on Station Approach.* Nausea builds in her stomach as she pictures Jamie setting fire to Surinder's shop. Surinder's *home.*

Scott comes back inside, swinging shut the front door with a slam. 'I didn't find a bug.'

Nadeeka is trying to make sense of the timeline. Lauren had interrogated her about Jamie's movements the week of the fire – had Nadeeka seen him buying lighter fuel? A face mask? – but the cashpoint withdrawal was *after* the fire, and Nadeeka suddenly remembers something Surinder said, when he'd seen her the day after the murder.

People have been very kind. We even had money pushed through the door. It's not a bad neighbourhood, really.

'Is this his?' Scott is holding up Jamie's coat between his thumb and forefinger, as though it's radioactive.

'Yes,' Nadeeka says shortly. She's too embarrassed to admit she's been wearing it, and anyway, a green dot on Shop Express's Messenger tells her Surinder is online. She sends him a message. He'll wonder why she's asking, but if she's right . . .

'Did you know this was in the pocket?' Scott says, and something about his tone makes Nadeeka look up from the dancing dots that tell her Surinder is typing. Scott's holding Jamie's woolly hat, except that he's unfolded it, and it isn't a hat at all – it's a balaclava.

'I . . .' She stares at it. Imagines Jamie pulling it down over his face; imagines him among a group of other masked men, jeering and hurling missiles, the way she's seen on the news. But Jamie wasn't like that, she thinks, and when she glances at her phone and reads the response from Shop Express she feels a surge of conviction.

It's Not What You Think

The money I mentioned was in an envelope pushed through our door the day after the fire, reads Surinder's message. *There was £300.*

'If Jamie was part of New Dawn – ' Nadeeka pushes back her chair ' – he didn't want to be.'

'You can tell yourself that all you want,' Scott says. 'The evidence says otherwise.'

'No.' She shakes her head. Goes into the kitchen and looks again at the printout of places encompassed in Jamie's step count. Scott had emailed it to her along with more scathing comments about Jamie's *shit watch*. Nadeeka had hit up Google right away, searching the street names to build a picture of where Jamie had been. Maybe she could track down other members of New Dawn – the people who had groomed him. If she could present Lauren with hard evidence . . .

She had stopped when the search engine had thrown up the Lord Admiral pub.

Did Jamie ever mention any of these places to you? Lauren had said. *The Lord Admiral, the King's Arms, the British Legion?*

They were presumably all places the police knew to be connected to New Dawn. One by one, Nadeeka found them all among the data Scott had managed to retrieve from Jamie's 'shit watch'. She so desperately wanted to clear his name, but everything she found made things ten times worse.

Nadeeka stares at the data now, willing it to show her something new. Is there a pattern? Some place he was going to regularly?

'Where are the kitchen scissors?' Scott says suddenly.

'In the drawer next to the hob,' Nadeeka says distractedly. *Beech Street*, she thinks, looking at the list. *Why does Beech Street ring a bell?* Jamie had gone there a month before he died. 'Where they've always been,' she adds. When Nadeeka puts it into the map, she realizes Beech Street is where the police station is. The job centre is next door, she remembers, and the magistrates' court across the road; there are no shops, no residential buildings.

'Could Jamie have gone to the police station?' she says, half to herself.

Scott snorts. 'Maybe he was answering bail.'

'He'd never been in trouble with the police.' *Unlike you*, Nadeeka wants to add, but doesn't. Scott's helping her out, even though she suspects he's only doing it to prove she was wrong to trust Jamie. 'That's why they didn't have his DNA on file. They had to take it from his toothbrush.'

'Asking for the time, then?' Scott shrugs. 'I dunno.' He's fiddling with the balaclava, pulling it between his fingers.

'Can you take this seriously? And leave that alone.' Nadeeka bats at the balaclava. 'It might have important evidence on it.'

She stares at the map. What would Jamie be doing at a police station, that he couldn't do online? Lost property, neighbourhood disputes, even crime reports – they're encouraged to do almost everything via a contact form nowadays.

'What if he wanted advice?' she says, but Scott isn't listening. He's hacking at the balaclava with the scissors. 'What are you doing?' Nadeeka says, outraged.

Scott doesn't answer. Instead, like a magician with a rabbit, he pulls a small black disk from the knitted seam. He places it on the table between them.

The bug.

'Then he wasn't recording me,' Nadeeka says slowly. Scott opens his mouth, and she holds up a hand, blocking his retort. 'I know you think I'm in denial, but I think I'd have noticed if Jamie wore a balaclava in the bloody house.'

'Where did he wear it, then?' Scott flips the bug over tentatively, as though it might move of its own accord.

'Protests?' One by one, the pieces are clicking into place. The cash Jamie had taken out wasn't to fund terrorist activity but to mitigate the terrible crime he'd committed against Surinder – a crime Nadeeka increasingly believes Jamie was compelled to carry out. 'He didn't buy a recording device to spy on me,' she says. 'He got it to spy on New Dawn.' Jamie must have worn the balaclava when he carried out the arson, and when he met with other members of the group.

'Going undercover in a white supremacy meeting?' Scott whistles. 'That's a sure-fire way to get yourself—' He breaks off abruptly, eyes fixed on the table.

'Killed.' Nadeeka says quietly. 'Maybe that's why he was at Beech Street police station. Because he knew they were after him.'

How to conceal your identity.

Jamie wasn't trying to hide from the police, he was trying to hide from New Dawn.

'Jamie was behaving strangely because he was scared,' Nadeeka says, everything coming together with blinding clarity. 'He distanced himself from me to protect me – even tried to walk away, but he couldn't bring himself to do it.'

Scott tears his eyes away from the table. He nods slowly, reluctantly. 'I think you might be on to something.'

'I know I am.' Nadeeka feels strangely disassociated, as though she's watching herself come to a conclusion she's known all along. She dials Lauren's number. There's a lot Nadeeka still doesn't know, but she's certain the police have it wrong about New Dawn.

Jamie hadn't been *one* of them.

He'd been trying to stop them.

PART FOUR
JAMIE

CHAPTER 28

Two months earlier

Jamie gets out of the taxi first. He holds out a hand for Nadeeka, who had reached her self-imposed limit of three vodka-and-tonics two hours ago, then declared *It's the weekend!* and ordered another round. Followed by two more. He taps the flat of his hand twice on the roof of the cab.

'Why do men always do that?' Nadeeka stumbles as she steps on to the pavement. 'Oops!'

Jamie puts one arm around her, taking a firm hold of her elbow with his free hand. 'So the driver knows everyone's safely out and he can drive off.' He steers her towards the house.

'I've literally never seen a woman do it. Do they teach you it in boy-school?' Nadeeka stops, seemingly incapable of talking and walking at the same time. 'Also . . .' She hiccups loudly. 'You called him "chief". You never call anyone chief. Is that a boy-school thing too?'

'Ah, you've rumbled us.' Jamie coaxes a few more steps out of her, then hunts for the house keys amid the eclectic contents of her handbag. 'You brought wet wipes on a date night?' He holds them up. 'Were you expecting something more adventurous than drinks and a pub quiz?'

'Mums never go anywhere without wet wipes.'

'You learn that in girl-school, I suppose.' Jamie opens the front door.

'Don't be so sexist!'

Jamie is about to point out Nadeeka's double standards when she trips over her own feet and faceplants on to the hall carpet. She lies there giggling to herself and making no attempt to move. Jamie can't help but laugh too as he hauls her upright and shepherds her up the stairs to bed.

Nadeeka starts pulling off her clothes, throwing them with abandon across the carpet. 'The girls are at Scott's.'

'Yes.' Jamie takes off his T-shirt and drops it into the laundry basket.

Nadeeka flings herself on the bed, both arms in the air. She has taken off her knickers but still has on her bra and a single sock. It is an interesting (if not unappealing) look. She beams at him. 'You know what that means.'

Jamie and Nadeeka's sex life falls into two distinct categories. There is the quiet and slightly furtive kind which happens when Maya and Nish are home: breathless under the covers, one eye on the closed bedroom door. And then there is the kind they have on a Wednesday night and every other weekend; the sort of rampant, uninhibited sex enjoyed at the start of a relationship – or after two bottles of wine.

Jamie sometimes feels guilty about how much he looks forward to the girls going to their dad's. It isn't only the sex (although the fear of being interrupted by someone else's child isn't exactly conducive to a great performance); it's because on those days Nadeeka gets to be Nadeeka, not Mum. And she really is different. More relaxed, more spontaneous. She laughs more; she's more affectionate. She even sits down to eat breakfast, instead of standing up by the sink.

It's Not What You Think

'Do you *feel* different?' Jamie asked her once.

'Kind of.'

He had found it fascinating, this idea that someone could be two people.

'Three,' Nadeeka had said. 'I think I'm three people. There's Work Nadeeka, too. I'm much more efficient there than I ever am at home. More confident, too. I can fire someone for poor performance without breaking a sweat, but when my hairdresser gave me that horrendous fringe last month, I told her it was perfect then gave her a massive tip.'

Jamie had wondered if this was a male/female thing; if women were more chameleon-like by nature. 'I think I'm just Jamie,' he'd said. 'I wouldn't know how to be any different.'

'Good job I like Jamie.'

'I like Nadeeka too.' Jamie had pulled her in for a kiss. 'All three of them.'

She's asleep when he comes out of the bathroom, snoring gently with one arm flung across his side of the bed. Jamie finishes undressing her (he has never worn a bra, but he imagines they are extremely uncomfortable to sleep in) and carefully pulls the duvet out from beneath her so he can lay it over them both. 'Goodnight, my love,' he whispers. 'Thanks for a great night.'

The alarm wakes Jamie rudely at eight the following morning. Theoretically, Scott drops the girls to school the Monday after his weekends with them, but in race season (and it always seems to be race season) he returns them to Nadeeka on Sunday morning.

Jamie screws up his eyes then drains the glass of water on his nightstand. He glances at Nadeeka, but she's sprawled face-down, a smear of mascara visible beneath a tangle of hair and duvet. He kisses the back of her head then goes for a shower. If he has to deal with Scott Hadley, he needs to be properly awake.

The dating apps should have a section specifically about exes,

Jamie thinks. A series of tick box questions like *Are you on good terms with your ex? Does he help out with the kids?* or *Is he insanely jealous of you dating again and liable to throw a punch at your new partner?*

That last gift had left Jamie with a painful jaw and a bruised ego. He'd been proud of himself for not raising a fist in return, but his cool response had enraged Scott, who had taken Jamie's lack of reaction as a personal challenge. Their encounters had always been uncomfortable, and after the punch they became laden with tension, the sinews on Scott's forearms continually pulsating as though he'd stopped around the corner to press out some push-ups in preparation. Frankly, Jamie wouldn't be surprised if he had.

'Stay out of his way,' Nadeeka always tells Jamie. 'He's not worth it.'

He isn't, but with Nadeeka out for the count Jamie has no choice but to face Scott alone. He fuels himself with a strong coffee and watches the clock until he hears a car door slam, swiftly followed by Maya's distinctive voice bossing Nish about.

'I'll ring the bell – you can't reach.'

'I can.'

'You can't, look.'

Jamie opens the door. 'Hey, girls, did you have a good time?'

'We had popcorn!' Nish says. Maya says nothing. She is always wary around Jamie when she comes back from her dad's, and Jamie wonders what poison Scott drips in her impressionable ears. As they run in the house, Jamie gives Scott a tight nod to bring an end to their interaction, but Scott takes a step forwards. 'Where's Nads?' His arms are folded across his chest like a bouncer outside a nightclub.

'Having a lie-in. We had a late one last night.'

The second it's out Jamie knows it was a stupid thing to say; that anything even vaguely hinting at a personal life between Nadeeka and Jamie makes Scott see red. On cue, a crimson flush creeps from the neck of his crisp white T-shirt.

It's Not What You Think

'I'm not fucking interested in what you get up to with my ex-wife.'

It is so patently a lie that Jamie almost laughs.

'My only concern is making sure my daughters are looked after, and don't come second to whatever *this* is.' Scott waves his hand, encompassing Jamie, the house . . . presumably Nadeeka too.

'*This* is pretty good, actually.' Jamie grips the doorframe so hard he can feel the grain of the wood. 'You should try it – oh, wait, you have. And you chucked it away.' *What is he doing? Shut up now . . .*

'Couldn't have your own kids, is that it?' Scott takes a step forward. 'Had to muscle in on someone else's?'

'Fuck off.'

'Thing is, when you have kids, you're bound together for life. Doesn't matter how long *you* stick around for, every time Nads looks at the girls, *I'm* in her head.' He taps the side of his skull. 'You could never understand.'

The words form on Jamie's lips before he has a chance to stop them. 'I guess I'll find out when we have kids of our own.'

Why did he say that? He and Nadeeka have touched on the subject of children lightly – almost jokingly – like toeing ice on a pond to see if it will bear weight. *I'm open to the idea*, Nadeeka said once, Jamie offering up *I wouldn't rule it out*. It is still early days, but when Jamie imagines having a baby – with Nadeeka's dark eyes; with his nose, perhaps – it fills him with a glow he hasn't felt before.

Jamie braces himself for another punch, but Scott doesn't move, only stares at Jamie with fury in his eyes. Then he turns and gets into his car, revving the engine as he pulls away.

Later, after Jamie has told Nadeeka that yes, the handover went fine, and no, Scott didn't start anything, he opens a text message from an unknown number.

You're fucking dead.

Jamie deletes the message, but he can't stop thinking about it, and when Nadeeka mentions that Jamie seems 'off' with her, he snaps back that maybe it's because he's got up at eight to deal with *your prick of an ex*.

Nadeeka raises an eyebrow. 'So it's my fault?' She's cranky too, hungover and sleep-deprived despite her later start.

'That's not what I said.'

'That's what it sounded like.'

Jamie taps Maya's plate. 'Your lunch is getting cold.'

'I don't like pasta.'

'Since when?'

'I don't like how you cook it. Only when Mum or Dad do it.'

Jamie pushes back his chair. It's that or say something unforgivable about Scott in front of the girls; that or end up fighting with Nadeeka – and isn't that exactly what Scott wants them to do? He goes upstairs and paces the bedroom, his fingers bunching into fists as he pictures Scott's sneering face.

Nadeeka is the best thing to have happened to Jamie in years. When Jamie had tentatively stepped back into the dating pool several years after his ex left him, he had despaired of ever finding love again, but the moment he met Nadeeka he knew he never wanted to date anyone else. Admittedly, he'd been daunted by the idea of acquiring two children as well, but Maya and Nish were (mostly) amazing, and Jamie had slowly fallen for them, too. But Scott does everything in his power to turn them against Jamie, and it's starting to cause friction between Jamie and Nadeeka.

Jamie sits on the edge of the bed. For the first time since he left Sheffield, he voices to himself the doubt that has been growing inside him. Scott Hadley isn't going anywhere. And if Jamie can't handle that, packing up his life and moving in with Nadeeka had been a big mistake.

CHAPTER 29

As Jamie's colleagues are preparing to leave the office at the end of a busy day, Jamie pulls up a forty-page inspection report and begins reading.

'Don't stay too late,' says Emma, from the neighbouring cubicle.

'No rest for the wicked.' Jamie pulls what he intends to be a rueful expression. 'Just need to get this squared away.' He turns back to his screen, frowning intently. The report is practically finished, and in any case isn't due for a fortnight, but Emma doesn't know that.

'See you, Jamie!' someone calls from across the room.

'Haven't you got a home to go to?' The boss, Adam Bennington, his coat already buttoned up against the autumn chill.

'Almost done.'

As the office slowly empties, Jamie drops the pretence and leans back in his chair, letting out his breath in a long, audible sigh. His thumbs hesitate over his phone for a few seconds, before he taps out a message to Nadeeka.

Need to stay late at work, sorry xxx

She doesn't reply right away, and Jamie goes back to his report, only half-concentrating. Things between them have been strained since the girls came back from Scott's. On Sunday evening, Maya had refused Jamie's offer of help with her homework, and so Nish had refused too, and although Jamie had told Nadeeka it was no big deal, the rejection had smarted.

'You're not still sulking, are you?' Nadeeka had said when they'd been getting ready for bed. Jamie had recalled her spread-eagled on the bed with come-to-bed eyes the previous evening, and had marvelled at the difference twenty-four hours could make.

'I haven't been sulking at all.'

'The girls are still getting used to having you around. Don't let it get to you.'

'I'm not.'

'Yeah, right.' Nadeeka had laughed, but it hadn't felt funny, and when she'd reached for him later, Jamie had pretended to be asleep.

By the time Maya and Nish got home from school yesterday, Scott's poison had been sufficiently diluted for Nish to tell Jamie a joke she'd learned at school, and for Maya to ask for Jamie's help with a science project. But now it's Wednesday and the girls are with Scott, and the exhausting and demoralizing cycle will start again.

Jamie's phone beeps with a reply from Nadeeka.

Okay, see you later. Don't work too hard! Xx

He checks his watch. He can't avoid the fallout from Scott badmouthing him, but he can avoid Scott. Another half an hour, then he'll go home.

When Jamie gets to the bus stop, the digital screen shows *Cancelled* in place of the bus he'd been planning to take. Karma for lying to Nadeeka, he thinks wryly. He hasn't owned a vehicle for years, opting for more environmentally sound options where possible, and renting a car when driving is the only option. His commute to work from Nadeeka's house is inexpensive and easy . . . when the bus is running.

He crosses the road to the Two Princes pub. There are worse ways to kill some time before the next bus, and at least now he doesn't risk running into Scott if he's late dropping Maya and Nish home.

Jamie is carrying his pint and a packet of crisps to an empty table in the corner when he hears someone call his name. He turns and smiles, recognizing Carrie Finder, the perennially sociable head of 'People and Culture'.

'Did you get your report done?'

It takes Jamie a second to remember his lie. 'Yes, all done.'

'Cheers to that!' She raises her wine glass. 'Join us, if you like?' She's sitting with two men, each with half-drunk pints and uninterested expressions.

'Oh, no – I won't intrude.'

'Nonsense! I insist. You're not intruding at all. Alan, Chris, this is Jamie from work.'

Jamie can't figure out a way to refuse without being rude, so he pulls out a chair and nods a hello to Carrie's friends. 'Hi. My bus was cancelled, so . . .' He takes a sip from his pint.

'It used to be a great service around here,' Alan says. He's in his fifties, with ruddy skin beneath an untidy greying beard. 'Bloody cuts.'

'Nightmare,' Jamie says, for want of anything else. The TV on the wall is showing Sky News, the sound too low to hear more than a murmur. 'So, what do you guys do?'

'I'm a teacher,' Alan says.

'Oh, what subject?'

'ICT. Secondary.'

'Enjoy it?'

'I spend most of my time stopping the lads using VPNs to watch porn.' Alan grins. 'It's eye-opening, I tell you.'

Jamie turns to Chris. 'Are you a teacher, too?'

'God, no.' He's younger than Jamie – in his early thirties – and wearing the joggers-and-hoodie uniform of a lad even younger. His dark hair is shaved to grade two, and a small gold stud glints from one ear. 'I'm at Hex Precision. The factory by the ring road? We make car parts.'

'I got to know Chris when he was going out with one of my mates,' Carrie says. 'We've been trying to shake Alan off, but he's persistent.' She and Chris laugh, and Alan joins in; it's clearly an old joke. 'So, Jamie.' Carrie nudges his arm. 'How are you settling in?'

'Yeah, good.' Jamie is thumbing a quick text to Nadeeka.

Bus was cancelled, so having a quick drink with someone from work xx

'One more for the road?' Carrie says. 'It's my round.'

'Take the chance while you can,' Alan says. 'I can't remember the last time Carrie opened her wallet.'

'I bought you a pint last week!'

Jamie's phone pings with a text from Nadeeka.

That's brilliant! Told you it wouldn't be long before you found some drinking buddies! Have a great time! xxx

The exclamation marks are a measure of how much Nadeeka wants him to be happy; how she's been hoping he'll join clubs, make friends, put down roots. Stay.

Carrie points at Jamie's glass. 'Foster's, was it?'

'Go on, then. Cheers.' How ironic, he thinks: most girlfriends want to get their partners *out* of the pub, not encourage them to stay.

'. . . bound to be approved, with that kind of agenda.' Alan is talking to Chris. He looks at Jamie as though he expects an answer. 'Don't you think?'

'Hard to say,' Jamie says, which is true enough.

'What happens afterwards, that's what I want to know.' Chris picks up a beer mat and turns it around in his hands. 'Once

It's Not What You Think

they're all given leave to stay, and there's no more room in the centre, where will they live? What jobs are they going to have?'

'Ours,' Alan says grimly.

'Oh – you're talking about the new immigration centre?' Jamie takes his pint from Carrie, who's carrying all four drinks at once and is perilously close to dropping one. 'Thanks.'

'Five hundred rooms, it's going to have,' Alan says. 'Not beds, rooms. With en-suite bathrooms and "kitchenettes".' He makes quotes with his fingers. 'I'm on thirty-six grand a year and my house doesn't have an en-suite, but these buggers are getting one for free!'

'I haven't even got my own house,' Jamie says. It's an attempt to lighten the mood, but Alan bangs his fist on the table.

'Exactly! Because you're not called Abdul and you didn't come here on a boat.' He holds up his palms, nodding as though graciously acknowledging applause. 'Am I right or am I right?'

Jamie dips his head to one side in a gesture he hopes Alan will take for agreement, then picks up his pint and takes several deep swallows. There's no point arguing with people like Alan; their views are firmly entrenched, fuelled by tabloid hysteria and generations of judgemental ignorance.

'That's a bit of an assumption.' Chris breaks into a grin. 'Maybe his middle name's Abdul.' He laughs uproariously. 'Well, is it? Is your middle name Abdul, Jamie?'

Carrie giggles. 'If it is, I'll have to get you a new ID badge for work.'

'My middle name is not Abdul,' Jamie says tightly. He takes another swig of his Foster's. A couple more, and he will make his excuses.

'Glad to hear it,' Alan says.

'It's Mohammed.' As the rest of the group roar with laughter, Jamie swallows the dregs of his pint, then places the glass firmly on the table. 'Right, I'm off,' he says. 'Thanks again for the drink, Carrie. It's been . . . enlightening.'

As Jamie leaves the pub, he passes a chalkboard menu propped on the bar. The day's special is gammon and chips, and Jamie wonders if Alan and Chris have seen it, although perhaps they wouldn't get the joke. Bigots never see themselves as bigots, do they?

He's glad to finally be on the bus; even gladder to put his key in the lock of 10, Cedar Walk twenty minutes later and be greeted by Nadeeka's arms around his neck, softly scented from the shower.

'Did you have fun?' She leans away from him, scrutinizing his face.

Jamie takes in her anxious expression; her desperation for him to be happy. 'It was great.'

'Who did you go with?'

'Um, Carrie from work – she's the HR manager – and a couple of friends of hers. Alan and Chris.'

'Nice blokes?'

Jamie thinks of Alan's ruddy face becoming more agitated as he considered the five hundred refugees who had the temerity to need basic cooking and bathroom facilities. He thinks of Chris's guffaw as he ribbed Jamie about being called Abdul. He turns away to take off his coat. 'Yeah. Nice blokes.'

'Oh, I'm so pleased!'

Nadeeka will worry less now she thinks he has friends, Jamie knows, and if she asks if he's going to see Alan and Chris again he can easily give an excuse. He doesn't have their numbers, or they live too far out of town.

Whatever story he gives Nadeeka, one thing is certain: Jamie has no intention of spending any more time with Alan and Chris.

CHAPTER 30

'It was great to hang out with you last night.' Carrie Finder is leaning on the blue partition fixed to Jamie's desk, so that all he can see is a pair of forearms and a head. 'Alan and Chris are cool, aren't they?'

'Interesting guys.' Jamie carries on checking his emails, hoping Carrie will take the hint.

'They thought you were great, too . . . Mohammed!' She laughs. Jamie glances around the office. He had intended his response to be cutting – a sarcastic riposte that would prompt an awkward silence, maybe even cause Alan and Chris to reflect on their so-called jokes. Instead, Jamie had been taken as one of them; someone ready to take the piss out of refugees.

'We wondered if you fancied coming with us to a protest against the immigration centre at the weekend,' Carrie says. 'The petition's had more than seventy-four thousand signatures, but we need feet on the ground to make a real impact.'

'I actually don't know much about the centre,' Jamie says. 'I haven't read up on the background, or what the need is around here for—'

Carrie stops leaning on his partition. 'The *need* is for local housing.' She walks around into Jamie's cubicle, and he tenses as though bracing himself for a punch. 'Did you know that eighty-two per cent of young people who leave the area do so because they can't find suitable housing?'

'I didn't know that, no.'

'So will you come?' Carrie puts a leaflet on his keyboard. The top half has the words *Charity Begins at Home* superimposed on to a Union Jack flag. Beneath it is a photograph of a man and a woman with two fair-haired children, the whole family looking almost comically glum. It's captioned *Mr and Mrs Williams have been waiting for local authority housing for three years.*

'They're all living in one room,' Carrie says. 'They were supposed to get a three-bed near the kids' school, but the council decided to put migrants there instead.'

'Carrie . . .' Jamie looks around the office again. 'I've got to say, I'm not really very comfortable—'

'Talking about this at work?'

'Well . . .'

'That's why I hang out with Alan and Chris, plus a few others . . . they *get* it, you know? But don't worry.' She nudges Jamie's shoulder. 'You can speak freely with me.' She turns over the leaflet. 'So, what do you think?'

Facilities at the new £200m immigration centre will include a state-of-the-art gym, cinema room, library and FREE WIFI, Jamie reads. *If you agree that foreign migrants shouldn't be housed in luxury hotels while homeless British military veterans are left to beg on the streets, march with us and make your voice heard!*

'Eleven a.m. Saturday,' Carrie says. 'It would be great to have you with us.' She smiles at him as she leaves, as though she's just delivered a training guide on manual handling instead of a leaflet packed with racist rhetoric.

It's Not What You Think

Jamie picks up the flyer between thumb and forefinger and drops it into the bin beneath his desk. He tries to concentrate on his emails, but nothing's going in. He keeps hearing the fervour in Carrie's voice; keeps seeing the words on the back of the leaflet. *March with us and make your voice heard!*

Jamie hesitates. Then he bends down and retrieves the flyer from the bin.

At lunchtime, he walks to the nearest police station, a small outpost which looks as though it might once have been someone's house. The front door is locked, a sign taped to the glass telling visitors to use the yellow phone to report a crime. Jamie turns the leaflet over in his hands. What if he just wants to pass on information? Can he use the yellow phone for that?

Just as he's deliberating, a police car turns into the driveway.

The driver opens his window. 'This isn't an operational station any more, mate.' He has deep grooves under his eyes. 'You can use the yellow phone to—'

'Report a crime. Thanks. Actually, I just wanted to give you this.' Jamie hands him the leaflet. 'Someone at work invited me to a protest against the immigration centre they're building near the bypass, and I thought you should know about it.'

'Saturday, right?' The police officer drops the leaflet on to the passenger seat beside him. 'It was mentioned in morning briefing.'

'Great. Do you need anything from me?' Jamie waits. 'A statement . . . or . . .'

'You're all good, mate. Cheers.'

Jamie feels rather flat as he walks back to the office. He had psyched himself up to deliver the leaflet, feeling faintly subversive, like a member of a resistance movement. But of course the police already know about it; that's what they're there for.

*

He doesn't see Carrie again until the end of the day, when she runs to catch up with him as he's leaving the office. She mimes tipping a glass to her mouth. 'Quick one? If we hurry, we'll make Happy Hour.'

Jamie makes an apologetic face. 'Thanks, but I have to get back. Some other time, maybe.' *When hell freezes over*, he thinks.

'And you'll think about the protest?'

'Yeah.' Jamie pictures Carrie's leaflet on the passenger seat of the police car. 'Do you reckon you'll get any trouble from the police?' he says, as airily as he can manage.

'Bound to,' Carrie says darkly. She starts walking, and Jamie finds himself walking alongside her. 'They can dump an immigration centre on us without any consultation, but if we dare to fight back, we're the ones getting kettled.' She gives a hard laugh.

'It *is* quite an extreme reaction,' Jamie says mildly. He's thinking Carrie might be less militant than Alan and Chris – that he should at least *try* to challenge her views – but, before he can say anything else, Carrie stops walking and clutches his arm.

'Exactly!' Her eyes are shining. 'It's totally disproportionate. I went to a demo once when it was almost all women and kids, and the local force sent about sixty cops, all in riot gear.'

Jamie tried again. 'That's not quite what—'

'So much for freedom of speech, right? What they don't seem to get is that it's not immigration centres *per se* we have an issue with.'

'It's not?'

'Of course not!' Carrie laughs. 'We're not monsters!' She starts walking again. 'But these people . . . they come by boat, right?' She doesn't wait for an answer. 'But they don't get those boats from Syria, or Pakistan, or Iran, do they? They go to Turkey first, then maybe Germany, then France; and they'd be perfectly safe in any of those countries.' She throws out her hands like a barrister delivering a closing argument. 'So let them claim asylum there. Let someone else pick up the bill. We don't have room.' She looks at Jamie expectantly. 'Do we?'

'It's a difficult balance,' he says. 'We're a small nation—'

'Exactly.' Carrie nods, satisfied, even though Jamie hadn't finished. A small nation *but a compassionate one*, he'd wanted to say; but there's no point. People like Carrie – people like Alan and Chris – don't change their minds.

'There aren't enough jobs for our *own* citizens,' Carrie says, 'let alone another country's.'

They've reached the bus stop now. Jamie feels grubby, not only as a result of Carrie's rhetoric but from his own cowardice in not challenging it. He tries again.

'We've got quite a few lower-level vacancies at ATP, haven't we? Adam said we've been struggling to fill them.'

A mischievous expression lights up Carrie's face. 'Shall I let you into a secret?' She leans closer to him, even though there's no one else around. 'When the applications come in, I sift out the foreign names.'

Jamie's mouth drops open. 'That's . . .'

'Just doing my bit for patriotism.' Carrie stands to attention, bringing up a hand in mock salute. 'We might stand a chance of getting this country back on its feet if more companies did the same, but far too many seem to be doing the reverse. "Affirmative action",' she adds scathingly, making quotes in the air with her fingers.

'I think that's my bus.' Jamie has never been so relieved to see the familiar yellow double-decker trundle around the corner.

'I've started a list.' Carrie thrusts her phone in front of Jamie's face. The Notes app is open, showing a list of company names. *Coldharrow Estates, Omnivise Analytics, Echelon Warehousing, Lumen, Ashmere Associates—*

Jamie goes back. *Echelon Warehousing?* He manages to stop himself saying it out loud, but what the hell is Nadeeka's company doing on this list? 'What—' He clears his throat, his mouth suddenly too dry. 'What will you do with these names?'

'Pass them on,' Carrie says simply. The bus pulls up beside them and the doors open with a loud hydraulic hiss.

'To who?'

She narrows her eyes, appraising him. A woman with a baby is boarding the bus, bumping her pushchair backwards up the step. Jamie leans forward and lifts up the front for her, and she smiles gratefully.

The bus driver calls to Jamie. 'You getting on, or what?'

'Let's have that drink some time.' Carrie holds his gaze challengingly. A small smile plays at the corners of her lips. 'I'll tell you then.'

Jamie hesitates, his right hand on the bus's grab rail.

'On or off, mate?'

Carrie winks at him, then turns and starts walking away.

'On,' Jamie says.

As the bus pulls away, he stays standing by the door. He watches Carrie get smaller and smaller until she's out of sight entirely, and with a growing sense of dread he realizes he will have to go for a drink with her. He has to find out why Nadeeka's company is on Carrie's list; and, more importantly, what Carrie plans to do about it.

CHAPTER 31

Nadeeka looks at him sympathetically when he gets in. 'Tough day?'

'A few issues with the foreman on the Bradstone development, that's all. It'll get sorted.' It's alarming how easily the lie trips off his tongue, but what else can he say? *I think my HR manager is a fascist and your company is on her hit list . . .* He doesn't even know what Carrie's list means yet. He turns away to hang up his coat. 'How was yours?'

'Great!' Nadeeka walks into the kitchen, raising her voice as she moves away from him. 'I had this idea for a recruitment day, and corporate are running with it. I've even been given a budget.'

'What are you planning?' Jamie follows her, his mind still on Carrie's list. If he asks Carrie outright about Echelon, she'll wonder why he's singled out that one in particular, and the last thing Jamie wants is to make Nadeeka's employer even more of a target.

Nadeeka flicks on the kettle. 'I'm thinking stalls for each

career pathway, a staff rep for each department . . .' She grins. 'Like a Freshers' Fair, but without the booze and shagging.'

Jamie manages to smile. 'You've, er . . . got a pretty diverse workforce at Echelon, haven't you?'

The question sounds forced but Nadeeka doesn't seem to notice. She wrinkles her nose. 'Not really. We don't have a single female forklift operative, even though the hours are really flexible.'

'But you have loads of different nationalities?'

'Oh, right. Yeah, over twenty, last time I counted.' Nadeeka takes out two mugs. Hers is the *Best Mum* one Jamie helped the girls buy for her birthday; his says *Health and Safety Inspectors do it with protection*. 'We've got a fair number from Poland and Bulgaria, here under the EU Settlement scheme, plus a few on skilled visas. And a couple of dozen refugees.'

'Refugees?' An uncomfortable sensation forms in Jamie's throat as he thinks of the immigration centre protest. 'I didn't know they were allowed to work.'

'They can once they've been granted asylum.' Nadeeka waits for the kettle to boil. 'Or they can apply if they've been waiting over twelve months for a decision.' She laughs. 'I bet you're regretting asking now. I can talk you through the intricacies of hiring someone with Resettled status, if you really want.' She grins.

Jamie gives a faint smile. 'You're all right. So your recruitment drive is to bring in, what, more local people?' He wonders if Carrie already knows about the job fair, or whether Echelon is on the list purely because of their inclusive hiring policies.

'Local, English, Ukrainian, Eritrean . . .' Nadeeka gives an exaggerated shrug. 'It's all the same to me as long as the work ethic's there. Corporate have given the go-ahead for a month-long recruitment drive, finishing with a job fair on site. It's going to be great.'

'I wonder if you'll get any backlash from it,' Jamie says, as though the thought has just occurred to him.

It's Not What You Think

Nadeeka looks at him in surprise. 'Why would we?'

'People can be narrow-minded.'

'Oh, you mean the "Johnny foreigner stole my job" brigade?' Nadeeka hands him his tea. 'Fuck 'em.' She laughs at Jamie's surprised expression. Nadeeka hardly ever swears. 'I mean it, Jamie. I've lost count of the number of local lads I've put in the warehouse only for them to turn up late or not at all. Don't get me wrong, we've got some great Brits on the payroll, but some of our best and most reliable workers are from other countries. I bet it's the same for you at ATP.'

'I guess,' Jamie says weakly. Should he tell Adam about Carrie filtering the resumés? Carrie has worked at ATP for years; she and Adam are pretty tight. What if it backfires and it's Jamie who loses his job?

Nadeeka leans against the counter, cradling her tea. 'When my parents came to the UK in the Eighties, they were literally spat at in the street. People thought nothing of calling them Pakis, or refusing to serve them.'

'I'm so sorry.' Jamie cringes a little at his response, which sounds so insignificant, even though he means it wholeheartedly.

'Yeah, well, if Mum and Dad can put up with that, I can deal with a few small-minded bigots.'

'Even so, maybe it would be better not to focus too much on the foreign-born workers in your recruitment campaign.' Jamie swallows. 'Just . . . you know, in case anyone has a problem with it.'

There's a long and uncomfortable silence.

Nadeeka studies him. 'It sounds a little bit as though *you* have a problem with it,' she says slowly.

'Me? God, no.' He shakes his head. 'Not for a second.' His revulsion at the suggestion makes his protestations so vehement he fears they sound insincere. He takes a deep breath. 'Absolutely not,' he says, more calmly. 'I just don't want you to attract any undesirable attention, that's all.'

Just as Nadeeka opens her mouth to form a retort, Nish careers down the stairs. 'Maybe you should stick to construction sites,' she says instead, and despite the lightness there's a sharp undercurrent. 'I don't think you're cut out for recruitment.'

Carrie pronounces herself 'thrilled' when Jamie asks when she's free for a drink, immediately proposing they join Alan and Chris after work that evening. Jamie would willingly go the rest of his life without seeing either man again, but Carrie's flirtations make him nervous, and he doesn't want to give her the wrong idea. Better to have chaperones – even obnoxious ones.

Jamie half-hopes Nadeeka will say he can't go, or at least hint at some displeasure, but when he calls her at lunchtime, she's almost as delighted as Carrie.

'It's so great you're making local friends,' she says. Jamie has been careful not to bring up the recruitment fair, or anything to do with Echelon's hiring strategies, and the tension between him and Nadeeka has dissipated. She tells him to enjoy himself and not to rush home. 'Maybe we could have them all over for drinks some time,' she adds.

Jamie imagines opening the front door to Alan, Chris and Carrie – imagines their faces when they see Nadeeka – and sweat trickles down his spine.

The day passes all too quickly, and soon Jamie finds himself back in the Two Princes, his palms slick with nerves.

'Good to see you again, Mohammed,' Chris says. Jamie forces himself to laugh. They shake hands, and Jamie notices Chris surreptitiously wiping his on his trousers as he sits back down.

'Carrie said you're up for joining the march.' Alan raises his pint towards Jamie. 'Good man.'

Jamie lifts his own pint in acknowledgement. 'You have to vote with your feet, right?'

'Right!' Carrie nods enthusiastically. 'Here's my mobile

number; give us a bell when you get there and we can meet up.' She scribbles it on a beer mat and hands it over.

'Thanks. And if . . .' Jamie clears his throat. 'If I come across any companies that deserve to go on *the list* . . .' He gives Carrie what he hopes is a knowing look.

The silence that follows makes the hairs on the back of Jamie's neck stand up.

'The list?' Alan says eventually.

Jamie attempts a more meaningful look towards Carrie. 'You know, *the list.*'

Another silence. Jamie's nausea intensifies.

'You absolute tit, Carrie,' Alan says. 'What have you told him?'

'Nothing.' She looks up through her eyelashes at him. 'But it's okay – I've got a good feeling about him.'

There's another pause – another exchange of glances between the three friends – and Jamie feels suddenly out of his depth, as though he's stepped off a sandbank and is flailing in the water.

Alan rests his forearms on the table and fixes Jamie with a gaze so intense it feels like a burn. 'You one of us, then?'

'Maybe.' Jamie tries to sound nonchalant, as though his reticence is because he can't be arsed, and not because he doesn't have a clue what Alan's talking about. *One of us?* One of who?

'The marches are only part of it, you know,' Chris chips in.

'I know.' Jamie's heart rate quickens.

'You interested in getting involved?' Alan's still staring at him. Jamie has to force himself not to look away.

'Maybe,' Jamie says carefully. His pulse is a drumbeat now, thrumming in his ears, and he doesn't dare lift his glass in case the tremor extends to his hands.

Alan glances at Carrie, then at Chris, then back to Jamie. There's a long silence, then he breaks his gaze away, takes a sip of his pint, and leans back in his chair. 'D'you catch the news this morning?'

Jamie exhales. Alan's moved on. Jamie must have passed the test – whatever it was.

'The RNLI story?' Chris says.

'Yeah. Boats being used to rescue migrant scum.' Alan looks directly at Jamie as he says this, and Jamie's pulse surges once more. That hadn't been the test . . . *this* is the test.

'Loads of people have cancelled their direct debits over it,' Carrie says.

'Course they have.' Alan shakes his head. 'Old Mrs Miggins doesn't give up a tenner of her pension each month for the RNLI to nanny a bunch of scrounging shitbags who decide it's a good idea to cross the Channel on a lilo.' He looks at Jamie. 'Does she?'

Jamie swallows. It's clear there is only one acceptable answer. 'She certainly doesn't.'

'You agree they shouldn't launch the lifeboats, then, if it's for migrants?'

Fuck. He wants him to actually say it. He wants to know if Jamie can be trusted, if his views are aligned with their own. 'Exactly.' Jamie's voice feels pinched. 'Like you say, it's not what they're funded for.'

'So if they see migrants in the water, they should . . .' Alan gestures for Jamie to finish the sentence.

The pub is suddenly too hot, too crowded. Jamie blinks hard, takes a sip of his pint to buy time. 'They should . . .' God, they're all looking at him. Waiting for his answer; for the answer he knows they expect. 'Let them drown,' he finishes quietly.

A broad smile spreads across Alan's face, and Jamie swallows his nausea with a chaser of Foster's.

'Saves doing the job once they reach dry land, right?' Chris chuckles. He leans forward conspiratorially, drawing in Carrie and a reluctant Jamie. 'The other night, right – must have been gone eleven, it was after last orders – Alan and me found one of them in the entrance to the shopping centre.'

It's Not What You Think

He glances at Alan, as though seeking his permission to continue with the story. Jamie's stomach hollows in trepidation.

'He asked for a quid so he could get a drink.' Chris pushes back his chair and half stands, and the corners of Alan's mouth twitch. 'So we gave him one for free!' Chris holds one hand in front of his crotch, spraying an invisible hose across the table. Alan and Carrie roar with laughter.

Jamie fights to hide his revulsion. He pulls out his phone and frowns at an imaginary message. 'I'd better be off.' He can't stay in this pub a second longer. Racist rhetoric is bad enough, but pissing on a homeless guy? They're psychotic.

'Is everything okay?' Carrie asks.

'Yeah, fine, just . . .' Jamie can't finish.

'You know . . .' Alan glances at the others. 'There's a few of us – like-minded individuals who want this country back the way it used to be . . . You should join us.'

Jamie pushes back his chair. 'I've got to shoot, sorry. My girlfriend wants me home.'

'Under the thumb, much?' Chris is trying for a rise, but Jamie isn't biting. He just wants to get the hell out of the Two Princes.

'I forgot we were having dinner,' Jamie explains. 'My bad.'

'You should bring her next time.' Carrie smiles. 'It would be nice not to be the token female.'

'She's got young kids – it's tricky to get a babysitter.'

'What's her name?' Carrie asks.

'Nad—' Jamie bites back the foreign-sounding name just in time. '—ia,' he finishes. 'Her name is Nadia.'

CHAPTER 32

The police station in Beech Street is sandwiched between the job centre and the magistrates' court, and Jamie wonders if the location is intentional, designed for those who spend their lives bouncing between the three institutions. He takes a numbered ticket from the machine by the door and stands by a poster condemning modern-day slavery. The seats are all full. There's a distinct smell of unwashed bodies, but Jamie can't identify the source. Perhaps it's always present, this cloying, throat-catching scent of feet and fluids. Jamie feels sorry for the woman on the front desk, and not only because of the smell – in the twenty minutes he's been waiting she has been called a bitch; been blamed for a missing bicycle, a delayed solicitor and a parking ticket; and had two separate people remind her they paid her wages.

'Seventy-eight?' She calls Jamie's number without looking up.

'I'd like to report a crime, please.' The counter is around Jamie's shoulder height, the floor behind it raised so that the woman is looking down on him.

'Is it happening at the present time and is there a threat to life to either yourself or a third party?' She rattles it off so fast Jamie takes a second to process it.

'Er, no. It happened . . . actually, I'm not sure when it happened.' Chris had just said *the other night*. 'In the past week, I think.'

'Name?'

'Mine?' Jamie hesitates. Would the police tell Alan and Chris who had grassed them up? They know he works with Carrie; it would be easy enough for them to wait for him to leave work, follow him and then . . . 'Um. Richard Smith.' He feels himself redden, but she isn't looking at him.

'Details of the crime?'

'Two men urinated on a homeless man.' Another wave of revulsion washes over him. He wishes he could be there to see the police confront Chris and Alan.

'Contact details of victim?'

'I don't know, sorry.'

'What's his name?' She raises her voice a touch, as though Jamie is a bit slow.

'I don't know him. I just . . . I heard about it from the people who did it.'

'And what are *their* names?' Jamie can sense her irritation now, sees her take in the packed room behind him.

'Alan and Chris.'

'Last names?'

'I don't know. And I don't have their addresses, either.' Jamie gets in there before she can ask. 'But they drink in the Two Princes. Alan's in his fifties, he teaches ICT at a secondary school – I'm not sure which one. And Chris is early thirties, I think. Gold earring. I think he said he worked in a car factory. They're both involved in today's protest against the new immigration centre, and this assault was definitely racially motivated. They keep a list of what I think are potentially targets and my—' Jamie just stops himself saying *my partner's employer*. 'There are local businesses on it. Echelon Warehousing is one of them.'

'Where did this assault happen, exactly?'

'They said it was in the entrance to a shopping centre.' *The* shopping centre, Chris had said, but Jamie had looked on Google Maps and found four of varying sizes within striking distance of the pub. And that's assuming it was the Two Princes they'd been drinking in that evening.

'Nothing's been reported.' The woman's looking at her computer screen, long nails tapping at the keys.

'*I'm* reporting it.'

'I've made a note. Thanks.' She presses a button to her right. 'Seventy-nine?'

'Is that it? Don't you want a statement?'

'Someone will be in touch if the victim comes forward. Seventy-nine!'

'But they admitted it! Surely it's an assault to piss on—'

'Unfortunately, someone mouthing off in a pub isn't evidence. We need a victim or a witness – ideally both.' She presses the button next to her and calls out the next number. 'Eighty!'

Jamie crumples his ticket into the overflowing bin and pushes open the heavy door, letting it bang behind him. What a waste of time! He's under no illusions the police will bother tracking down Alan and Chris; Jamie could probably frogmarch the pair of them into the station with signed confessions and the police would still say there isn't enough evidence to proceed. Can't they *get* evidence? Ask shopping centres for CCTV, speak to the homeless community to see if anyone heard about what happened? Isn't that what the police are supposed to do?

Jamie pushes his hands into the pockets of his jacket as he makes his way back to work. He can't stop thinking about Chris and his crude mime, his face contorted in laughter, as it no doubt had been during the assault itself. Had their victim tried to get away? Had he sworn at Alan and Chris? Kicked at their shins? Or had he simply curled into a ball and taken the humiliating attack, knowing the odds were already stacked against him?

It's Not What You Think

Anger surges inside him. Men like Alan and Chris, who target the most vulnerable people in society, are cowards. Their victims are easy targets, unwilling to draw attention to themselves, unable to go to the police. And so the perpetrators get away scot-free.

Jamie calls Carrie. If the police want evidence, he'll get them evidence. He'll coax more details of the assault out of Alan and Chris; he'll find out from Carrie what happens to the company names she passes on. He'll get the name of the organization they're working for.

Then he'll give everything to the police.

'Hey!' Carrie sounds delighted to hear from him. 'Are you on your way?'

Jamie speaks quickly, before he can change his mind. 'Listen, I'm really sorry, I can't make the march – family crisis. But what Alan said, about joining a group of like-minded people . . .' Jamie stands by the crossing, waiting for the lights to change. He takes a deep breath, the noise of the traffic drowned out by the thunder of blood in his ears. 'I'm in.'

CHAPTER 33

'The organization is called New Dawn,' Carrie says. They're in the small park near the office, where Carrie had suggested they meet before work on Monday, in order to talk more easily.

'I don't think I've heard of them.' Jamie wonders if his voice sounds strange to Carrie, or if it's just in his head. He feels weirdly conscious of every movement he makes, every expression on his face.

'Nor had I, but honestly, it's like a breath of fresh air. It's just great to have somewhere to speak our truths, if you get me?' They're walking loops of the tiny park, passing the fountain for the second time. 'You joining is great timing actually; we're meeting tonight, and the boss says it's okay to bring you along, as long as I can vouch for you, which obviously I can. You'll get a text message later with a what3words location – you have to reverse it – but we can just go together, if you like?'

'Who's the boss?'

'*The Boss*. That's literally his name.' Carrie laughs. 'I mean,

It's Not What You Think

it's not, but that's what he likes to be called. He heads up the local chapter of New Dawn, and he works with head office, so we know what's happening at a national level.'

'And is that who you give your list to?' Jamie's ribcage is tight. He's glad they're walking, so Carrie can't see his face. 'Of companies who hire . . . *non-whites*?' He's amazed she can hear him, he's dropped his voice so low, terrified someone will hear him and think he's saying this stuff for real.

'Not just companies. People, too. But yes, we all give our intel to the boss, and he adds it to the master list and grades it in terms of priority.'

Priority? Jamie needs to see this list. He needs to know where Echelon is; how much danger Nadeeka could be in.

'Sounds very organized.' Jamie risks a laugh, but it comes out thin and false. 'Do you get to see this master list? Must be interesting, seeing what other people have added.' He swallows.

'Yeah, I got access once I was through my initiation.' Carrie turns to him. 'So tonight, then. You're up for it?'

Jamie just nods. If he goes too hard for the list, she'll be spooked. 'What happens in the meetings?'

'We discuss business – like if we have a protest coming up, or some direct action – but for a lot of us it's just an opportunity to socialize with people who don't shoot you down for speaking your mind.'

'Sorry – direct action?'

'Sometimes words and marches aren't enough.' Carrie looks at her watch. 'We should get to the office.'

'This *direct action*,' Jamie says. 'Is it against the law?'

Carrie stops abruptly, turning to face him. 'I'll tell you what's against the law: Pakis grooming schoolgirls. Jihadis funding their terrorism with state benefits. Mosques radicalizing vulnerable British citizens.' A flicker of uncertainty crosses her eyes. 'You do get that, don't you? Because as your sponsor—'

'Absolutely.' Jamie nods vehemently. Does he sound convincing?

'It's a national disgrace,' he adds for good measure. 'I just wanted to check how far you – *we* – are able to go.'

Carrie holds his gaze. 'We go as far as we need to.'

As they draw close to the office, Carrie begins talking about whether they should replace the coffee machine, and which charity partner they should support this Christmas. Jamie marvels at her ability to segue so smoothly from xenophobia to office politics. He's never really questioned his colleagues' political leanings, and he tries to imagine where he would have placed Carrie had he thought about it. Centre? Maybe even slightly left of centre, perhaps because most of the women he knows position themselves there. He finds it hard to reconcile Carrie's cheerful demeanour with what he now knows lies beneath.

Carrie has to pass Jamie's cubicle to reach her office, and so they continue chatting as they cross the open-plan space. The cleaners have been, and the air is filled with a citrus tang. Jamie's chair has been pulled out and is facing the wrong way, and the contents of his desk have been shuffled about. Jamie feels a lurch of panic. The silver-framed photograph that has over time been pushed to the back of his desk amid a tower of files has been given pride of place again on his monitor stand. The photo is of him with Nadeeka and the girls, their heads pressed tightly together. Maya and Nish have skin a shade or two lighter than their mother's, but all three are very clearly not white.

Jamie quickens his pace, his body angled to block Carrie's view of his desk. He backs into the cubicle and fumbles with one hand for the photo, sliding it face-down off the stand and on to the desk. He'll have to take it home to avoid anyone at work seeing it and dropping into conversation that he has a brown-skinned partner with mixed heritage children. 'So I'll wait to hear about tonight, then?' he says.

'You'll get a message.' Carrie drops her voice, and the secrecy

It's Not What You Think

sends a shiver down Jamie's spine. He isn't sure what he finds more disturbing: the cloak-and-dagger arrangements or Carrie's breezy talk of direct action. She looks around, checking to see if anyone's listening. 'It normally comes before lunchtime.'

It comes at eleven; a text from an unknown number with three seemingly random words. *Broken tide ember.* Jamie swallows hard. What if he goes to the police now? Would it be enough? He dismisses the idea instantly. He only has one shot at this, and he doesn't know what tonight's meeting will look like. He imagines the police charging in – riot helmets on and batons raised – only to find a dozen Carries in a village hall. What would they arrest them for: harbouring racist thoughts? No. The police have already fobbed him off twice. When Jamie contacts them again, he needs to have irrefutable evidence of a crime. That way, the police can't fail to act.

He's relieved when Carrie suggests they go together to the meeting. Her incessant chatter is a welcome distraction from Jamie's racing thoughts, as apprehension forms a knot of anxiety in his stomach. What if they won't let him in? What if it's a trap, and they let him in only to turn on him? What if, by attending the meeting, Jamie is himself committing a criminal act?

The gathering is in a British Legion hall, a single-storey building with an outside toilet, squatting at the back of scrubby parkland. Jamie follows Carrie inside. The man on the door – well-built and watchful – nods in recognition at Carrie, then fixes his gaze on Jamie.

'He's with me,' Carrie says. 'I've cleared it with the boss.' The man nods, although his gaze rests on Jamie a second longer than it needs to.

Inside, the space is the size of a school gymnasium, the chairs laid out in church-service rows. Most are occupied. At the front of the room is a small, raised platform on which are a lectern and several more chairs, all empty. It could be a meeting of any kind, Jamie thinks, from the Women's Institute to a parish council AGM, were it not for the fact that at least half of the attendees are wearing face coverings.

'That's optional,' Carrie whispers, following Jamie's gaze to a man with a red bandana fixed above his nose. 'I've never bothered.' They take seats at the back, and Jamie scans the room until he sees Alan and Chris. Neither of them is wearing masks. Jamie is about to ask Carrie if she knows many people here, when four men step on to the stage and the room falls silent.

A man with a moustache and wire-framed glasses walks towards the lectern. The other three men are wearing balaclavas, slivers of white skin just visible around their eyes and mouth. They survey the audience for a few seconds, before sitting down as one. Jamie's neck prickles.

Carrie leans into him, speaking in a low voice. 'That's the boss, in the middle.'

The boss wears jeans and a black quarter-zip sweater, his sleeves pushed up over muscled forearms. On his feet are a pair of grey and orange Adidas trainers; without the black balaclava, he'd look like any other bloke out for a pint. He gives a single nod, and the moustached man turns to the audience.

'The New Dawn is upon us,' he says.

'We step into the light.' The audience answer in unison, a low but fervent chant that sends a crackle of electricity around the room. Jamie tenses. His whole body wants to run.

'My brothers, the boss has asked me to commend you for your efforts this week. Those of you who have spent time leafleting, who have passed us information, who have recruited new members . . .'

Jamie feels Carrie's eyes on him.

'. . . we see you and we thank you. The boss would also like to thank our brother who informed us of radicalization taking place under the guise of "cultural awareness sessions".' The speaker makes quotes with his fingers. 'Thanks to swift action from several of you, the individuals concerned have been . . .' his lips twitch ' . . . *educated* in the error of their ways.'

The audience applauds.

'Regrettably, it has not all been good news.' The speaker pauses, and the energy in the room shifts again, as though someone has opened a door and let in the cold air. 'Someone we believed to be a true brother became loose-lipped. He has been dealt with, but the boss would like to take this opportunity to remind you that New Dawn meetings are sacred. Speaking about our activities jeopardizes the safety of everyone in this room.' He pauses again. 'And there will always be consequences.'

Sweat soaks into Jamie's collar. He can feel dozens of pairs of eyes burning into the back of his neck, and is it his imagination, or is 'the boss' looking directly at him? He barely takes in what comes next, so loud is the blood roaring in his ears.

When the meeting finally ends, Jamie forces himself to move slowly. He stands, stretching as though he's spent the last hour soporific, instead of wound tight as an eight-day watch. As he makes for the door, Carrie catches his arm.

'The boss wants to see us.'

'What? Why?'

'He meets all the new members. It was the same when Chris brought me along for the first time.'

They're moving slowly towards the front of the room, where the boss and his two henchmen are still sitting on the dais. Jamie thinks he might throw up. He wishes fervently that he'd known so many people would have their faces covered; he would feel so much less vulnerable with a disguise of his own.

Stepping on to the dais, Jamie stumbles, and a smirk plays at the corners of one of the henchmen's lips.

'Name,' the boss says. It's the first time he's spoken, and Jamie notes the lack of inflection at the end of what is clearly a command, not a question.

'Jamie Golding.' He can hardly give a false name, not with Carrie standing beside him.

'Sponsored by?'

'Carrie Finder, boss.' Even Carrie seems nervous, a breathy quality to her voice.

A long silence follows. Around them, conversations are beginning and ending, and Jamie hears the scraping of chairs as they're moved and stacked. And, all the while, the boss stares at Jamie. Only when Jamie glances away, the intensity of the boss's gaze almost physically painful, does the boss speak. He'd been waiting for him to give in, Jamie realizes. Round one to the boss.

'Give him the initiation.' The boss folds his arms high across his chest.

'Initiation?' Jamie has a sudden flashback to his first day of secondary school, when he and another boy had been dragged into the toilets and made to 'dive' for coins.

The moustached man steps forward. 'There's a Paki shop near your house.'

Jamie is so horrified to realize that New Dawn know where he lives, he almost misses what comes next.

Almost, but not quite.

'Burn it down.'

Jamie's mouth opens, but nothing comes out. Carrie makes a small sound, but Jamie's rooted to the spot; can't turn to see if she is as horrified as he is, or whether the noise she made had been one of approval.

The man with the moustache looks at the boss, waiting for another of the short nods with which Jamie is already uncomfortably familiar before he continues. 'Burn it down, and you're one of us. A brother in the new dawn.'

'And if I can't?' Jamie's voice is shaking.

The man holds his gaze. 'You don't want to find out.'

CHAPTER 34

'You eat dinner off it!' Maya hops from one foot to the other. The four of them are playing a word game, Nadeeka's eldest waiting impatiently for Jamie's guess.

'A plate?' Jamie is struggling to stay present, his head still reeling from his first encounter with New Dawn. 'A table?'

'No!' Maya flaps her hands in frustration. 'When Mum says we can eat in front of the TV! We eat off them!'

'I know it!' Nish leaps up. 'It's—'

Nadeeka shushes her, laughing. 'Don't give them the point!' She holds up the little plastic hourglass. 'Time's up.'

'It was a tray!' Maya rolls her eyes dramatically. 'Now they're going to win.'

'Sorry, mate. You'll have to be on Mum's team next time.'

'It's okay. It's not your fault you're rubbish.' She pats him on the head, a daring glint in her eyes, and Nish bursts out laughing. Jamie makes himself laugh too, one hand clasped to his chest in *faux* outrage. He catches the shadow of a frown on Nadeeka's face before she joins in with the good-natured teasing. Is she suspicious? Does Jamie look as though he's hiding something?

He gets up, ruffling Maya's hair. 'I'm going to put the kettle on. Anyone want anything?'

'Coffee please!' Nish calls, then falls about in hysterics at her own audacity.

'Okay . . . I think it's time for bed,' Nadeeka says, scooping up her youngest.

'But Jamie said we could play hide-and-seek!' Maya follows Jamie into the kitchen. 'Tell her, Jamie!'

'Your mum's the boss, you know that.' He shoots an apologetic look at Nadeeka. 'Although I did say we'd have a game before bed.'

'*One* game of hide-and-seek. Then bed.' Nadeeka uses her stern voice, but her eyes are dancing – she loves seeing them all getting on.

One game turns into three, and then Maya hides so well, Nadeeka calls a stop to proceedings before bedtime is pushed any later.

'Maya!' she calls from the hall. 'Game's over!'

'She won't come out,' Jamie says. 'She'll think it's a trap.'

'It's not a trap, Maya!' Nadeeka calls.

'Now she'll definitely think it's a trap.' He takes up position at the bottom of the stairs and raises his voice. 'Olly olly oxen free!'

'Olly *what*?' Nadeeka erupts into laughter. A door opens upstairs, feet pounding along the landing.

'Did I win?' Maya shouts.

'It's what you say when you're calling a truce,' Jamie says. 'Didn't you say it when you were a kid?'

'Nope, must be a weird Golding thing.'

'Well, now it's a weird Prasanna thing.' He grins at Maya as she appears at the top of the stairs. 'You won! Where were you?'

'In the bathroom.'

It's Not What You Think

'I looked there!' Nadeeka says in outrage.

'I was under the dressing gown on the back of the door!' Maya is triumphant. 'Come and see how I did it!'

'Show me while you're brushing your teeth. You too, Nish.' Nadeeka herds the girls upstairs.

Jamie retreats to the kitchen, where he leans on the counter, palms either side of the sink, and exhales. It's been a week since he was told to burn down the corner shop. There was a meeting tonight, he got the what3words location through, but he had made an excuse, unable to come up with a good reason why he hadn't yet carried out his initiation task.

'You are going to do it, aren't you?' Carrie had said as they'd left the British Legion a week ago.

Jamie had stared at her, incredulous. 'Of course I'm not going to do it!'

'It's just a fire. No one needs to get hurt.'

'They *live* above the shop!'

'Fifteen of them in a one-bed flat, no doubt. Milking the child benefit payments.'

He'd almost blown it then – forgotten what sort of man he was pretending to be – but he'd bitten his tongue just in time. 'Yeah,' he'd managed, bile rising in the back of his throat. 'Probably.'

'Listen, Jamie,' Carrie had said, and for the first time since she and Jamie had started talking he sensed a flicker of nerves. 'The initiations . . . they aren't exactly optional.' Jamie had wanted to ask if she'd had one herself, but he'd suddenly remembered what she'd told him in the park about the master list. *I got access once I was through my initiation.*

If Jamie wants to give the list to the police, he has to go through with his initiation.

He has to set fire to Surinder's shop.

His phone pings, making him start. He's noticed Nadeeka looking sharply at him when that happens. Maybe he should turn it off when he's at home; or would that prompt just as much suspicion?

The message is from Carrie. *The boss wants that project across the line by tomorrow morning. Okay with you?*

It's so far from okay, it would be laughable if it wasn't so horrific. Jamie's cursor blinks in the empty *reply* box.

'Nish is bouncing off the walls.' Nadeeka's voice comes suddenly from behind him, and he slips the phone into his pocket. She laughs. 'I'm not sure hide-and-seek immediately before bed was the best idea.'

'S-sorry.' Jamie's heart is thudding so loudly he's amazed she can't hear it. 'My fault.'

'You're forgiven.' She comes close; kisses him lightly on the lips. 'Apparently we're having a rematch tomorrow night.' She shoots him a sidelong look. 'Maya wants to be on my team.'

'I knew it,' Jamie says. 'Traitor.'

'Can you stick something on TV? I need to get on with the girls' nativity costumes.'

They watch re-runs of *Frasier*, Jamie's eyes fixed on the middle distance.

Okay with you?

What if it isn't?

Nadeeka laughs at something on the television, so Jamie laughs too, the sound hollow in his ears. He should never have got involved. If he tells the police now, New Dawn will know it had come from him. Maybe if he lived on his own he could ride out the consequences, but he has Nadeeka to think about, and Maya and Nish. They never asked to be mixed up in this.

How could he have been so stupid?

He's trapped.

The second episode finishes, and Jamie's still going round in circles, no closer to knowing what to do. He picks up his phone, thinking about messaging Carrie to say . . . what? *I can't do it? I'm emigrating to Australia?* Or how about the truth? *I was pretending to be scum like you, so I could gather enough evidence to grass you all up to the police?*

'Is something wrong?' Nadeeka's voice cuts through his thoughts.

'What?' The television's been turned off. When did she do that? 'Nothing's wrong.'

'You seem distracted.'

'Just tired.' He yawns, stretching his arms above his head. 'In fact, I'm going to turn in.'

'You would tell me?' Nadeeka searches his face. 'If something was wrong, I mean?'

'Nothing's wrong.'

'That's not what I asked.' Her words are clipped.

'Of course I'd tell you.' Jamie can't look at her. Can't lie to her face. It was the one thing she'd asked him, the moment things started getting serious between them. *Please don't ever lie to me. I couldn't deal with that again.* She felt vulnerable after what Scott had done to her, she'd said, and Jamie had rushed to reassure her that he wasn't like that, that he would never lie. It wasn't in his nature.

Of course I'd tell you.

But what other option does he have? The words of the boss's moustached spokesman are ringing in Jamie's ears. *There will always be consequences.*

As the clock on his nightstand ticks from eleven to midnight to one a.m., Jamie lies awake. Nadeeka sleeps soundly, the duvet pulled tight around her as though someone might steal it in the night, and the softest of snores coming with every third breath. He watches her, his heart full of everything they have together, everything they're building together.

Then, when he is completely certain she's asleep, he gets out of bed, pulls on his clothes and slips out of the house.

CHAPTER 35

The twenty-four-hour garage sells lighter fluid in lurid yellow tins on a shelf behind the cashier. As she rings it up, Jamie picks up a cheap balaclava from a basket by the till, and drops it on the counter with a casualness he doesn't feel. 'I'll take one of those too.' Too late, he realizes he should have bought the two items separately. *Idiot! Why not add a kitchen knife, a roll of duct tape and six packs of paracetamol to your order while you're at it?* But the cashier either doesn't make the connection, or doesn't care, and soon Jamie is walking out of the garage with a plastic bag clutched in one hand. He is, he knows – having extensively researched it – now committing the criminal offence of *Going Equipped*.

Assuming he's going to go through with this.

Which he isn't.

He can't.

And yet, if he doesn't, he won't be granted access to the list; won't be able to see if Echelon is a target.

Jamie removes the plastic safety seal from the lid of the

It's Not What You Think

yellow tin. The balaclava fires sparks of electricity when he pulls it over his head. He has rolled up the bottom half and is wearing it like a hat, but his fingers itch to tug down the wool and hide his face.

The corner shop is double-fronted, with two full-height windows obscured with vinyl stickers sporting images of fruit and veg. The floor above, where Surinder lives with his wife and their twin sons, is in darkness. The boys go to the same school as Maya and Nish; Jamie has seen them at the school gate when he's done the drop-off with Nadeeka. They're a boisterous pair, their parents frequently chastising them for running too far ahead or kicking a football too near the road.

Jamie passes the shop on the opposite side of the road, his eyes flicking from house to house, checking for lights, for movement, for cameras. The street is in darkness, but he keeps walking, his quickening steps keeping pace with his racing heart. His breath's coming too fast, his head filling with a pressure so intense he feels it could crack open his skull.

How could he have put Nadeeka and her daughters in danger like this? If Jamie doesn't complete his 'initiation task', who knows what New Dawn will do? An eye for an eye? Jamie pictures a New Dawn 'brother' sauntering up Cedar Walk at three in the morning, pouring petrol through Nadeeka's letterbox. He stumbles against a wheelie bin, leaning on the filthy plastic as his knees buckle under him.

Think, Jamie!

There has to be a way to satisfy New Dawn and keep Nadeeka out of it without risking the lives of Surinder and his family. There has to be another way to get hold of the list.

A drop of water hits the wheelie bin with a dull *splat*. As Jamie looks up, another falls, then another and another. *Splat, splat, splat.*

Rain!

Within seconds the heavens have opened, and Jamie is soaked

through, his balaclava so waterlogged he has to slide it off his head and wring it out.

I couldn't light it, he'll tell Carrie. *The matches got damp.*

It feels like a miracle. He holds out the box – opens it and lets the rain soak into the red-tipped matches – so he can look Carrie in the eye and say he tried.

'Not hard enough,' Carrie says, the following day. 'You realize it's me who'll get it in the neck for this?' They're in her office, the sign on her door flipped over to *Meeting*.

'You?' Jamie's head is thick from lack of sleep. 'How would the police know you—'

'Not from the police!' Carrie snaps. 'From the boss. I'm your sponsor – it's my responsibility to make sure you go through with it.'

Jamie doesn't know what to say. 'I'll try again,' he manages eventually, but Carrie is only partly mollified.

'I think I should come with you.'

'No, you don't have to—'

'It'll keep the boss off our backs if he knows I'm on the case. Cedar Walk, right?'

The reminder that, as his Human Resources manager, Carrie has access to his personal data renders Jamie incapable of speech.

'I'll meet you at the end of the road. Three a.m.'

All he can do is nod.

He goes to the library after work. Carrie has given him a reading list, warning him that the boss likes to pick on group members to finish key quotes from his favourite texts. Jamie reddens as he asks the librarian to order a copy of *Mein Kampf* from another branch, but she doesn't bat an eyelid.

Logging on to a library computer, Jamie searches for buzzwords he can use in conversation with other New Dawn members. He falls down a rabbit warren of Reddit threads on the woke agenda, and reads a terrifyingly academic article claiming to prove the genetic superiority of white people. He lifts whole sentences and practises them in his head. He may have convinced Carrie, but what about the others? What about *the boss*?

Jamie Googles *how to conceal your identity*, but it's all blog-posts about going off grid and buying fake passports on the dark web. He searches *How do you make people like you?* instead and wonders how much he'll remember when he's in a New Dawn meeting trying not to throw up. *Ask questions about the other person's interests*, he reads. *Mirror the other person's body language to foster a sense of empathy.*

That evening, when Nadeeka yawns and suggests they call it a night, Jamie says he'll stay downstairs for a while.

'I'm not feeling great,' he tells her, and it feels like the first truth he's spoken for weeks. 'I'll take some painkillers. Wait for them to kick in before I come up. I'll only disturb you otherwise.' He slides his gaze away from hers, avoiding the uncertainty he knows he'd see there. She's scared he's going off her, when the reality is that he loves her too much to let her get hurt.

He listens to her footsteps upstairs; hears the loo flushing and the floorboards creaking as she gets into bed. He pictures her lying awake worrying, before giving in to the fatigue of a long day. And, as the clock ticks closer to three a.m., his desperation grows.

He can't go on like this. If he doesn't do New Dawn's bidding, he's a dead man walking. The police won't protect him; Jamie will be looking over his shoulder for the rest of his life.

Unless he disappears.

It takes him an hour to write the note, the nib of his pen hovering on the borders of clichés Nadeeka doesn't deserve. *It's not you, it's me.* He doesn't want to hurt her any more than he has to.

You deserve more, he writes eventually. *I thought I could be enough for you, but I'm not the man you think I am.*

She'll come after him, he thinks. Try to win him back. He doesn't kid himself he's any great catch, but what the two of them have together is special. What they *had* together. Jamie stops writing, screwing his eyes shut until the threat of tears has passed. There's only one thing he can write that will stop Nadeeka in her tracks, but once he sets down the words, there's no going back. She has too much self-respect for that.

Jamie picks up the pen.

I'm so sorry, Nadeeka. Please believe me, I never meant to hurt you. I love you, but I think it's best if I move out. J x.

He exhales. Underlines *I'm so sorry*, as though those three words could ever soften the brutality of his blow. He sets the letter on the coffee table. That's that, then. The grenade that will destroy the first good thing to happen to him in years. A stunning, intelligent, funny woman. Two equally clever and funny kids, just when Jamie had given up hope of having a family of his own.

He stares at the note until the words swim. He'll have to quit his job, of course. Start again somewhere else; homeless, jobless. Forever running from New Dawn.

Will they try to find him? Ask Nadeeka where he is? Jamie pictures Alan, Chris, Carrie, 'the boss' . . . closing in on Nadeeka. Will they follow her to work? Fall into step with her as she leaves her car, a firm grip to each elbow?

Or will they come to the house? Jamie imagines Maya running to the door – expecting her dad, perhaps; her grandmother – and instead finding . . .

No. Jamie swallows. He can't do it. What kind of coward leaves his family to face the consequences of his own actions? He screws up the note. Tomorrow, he'll tell Carrie he's sorry he stood her up, but he's changed his mind about the initiation. Perhaps if he makes out he's still committed to the cause but is scared of getting caught, they won't come after him.

Jamie waits another fifteen minutes, until he's certain Carrie

It's Not What You Think

will have given up, then he gets up and stretches, stiff from the hours spent tensed on the sofa. He turns off the light. He has a sudden longing to be with Nadeeka, to wrap himself around her warm body and feel her sink into him in her sleep. Moonlight sends a strip of pale white through a gap in the curtains, and Jamie goes to close them.

He freezes. Carrie is standing at the end of the cul-de-sac, a long puffa coat zipped from ankles to neck. She's looking directly at No. 10. Jamie's pulse quickens. *She can't see you*, he tells himself. The house is in darkness; he'll be nothing more than a shadow in the window. *She'll leave soon. Give up.*

But Carrie doesn't leave; she starts walking towards the house.

No, no, no! Jamie's panic stops his brain working. All he can think about is Carrie ringing the bell; Nadeeka stumbling bleary-eyed down the stairs, wondering who would call at such an ungodly hour. Carrie seeing Nadeeka, knowing Jamie lied to her, realizing that New Dawn's rhetoric is against everything he truly believes in.

He grabs his coat and opens the front door.

CHAPTER 36

Jamie gets to Carrie just as she draws level with the house.

'I was beginning to think you'd bottled it!' she says.

'Sorry.' He glances up at the bedroom window, knowing how easily sound travels at night. 'I dropped off.' He starts walking, so fast she has to run to catch up with him. Anything to get her away from the house.

'The boss says once you've done this, we can brief you on our next operation.' Carrie delivers this promise as though she's bribing a child. *Eat your greens, and I'll give you ice-cream.*

Jamie looks at her. 'What operation?'

'He says it's our biggest yet; not like anything we've done before. He reckons it's the one that's going to make everyone see that New Dawn means business.'

A cat yowls from the bushes, making them both start. *Not like anything we've done before.* Not a protest, then. Not arson. Despite everything, he feels a dart of adrenaline. This is why he got himself into this nightmare – to gather information.

It's Not What You Think

All he needs to do is find out what they're planning, then he can go to the police.

They're getting closer to the corner shop. Jamie desperately tries to think of a way to seemingly go through with his 'initiation test', without putting anyone at risk. Could he light the fire then somehow put it out without Carrie seeing? Suggest they burn down something else? A derelict building he could convince her is full of refugees?

'The boss has wanted this Paki shop done for ages,' Carrie says. 'Apparently the owner's brought his parents over. That's the problem, isn't it? You open the floodgates, and they swarm in.'

Jamie remembers Nadeeka mentioning Surinder's parents. His mother was ill and Surinder had been worried about being so far away from them. As his hand clenches around the tin of lighter fuel in his pocket, an idea hits him. 'Damn!' He stops walking. 'I've left the lighter fuel at home.'

'Oh, Jamie!' She turns back the way they came, but Jamie puts a hand out to stop her.

'It's fine, there's a twenty-four-hour garage around the corner; it'll be quicker than going home. I'll see you at the shop.'

'I'll come with—'

But Jamie is already sprinting. This isn't a way out, but it might just save Surinder and his family from losing everything – including their lives.

There's a phone box next to the petrol station – one of the few not to have been taken out or turned into lending libraries. It stinks of piss, and Jamie breathes through his mouth as he Googles the corner shop's number.

A man's voice answers, thick with sleep. 'Hello?'

Jamie stays on the line, needing Surinder to be fully alert.

'Who is this?'

How long to get back to the shop, to light the fire? How long for the smell of smoke to drift upstairs? Five, ten minutes? Jamie can't risk Surinder falling straight back to sleep again.

'Fuck you very much.' Surinder sounds properly awake now. 'Who is—'

Jamie hangs up.

Carrie is waiting for him across the street from Shop Express. 'Did you get it?'

He nods. Surinder's shop is sandwiched between a residential house and a launderette that has been closed 'for refurbishments' for at least a year. The remainder of the red-brick row is a mix of houses and flats, and the sight of birthday balloons through a front room window makes Jamie's breath catch. How many families live within those walls? How many children, old people, animals? The whole terrace could go up.

Carrie pulls up her hood. 'Come on, then.'

Jamie takes a deep breath. If he does this, he'll gain the boss's trust and then he'll be able to do what he's wanted to do all along: pass evidence to the police that will bring New Dawn down. He pulls the lower half of his balaclava over his face, and they cross the road together.

'Great,' Carrie says, peering through the glass door of Shop Express. 'There's a doormat. Try and get as much of the lighter fluid as possible on that.'

Jamie hasn't prayed since he was a child, and he's pretty certain that, if God exists, he doesn't respond to prayers sent up during the commission of a serious crime. Nevertheless, as he pours the lighter fluid through the letterbox, he prays that Surinder is still awake; that he and his family will be spared.

'Now light it.' Carrie's eyes glint in the dim light, her voice fervent, almost manic.

But Jamie's hands won't stop shaking. He fumbles with the box of matches, spilling several on to the pavement. The first match he strikes snaps in two; the second extinguishes in his trembling hands. He tries a third time, and again the flame dies before he can move the match towards the door.

'Give it here,' Carrie says, exasperated. She takes the box of matches, lights one expertly, and drops it through the letterbox. There's a beat, then a sudden flare as the lighter fuel catches. 'That'll show them,' Carrie says gleefully. She looks at him, her face ablaze with excitement. 'You did it!' Without warning, she reaches up and kisses him, hard and fleeting. Then she runs.

Jamie runs too; towards the piss-stained phone box to call 999. Behind him, the glass door shatters with a gunshot *crack* that echoes in the empty street.

CHAPTER 37

He's home eight minutes later, his chest heaving with fear and shame and the full-pelt run back to Cedar Walk with the sound of sirens ringing in his ears. His hand shakes as he silently unlocks the front door. The smell of lighter fluid clings to him, but he daren't risk waking Nadeeka by having a shower, so he bundles his clothes into a plastic bag and stuffs it under the sink. Then he slips into bed, where he lies awake, consumed with guilt. He plays out scenarios in his head, each one ending with no one getting hurt. Maybe the fire burned itself out by the door. Maybe the shop has a sprinkler system. Maybe the fire engines got there before the flames took hold.

At breakfast, Nadeeka is shocked to read about the fire on Facebook. 'The police say it was arson,' she says. 'Apparently, they're *not yet classing the incident as racially motivated*.' She reads this from the press release, her tone loaded, then shakes herself like a dog ridding itself of unwanted water. 'I thought things were better now than when I was growing up, but maybe it's just better hidden.'

It's Not What You Think

'I'm sure it was an isolated incident.' Jamie's phone – on silent permanently now – flashes with a message from Carrie. 'Try not to worry.' He wonders if his words sound as hollow as he feels inside.

Nice work, the message reads. *The boss appreciates you working out of hours to get the project signed off. You've proved yourself to be a real team player.*

'Are you still okay to walk the girls to school this morning?' Nadeeka says. He often takes them when she's working from home.

'Actually, no. Sorry.' Jamie stands. 'I have to go in early today.'

'Oh. Right.' She turns and tips the dregs of her coffee into the sink, and for the first time since Jamie moved in, he leaves without kissing her goodbye.

He isn't going to work. At least not yet. He walks instead to the corner shop, where a single strand of police tape has been tied across the front of the shop. A yellow fire service notice is tacked to the charred front door. The door and both windows have been boarded with sheets of plywood, and the pavements beneath them sparkle with the crushed remnants of shattered glass. Jamie walks around to the shop's small concrete yard, where black plastic crates are neatly stacked next to a white van. Checking to make sure no one is around, he pushes £300 in cash – the maximum he was able to withdraw from the ATM on the way – through the back door.

The next few days pass in a blur. At home, the atmosphere continues to be strained. Jamie sees the confusion and hurt on Nadeeka's face when he turns away from her at night, but he can't bring himself to accept her embrace when he's leading a double life, and he can't tell her the truth. She'll insist on Jamie leaving New Dawn right away, but he won't do that until he knows what they're planning. The only way he can come to terms with what he did to Surinder is by using it to bring down New Dawn.

At work, the picture is only slightly better. He stops himself snapping at his colleagues by avoiding them as much as possible, stretching out his site visits and eating lunch at his desk. Adam Bennington makes a point of seeking him out and asking if everything is all right at home. 'You've seemed a bit out of sorts lately.'

Jamie brushes it off. 'I think I'm coming down with something.' It feels like the truth. Maybe even *is* the truth. He wakes every morning with a tightness in his chest and a scratchy throat that makes swallowing an effort. Every night he lies awake in the dark, listening to the blood rushing in his ears; every day he struggles to focus on his work, trying to avoid Carrie, who seems to revel in conspiratorial glances during meetings.

On Monday morning, she stops by Jamie's desk on her way back from Adam's office. 'All right for tonight?' It will be the first meeting since the arson. Jamie is both dreading it and anxious to learn more about New Dawn's new target.

'See you there.' He tries to smile.

'Great.' Carrie glances around, then lowers her voice. 'The boss wants to thank you personally.'

'I don't need . . . He doesn't need to do that.'

'I'm going straight from work if you want a lift,' Carrie says. 'We could have a cheeky drink with Alan and Chris first.' She starts walking away. 'It'll be nice!' she calls over her shoulder.

Nice is not the word Jamie would use to describe his current situation. They're in the function room of another pub, dingy and damp-smelling, and presumably owned by a landlord who asks no questions as long as the right amount of cash passes hands.

Once again, Jamie is sitting in the middle of a row, surrounded by men and women in an array of balaclavas, scarves and hats. He wonders if extremists have seasonal alternatives, or if they spend August heatwaves sweltering in wool. Jamie is wearing his own balaclava, and even though everyone in the room has already seen his face, he still feels reassured by the layer of anonymity.

'. . . our new brother, Jamie.'

At the sound of his name, Jamie jerks his attention forward to where the boss's moustached mouthpiece is looking expectantly in his direction.

Carrie elbows him. 'Go on!'

'What?' Sweat prickles beneath Jamie's collar. Around him, other members of the audience are turning to look at him and he realizes with horror that he's expected to speak.

'Was it you torched the Paki shop, then?' The voice comes from somewhere behind Jamie. 'How did that feel?'

'Yeah. Good.' He almost chokes on it.

'Shame the barbecue didn't get going,' comes another voice. 'What did you use? Petrol?'

'Lighter fluid.' How has this happened? He had planned to infiltrate the group quietly, to stay undercover, unobtrusively gathering evidence. Yet now he's in the spotlight, fifty people staring right at him.

'Petrol would have taken better,' says a woman to his left, as casually as if they were swapping recipes. She smiles. 'Great job, though. I can't believe how many Paki shops there still are around here.'

'Right.' Jamie wishes he had more confidence in his voice, his body language. Does he look nonchalant? Perhaps a little proud? Or do his hunched shoulders betray the disgust he feels inside? Disgust with the New Dawn movement; with everyone in this room; but most of all with himself. A couple of rows in front of him, Alan and Chris are talking in low voices. At precisely the same moment they glance at Jamie, before looking swiftly away when they see him watching them. Unease forms a tight knot in Jamie's stomach. Are they talking about him?

The agenda moves on – more celebrated acts of petty violence; more warnings about dissension in the ranks – but the information Jamie has come here for remains frustratingly out of reach.

'Soon,' the moustached spokesman says, 'we will share the location of our next operation and allocate roles to those of you who have proved themselves trustworthy.'

Carrie nudges Jamie. 'That's us!'

'Recent direct action has brought awareness at a local level,' the spokesman says, 'but the next target will put the issues that matter on the front page of every national newspaper.' He raises a fist. 'The New Dawn is upon us!'

'We step into the light!' choruses the audience. Jamie mouths the words silently, distraught that he can't make this his final meeting. He's not sure how many more he can bear to sit through; each one makes him feel more complicit.

As the meeting breaks up, Jamie heads straight for the door, but, just as he gets there, he hears his name. Every fibre of his body wants to run. He makes himself turn around.

'You got a minute?' Alan is walking towards him, Chris by his side.

'Sure.' Jamie tries to act casual, but his throat clamps around the word, releasing it several notes too high.

'Chris here said a mate of his saw you in town with a Paki woman.'

All around them, people are moving, talking. Their conversations bleed into a dull hum, as though Jamie is underwater, his own breathing seemingly louder than anything else in the room. He forces his face to show confusion rather than the abject fear he's feeling. 'Paki?' He supposes people like Alan and Chris apply the slur freely to anyone brown-skinned, which means they could easily be referring to Nadeeka.

'Yeah. In Homebase,' Chris says. 'Saturday.'

Shit. Definitely Nadeeka. They'd gone to look at outdoor Christmas lights for the garden. Sweat trickles down Jamie's spine. 'Yeah,' he says, trying desperately to sound casual about

It's Not What You Think

it. 'That was the woman from the corner shop. Call me sick, but I couldn't resist asking her about the fire. How it had shit them up, you know?' He laughs, the action so unnatural he almost chokes on it.

Alan doesn't say anything. His eyes narrow a fraction, as though he's puzzling something out.

'I'd better . . .' Jamie looks at his watch. 'See you next week.' As he walks away, he bangs into a chair and sends it skidding across the slate floor. Did they believe him? All his senses are on fire, his limbs awkward, as though they've forgotten how to work together. He nods to the man on the door and then finally he's out, gulping fresh air and taking deep, slow breaths in an effort to quiet his heart.

It's fine, he tells himself. *There's no reason for them to know the woman was my partner.*

But as he leaves the yard and glances back, Alan and Chris are standing there.

Watching him.

CHAPTER 38

Jamie pushes the needle through the cheap fabric of his balaclava, cursing as he accidentally jabs his thumb. He considers himself relatively domesticated, but he has never mastered sewing, and he can hardly ask Nadeeka. He's borrowed the needle and thread from the basket next to the sofa, where she has been working most evenings on Maya's and Nish's nativity costumes. He sucks a bead of blood from his thumb. How does she make it look so easy?

The covert microphone is a wireless plastic disk that records via Bluetooth to his phone. It looks cheap – it *was* cheap – but Jamie has tested it and played back a recording of two men talking on the radio, at the approximate distance Jamie is likely to be from New Dawn's leaders and their confederates at the next meeting.

'What's this?' Nadeeka had said, when she'd picked up the package from the doorstep three days ago. She had turned it over, her interest piqued by the Chinese writing on the label.

'Just some supplements I saw advertised on Facebook.' Jamie

had wanted to snatch it out of her hand. 'Probably a load of rubbish.' His answer had seemed to satisfy her; she hadn't questioned him further.

Recording a New Dawn meeting fills Jamie with fear, but he's been to several meetings now and has never seen anyone being searched. The hidden bug has no incriminating light, makes no noise . . . there's no reason for anyone to know it's there. And when Jamie passes the resulting evidence to the police, they'll have more than just his word to go on.

He's just putting the needle and thread back in Nadeeka's sewing basket when she and the girls come back from rehearsal. He closes the needle case with a snap.

'What are you up to?' Nadeeka says from the lounge doorway, an amused look on her face. She throws her coat over the banister and helps Nish out of hers. 'Maya, hang yours up, please – coats don't live on the floor.'

'I thought I might be able to help, but I think it's beyond my skill set.' It troubles Jamie how easily the lies come to him nowadays.

'You're a sweetheart for thinking of it.' She comes in and kisses him. 'I'm almost done, anyway.' She pulls out a shimmering white dress. 'What do you think?'

'Beautiful.' Jamie turns to Nish, who has run to see the dress. 'You're going to look wonderful.'

'I get to hide behind a secret door until it's time for my lines!'

'How exciting.' Jamie smiles.

'But we can't use the stage till the real thing, so we're just pretending for now.'

'Can I have a biscuit?' Maya calls.

'No,' Nadeeka says, without missing a beat, 'you'll spoil your tea.'

'But I'm hungry!'

'Then you'll enjoy your meal . . .' Nadeeka goes into the kitchen to intercept the inevitable attempt to open the biscuit tin, and Jamie lets out a slow breath. There's a permanent tightness in his chest nowadays, like indigestion that won't shift. 'Go change out of your school things, then we can eat.' Nadeeka raises her voice. 'Do you mind watching the girls tomorrow night?'

She's talking to him, Jamie realizes suddenly, and he walks towards the kitchen as Maya and Nish slope reluctantly upstairs to change. His coat is hanging on the rack in the hall, the balaclava stuffed into one pocket. 'Sorry, I might not be back till late tomorrow.'

'You're working late?' Nadeeka looks at him. 'Again?'

'Probably.' Jamie holds her gaze. 'I have to get a report in – Adam's cracking the whip on this one.'

'What time will you be home?'

'Eight maybe. Nine? I'll let you know.'

There's a beat.

'And you'll be at work?'

'That's what I just said.' Fear makes Jamie defensive, and he sees a flicker of unease in Nadeeka's eyes. She opens her mouth to say something, then closes it again. They stare at each other. Jamie looks away first, straightening a chair that had been perfectly straight to begin with. 'Do you need any help with dinner?' he asks.

'What's happening to us?' Nadeeka's voice is small.

'What do you mean?'

'I feel like you're pulling away from me.'

'That's ridiculous.'

She sets down a pan hard on the counter. 'I'm ridiculous?'

'I said *that's* ridiculous.' Jamie goes to her, intending to put his arms around her, but she steps away.

'If you don't want to be with me—'

'Of course I want to be with you!'

'—I'd rather you just said.'

'Nadeeka, please . . .' He touches her lightly on the shoulder. 'I love you.'

It's Not What You Think

'Do you?'

For a split-second, he thinks about telling her he's risking his life to expose the sorts of scumbags who would do her harm. He thinks how much better he would feel to release the tension inside him instead of keeping it to himself.

Then he thinks about setting fire to Surinder's shop, and Nadeeka's abject horror that someone would do such a terrible thing. And he doesn't say a word.

'I guess that's my answer,' Nadeeka says.

You idiot! Jamie thinks. 'No, I—'

But Nadeeka marches past him and into the hall, calling upstairs to the girls. 'Tea's ready!' The conversation is over. Jamie can almost feel his life dissolving around him, minute by minute. He needs to bring down New Dawn before his lies destroy Nadeeka's trust in him completely.

The meeting the following evening is in the back room of a pub called the King's Arms. Jamie meets Carrie outside. He's disconcerted when she gives him a hug, although he supposes being seen with another woman is the least of his problems right now. She grins as Jamie pulls on his balaclava. 'I'm loving the *international man of mystery* vibes.'

Jamie gives a weak smile. He can feel the microphone against his scalp. What if it shows from the outside? A lump in the seam, or a darker patch through the weave of the fabric? He fights the urge to touch it. If someone sees it, that's it. They'll kill him.

It gives him some small comfort to know that, if things go badly wrong tonight, the bug will capture everything. He imagines the police examining his body, emptying his pockets, interrogating his phone. They'd find the recording, wouldn't they?

He shakes himself. *Nothing will go wrong.* He'll get in, record the meeting, get out. Then he'll write everything up and present all the evidence to the police, and this nightmare will be over.

'There are a couple of seats there,' he says, steering Carrie towards the front of the room.

'You're keen,' she jokes. 'Do you have an apple for the teacher as well?'

Jamie forces a laugh. It goes against all his instincts to put himself in the front row, so far from the exit, but he needs to be close for the recording to work. He glances around, hoping Alan won't be here, but finds the older man is already watching him. Jamie nods to him in greeting, but Alan simply stares at him, and Jamie's blood runs cold. He wonders if the microphone will pick up anything above the rapid drumbeat of his own heart.

The boss and his sidekicks take up their usual positions at the front of the room, a mere three metres from where Jamie and Carrie are sitting.

'The New Dawn is upon us!' says the man with the moustache.

Jamie is too close not to join in with the response. He imagines his voice being played in court, and he wonders if people will believe his story, or whether they'll think he really was part of New Dawn.

A large screen has been set up beside the leaders, the reason for which doesn't become clear until halfway through the meeting, when the moustached man picks up a remote.

'Our next action is not taken lightly, but the time for quiet resistance is over.' His gaze sweeps the room. 'They're hosting it in plain sight. No shame. No attempt to hide their agenda. A celebration of so-called "diversity". Foreign languages, foreign cultures taking precedence over our own. And we're expected to smile and clap along?'

There are jeers from the back of the room; shouts of 'Never!' heralding applause.

'They say it's about opportunity. Inclusion. But it's erosion, plain and simple. Another chisel-blow to the foundations of what this nation is.' He presses a remote and the TV displays a picture of an imposing building. 'This is where they'll gather. Where they'll showcase their vision of Britain's future.' He pauses, the silence so heavy it's almost painful. 'This is our next target.'

The room is electric with anticipation. A chair scrapes against the floor as the boss stands up, and the hum in the air intensifies. He's dressed in black; combats tucked into boots, military style, with a ski mask obscuring most of his face. His gaze moves slowly across the room, then he raises one arm, his fingers clenched in a fist. 'The New Dawn is upon us!'

'We step into the light!' the audience cries.

Jamie's lips follow the words, but no sound escapes. Because the building on the screen is one Jamie recognizes.

CHAPTER 39

'Why don't you take some time off work?' It's Sunday night and Jamie's doing the washing up, his back to Nadeeka. Things between them are still strained, but when he got back from the King's Arms two nights ago he'd found she'd left a plate of cottage pie out for him. A peace offering, he thought. Hoped.

'I am. You know I am.' She picks up a tea towel and comes to stand next to him. 'I stop on December 23rd and I don't go back till the first week of January.'

'Sooner, though.' Jamie scrubs at an already clean plate. 'Maybe the week after next, or better still the one after that? We could go away.'

Nadeeka laughs. 'I can't go away a week before Christmas! Besides, there's the job fair.'

'Can't someone else handle it?'

'Are you joking? I've asked my own recruits to staff the stalls – some of whom don't speak much English – and we're expecting well over a hundred prospective employees. There's a coachload coming with an asylum charity. I can't just wash my hands of it because I fancy a few days off.'

'You could work remotely.' Jamie shakes the soapy water from his hands and wipes them on his jeans. 'From here.' He takes out his phone and shows her the screenshot he'd taken earlier. His heart is pounding. *Please say yes. Let's take the girls and get out of here . . .*

'Lapland?' Nadeeka looks at him, incredulity on her face.

'The girls would love it.'

'I'm sure they would, but we can't afford to—'

'I'll pay. It's a great deal. A once-in-a-lifetime trip. Five nights, and you get to go sledding with huskies, and meet Santa, and—'

'The girls have got school!' She's still half-laughing, as though Jamie has gone mad; as though this were simply a crazy whim, instead of a desperate attempt to keep Nadeeka and her daughters out of harm's way. 'They'd miss the school show, and there's parents' evening and Christmas shopping night . . .' Nadeeka takes the phone from him and puts it firmly on the counter. 'And that's on top of the job fair.' She loops her arms around Jamie's waist and looks up at him. 'I love you for wanting to do this, but it's too short notice. I'm sorry.'

'I'm sorry too,' Jamie says fervently.

Nadeeka rests her head on his chest. 'Next year, yeah?'

Jamie stares into the window at the reflection of his pale, drawn face. Next year will be too late.

The following morning, Jamie leaves home at the usual time, waits until he's sure Nadeeka will have left for work, then doubles back and lets himself into the house. He's relieved that Cedar Walk, although friendly enough, isn't one of those streets where everyone knows everyone else's business. Even if one of the neighbours has seen Jamie return, it would be unlikely to arouse suspicion.

He sits at the kitchen table and opens his laptop. He registers as sick via ATP's employee portal, then gets to work. Time to tell the police everything.

He downloads last night's recording from his phone to his laptop. The sound is muffled, but it's possible to make out almost everything. Then, in a fresh Word document, Jamie begins to document what he knows. He describes everyone he can think of: 'the boss', the moustached spokesman, the thug on the door, Alan, Chris, Carrie. He lists all the meeting venues, and rough-counts the attendees he's seen at each. He records New Dawn's battle cry, his blood running cold as he types the words.

Step into the light.

Jamie is just detailing what he knows of the forthcoming operation when the doorbell rings. He wants to ignore it, but there is a constant stream of deliveries in the run-up to Christmas, and it will be a matter of seconds to sign for it then get back to his . . . He walks into the hall, trying to think of the right word for it. *Exposé*, he decides. An exposé that will not only bring down New Dawn, but will also provide some small mitigation for his own horrific act. He checks his watch. By midday, he'll be able to present his dossier to a police officer. He'll be putting his fate in their hands, but at least it will be over. Everyone he loves will be safe, and he can finally come clean to Nadeeka.

He opens the door.

'All right, Jamie?' Alan stares at him, unsmiling. 'A little bird told me you weren't feeling so good.' Carrie and Chris stand either side of him, their expressions unreadable.

Jamie starts to run through his options. A highly contagious infection, perhaps? Anything that will allow him to close the door and—

But Alan is already taking a step forward.

Jamie watches helplessly as the three members of New Dawn shoulder their way past him and into the house.

CHAPTER 40

'It was nice of you to pop round,' Jamie follows the trio into the sitting room. Carrie must have told them he'd signed in sick. 'I hope you brought grapes and a bottle of Lucozade.' He forces a laugh, but it dies as soon as it leaves his lips, and he's left with an odd, heavy sensation in his throat, as though he might cry.

'I brought Alan and Chris with me,' Carrie says. 'I hope you don't mind.'

'Not at all.' Of course he fucking minds, but what's he going to do about it? 'It's very thoughtful of you to check in on me, but I'm fine, really. Just a stomach bug, I think.'

He wishes they'd sit down. Carrie's standing still, but the other two are roaming restlessly around the room, looking out of the window, touching the sofa, the cushions. What do they want?

His phone buzzes in his pocket.

'Aren't you going to get that?' Chris says.

Act normal, Jamie tells himself. 'Oh. Yeah. Okay.' He takes out his phone. *Nadeeka*. Jesus, of all the times to call . . . 'Hiya, can I phone you back?' He keeps his eyes on Carrie, who's saying something to Chris. 'I'm just in the middle—'

'Are you in the office?' Nadeeka says.

'Yes. I'll call you—'

'Who's that talking?'

'The HR manager. We're in a meeting. Look, sorry, but I have to go.' He ends the call and turns his phone to silent.

'Alan and Chris have raised a few concerns.' Carrie takes no notice of the interruption. 'And instead of going straight to the boss, they came to me. I'm your *sponsor*, Jamie.' She waits expectantly, and a frown shadows her features as it becomes clear he isn't following. 'If you're not fully aligned with New Dawn's ethos, it's not just your neck on the line, it's mine too.'

'B-but I am aligned.' Jamie's trying to keep control, but a tremor runs through his body and chatters his teeth. He's made them suspicious, that much is obvious. He doesn't know what they know, but he needs to get them out of the house before his cover is blown completely. 'Shall we . . . we could go for a coffee? A drink?'

'I don't think so.' Alan's suddenly at his side, looming over him, his face no longer blank but full of rage. He jabs Jamie hard in the chest and Jamie stumbles backwards, falling on to the sofa. 'Who the fuck are *they*?' He thrusts a silver oval picture frame in Jamie's face.

The photograph had been on the windowsill. It pre-dates Jamie – Maya and Nish had been around five and three – but Nadeeka looks the same in the picture as she does now. Shoulder-length glossy black hair, dark eyes, two tiny dimples either side of her smile. Her skin a touch darker than her daughters.

Jamie opens his mouth, but nothing comes out. What can he say? A friend? A cousin? A stock image bought with the frame and never replaced? He suddenly realizes he can't see Chris. Where is he? Upstairs, looking for more photos?

'I said, who the fuck are they?' Alan says, louder now. 'Is your wife a fucking Paki? Are these your fucking bastard half-castes?'

It's Not What You Think

Perhaps it's the knowledge that there's no longer anything to lose. Perhaps it's the slurs, which are hard enough to stomach when generic; impossible when directed at three people Jamie knows, respects and loves. Either way, Jamie can pretend no longer.

He half-stumbles, half rolls off the sofa. 'Don't call them that, you racist piece of shit!'

'I *knew* you were lying.' Alan grabs Jamie's collar, yanking him to his feet. 'I fucking told you, Carrie.'

'I know, I know you did . . .' There's something else beneath Carrie's anger. Tears? Fear? 'I thought I could trust him, I thought he—'

'He was going to grass us up.' Chris's voice cuts through the chaos, and for a moment there's silence. Alan turns to look at him, pulling Jamie's shirt with him, his knuckles pressing into Jamie's windpipe. Chris holds up Jamie's laptop, and any last vestige of hope Jamie might have had vanishes. 'He's written it all down. Names, dates, descriptions. All our plans.'

Carrie gasps. 'We need to call the boss.' She takes out her phone.

'And do what in the meantime?' Chris snaps the laptop shut and frisbees it on to the armchair. 'We can't let him go.'

'I won't say anything.' Jamie tries to wrench himself free, but Alan pulls him close and drives a knee into his stomach. Jamie cries out. He thinks he might vomit.

'The boss's phone is off,' Carrie says.

'Call his personal number.' Chris is mirroring Alan now, both men gripping Jamie's shirt, manhandling him away from the sofa, slamming him up against the wall.

'That's only for emergencies.'

'This is a fucking emergency, you stupid bint.' Flecks of Alan's spit land on Jamie's face. He can smell their breath now, see the mix of rage and panic in their eyes.

'Okay, it's ringing.'

Jamie summons all his strength. He twists to the side, launches himself at the two men pinning him against the wall, but Chris lands a punch to his stomach and—

'Boss, it's Carrie. I'm sorry to call this number, but we've got a problem.'

'What the fuck?' Alan releases his grip. Chris too. Suddenly unsupported, Jamie slides to the floor. His insides have turned to liquid, the pain in his gut like nothing he's ever felt before. He presses his hands to his stomach.

'Oh, my God . . .' Carrie's voice breaks and when she speaks again it's small and scared. 'A really big problem, boss.'

Alan's backing away. 'Jesus, Chris, what did you do that for?'

'He was going to grass us up.'

Jamie's fingers are warm and slippery. He looks down.

Not a punch.

He's been stabbed.

Chris is holding the knife away from his own body, as though it's nothing to do with him, as though Jamie's blood dripping from the blade is incidental.

'We're going to need a clean-up.' Carrie is still on the phone, although her voice sounds far away, coming to Jamie through water, through a metallic sound in his ears like the ringing of a bell. He can't see anything now, his vision clouded with black stars that dance across his eyes. He tries to summon a picture of Nadeeka, but the black stars are thickening and quickening and—

'A full clean-up,' comes Carrie's distant voice. 'He's not going to make it. Can you sort it, boss?'

Everything is muffled now. Soft. Wrong.

He blinks, once, twice, trying to clear the blur from his eyes, but the darkness is creeping in fast. The stars burst and scatter across his vision, each one growing larger, swallowing the world in flickering patches. He tries to hold on to something – someone – Nadeeka's face, her laugh, anything to anchor him. But even that is slipping.

It's Not What You Think

I can't die.

The thought slices through the fog, sharp and sudden. *I can't die, not now.*

Because no one else knows what New Dawn are planning.

It's all in his head and on his laptop, but they'll destroy that now, won't they? The blueprint for the next target. The chilling, clinical plan to devastate a community. Jamie's chest convulses as he tries in vain to suck in air.

Explosives.

Enough to kill hundreds of innocent people.

And Jamie's the only person outside New Dawn who knows when and where.

He coughs. Chokes. Tries to speak. Nothing comes. The black stars merge into a single blanket of darkness.

And then it's over.

Jamie has failed.

PART FIVE
LAUREN

CHAPTER 41

'Jamie wasn't *one* of them,' Nadeeka says, as soon as Lauren answers the phone. 'He was trying to *stop* them.'

'What makes you think that?' Lauren is non-committal, knowing how common it is for families to reject the possibility that their relatives engaged in criminal behaviour. Lauren sympathizes – she'd find it equally difficult to believe about her own loved ones – but in Jamie Golding's case the evidence speaks for itself. His phone puts him in the vicinity of multiple New Dawn meetings. His DNA was on the bottle of lighter fluid used to torch the convenience store. Golding is a murder victim . . . but he was also a criminal.

'I don't think,' Nadeeka says. 'I know.'

Lauren listens patiently as Nadeeka recounts her visit to Jamie's parents, then reads out the list of books he'd reserved from the library. Lauren clamps her phone between her shoulder and ear as she doodles a church in the margin of her notebook.

' . . . and *Mein Kampf*,' Nadeeka finishes.

Seriously? Everything Nadeeka is telling her serves only to

strengthen the case against Golding. 'I see,' Lauren says. She adds a tiny bride to the side of her church. *Something borrowed* . . . she remembers the rhyme and jots down the items she needs to find. *Borrowed, blue, old, new.* Later, she'll tell Fraser he can be her 'old', she thinks, suppressing a chuckle.

' . . . sewn inside a balaclava.'

Lauren stops doodling. 'What did you say?'

'A bug. He must have recorded their meetings.'

Lauren puts down her pen, leaving her bride jilted at the church. Golding might have worn the balaclava to commit crime. Had he recorded himself to prove to New Dawn he'd carried out their bidding?

'There's more,' Nadeeka says. 'I think he went to the police for help before he died.'

Two officers walk past the open door to Lauren's office, laughing. She sits very still. 'Go on,' she says quietly. She thinks of the times the police have got there too late; haven't listened; haven't acted. She listens to Nadeeka, then she pushes back her chair.

'I'm going to make some calls,' she tells Nadeeka. 'I'll come back to you as soon as I have some answers.'

Three hours later, Lauren pulls an unmarked car on to Nadeeka's drive. She looks at Fraser and grimaces. 'This isn't going to be easy.'

'When are murder investigations ever easy?' Fraser laces his fingers through hers, and the simplicity of his touch fills Lauren with the confidence she needs.

She nods. 'Let's do it.'

There's a new carpet in Nadeeka's living room, a grey fleck that doesn't quite match the one in the hall.

'It was the only one they could fit right away.' Nadeeka follows Lauren's gaze. Her voice sounds flat, and, when Lauren says how nice it looks, she doesn't smile. The skirting board has been replaced, and the smell of paint lingers in the air. Lauren thinks about the blood seeped into the concrete floor. She imagines another family, in years to come, pulling up the carpet and wondering what caused the stain.

Hanging on the handle of the door are two costumes.

'The girls' nativity outfits look great,' Lauren says. 'You've done so well to get them made, with everything that's happened.'

'I think it's kept me going. Something *normal*, you know? The girls are so excited – the show's been sold out for weeks. Scott can't make it, he's got a race, so he's going to the dress rehearsal the day before.'

Lauren picks up a shimmery white dress with what looks like LED lights threaded across the shoulders and down each arm. 'Let me guess – Maya's an angel?'

Nadeeka gives the ghost of a smile. 'A drone, actually.' The smile grows as she clocks Lauren's confusion. 'The modern-day equivalent of the star of Bethlehem.'

'A drone that guides the shepherds and wise men to the stable?'

'Yes . . . except the shepherds are buskers, and the wise men are a rabbi, a Buddhist monk and a Hindu priest.'

'And the stable?'

'A library.' Nadeeka picks up the second costume, which consists of black leggings and a T-shirt under thick card painted with the cover of a book. 'Nish is in the choir. When they all stand sideways at the end, their spines spell out "peace and goodwill to everyone".'

'This sounds incredible.' Lauren's memories of her own school nativity plays are mostly tea-towel headdresses and Sophie Harrison getting to be Mary for the third year running.

'There are seven schools involved,' Nadeeka says. 'The teachers deserve medals.'

'Or gin,' Fraser says.

Lauren puts the drone costume back on the doorknob. She turns a level gaze on Nadeeka. 'Shall we sit down?'

There's a beat. Nadeeka nods.

'Jamie *did* go to the police station in Beech Street,' Lauren says, once they're settled. Nadeeka takes a sharp breath. 'He didn't ask for help, but he did report a crime.'

'How come you didn't know that sooner?' There's a sharp edge to Nadeeka's voice.

'We would have done if Jamie had made the report under his own name, but he gave a false one – Richard Smith – perhaps through fear of recriminations.'

'What did he report?'

'A racially motivated assault on a homeless man.' Since Nadeeka's call, Lauren has found a second intelligence report on the assault, made by a PCSO following a conversation with a night shelter volunteer. The PCSO had made perfunctory enquiries but no victim had been identified, and, although a link had been made with 'Richard Smith', no solid leads had been identified and the incident had not been recorded as a crime.

Fraser clears his throat. 'Intelligence suggests the assault was carried out by members of New Dawn.'

'We think Jamie was in over his head; that he was trying to extricate himself from the organization,' Lauren says. 'I've spoken to our digital forensics team, and, on the date you say Jamie received the package containing the recording device, he also downloaded an app called ShadowTek.'

'That's it.' Nadeeka sits up. 'That's the name on the instructions.'

'We don't know if recordings can be retrieved from the cloud, or whether they're only saved locally on the phone itself,' Fraser says. 'The team's working on that now.'

There's a long silence, then Nadeeka looks at Lauren. 'Did you find the people responsible for the assault? The people Jamie was reporting?'

It's Not What You Think

'Not yet.'

'Was it investigated?'

'It was recorded on the intelligence system, but without specific dates or locations we were unable to—'

'So it *wasn't* investigated?' The words are shot with steel. 'Jamie came to you for help, and you did nothing?'

'If Jamie had disclosed that he was in danger, we absolutely would have—'

'You could have prevented Jamie's murder!'

'Maybe,' Lauren says, and her honesty seems to surprise Nadeeka, who falls suddenly silent. 'Would you be able to let us have Jamie's watch?' she asks gently. 'Phone triangulation isn't as accurate as TV shows would have us believe, and the information you've been able to get from his watch—'

'Scott did it. He's into his tech.'

'—will be very helpful for us to cross-reference with our data,' Lauren finishes. She glances at Fraser, who raises an eyebrow to signal that he's on her wavelength. Interesting for Scott Hadley to be so helpful, given his feelings towards Golding. 'I hear from Kath that Scott's moved back in,' Lauren says.

'He's staying here, yes. Kath insisted, and Scott was worried about the girls. To be honest I wasn't keen at first, but I do feel safer having someone in the house, especially now I know what New Dawn are capable of.'

'That's good,' Lauren says, although she isn't at all sure it is. It's possible, she supposes, that Hadley's here because he's genuinely worried for his daughters, or because he gets a kick out of playing the hero. But it's equally possible he's here with more nefarious intentions.

One thing's for sure: Lauren wants to take a closer look at Scott Hadley.

CHAPTER 42

There are no longer sufficient chairs in the briefing room for everyone to sit down. Detectives seconded to Lauren's team lean against the walls, perch on windowsills and roam restlessly by the door, as though keen to get going with their enquiries – or perhaps to get to the canteen before breakfast ends, Lauren thinks wryly.

Sitting beside her at the front of the room is DI Stratman. The moment Golding's murder had been linked to an extremist organization, there had been pressure on Lauren to hand over ownership of the investigation to the counter-terrorism unit. Lauren had stood her ground. She'd argued that her previous time on the CTU, and her team's experience of complex murder investigations, made major crime perfectly placed to oversee the case. The detective superintendent had eventually agreed on the condition that Stratman be given access to everything Lauren's team did. Lauren had – somewhat reluctantly – agreed.

'The post-mortem has confirmed Golding died as a result of a single puncture wound to the stomach,' she tells her team, 'caused by a thirteen-centimetre stiletto blade with bevelled edges on both sides. It perforated the stomach and bowel and caused a fatal internal haemorrhage. Bruising around the incision suggests that whoever stabbed him pushed it right up to the hilt.'

'Brutal,' Kenric says.

'The type of knife adds weight to our theory that this was premeditated, right?' Fraser says. 'I mean, they didn't just grab a kitchen knife – they came prepared.'

'Right.' Lauren looks around the room. 'So, assuming it *was* New Dawn who killed him, that tallies with the rest of their operation. They're slick. Well prepared.' She taps a key on her laptop and brings up the slide with their list of suspects. 'We don't know if the individuals purporting to be police officers and mortuary staff were responsible for Golding's murder, or if they were a separate clean-up crew, but it's fair to assume they're all connected to New Dawn.' She looks around the room. 'Find one, and we'll find the rest.'

'We're still looking at Jamie's line manager, Adam Bennington,' Fraser adds, 'as well as Nadeeka's ex-husband, Scott Hadley, who recently moved in with her for "security reasons".' His emphasis prompts a murmur of cynicism from his colleagues.

'I can do some more checks on Hadley,' says one of the intelligence officers.

'Thank you.' Lauren wishes she had something more concrete to go on than a *feeling*. 'Find out if he's affiliated with any political parties, if he's ever attended a protest or demo. And take a look at his socials. See what he's followed, liked and shared.'

'Surely we've got the same issue we ran into with our theory on Golding,' Matt says. 'Hadley was married to Prasanna; they've got kids together. Why would he suddenly target her?'

'Because he's bitter?' Fraser suggests. 'Remember that Fathers for Justice guy who went berserk when he was refused custody? Mr Nice Guy for a decade and then . . .' He aims an invisible rifle at Matt.

'Hadley looks the type, to be fair.' Kenric is looking at his phone. He spins it round, flashing a Facebook profile picture. 'White – no offence, hashtag-not-all-whites etcetera – shaved head, tatts . . .'

Sonya takes the phone and squints at the photo. 'You can't tell where his face ends and his neck starts.' She hands it back. 'I hate to break it to you young ones, but once you hit forty the dating apps are full of bald men who look like thumbs.'

'Can we get back on track, please?' Lauren's relieved she doesn't have to worry about an online world full of thumb-men. 'Kenric, how are you getting on with fancy-dress shops?'

'I've made some enquiries, but all the police stuff they hire out is very obviously fake – plastic hats, rubber batons and the like. I've got a potential lead with a company called Blue Light Wardrobes, which supplies military and emergency service costumes to film and TV companies. I'm seeing the owner later today.'

Bahnaz puts a hand in the air, as though she's at school. 'I've got an update on the body bag, ma'am.'

'Go on.'

'The manufacturer says the serial number on the bag was part of a bulk order placed by Fletcher & Sons Funeral Services, in Elmsfield.'

'Have you spoken to them?'

'No, ma'am, I thought it would be better to surprise them. I'm going there after briefing.'

'Excellent. I'll come with you.' Lauren turns her gaze on to a man in his late fifties, wearing jeans and a navy bomber jacket over a grey T-shirt with a stain on the collar. 'Whitty?'

'Ta. I'll keep it brief.' DC Craig 'Whitty' Whitfield has a physique honed from a career working round-the-clock surveillance shifts, snatching snacks from service stations, and (now that he is nearing retirement) a sedentary job on the source management unit as handler to a number of fiercely protected informants.

It's Not What You Think

Unshaven and with hair in need of a comb, Whitty looks, Lauren always thinks, more like a source himself than a handler.

'New Dawn switch up their meeting locations, as you've discovered.' Whitty speaks at a volume the entire room has to strain to hear. Every SMU detective Lauren has ever met has spoken in a similar way, as though they're wary of being overheard, even if the conversation is a request to use admin's photocopier because the one in SMU is broken. 'No connection to the Freemasons, but my source says it keeps people from asking questions.'

Lauren wonders if Whitty has an undercover officer in New Dawn, or whether his intelligence is coming second, or even third, hand.

'Each chapter decides on their targets independently. Locally my source tells me there's been a focus on recruitment, with at least a dozen new members brought in over the last year.'

'Do we have any names?' Stratman interrupts.

'Working on it.' Whitty turns pointedly back to Lauren, and she appreciates the old-school respect for her rank and role. 'New Dawn have plans for more of what they call "direct action", and my source reckons it's due to kick off in the next week or so.'

'Can he give us a steer on what their target is?' *Or who*, Lauren silently adds, thinking of Nadeeka and her two young daughters.

Whitty shakes his head. 'All he knows is . . .' He raises both hands for absolution. 'Forgive my French, boss, but I'm quoting here: he says it's going to be a fucking bloodbath.'

The room falls silent.

A bloodbath in an unknown location at an unknown time.

And they have a matter of days to stop it.

CHAPTER 43

Fletcher & Sons Funeral Services is incongruously positioned between a pet superstore and a pound shop. Gold-etched marble headstones are lined up in the window, and Lauren wonders if they were carved especially for the display or ordered by grieving relatives and never paid for.

'Do you want to be buried or cremated, boss?' Bahnaz says as they get out of the car.

'The word *want* is doing some heavy lifting there.' Lauren pushes open the door and a sombre chime rings out. 'Cremated, I think. You can stick the urn in the briefing room so you don't forget me.'

They wait on sticky plastic-covered chairs in a sad grey room, while a diffident receptionist goes to find the boss, before leading them into an equally sad and grey office.

Mr Fletcher interlaces his fingers. 'How can I be of service?'

'I understand you order your mortuary bags from a company called Summit Manufacturing,' Bahnaz says.

'That's right. We've used them for years.'

It's Not What You Think

'A bag with a serial number from your last order has been seized as part of an active murder investigation. Have you had any go missing?'

Lauren keeps her gaze on Fletcher, but, although his brows lift a fraction, he doesn't seem unnerved by this revelation.

'We've not had a break-in, if that's what you mean?'

'What do you do with the bags after you're done with them?' Bahnaz asks.

'They're single-use; we incinerate them. Although not all the bodies come back here, as you know; in the case of sudden deaths, we're merely the . . . chauffeur.' Mr Fletcher looks pleased with the word. 'I imagine the hospital mortuary disposes of the used bags with the rest of their hazardous waste.'

Lauren undoes her jacket. It's stifling in here; the radiators must be up full whack. 'What vehicle do you use to collect dead bodies?'

'It's what we call a hearsette. Very discreet. It's a Mercedes Vito; they look more like a people-carrier from the outside. Black, of course.'

Lauren takes out her phone and opens her emails.

'The windows are fully tinted, and the seats have been replaced with a two-tiered deck.'

Lauren shows Fletcher the CCTV still of the black Mercedes van at the petrol station. 'Like this?'

'Exactly like that. Although that one's older – we only bought ours last year.'

'The plates are false,' Lauren says. 'Mr Fletcher, where was your Mercedes Vito on December 1st?'

'I hope you're not suggesting it was being used for disreputable purposes?'

'December 1st, Mr Fletcher.' Lauren holds his gaze, and for a second she thinks he's going to kick up a fuss; but he sighs loudly and opens a large leather-bound book on his desk at a page marked with a scarlet ribbon.

He flicks back a couple of weeks. 'Ah!' He looks up and smiles. 'I can put your mind at rest, DCI Caldwell. The vehicle was being serviced. My son took it to the garage.'

'Does your son work for the business?' Bahnaz asks.

'Both my sons do. Damian's our driver, and Peter's training to be an embalmer.'

Lauren catches her breath. Two men taking Jamie Golding's body away from the murder scene. Two sons at Fletcher & Sons Funeral Services. Could it be that simple? 'Are they around? I'd like to speak to them.'

'Well, yes, but—'

'Now, please.' She stands, and Bahnaz follows her lead, and after another heavy sigh Fletcher gets to his feet.

When Damian Fletcher sees Lauren's warrant card, he turns the colour of bleached bone. His younger brother, Peter, makes a bolt for the door.

Bahnaz steps into his path, an outstretched palm striking his chest. 'Where are you off to in such a hurry?'

'Damian, how long was the Vito at the garage for on December 1st?' Mr Fletcher says. 'These officers seem to think it might have been involved in some sort of criminal activity.'

'It . . . I . . . we . . .' Damian looks as though something's stuck in his throat.

'Cat got your tongue?' Lauren has heard enough. She reaches for her cuffs. 'Damian Fletcher, Peter Fletcher, I'm arresting you on suspicion of murder and concealing a body. This arrest is necessary in order to prevent the investigation from being obstructed.'

'Now look here—' Mr Fletcher tries to intervene, but Lauren already has Damian cuffed, and Bahnaz is snapping her own set on Peter.

'You do not have to say anything,' Lauren says, 'but it may harm your defence if you do not mention when questioned

It's Not What You Think

something which you later rely on in court. Anything you do say may be given in evidence.'

Peter looks wretchedly at his brother. 'You said they'd never know we were involved.'

'Shut up, you dick!'

'You're a right pair of master criminals, aren't you?' Bahnaz says. She turns to Mr Fletcher. 'Where's the Mercedes?'

'Parked at the back.'

'Keys, please. We'll be seizing it as evidence of a serious crime.'

'But we need it!'

'So do we.' Bahnaz gives him a cheery smile. 'We'll give you a receipt.'

The Fletcher sons travel separately to custody, installed in the back seats of two marked police cars, while Lauren and Bahnaz wait outside for the recovery truck.

'Do you want to sit in on the interviews with me?' Lauren asks her.

Bahnaz looks awkward. 'I've got to pick up the kids at three.'

'No problem.'

'I'm really sorry, I—'

'Hey – you don't need to apologize. You did a great job today. We'll get the Merc away, then you can go and do a great job at home, too.'

'Thanks.' Bahnaz hesitates. 'Do you think you and Fraser'll have kids?' She screws up her face. 'Sorry. None of my business. Forget I asked.'

'It's fine.' Lauren shrugs. 'Neither of us feels the urge, to be honest, so I guess not. It's a shame in a way, I think Fraser would make a great dad, but he reckons there are too many kids in the world already. No offence.'

'To be fair, that thought crossed my mind at four o'clock this morning after the baby had woken up for the third time.'

They laugh, just as Lauren's phone starts ringing. 'Kenric,' she says, pressing accept.

'Boss, do you remember you asked me to check for intelligence reports about anyone buying a lot of bleach?'

'For cleaning the murder scene, right. But we know now they didn't do it themselves; they paid for Safeguard Solutions to do it.'

'On December 6th, a man bought large quantities of hair bleach from Costco in Ashfield Mere.'

'December 6th?' Lauren shakes her head, and Bahnaz looks at her quizzically. 'That was five days after the murder, Kenric – the scene was long gone by then.'

'They bought citric acid, too,' he says quietly. 'And a large quantity of three-inch nails.'

The recovery truck pulls up outside the gates and begins backing up, a loud *beep beep* cutting into the silence.

'Shit . . .' Lauren murmurs.

Citric acid has a number of uses, she knows. It's found in cleaning products and in cosmetics, and it'll descale a kettle in the time it takes for the water to boil. More significantly, when citric acid is added to something containing hydrogen peroxide – such as hair bleach – and a handful of other easily obtainable ingredients, it creates an effective explosive.

'Call DI Stratman,' Lauren says. 'Now.'

Add in shrapnel flying at a thousand metres per second, and the impact of that explosive becomes catastrophic.

CHAPTER 44

While the Fletcher brothers consult with their solicitors, Lauren gathers the key members of her team in the major crime office. DI Stratman has brought with him a counter-terrorism intelligence officer, who gives a rapid update on the limited information they have about New Dawn's forthcoming attack.

'The group targets individuals they perceive to be immigrants.' She pushes a pair of black-rimmed glasses on to the top of her head. 'So we're prioritizing places of worship, community groups and so on.'

'We've drawn up a list of potential targets,' DI Stratman says, 'and we'd like local units to step up patrols in those areas.'

Lauren nods. 'I'll speak to the area commander.'

'We don't want to cause widespread panic,' the intelligence officer says, 'especially given the current concerns around public confidence, but we've asked the community and diversity officer to reach out to vulnerable groups. They'll also be establishing if any of them have events coming up.'

'I don't know how big the Pagan community is around here,'

Fraser says, 'but it's the Winter Solstice this week. That might be seen as being against Christian values?'

'We're also in the middle of Hanukkah right now.' Matt's looking at the calendar on his phone. 'Isn't there a menorah-lighting ceremony in town?'

'Leave that with us,' DI Stratman says. 'What progress has been made in relation to the purchases made from Costco?'

'CCTV shows the purchases were made by a white male,' Matt says.

Kenric gives a dry laugh. 'Shocker.'

'He used a cloned card, which fraud investigations are working on now, and it looks like he was picked up by an Uber. We're trying to get the account details, but they're a nightmare to deal with, as you know.'

'Anything more from your source?' Lauren looks at Whitty.

He nods. 'As you suspected, your man Golding was taken out because he was about to blow the whistle. It's shaken them up, and the boss has put a temporary stop on all digital comms, so my source is out of the loop.'

'"The boss"?' Lauren asks.

'New Dawn don't like to compromise their key players,' Whitty explains. 'Each chapter is run by "the boss".'

The boss . . . Something snags at Lauren's mind. *The boss appreciates you working out of hours . . .* 'Golding's HR manager sent him a text,' she says. 'Something about getting a project across the line . . . proving himself to be a team player. Her message referred to "the boss".'

'You think we should talk to Adam Bennington?' Matt says.

'No, I think we should talk to Carrie Finder.' Lauren thinks out loud. 'I want to know what she meant by Jamie working out of hours, and I'd like to know more about Adam Bennington.'

'I can go and see her after we interview the Fletchers,' Fraser says.

'Great. Don't spook her – just sound her out.' Lauren's phone vibrates with a text message from custody. 'Damian Fletcher is ready for interview,' she tells Fraser, then she turns to the others. 'If he gives us any information about the upcoming attack, I'll update you right away.'

In the interview room, Fraser presses record.

'My client has a prepared statement,' the solicitor says, after Lauren has reminded Damian of the reason for his arrest. He takes out an A4 sheet of paper, with a few lines written in scratchy blue ink. '*On December 1st I provided private ambulance services following what I believed was the murder of a white male. I was not told his name or the circumstances of his death, and I do not know the names of the police officers I spoke to. I was asked to take the body to a car park, where the body would be transferred to a different private ambulance. I was told the police had requested this, and so I did not question it. I do not recall the details of the other ambulance.*' The solicitor puts the paper on the table.

Lauren is about to say – albeit in more professional terms – that she's never heard such utter bullshit in her life when she realizes the recording equipment isn't working. She nudges Fraser and nods towards it. He frowns and presses record again. Damian smirks.

Fraser waits for the red light. 'Okay, good to go.'

'I'm so sorry,' Lauren says to the solicitor. 'I'll need you to read that again.' He tuts, then picks up the statement and repeats Damian Fletcher's bullshit. The false start has thrown Lauren, and she feels uncharacteristically irritated with Fraser. The whole team is running on empty, but they can't afford to make stupid mistakes. 'Do you have anything to add to your prepared statement?' she asks Fletcher.

'No comment.'

'In that case, I'd like to dig a little into your account.'

'No comment.'

'I haven't asked you anything yet.'

'No comment.'

Lauren folds her arms across her chest and stares at Damian, who stares back, seemingly untroubled. 'Your father, Roger

Fletcher, tells us that when the police request your attendance at a sudden death you are provided with a URN – a unique reference number. Were you provided with that information?'

'No comment.'

'I understand these jobs are entered into a spreadsheet which forms the basis for your company accounts. Correct?'

'No comment.' Damian gives an extravagant yawn.

'He was kind enough to show me December's spreadsheet.' Lauren pauses. 'There is no entry for Cedar Walk; in fact, there's no entry for December 1st at all. How can you explain that?'

'No comment.'

'Can you describe any of the police officers who were at the crime scene when you collected the body?' Fraser asks.

'No comment.'

'Male? Female? White? Black? Tall? Short?' Fraser's voice grows louder with each question, his patience clearly evaporating.

'No comment.'

'I'd like to point out,' Lauren says, 'that this may be your only opportunity to put across your side of the story. The next time you're asked questions about this, you may very well be in court, where the judge won't take kindly to a defence appearing from nowhere.'

Fletcher's solicitor clears his throat. 'My client has provided you with an explanation for the events of December 1st.' Even he doesn't sound convincing, Lauren thinks.

'You claim you were asked to transfer the body to a different vehicle,' Fraser says. 'What can you tell me about that second vehicle?'

'No comment.'

'Is that standard practice?' Lauren twiddles her pen between two fingers. 'Swapping a body between ambulances? Granted, my mum and her sister used to pass Granny over in a service station car park, but she wasn't dead.' This time, the solicitor's cough sounds suspiciously like a laugh.

'No comment.'

It's Not What You Think

'At least, not then,' Lauren adds, and now the solicitor's lips twitch. 'Look, if you're not going to give us the full story, I'm going to have to fill in the blanks.' She leans back, appraising Damian for a few seconds. 'I think you knew full well when you collected the body of Jamie Golding from 10, Cedar Walk that this wasn't a legitimate police request. I think you knew the "officers" you spoke with weren't warranted officers. I think you drove to the drop-off point you mention in your statement, but, instead of transferring the body to another vehicle, you and your brother carried it into the woods, where you buried it.'

'This is pure supposition on your part, officer,' the solicitor says.

'And I think you did all that because you're part of an extremist organization called New Dawn.'

Until now, Damian's expression hasn't changed. He's answered Lauren's questions – albeit without substance – with a laconic, almost sarcastic boredom, meeting her gaze without hesitation. But, when Lauren mentions New Dawn, he frowns. It's fleeting, but she's pretty sure it's genuine.

'Do you know what New Dawn is?' Fraser must have seen it too.

Damian looks at his solicitor. 'No comment?' he offers, but he seems thrown.

The solicitor closes his laptop. 'I'd like to speak with my client, please.'

'What do you reckon that's about?' Lauren says, once Damian and his lawyer have been shown to a consultation room.

'I don't know,' Fraser says grimly, 'but I don't like our chances of getting it out of him.'

They're heading out of custody when Kenric appears at the top of the stairs. 'Ah, just the person, boss. I've got an update from the costume company I went to see.'

'A good one?'

'That depends on your perspective.' Kenric walks towards them. 'First off, the hire place doesn't do one-off rentals – they deal with big production companies they've known for years. He's not had any randoms phoning up for a single copper's outfit.'

'I guess it was a long shot,' Lauren says.

Kenric produces the still image of the young uniformed 'officer' who had been guarding Nadeeka's house when she returned home. 'But when I showed him this, he pointed out this badge.' He indicates the sew-on patch on the breast of the officer's stab vest: a black and white version of the Union Jack, but with a cobalt line across the centre.

'So what?' Lauren says. 'The thin blue line. For colleagues who've lost their life. Loads of coppers have those – you can buy them online.'

'Not like this.' Kenric is zooming in on the patch. 'None of us noticed because we're so used to seeing them around the nick . . . but look.' At the bottom of the emblem, below the blue stitching, are three stars.

'Oh, my God.' Lauren's eyes widen. 'I've got this badge.' She turns to Fraser, who looks as stunned as she feels. '*You've* got one.'

'We've all got one,' Kenric says. 'At least, those of us who were in the job back then.'

'When was it?' Lauren tries to remember. '2018?' It had been a bleak year: a promising probationer hit by a stolen car, an officer who dropped dead from a heart attack during briefing, and finally a much-loved sergeant who died by suicide.

'2019,' Kenric says. 'I was on team two at the time.'

The badges had been commissioned by the sergeant's team and sold to raise money for the charity Care of Police Survivors. They'd been so popular they'd had to order more, the small fabric patches soon so much a part of the force uniform, it was rare to see a frontline copper without one.

'There's literally only one explanation,' Kenric says. 'That stab vest could only have been issued to a copper in our force who was serving in 2019.' He looks up and down the corridor, making sure no one can overhear them. 'Which means they could still be in the job now.'

CHAPTER 45

Lauren looks at the list of names in front of her. In 2019 the force had 1,865 uniformed officers, 1,119 of whom are still serving.

'And 783 of those are now in specialist roles,' Kenric says, 'which means they're not using their uniform on a regular basis and could feasibly have passed their stab vest to New Dawn without anyone noticing.'

'What are we going to do: interview 783 coppers?' Fraser doesn't wait for an answer. 'We're off on a wild goose chase here – that patch could have come from anyone, including officers who've left the job.'

Lauren motions for him to keep his voice down. The door to her office is closed – she's keeping this latest information on a strictly need-to-know basis – but who knows who might be in the corridor? Given the speed with which the original story reached the press, Lauren's not taking any chances.

'Stores say all the officers who resigned or retired handed in full kit,' Kenric says, 'including stab vests.' He checks his notes. 'They've registered eighteen destroyed because of damage or contamination, and another thirty-seven due to wear and tear.'

'Eighteen, thirty-seven, seven hundred . . .' Fraser blows out his cheeks. 'We're just throwing numbers around – it doesn't *mean* anything.'

'It does if one of these officers matches the description of one of our fake cops.' Lauren turns to Kenric. 'Ask stores to run an audit via line managers. Say it's a resilience exercise . . . that we need to know who could feasibly deploy if we need to boost the frontline.' It doesn't feel too far from the truth. Tensions have been simmering across the country since the murder; if the public finds out that one of the fake cops was actually a real one, there'll be full-scale riots. She presses the heels of her hands against the headache forming at her temples. 'Vetting!' she says suddenly. 'Kenric, I want all these officers' recruitment files looked at. Make sure they were properly vetted when they joined, and flag anyone who might have slipped through the net.' Her temples throb. 'Fraser and I need to get back to custody.'

In stark contrast to his brother, Peter Fletcher starts talking before they're even in the interview room. 'I'd never have got involved if I'd known—'

'Whoa . . .' Lauren puts up a hand. 'Hold your horses, mate, let's get the tape rolling, shall we? Don't want to have to do this twice.' She waits for Fraser to record – both of them looking for the confirmatory red light – before cautioning Peter and reminding him of the reasons for his arrest. She rests her forearms on the table and leans forward. 'Peter, why don't you tell us what happened on December 1st?'

Peter glances at his solicitor, who gives a brief nod, then he turns back to Lauren and Fraser. 'I knew it was bad, but I didn't know how bad until afterwards.'

Lauren feels a surge of emotion – a mix of excitement and relief – but she simply makes a few notes on her pad, not wanting to put Peter off.

'They said there'd been an accident, and some bloke had died.

Not murder.' Peter squeezes his fingers together. 'They didn't say it was murder.'

'Who is "they"?' Fraser says.

'Damian got a phone call. A mate of his. Alan.'

Alan. The teacher Jamie had mentioned when he'd reported the assault on the homeless man?

'Damian said he owed Alan a favour, and we had to do it, or Damian would get into trouble over something on his computer.'

Interesting. In Lauren's experience, when people talk about *something on a computer*, there's only one *something* they mean. She will take great delight in passing this information to the Child Exploitation and Online Protection team to wipe the smug grin off Damian Fletcher's face.

'What favour did he want from you?'

'He wanted us to collect the body and . . .' Peter looks at the floor. 'Get rid of it.' His voice has dropped to a whisper.

'And did you?'

Peter nods.

'How?'

'We buried it in the woods.'

'Peter.' Fraser takes over. 'Have you heard of an organization called New Dawn?'

'No.'

'Are you sure? Think carefully.'

'I'm sure.' Peter chews his bottom lip.

'You've never heard anyone say those words to you? *New Dawn.*'

'DS Hogan, my client has answered your question.' The solicitor's tone carries a warning; Fraser's gone in too hard. Lauren looks at him, trying to convey that she wants them to tread carefully, that Peter's already giving them what they need. They can't afford for him to close down now.

'New Dawn is a far-right extremist group,' Lauren explains. 'We believe Alan is working with them, and it's very important we find him. Do you understand?'

Peter nods.

'Great.' Lauren smiles reassuringly. 'Tell me everything you know about him.'

'Alan Ellis.' Lauren looks around the office at the same group of people who had gathered earlier that afternoon. 'ICT teacher at Millfield Academy, where he's listed as also being responsible for pastoral care.' She turns her laptop around and shows them a website featuring a white man with thinning hair and an even thinner smile. 'Let's bring him in.'

'Apologies for stepping out of my pay grade, but – ' Fraser looks between Lauren and DI Stratman ' – could we put him under surveillance first?'

'New Dawn's planned attack could only be few days away,' Lauren says.

'Exactly. If Ellis goes *no comment*, we're left with whatever we can get from interrogating his phone, and all that will take time.' Fraser pauses. 'And we don't *have* time. But we know he's an active member of New Dawn. If we follow him for a couple of days, he could lead us straight to the others.'

Stratman nods slowly. 'I'll put in a request for the surveillance team.'

'Hang on,' Lauren says. 'I'm not comfortable delaying this arrest. We're talking about a terrorist attack that could kill or maim dozens – maybe even hundreds – of people. Do you seriously want to explain to a grieving relative why we didn't arrest someone we knew was involved in the planning of it?'

'We could easily end up talking to grieving relatives for another reason if we bring Ellis in too early and he doesn't give us anything.' Stratman's gaze is challenging. 'Twenty-four hours,' he says. 'Then we review.'

Lauren knows the plan makes sense, but all her instincts are telling her to act swiftly. 'Twenty-four hours,' she concedes. 'Then we bring him in.'

CHAPTER 46

As the briefing breaks up, Fraser leans towards Lauren. 'Foxleigh Manor have just emailed. They need the name cards for the tables; I'm going to have to nip home and get them.'

'What, now? We're up to our ears! They'll have to wait till tomorrow.'

'Apparently we should have delivered them two weeks ago.' Fraser raises his eyebrows. 'Look, I agree it's unreasonable, but given they almost fucked up the entire wedding by double-booking us, I'd rather not piss them off over something as small as name cards. I'll interview Carrie Finder on my way back – kill two birds with one stone.'

Lauren closes her eyes for a second. The wedding planner at Foxleigh Manor takes days to reply to her perfectly straightforward emails about things like parking and room rates, yet she expects Lauren and Fraser to respond immediately. 'I guess we don't have a choice.'

'It'll take an hour, tops.' The corners of Fraser's eyes are pinched, and Lauren wonders if he's keeping something back. At this stage, it wouldn't surprise her if the entire venue had burned down.

'Maybe it's an omen,' Lauren says, deliberately bleakly. Fraser's face makes her smile. 'Go on, then. But be quick. I've given the others a three-line whip and they won't be happy if they know I've let you swan off to—'

'—save our wedding?' Fraser raises an eyebrow. 'May I remind you that you were the one who wanted the big dress—'

'It's not that big!' Despite everything, Lauren laughs.

'—and a hundred of our nearest and dearest? I was all for whisking you off to a deserted beach with a registrar and a couple of hotel guests as witnesses.'

'To be fair, it's my mother's fault the guest list is so big.' Lauren groans. 'But you're right.'

'Of course I'm right.' Fraser grins at her. He turns to leave, then hesitates. 'That list you gave Kenric for vetting . . .'

'What about it?'

'He's had the first tranche checked and the results are in HOLMES. It's probably nothing, but . . .' He rubs the side of his nose, then looks at her for a second or two before continuing. 'Matt never went through vetting.'

'Our Matt? Matt Draper?'

'The forms were posted out to him, but he never sent them back, and it was never chased up. He had a basic PNC check when he applied for the job, but none of the checks around debt, family, political affiliations and so on.' Fraser pauses. 'And he was in a uniform role in 2019.'

A chill runs through Lauren. 'What are you saying?'

'I'm not saying anything . . .' Fraser checks himself. 'Okay, I guess I am saying something. I'm saying we should look at him more closely.'

'Matt's straight as a die.' Lauren shakes her head. 'You've worked with him longer than I have: you know he's sound.'

'Remember when he went on about extremism being

nuanced? That even in an organization like New Dawn, there would be people at both ends of a spectrum?'

'He was playing devil's advocate, that's all.'

'It sounded as though he was defending them.'

'Matt's not a fascist!'

'I'm not saying he is, I'm just saying we should look at him.' Fraser keeps a level gaze on her. 'You know as well as I do that some of the biggest threats hide in plain sight.'

Damian Fletcher is so keen to distance himself from New Dawn that Lauren has to ask him to slow down, worried the recording won't capture his chaotic half-confession. He *did* bury the body, but only because he'd been told Golding had died in an accident, and then only because Damian had felt intimidated by Alan.

'Alan the secondary school computer teacher?' Lauren clarifies.

There's a beat, then Damian nods. 'Yeah.'

'Your brother described Alan as "around five foot seven, with weedy arms and a beer belly like he's swallowed a ball".' Lauren looks up from her notes. 'Not exactly Tyson Fury.'

'No, but . . .' Damian looks at his solicitor, but it's clear he's on his own with this one. 'He's a Nazi, though, isn't he? That's not something you wanna mess with.'

'Ah! So you knew that at the time he asked you to dispose of the victim's body, then?'

'No . . .' Damian's eyes flick rapidly in their sockets as he tries to match up the truth with the version he's currently trying to tell Lauren. 'Like I said before, I don't know nothing about this New Dawn.'

'Then why were you intimidated by Alan?'

'I just . . .' Damian blinks. 'I got a *sense*.'

'Is that right?' Lauren leans forward, dropping her voice as though she's about to impart a secret. 'I've got a *sense* right now, Damian. I can *sense* you're going to be charged with a very serious indictable offence.'

Sure enough, the on-call Crown Prosecution Service lawyer approves charges for Damian and Peter Fletcher, both of whom are remanded in custody and denied their right to phone calls on the grounds that it could jeopardize the police investigation.

'On balance, I'm inclined to believe they aren't in New Dawn's inner circle,' Lauren tells Fraser, when they're both back in the major crime office. 'They're too thick, for one. But they're only one degree of separation from Alan Ellis, who has frustratingly behaved entirely non-suspiciously since he was put under surveillance.'

'It's only been a few hours!' Fraser laughs. 'Give it time.'

'I don't want time; I want him nicked. Did you get the name cards across to Foxleigh Manor?'

'I did.'

'And did you—'

'—tell them the boss isn't happy?' Fraser gives a mock salute. 'You bet.'

Mention of *the boss* reminds Lauren of Carrie's text to Jamie. 'What did Carrie Finder have to say?'

'That Golding had worked late a few times to clear a backlog left by his predecessor, and Adam Bennington had mentioned to Carrie that he'd done a good job.' Fraser sits on the edge of his desk. 'She claims to have messaged Golding in her capacity as a wellbeing manager, but, reading between the lines, I think she had a bit of a crush on him and she saw it as an excuse to use his personal number.'

That fits, Lauren thinks, as she remembers the way Carrie became flustered in front of Fraser. One of those socially awkward women who don't know what to do with themselves when they're around a good-looking man.

There are only a handful of officers left in the office now, half-heartedly updating actions and glancing hopefully in Lauren's direction. No one has bothered to close the blinds, and the pitch-black night is streaked with lights from passing cars.

'Forensics said they had an update on the rags we seized from Safeguard Solutions.' Lauren looks around the room. 'Did they send it in?'

'Do you want the good news or the bad?' Kenric says.

'Both.'

'The good news is we got a DNA hit on one of them. Chris Morley, white male, previous for violent disorder.'

'That's great! What's the bad news?'

'The evidence bag with the rags in has a tear in it.'

'What? How?' Lauren groans. Where forensics are involved, the chain of evidence is everything. A compromised bag means the defence can argue the sample is contaminated and refuse for it to be presented in court.

'The property store's been rammed lately,' Sonya says. 'Someone must have shoved something sharp against it.'

Lauren looks at her exhausted team and makes a decision. 'Right, everyone, go home, get some kip, and we'll pick this up in the morning.' She holds up a finger, keeping them back until she's finished talking. 'I'm sure I don't have to remind you of the importance of keeping everything within the team.' She makes eye contact with each of them in turn: Kenric, Sonya, Fraser, Matt. 'Don't even talk to your partners: got it?'

'Yes, boss.' The response comes as one.

Lauren lets them leave, then she turns off the lights and locks up, and walks with Fraser to the staff car park. It's almost empty, only Matt still there. He's sitting in his car, one side of his face illuminated by the phone he's holding to his ear.

'Two secs,' Lauren tells Fraser, and she walks over to Matt's car.

When Lauren had arrived on major crime, she had instantly picked up on how well-respected Matt was by the rest of the team, and she's seen for herself since then what a good detective he is. Matt hangs up as Lauren approaches.

A good detective . . . but is there another side to him?

'I forgot to ask if there'd been an update on the cloned cards,' she says, as Matt gets out of his car. 'You said you were speaking to financial investigations.'

'I updated HOLMES earlier – did you not see it?'

'Sorry, no.' She had, but it had been the first thing that came to mind to say as she walked over.

'One of the cloned cards was used to buy a burner phone from a kiosk at Sainsbury's. The CCTV isn't great, but the woman who made the purchase was wearing a distinctive coat and the security guard was able to find her on the outside camera. He's sending through a still of her getting into a red Fiat 500. No reg number, but it's a start.'

Matt's phone rings. Lauren waits a beat, but Matt silences his phone without looking at it. 'Okay,' Lauren says eventually. 'See what VODS throws up on red Fiat 500s in the local area.' She's stalling. *Just do it, Lauren!* 'Hey, Matt?'

'Yes?'

'You were on shift in 2019, weren't you?'

'Yeah. Team four. Good times, although I couldn't do it nowadays. Night shifts almost killed me.' He rubs at a mark on the car window.

'Did you have one of the thin blue line patches?'

'We all did. I've still got mine somewhere.'

'Matt . . .' Lauren pauses. 'There aren't any vetting details on your HR file.'

He frowns. 'I don't understand.'

'You never returned the form to recruitment.'

'No, I mean, I don't understand the relevance. Why are you telling me this? I've been in the job for over thirty years; does it really matter what paperwork was or wasn't done when I joined?'

It's Not What You Think

It does if it would have revealed something you didn't want people to know, Lauren thinks. 'I guess not,' she says lightly. 'The system wasn't as robust back then, I suppose.'

Matt's jaw drops a fraction. 'You think I'm connected to this job, don't you?'

'No. That's absolutely not what I think.' *Is it?*

'Then why the third degree?'

'Everyone's being checked.' Lauren tries for a smile, but it feels fake, even to her. 'No stone unturned, right?'

'Right.' Matt stares at her for a second, then he gets behind the wheel and slams the door.

CHAPTER 47

Lauren sleeps fitfully. Each time she wakes, she checks her messages to see if the surveillance on Alan Ellis has led to anything. At 4.30 a.m. when she reaches for her phone, she finds Fraser doing the same.

'Can't sleep?' She scoots closer to him, resting her head against his chest as she squints at her screen.

'Nothing from the surveillance team,' Fraser says.

'Might have something on phones, though.' Lauren chucks her own on the bed. 'The analyst wants to see me first thing.'

'Will you push to arrest Ellis tomorrow?'

'Today, you mean? A hundred per cent. If Ellis knows where New Dawn plans to plant explosives, we have to get that information out of him – there's no time to waste.' She throws back the covers. 'I'm giving up on sleep. Coffee?'

Fraser swings his legs out of bed with a groan. 'Make it a strong one.'

*

It's Not What You Think

By seven, Lauren has had five cups of coffee and her brain is crackling with static. She's sitting in the analyst's office, struggling to make sense of a spreadsheet packed with telephone numbers.

'Each page shows the phones that were in the vicinity of a New Dawn meeting from fifteen minutes before it began to fifteen minutes afterwards,' the analyst says. He clicks rapidly through the pages. 'The greyed-out numbers are linked to a single meeting, those highlighted in yellow correlate with two meetings, pink with three, purple with four . . .'

Just as Lauren is starting to feel dizzy, the scrolling numbers stop dead. In the centre of the screen is a phone number with a thick black box around it. She looks at the analyst. 'What's so special about that one?'

'That number appears in the vicinity of every New Dawn meeting we know about, which means there's a high probability it belongs to someone attending. And luckily for us – ' the analyst taps his pen lid against the number ' – it's not a burner phone. It's on a contract.'

Lauren's heart leaps. 'Do you know who it belongs to?'

'Yes.'

'Have you thought about telling your face?' Lauren grins. 'I can't tell you how happy I am to have a bit of good news. It was starting to feel as though we'd never get a breakthrough.'

'You won't feel like that in a minute.'

'What do you mean?'

He minimizes the spreadsheet and clicks on a different document. 'As soon as we got a name, Intel did the usual checks – PNC, intel, some open source.' The document opens, and Lauren takes in the photograph of the man on the screen, captioned with his name, address and last known occupation.

'Shit,' Lauren says.

'Police officer. Ex-police officer, technically,' the analyst adds, 'although he only retired a year ago. His name's Mike Bishop.'

'Is he one of ours?' Not that it will make any difference to the public, Lauren knows. A bad apple is a bad apple, no matter what barrel it's in.

'Detective inspector in the Met. Moved here when he left the job. And if you compare his photo to our so-called DI Burton...' The analyst brings up the e-fit and drags the corners so it's the same size as Bishop's photograph, then positions them side by side. The similarities are striking.

'No wonder he was so convincing.' Lauren can't stop staring at the two images; at the narrow eyes, the full moustache. She thinks of Nadeeka arriving home to find her world destroyed, putting her trust in the very man who had destroyed it. She thinks about the damage done to the police's reputation – damage which could take generations to undo – and she feels a wave of anger so intense it pushes her out of her chair. 'Who knows this information?'

'Just you and Intel at the moment.'

'Keep it that way. I'll ask Fraser to put an arrest team together.'

She finds him coming back from the kitchen, three over-full mugs of coffee in each hand.

'Don't let me have one of those,' Lauren says. 'I'm operating at a level of caffeine that should probably be illegal.' She fills him in on this latest development. Fraser's eyes narrow as he learns that Mike Bishop was a serving police officer, his jaw taut with barely contained anger. Lauren gets it. No one hates corrupt cops more than other cops. 'Hard to stomach, isn't it?'

Fraser gives a tight nod. 'What's the plan?'

'I want arrest teams ready to go in an hour. I'd prefer to do a dawn knock, but we can't afford to lose any more time; I'm worried Bishop will get wind of what's going on. The DNA hit on the cleaning rags gives us enough to bring in Chris Morley, and, given he and Alan Ellis come as a pair, we should do the arrests simultaneously. Stratman's just going to have to lump it.'

'Three arrest teams, then?' Fraser says. 'Let me get shot of these, and I'll put them together. Team two are on earlies this week – they're a good bunch. And I'm thinking Kenric and Matt?'

'Sonya,' Lauren says. 'Leave Matt out of this one.'

Fraser raises an eyebrow. 'So you *do* think—'

'Let's just get these three nicked,' Lauren says, calmly but firmly. 'Fast.'

They gather for a briefing in the back yard an hour later, police vans parked on three sides of a square, their doors pulled back so the arrest teams can see Lauren and DI Stratman.

'Radio up when you're in position,' Lauren says, 'but wait for my signal before going in. Team one, Chris Morley's due to start work at nine, so get the factory foreman on-side and you should be in and out with no drama. Teams two and three: it's big red key time.' The heavy metal enforcers will make short work of the doors Lauren has already scoped out on Google Street View, minimising the risk of Mike Bishop and Alan Ellis disposing of crucial evidence.

'Did the surveillance throw up anything, boss?' Bahnaz asks.

Lauren defers to Stratman. It irks her that she capitulated yesterday when they could have had Ellis in the traps overnight. She should have stood her ground.

'Ellis's behaviour changed an hour or so after surveillance started,' Stratman says. 'He began looking over his shoulder, crossing the road unnecessarily . . . behaviours common with individuals who know they're being followed.'

'Do you think he was given the nod?' Kenric asks.

'It seems that way.' Stratman flips open the cover of an iPad and swipes through a series of photographs. 'He was approached in the pub on Wednesday evening by a man who seemed to know him, and Ellis was visibly uncomfortable. Couldn't get away quick enough.' He turns the tablet around. 'We lost him soon after that; we think he switched jackets with another man,'

Stratman is saying, but Lauren's attention is on the man seen talking to Ellis.

Sonya's jaw drops. 'Isn't that thumb-man?'

'Scott Hadley,' Lauren translates, in case Stratman has expunged the memory of Sonya's peri-menopausal dating woes. 'Nadeeka Prasanna's ex-husband.' What had Hadley been doing talking to Ellis?

As the arrest teams make their way to their respective locations, Lauren messages Nadeeka. *Just checking in. How are you doing?*

The usual breakfast chaos, Nadeeka replies, *but I'm okay. Scott's taking the girls to school today, so I can get to work early. I'm running a recruitment event at the weekend and things are getting busy.*

Lauren's tension eases slightly now that she knows Nadeeka will be safe at work all day, and Maya and Nish at school. In the meantime, Lauren can get Ellis into interview and establish whether Scott Hadley is part of New Dawn.

Mike Bishop lives in a detached Victorian villa with a gravel drive and a hundred-foot garden, at the end of which two uniformed officers have been stationed. There are patrol cars waiting at either end of the residential street, and two taser-trained officers in an unmarked van with Lauren and Fraser.

Five miles away, at the car parts factory at which Chris Morley is a machine operator, a second arrest team is waiting for the nod, with the third team poised near Alan Ellis's door. Lauren watches Kenric and Sonya walk towards Bishop's gravel drive, then she presses the transmit button on her radio. 'Arrest teams: go!'

At the Victorian villa, a uniformed officer swings the enforcer. There's an almighty bang, and a second one, then the door smashes open. The arrest team charge in. In the van, Lauren and Fraser wait impatiently.

'I hope he's not out,' Fraser says.

It's Not What You Think

'His car's on the drive,' Lauren says – she has already confirmed that the black Mazda is registered to Bishop – but now Kenric is coming out of the villa, shaking his head. 'Damn!' She pulls back the van door.

'The neighbour's talking to him,' Fraser says. They watch as a woman in gym clothes, arms hugged tight to her body, walks closer to the fence separating the two driveways. A minute, maybe two, and then the neighbour's going back inside, and Kenric and Sonya are crossing the street to the van, and it's clear from their faces that it's not good news.

'The neighbour saw him half an hour ago getting into a taxi,' Kenric says. 'He had two large suitcases with him.'

'Holiday?' Fraser says hopefully.

'Negative result at Hex Precision.' The officer's voice crackles through everyone's radio simultaneously. 'Chris Morley didn't turn up to work today. His housemate works here too – says he didn't come home last night.'

Lauren is about to ask for an update from the arrest team at Ellis's home address when they call it in.

'No sign of occupancy, ma'am.'

'Shit,' Fraser says, his face echoing how Lauren's feeling. Sure, Bishop could have been taking his suitcases on holiday, but the timing's a hell of coincidence. First Ellis, now Bishop and Morley.

Someone's tipped them off.

CHAPTER 48

The door to Lauren's office is shut, the sign flipped to *In a meeting – do not disturb*. She's aware of constant movement in the corridor on the other side of the opaque glass, and the hum of conversation as more officers arrive to swell the investigation team.

Lauren stays where she is. She doesn't often feel as though there's no hope, but right now she's struggling to see how they can pull things together in time to stop whatever New Dawn are planning. Counter-terrorism say they're *making progress* on identifying the target for the explosives attack, but DI Stratman's set jaw had suggested the word 'progress' was an optimistic choice. In the meantime, all-ports warnings have been issued for Bishop, Ellis and Morley, and warrants obtained to search their abruptly abandoned properties.

Lauren goes back over the investigation from the beginning. She thinks about her first meeting with Nadeeka, and the investigation plan drafted at the kitchen table that evening. What has she missed? She takes out a sheet of blank paper and draws a timeline, starting long before the murder. When had Jamie first encountered New Dawn? In the first week of November, he'd gone to Beech Street police station to report the racially aggravated assault, so it must have been before then. Lauren makes a mark on her timeline.

It had been around that time that Jamie had begun telling Nadeeka he had to work late, or that he was staying to have a drink with colleagues. Nadeeka had been delighted he'd been making friends, but they know now that Jamie had been infiltrating New Dawn. She pulls up the messages retrieved from Nadeeka's phone's cloud account and marks the dates of each one on her timeline. The first message Jamie had sent about being late is dated October 29th.

Bus was cancelled, so having a quick drink with someone from work xx

Lauren looks at it intently, as though another layer might reveal itself if she just stares hard enough. Had Jamie really gone for a drink that night, or had he already been embroiled in New Dawn's activities by then? None of Jamie's colleagues has admitted to meeting him outside of work, so either it was a cover story, or one of them is lying.

She brings up Google Maps and finds ATP Construction. Nadeeka said Jamie used to get the 806 bus home from work, and it's a matter of minutes before Lauren finds the most likely bus stop, a few hundred metres from ATP. On the opposite side of the road, the map shows an orange tankard topped with frothy beer. She clicks on the icon to see the name, then she closes her laptop and puts on her coat.

Lauren is disappointed to discover there's no function room at the Two Princes.

'We don't even do bar snacks,' the landlord says, 'unless you count pork scratchings. We're just your basic pub.'

Lauren is just thinking that she's had a wasted trip – with no private room available, New Dawn won't have held meetings here – when she spots the CCTV above the bar. That settles it: New Dawn *definitely* won't have met here. She indicates the camera. 'Does that work?'

'Too bloody right it does. Not that it stops the bar staff from sticking their fingers in the till. They must think I'm stupid.'

'How long do you keep the footage for?'

'It records over itself every ninety days.'

Lauren smiles. 'I'd like to see October 29th, please.'

The camera is focused on the till, the small row of optics, and the section of bar where customers order drinks. It doesn't take long for Lauren to spot Jamie, ordering a solitary pint and taking a sip before carrying it away. It's frustrating that there are no cameras away from the bar, and Lauren asks the landlord to fast-forward, wondering if Jamie stayed for a second drink.

'Stop!' Her hand shoots out, even though it's the landlord who has the controls. 'Back up a bit. There!'

He pauses the footage. On the screen, a woman is tapping her card to pay for a round of drinks. 'I'm no detective, love, but that's not the bloke you were just looking at.'

Lauren knows this woman. But from where? 'Can you play it in slow motion?' She thinks perhaps it's the receptionist from Foxleigh Manor – she has the same style, at least – or is she just one of those girl-next-door women who always seem familiar? The landlord moves the footage forward frame by frame, and the woman gathers three pints in her hands with a practised air. Her blonde hair is styled in loose curls that fall either side of her navy blazer. She's too old to be the receptionist, Lauren realizes, but she's certain she knows—

And then the woman laughs, showing a surprising number of teeth, and Lauren recalls her instantly. *Carrie Finder.*

The boss appreciates you working out of hours . . . You've proved yourself to be a real team player.

It's Not What You Think

Carrie had told them she hadn't socialized with Jamie; that Jamie, in fact, had been positively *anti*-social. Seems rather a coincidence, then, Lauren thinks, that they should find themselves in the same pub at the same time . . .

Lauren heads back to the nick, where she asks for intelligence checks on Carrie Finder. Fraser's a good judge of character, but Lauren's certain Carrie hasn't given them the full story. Had she had a crush on Golding? Or was there something more sinister at play?

There's nothing on the system – no convictions, no stop-checks or cautions – and no obvious open-source intel that might hint at her political affiliations.

'She did briefly add an anti-vax banner to her Facebook page,' says the intel officer, clicking through Carrie's profile pictures.

'So did my cousin,' Lauren says. 'I don't think that's necessarily an indicator of far-right extremism. Does she have a car?' She waits while the intel officer runs a DVLA check.

'Yep, a red Fiat 500.'

'Can you run the index number through ANPR and see if—' Lauren stops short. The woman who bought the burner phone at Sainsbury's got into a red Fiat 500. Lauren needs to see that CCTV image.

Matt airdrops the still to Lauren's phone and watches as she scrutinizes it. It's a terrible image – no wonder the shoplifting figures at Sainsbury's are through the roof – but Lauren knows within seconds who she's looking at. If she'd seen this first – before her memory was jogged by the footage at the Two Princes – she might not have recognized the wavy-haired woman behind the wheel of the Fiat, but now she's in no doubt. Carrie Finder bought a burner phone with the same cloned card used to secure the village hall for a meeting of New Dawn.

'Who's the woman?' Fraser says, just as Lauren's swiping the image from her phone. She's about to tell him what she's uncovered when she sees Matt waiting too, and she can't shake the prickle of uncertainty that's followed her since Fraser cast doubts over his integrity. Could it have been Matt who tipped off Bishop and the others? Lauren can't take the risk of losing Carrie Finder too.

'No idea,' she says shortly.

Instead, she takes the information to the CTU, where, with a detachment that belies her churning insides, tells DI Stratman she no longer trusts her team enough to let them in on all aspects of the investigation.

He raises an eyebrow. 'I'm surprised; I assumed you ran a tight ship there.'

'I do.' Lauren battles to keep the indignation from her voice. 'But briefings are attended by representatives from several specialisms, and we have numerous officers on loan from other departments.'

'You don't suspect any one individual, then?'

There's a beat.

'No.'

Stratman's eyes narrow briefly, then he nods. 'Well, I appreciate you coming to us. I'll run it by the boss, of course, but I think it's best if we take control of the investigation in its entirety now.' He pauses. 'I seem to remember that was our recommendation after New Dawn's involvement had been confirmed.'

Lauren doesn't rise to the bait. 'Has anything been found at Bishop's house?'

'The searches are still ongoing,' Stratman says. 'The Home Secretary has authorized an intercept on calls coming into his contracted phone, so we'll see what that turns up.'

'And the planned attack? Craig Whitfield's source says it's happening this weekend – has there been any more intelligence on what the target is?'

Stratman doesn't say anything for a few seconds, then he gives her a polite smile. 'We're making progress. I'll let DC Whitfield know he can pass any updates directly to me from now on. Ma'am,' he adds, only just the right side of respectful.

Slowly, Lauren stands up. He's dismissing her. And although she knew this was the most likely outcome, it still smarts.

'How come they're taking over now?' Fraser asks, when they're on their way home. 'I thought you'd had the dick-swinging contest on that one already.'

'I don't know.' Lauren looks out of the window so he can't see her face. She doesn't like keeping things from him, but that had been part of the deal when she'd taken the DCI job; sometimes she would be privy to information she couldn't share with him. 'I guess whatever intel they've got has raised the threat level.'

'Stratman probably went crying to the boss.'

'Maybe.' She circles her neck, trying to ease the stiffness.

'Why don't you have a bath when we get home?' Fraser glances at her. 'And don't say you haven't got time.'

Sometimes Lauren thinks Fraser knows her better than she knows herself.

'Glass of wine, *Love Island* repeats, some of that pink glittery shit your mum gave you for your birthday . . .'

'Pink glittery shit?' She laughs. 'I'm sold.'

'I'll even run it for you. I know just how you like it.' He leaves a beat. 'Hot and deep, just like your men.'

'Fraser Hogan!' Lauren laughs so hard she can't stop for the rest of the way home.

True to his word, Fraser runs the hot water until the room fills with steam, and pink-tinged foam kisses the top of the tub. He puts a glass of wine and her iPad on the bamboo bath tray, and a fresh towel on the heated radiator. He even lights the Diptyque candle Lauren had decided was too expensive to ever use.

'Enjoy.' He kisses her. 'I'm going for a run.'

Lauren closes the door to trap in the steam, then steps into her gaudy bubbles. The water's so hot she has to hop from foot to foot until the temperature is bearable, before lowering herself slowly beneath the surface. She lets out a long, satisfied groan. Perfect.

At first she thinks she'll lie in silence, but her head is too full of Mike Bishop and counter-terrorism and Nadeeka's mistrust, and Lauren knows she won't relax without something to drown out the noise. She logs on to Netflix and half-watches *Emily in Paris*. She's midway through the second episode when she feels a vibration in the pipes beneath the bath. Lauren pauses the show. The vibration comes again – a tiny tremor travelling through the bottom of the bathtub – and she swears under her breath. She knows exactly what this is. The plumbing in their house is old and should really be replaced; last year the pipes in the separate ensuite shower room made a similar noise just before one of them burst, flooding downstairs and causing a stain on the kitchen ceiling she can still see despite several coats of paint.

Lauren hauls herself out of the bath and wraps herself in her towel. Still dripping wet, she kneels on the tiles and prises off the bath panel. She braces herself for the sight of water, but the tiles beneath the tub are dry and she's just about to put the panel back when she sees something tucked in the corner. She reaches for it.

It's a small black phone.

Lauren sits back on her heels and stares at it. It isn't hers, which means it must be Fraser's, and there's only one reason why a man in a committed relationship would want to hide a mobile phone. Lauren feels suddenly light-headed. They're getting married in less than a fortnight. Is Fraser having *an affair*?

Just as her head starts to reel with unanswered questions, the phone vibrates again, the screen lighting up with a message.

All ready for Christmas?

Christmas? Her mind spirals – a mistress? A second family? – but then Lauren sees the sender's name and suddenly she can't breathe. She drops the phone as if she's been scalded, and it skitters across the tiles.

Mike Bishop.

Lauren presses her palm to her heart, her breath coming in ragged gasps. A wave of nausea threatens to overwhelm her. Just then, there's a knock at the bathroom door and she claps a hand to her mouth, suppressing a yelp.

'Is there any hot water left?' Fraser calls through the door. 'I just *bossed* that canal segment we did a couple of weeks ago.'

'Sh-should be,' Lauren manages, her voice unnaturally high.

'Cool, I'll hop in the shower, then make a start on dinner.'

She hears his footsteps move away from the bathroom, and she draws her knees up to her chest, her eyes still fixed on the phone on the floor.

What the hell is she going to do?

PART SIX

CHAPTER 49

FRASER

Fraser had been nineteen when he'd joined the army. He'd been a plumbing apprentice working for his dad at the time, seduced by an advert which promised better pay, free accommodation and good promotion prospects. Fraser's mum had cried for ten days straight.

'She's frightened of losing you, son. She'll come round.' Fraser's dad might have been frightened too, but he hadn't been the type to admit it. Real men kept their feelings to themselves and besides, he was bursting with pride. 'Serving Queen and country,' he would tell his mates down the pub. 'No greater honour.'

In the weeks between signing up and starting his training, Fraser had occasionally thought about the risk of taking a bullet, or of stepping on a landmine and being blown to smithereens. But the concept had felt unreal, and he had focused instead on training hard in the gym, as though muscle alone would stop the shrapnel.

He'd been a good soldier. A team player with sound judgement and good instincts. Calm in a crisis. He'd done a tour in Afghanistan, then a second. A third in Iraq. A few years on German barracks. The first time he'd shot someone he'd thought he might throw up, and the green tinge on his comrades' faces suggested he wasn't the only one. But several hours later they had learned that two of their regiment had been killed in the same conflict, and Fraser's nausea had given way to anger. It had been this anger which had sustained him throughout the remainder of his service; from that point, Fraser had fought not only for Queen and country, but for his fellow soldiers. His fallen brothers.

A knee injury had put paid to his future in the army, and he'd been unceremoniously spat back out into society. There had been a certain cachet to being a serving officer, but now he was a civvy again, no one had seemed to care. There had been no 'thank you for your service' in Britain, the way Fraser saw veterans being commended in America. In fact, outside Remembrance Day, no one in the UK seemed to give a shit about soldiers at all. No one seemed to give a shit about their *country*.

I met a lad today didn't even know the national anthem, Fraser once posted in a Facebook group he'd joined for ex-military. The responses had come thick and fast.

This country's going to the dogs.

The snowflake generation wouldn't last five minutes in the forces.

Did you see that message Coventry City Council just put out? Happy 'festive season'. Not a mention of Christmas anywhere!

Many of the group's members had been struggling to find work. Several had PTSD; others had few transferable skills. They had shared their experiences online, taking the collective frustrations of the group personally.

'A mate of mine went for a security job last week,' Fraser had told his dad. The lads he chatted with online felt more like mates than anyone he saw down the pub. 'Lost out to some Albanian. Almost twenty years in the army and he's having to put in for benefits. How's that fair?'

It's Not What You Think

'It's a shocking state of affairs, son, but I can't say I'm surprised. You read about it all the time.' Fraser's dad indicated the tabloid newspaper he had bought every day for as long as Fraser could remember. 'There's you struggling to find somewhere to rent – and don't get me wrong, you can stay here as long as you need to – while the government give five-bedroom houses to any Tom, Dick or Mustafa.'

It had been Fraser's mum who suggested he join the police. The pay was good, she'd said, and he could transfer his pension. It would give him a sense of identity again.

Fraser had felt at home right away. The uniform had helped, as had the camaraderie he hadn't realized he'd been missing so much. There had been the usual political correctness to cope with, but he had soon got to know who he could trust to banter with, and who was liable to go crying to the guv'nor.

He had discovered New Dawn just over eighteen months ago, through an intelligence briefing at work. *A right-wing organization gaining ground in the UK*, the memo had said. *Members state they are on a 'crusade against wokeism and the left'*.

'Sounds all right to me.' Fraser had grinned, and there had been a few laughs around the table before the DS had raised a warning eyebrow to nip the joking in the bud. Later, Fraser had looked up New Dawn. The organization had been in its infancy, but Fraser had felt an immediate kinship with its patriotic values. He might have left it there, but then the UK had brought in a Labour government, and Fraser had joined New Dawn in protest. There hadn't been a local chapter, but head office had offered support if Fraser wanted to set one up.

And now here they are. A fully fledged chapter of New Dawn. They haven't yet made the impact Fraser would like, but that's all going to change. He tips back his head and smiles, letting the hot shower cascade down his face. The day after tomorrow, everyone will know what New Dawn stands for.

CHAPTER 50

LAUREN

This cannot be happening.

She's wrong. She has to be wrong.

The phone is . . . Lauren flails for a possible explanation . . . the phone is to contact a lover, and how absurd that what would ten minutes ago have been the end of the world is now a best-case scenario, but God, please let it be a lover. Let Fraser be cheating on her. Let him be a bigamist with seven children and a wife who wants to know everything's ready for Christmas. Let it be anything but what's staring her in the face.

Fraser is part of New Dawn.

Shock sends her into violent shivers, and she reaches for her towel and pulls it tightly around herself, waves of nausea threatening to overwhelm her. She thinks of Jamie Golding, naively thinking he could bring down New Dawn; thinks of the devastation it's brought to Nadeeka's life. She recalls Fraser's supportive words as Lauren had despaired of solving a murder when the evidence had already been destroyed.

Lauren picks up her own phone. She has an instinctive urge

It's Not What You Think

to call 999. Who should she go to? *DI Stratman? The chief constable? Whitty?* Her thumb floats over the screen.

Can she trust her comms are secure?

The investigation has been sabotaged by leaks and tip-offs which, she realizes now, must have come from Fraser. Mike Bishop, Alan Ellis, Chris Morley, all conveniently out of the way when the police had come knocking.

Sonya? Bahnaz? Kenric? Matt?

Can Lauren trust them? She'd trusted Fraser, and he has betrayed her twice over: once as her sergeant, and again as the man she'd planned to spend the rest of her life with.

Lauren tries to slow her racing heart. She needs to think like a DI, not a jilted bride. If this were a hypothetical situation – an exam question; a scenario on an interview board – what would Lauren do? What would give them the best chance of tracking down the rest of New Dawn? Of identifying the location of this weekend's terrorist attack?

Lauren gets unsteadily to her feet. She knows exactly what she has to do.

She has to say nothing.

CHAPTER 51

FRASER

'Did you fall asleep in the bath?' Fraser says, when Lauren comes downstairs. 'I almost put out a "fear for welfare".'

Lauren would usually be in pyjamas at this time of night, but she's put on grey joggers and an oversized sweatshirt, which means she's half-expecting to be called back to work. She's flushed from her bath, and clutching her phone as if her life depends on it. Always on-call, always working . . . If there's one thing Fraser would change about Lauren, it's her inability to switch off.

'I was watching *Emily in Paris*.'

'Put it on down here if you want.' He offers the remote. 'I stuck the news on, but I'm not watching it.'

Fraser is forever reminding Lauren to relax. He works hard himself, but he keeps his life in carefully separated sections. When he's at work, he's at work; when he's at home, he's with Lauren. And, when he's on New Dawn business, he's one hundred per cent dedicated to the cause. A thrill runs through him at the thought of what they have planned. It's been a long time coming, and the past few weeks have made things very difficult, but Fraser won't be beaten.

Golding's death had been a monumental fuck-up.

Fraser doesn't have an issue with the concept of neutralizing a threat, but it has to be handled in a controlled manner. New Dawn's policies are clear: the order to strike only ever comes from the boss. Yet Carrie and her gormless associates had crashed in and shanked Golding in his own house, of all places. At least in a public place there are ways of explaining away forensic traces, but in someone's home? Way more incriminating.

'You have got to be kidding me,' he'd said, when Carrie had phoned from Golding's house. She'd called Fraser's personal number – strictly reserved for emergencies – and as he'd listened to her halting confession Lauren had looked at him quizzically. *What is it?* she'd mouthed.

'Can you sort it, boss?' In his ear, Carrie had been close to tears, as though it hadn't been her who had fucked things up in the first place.

'I don't exactly have much choice, do I?' He'd ended the call.

'What's happened?' Lauren didn't go in for public displays of affection at work, but she had briefly rubbed his arm. 'Are you okay?'

Fraser had looked her in the eye. 'Don't freak out . . .'

'Why would I freak out?'

'Foxleigh Manor have double-booked the ceremony room.'

'Whaaaat?' Lauren had somehow managed to make the word stretch for several syllables, her voice rising in pitch and volume until it filled the whole office. 'This is a disaster!'

'You said you wouldn't freak out.'

'I said *why* would I freak out? I never said I wouldn't freak out. Our wedding is less than a month away and we no longer have a venue, Fraser. I think I'm allowed to freak out a bit.'

'I'll sort it.' Fraser checked his trouser pockets for his keys. 'Assuming you don't mind me ducking out of work for a bit?'

'Go!' She pushed him towards the door.

Head office blame him for the fuck-up, of course, even though Fraser never would have approved Jamie Golding so quickly if they hadn't been leaning on him to recruit. They'd intimated that other chapters were growing faster; that Fraser's chapter could be given incentives, more funding, if they had more members. The pressure had clouded Fraser's judgement and, besides, he'd trusted Carrie. She was a New Dawn stalwart who had proved herself loyal in numerous ways. She'd been adamant Golding was sound.

'I work with him,' she'd told Fraser. 'He's new in town, doesn't know anyone. We can make him one of us.'

Fraser should have followed his gut. 'I don't like it,' he'd said to Mike. 'It's too fast.'

Mike Bishop was ex-job: a detective inspector in the Met who had left London for a quieter life. Police officers have a sixth sense for their own ilk and the two men had sussed each other out soon after meeting. Fraser had been glad to have someone trustworthy as his deputy; gladder still that Mike had been happy to chair their chapter meetings. Fraser preferred to stay silent, his gaze moving ceaselessly over their congregation, alert for potential rebellion. How had he missed Golding?

'Let's make Golding's initiation a big one,' Mike had suggested. 'Test his mettle.'

Golding had visibly balked when he'd been asked to burn down the Paki shop and Fraser had half-expected him to bail completely. He'd been surprised – and grudgingly impressed – when the force briefing had included an arson with intent to endanger life at Surinder Bhatti's convenience store.

'I reckon he's a good find,' Mike had said. Fraser had concluded the same, until he'd spoken to the detective overseeing the arson investigation and discovered the occupants had been woken by an anonymous phone call shortly before the fire was started, and that the subsequent 999 call had come from the same phone box. Fraser had determined to keep an eye on Golding, but then the bastard had got himself killed, and Fraser had been forced to deploy the Clean Up.

Head office tell you that if you need the Clean Up it's already too late. The protocol had been developed to make crime scenes disappear, obliterating the 'golden hour' so prized by the police. Fraser's sponsor had told him about a pub fight in Norwich, after which a critically injured man had been rushed into a decommissioned ambulance by two convincing paramedics, while New Dawn members flashed police badges and took down particulars. Always handy to know where to find the witnesses you might later need to take care of.

Fraser had had no intention of ever deploying the protocol, but he had nevertheless taken it seriously. He had begun by assigning roles and creating an ops box with everything they'd need. Uniforms, crime scene tape, forensics suits, evidence bags, the vinyl stickers designed to transform a white car into something that would pass for a police vehicle. He'd added a fluorescent jacket he'd found hanging in the locker room to the police-issue shirt and trousers he no longer needed to wear. He'd hesitated before including his stab vest, but he had no intention of returning to uniform, so in it had gone. Fraser had made sure to remove the epaulettes that bore his shoulder number, replacing them with a pair he'd bought online. Finally, and despite the grumbles from Carrie and others, he had run a paper feed exercise to walk the team through several possible scenarios in which they might need to deploy a Clean Up. The same skills that made Fraser one of major crime's best detectives had made him the best possible person to make this murder disappear.

*

When Fraser had returned to the office after setting the Clean Up in motion, Lauren had looked sick with worry. Fraser had smiled reassuringly. 'All sorted. They've told the other couple they'll have to find another venue.'

'Oh, thank God for that! I mean, gutting for the other couple, but great for us. I'm glad they called you and not me – I think I might have lost it.' Lauren had put her arms around his neck, for once not bothering about who might see them, and squeezed him tight. 'I'm a lucky woman, Fraser Hogan.'

'I don't mind watching the news,' Lauren says now.

Fraser pats the sofa next to him. 'Come on, I'll get you a glass of wine.'

'No, I . . . I'm fine.' She's still standing in the doorway. 'I want to keep a clear head.'

'There's nothing more you can do till tomorrow. Try to relax.'

'Actually, I think I might go to bed.' She touches her head lightly. 'Headache. I had the water too hot, I think.' Her smile is faint and fleeting, and Fraser watches her thoughtfully as she goes back upstairs. Lauren's feeling the strain of the investigation, that's for sure, but is there something else?

He waits a while, then he goes upstairs. Their bedroom door is ajar, and Lauren is already asleep, lying on her side, facing the wall. He watches the rise and fall of her breathing for a minute, then he goes to the bathroom. He isn't worried, not really – if Lauren were on to him, he'd know – but nevertheless he's reassured when he quietly removes the bath panel and sees that his burner phone is exactly where it should be.

Being on the investigation team – and in the confidence of the senior investigating officer, no less – had enabled Fraser to ensure the Clean Up had been carried out satisfactorily. He had begun with the house-to-house enquiries.

'I can get uniform to do those,' Lauren had said, but Fraser had insisted.

'I'd rather know it was done properly. No short cuts.'

She'd nodded, and Fraser could tell she was pleased; that there would be a line in his next appraisal that would mention him *going the extra mile*. And so he had trudged from one house to the next, quizzing each of the neighbours to see if they presented a risk. On the whole, the Clean Up had been well executed. Doorcam footage had not only been seized but deleted from the hard drives and, in some cases, the system disabled altogether.

'The picture's been terrible since your boys came round,' an elderly gentleman had said. His son had installed a camera by the front door. Fraser had found a smear of Vaseline across the lens. Nice touch, he'd thought. Good to see New Dawn members with a bit of initiative.

He had wiped away the grease. 'Try it now.'

'Perfect!' The old boy had tried to give Fraser a tenner from a battered biscuit tin stuffed with cash, and Fraser had told him to put his money away and be careful, keeping that amount of money at home. This kind of house – bungalow, vertical blinds, a walking frame parked in the porch – was a distraction burglary waiting to happen.

'I'm going to ask the crime prevention team to pop over and see you, if that's okay? They'll fit a chain on your front door and have a chat with you about how to stay safe.'

'You're a good lad. Thank you.'

'Royal Signals?' Fraser had nodded to a faded photograph on the wall.

The old boy had let go of the banister he'd been holding and straightened. 'Fourteenth Regiment.'

Fraser had shaken his hand. 'Thank you for your service, sir.'

*

The only part of the Clean Up that hadn't gone to plan had been the disposal of Jamie Golding's body. When Fraser had called Danny, the site manager of a disused quarry ideal for making people disappear, he had heard the telltale long ringtone of a foreign network.

'All right, boss?' Dance music had been pumping in the background.

'Where the fuck are you?'

'Tenerife.'

'You didn't say you were going away.'

'Last-minute deal. Since when did I have to ask permission to go on holiday?'

'Since you became part of a Clean Up operation,' Fraser had said, his teeth gritted. Where was the commitment?

'Clean Up?' There had been a moment of silence. 'Shiiiit.'

'Precisely.' Thank God Fraser had had the foresight to build in back-up. 'I'll call Brian.' The two men worked together at the quarry, presenting Fraser with one of the more straightforward job shares on the Clean Up plan.

'Listen, boss—'

But Fraser had hung up. And it wasn't until he'd dialled Brian's number and heard the same long ringtone that he'd realized what Danny had been about to tell him. Brian had gone to fucking Tenerife as well.

It had been Alan who had sorted the body in the end. He had a mate who worked in a funeral parlour who owed Alan a favour. Something about some dodgy content he'd needed expunging from a hard drive.

Fraser hadn't wanted to know the details. 'All I need to know is: will he talk?'

'No, he's good as gold. I'll sort it, boss, I promise. Least I can do, given what's happened.'

Fraser should never have trusted him. Now the Fletcher boys are banged up and singing like canaries, and Golding's body is giving up evidence that should be rotting at the bottom of a flooded quarry.

It's Not What You Think

*

Fraser replaces the bath panel.

Lauren's breathing is deep and even, and he keeps the light off so as not to disturb her. As he brushes his teeth, he reads the neon sticky notes Lauren puts on the mirror in their shower room. *Bridesmaid gifts*, reads one. *Pick up rings!!!* says another.

Fraser feels the twinge of disquiet he always experiences when thinking about their upcoming wedding. His feelings for Lauren haven't changed over the years they've been together, but his work with New Dawn has become so important that it has filled much of the space previously occupied by her. It must be a little like working in the church, he sometimes thinks: devotion to one's faith ultimately trumps real-life relationships.

Soon after Lauren and Fraser had met, they had concluded that, where politics were concerned, they would have to agree to disagree. Lauren hadn't seemed fazed by the political gulf between them. She had grown up with parents who regularly argued about the perceived evils of Tony Blair versus William Hague, but who had loved each other dearly and had never gone to bed on an argument.

'Sorry about Dad,' Lauren had said after Fraser had met her parents for the first time.

'I thought he was great.'

Lauren had turned to him in horror. 'He likes Nigel Farage!'

'Exactly.' Fraser had laughed, and Lauren had too, and they'd gone back to Lauren's flat and shared a bottle of wine and uncomplicated sex. Over the years, whenever conversation drifted to immigration, or food banks, or matters of tax, Lauren and Fraser have changed the subject. *Let's agree to disagree*, one of them would remind the other, and soon neither of them could have said exactly how far apart their political leanings had drifted.

Fraser taps his toothbrush against the side of the basin and turns out the bathroom light. He and Lauren got engaged two years ago, before Fraser discovered New Dawn; and the wedding has since become an inevitability he couldn't stop even if he wanted to. And he doesn't. Lauren is clever, funny and gorgeous. In a perfect world her views would align more closely with his own, but as women go she's what his mum would call a *keeper*.

Which is why she can never find out about the work Fraser does for New Dawn.

He slides into bed and spoons around her, slipping an arm over Lauren's waist and resting it across her soft breasts. She tenses in her sleep, her breath hitching.

'Shhh,' he murmurs. 'It's okay.' He pulls her into him.

He needs to be careful. Not only to safeguard the important work they have yet to do, but to protect Lauren herself. Because, however unpalatable a thought it is, Fraser understands the assignment. If Lauren ever finds out about his work for New Dawn, Fraser will have no choice but to silence her.

CHAPTER 52

LAUREN

Lauren has to press her lips tightly together to stop herself from screaming. The man wrapped around her is a stranger – a monster – and yet it's also Fraser. The man she loves.

The man she *loved*.

She lies unblinking in the darkness, listening to Fraser's breathing.

He's still awake.

She wants to run. But she won't. Because Fraser has information they need.

Could we put him under surveillance? Fraser had suggested, when Lauren had wanted to bring in Alan Ellis. *If we follow him . . . he could lead us straight to the others.*

How ironic, Lauren thinks, for Fraser to now fall victim to his own advice.

She feels his breath on the back of her neck and forces herself to lie still. All she has to do is survive the next few hours, then the tables will turn. The hunter will become the prey.

CHAPTER 53

NADEEKA

Nadeeka's alarm went off half an hour ago, but she is still in bed, staring blankly at the ceiling, unable to move. She has been running on adrenaline; focusing on the girls, on work, on simply putting one foot in front of the other. Grief is more easily managed in motion. When Lauren had accused Jamie of being an extremist, Nadeeka had channelled her grief into anger, and it had fuelled her search for the truth.

But now?

Now the anger has burned itself out.

She has woken to an emptiness deep inside her; to a pain in her chest that feels as though something is pressing her on to the bed. Tears squeeze from the corners of her eyes and soak into her crumpled pillow. Jamie's gone. For a few brief months Nadeeka had been given a second chance of happiness, only for it to be cruelly snatched away.

'Mum!' Nadeeka's door opens, and she hastily wipes her eyes. 'Nish said I smell.' Maya looks at her mother curiously. 'Are you ill?'

'Yes.' Maybe she is. She *feels* ill. Her head aches. Her *heart* aches. 'Can you ask Dad to take you to rehearsal?'

It's Not What You Think

'He's not here.'

'What?'

'I heard your alarm, so me and Nish got up, but Dad's not here.'

That gets her up.

On Wednesday morning, Scott had left his bedding in a heap in the lounge. Nadeeka had folded it neatly and put it in the big blue IKEA bag behind the sofa, knotting the long straps to keep everything tidy and feeling like an idiot for playing housekeeper to a man who hasn't been her husband in years. That evening, he had told Nadeeka he had some *business to take care of*, and had still been out when Nadeeka had gone to bed. The following morning, she'd found his bedding folded in the IKEA bag, and naively thought he'd taken the hint.

He'd gone out last night, too, and now Nadeeka checks the bag and finds everything is exactly the way she'd left it. Scott hasn't slept here for two nights. She wonders wryly whether the *business* he'd taken care of was blonde or brunette, and feels a flash of anger. Not for Scott's nocturnal activities – his wandering eye is thankfully no longer her problem – but because he's supposed to be here to protect them.

Nadeeka tosses the bag back down. Well, he can bloody well move back in with Kath, or Gabriela, or whichever other woman is stupid enough to give him a free meal ticket. She doesn't need looking after.

She's on her own now.

Lauren will tell her she's not, of course. Lauren will say the police are just a 999 call away; that they're *this close* to a breakthrough and that, soon, the people who killed Jamie will be safely behind bars.

But what does Lauren know?

She'd been wrong about Jamie. She'd been wrong about the events leading up to his death. Lauren wouldn't know danger if it was staring her in the face.

CHAPTER 54

LAUREN

It's still dark when Lauren slips out of bed. Fraser is lying on his stomach, face in his pillow and one arm dangling off the edge. Lauren splashes water on her face and brushes her hair, but doesn't shower or bother with make-up. Her heart is pounding.

She's almost dressed when he stirs.

'What time is it?'

Lauren forces herself to speak normally, even though her heart is racing fit to burst. 'Not yet six. I'm going to head in early.'

'How come?' His voice is sticky with sleep.

Lauren pulls a sweater over her shirt. 'Meetings.'

Fraser pushes himself up on his elbows. 'Give me half an hour.' He yawns cavernously, distorting the words that follow. 'I'll come wi—'

'No need.' She's halfway out already. 'I'll see you at briefing,' she calls, and it's all she can do not to run from the house.

*

It's Not What You Think

When the chief constable arrives at work, Lauren is sitting at his PA's desk.

'How's your typing speed?' he says, chuckling, then he takes in Lauren's expression. 'Ah. Looks like we need coffee for this one.'

'I've asked counter-terrorism to meet me here,' Lauren says. 'And DC Whitfield from source management.'

'We definitely need coffee.' The chief flicks on the machine just as the *ping* of the lift announces the arrival of Whitty and DI Stratman.

When Lauren finishes speaking, the silence it leaves is so loud it feels like physical pressure.

'*All ready for Christmas . . .*' The chief looks at Whitty. 'Is there intelligence to suggest New Dawn might carry out activity on Christmas Day?'

'Not that we're aware of, sir.'

'We plan to bring in Carrie Finder this morning,' Stratman says. 'She might give us something.' He turns to Lauren. 'How long has Fraser been in the job?'

'Ten years,' Lauren says. 'He was in the army before that.'

'Has he ever given any indication of harbouring extremist views?'

Lauren's chest tightens. 'With respect, I wouldn't have been with him if he had.' She takes a deep breath. 'We don't often talk about current affairs. We've always been at opposite ends of the political spectrum, although – ' she shakes her head ' – not to this extent. I had no idea.' She digs her nails into the flesh of her palms.

'How long have you been together?' Whitty asks.

'Over four years. We're getting—' Lauren takes a steadying breath. 'We were due to get married the day after Christmas.'

It's clear no one knows quite what to say or where to look. From the PA's office, Lauren hears a computer being booted up.

'The phone's still under the bath,' she says. 'I didn't dare take it out before I left the house today in case he checked it this morning.' She feels oddly detached, as though she's watching from the sidelines. Thinking of Fraser as a suspect, not a fiancé, is the only way she will be able to get through this.

Stratman leans forward. 'You must be feeling so—'

'I assumed you'd want to put him under surveillance,' Lauren says crisply. *Don't be nice to me*, she thinks. *If you're nice to me, I'll cry.* 'We have less than twenty-four hours before New Dawn's planned attack, and we still don't know where their target is.'

Stratman meets her gaze. He gives an almost imperceptible nod. *Understood.* 'We'll get a team on him, and we'll ask for Home Secretary authority to intercept his phone calls.' He hesitates. 'It means you'll have to carry on today as if nothing has happened. Can you handle that?'

'Of course.' Lauren's attempt at a businesslike tone is only partly successful. 'At work, though, right? I can't—' Her voice cracks. 'I can't go home with him.'

'Don't worry about that,' the chief says grimly. 'Fraser Hogan won't be going home. Not for a very long time.'

CHAPTER 55

FRASER

Fraser feels tense. Three key team members – Mike, Alan, Chris – are now having to lie low, leaving Fraser to execute tomorrow's operation alone. Now that CTU have taken ownership of the murder investigation, Fraser no longer has access to the HOLMES file, so he can't see if other persons of interest have been identified. Should he bring in Carrie, or steer clear of her?

Before he leaves for work, he retrieves his burner phone from behind the bath panel and sends a quick reply to Mike's question about Christmas. *A few more presents to wrap*, Fraser types. *Shame you can't celebrate with us, but best to stay out of the way for now. Remember: no airports.* He sends the same reminder to Alan and Chris – the passport details of all three men have been widely circulated – then replaces the phone and clips the panel back into place.

On the way to work, Fraser goes over the plan for tomorrow. He had planned to be in the company of other police officers when the explosives were being laid – the ultimate alibi – but that won't happen now. He tells himself it's because it's too late to brief other members of New Dawn, but the truth is simpler.

Fraser wants to *be* there.

Being on scene is a risk, but Fraser's appetite for risk increases daily. He is consumed by New Dawn – by the righteousness of the cause – and it is slowly crowding out everything else. When he's on New Dawn business, he feels powerful. Invincible. No one can stop him.

At the station, Craig Whitfield is in the yard, cigarette in hand. He looks as though he's slept in his clothes and Fraser wonders whether the vibe is intentional, or if the guy just doesn't give a shit. 'All right?' Fraser says.

'Can't complain.' Smoke curls from Whitty's nostrils as he speaks.

'Anything fresh on New Dawn?' Fraser keeps his voice casual.

'I can't tell you that, mate.'

Mate. Was there an edge to that, or is Fraser imagining it?

'Course not. Sorry. Shouldn't even have asked.' He nods towards the nick. 'Lauren's pissed CTU have taken over.'

Whitty shrugs. 'That's the way it goes sometimes.' He draws on the cigarette. 'You guys are getting married, right?'

'Day after Christmas.'

'Rather you than me.'

'You not married?'

'Divorced.' Whitty flicks his cigarette end over the wall and walks off. 'Enjoy your final days as a free man.'

Fraser watches him leave, eyes narrowing. Something's off. Whitty can't *know* – if he knew, he'd arrest him – but does he suspect? Has one of his sources been talking? Fraser's always been careful not to use his real name, but a few members of the chapter know he's a copper. Carrie included.

Has Carrie been nicked?

It's Not What You Think

Fraser's pulse picks up. If they've got Carrie, he's in trouble. She's not good under pressure; it'll be obvious she's lying. She could tell them everything and all Fraser's hard work will have been in vain.

He steadies his breathing. Makes a decision. Too much can go wrong in twenty-four hours. If he waits until tomorrow to carry out the operation, he risks losing it all.

They'll go early.

They'll go today.

CHAPTER 56

LAUREN

Lauren enters the secure log-in on her laptop, granting her access to DI Stratman's interview with Carrie Finder. In the interview room, a light on the machine will illuminate to indicate the interview is being monitored. Lauren feels a pinch of resentment at not being there in person, even though this is about far more than departmental jurisdiction now. Lauren can no longer be objective about this case, not now Fraser's involved.

He had come to morning briefing, casually knotting his tie as he'd sat down, and triggering in Lauren a peculiar mix of fear and longing. She hadn't been able to make eye contact with him, and she'd rattled at breakneck speed through the sanitized update she'd agreed with counter-terrorism, before excusing herself to catch up with emails.

Fraser had caught her at the door. 'Everything okay?'

'Fine. Fine. I'd better . . .' Lauren had gestured vaguely towards her office, her heart hammering. She has no talent for deception, unlike Fraser. How long has he been lying to her? A year? Two? Since the beginning?

It's Not What You Think

On Lauren's laptop screen, Carrie Finder looks pale and anxious. She sits with her hands pressed under her knees like a child, her eyes fixed on the scratched Formica table.

She had been arrested as she'd arrived at work this morning, two plain-clothes officers swooping in and redirecting her to their car. In her jade-green silk blouse and wide trousers, she looks more like a solicitor than a criminal.

'How long have you known Alan Ellis?' DI Stratman asks her.

'No comment.' Carrie's so quiet Lauren has to turn up the volume on her headphones.

'How about Chris Morley?'

'No comment.'

'Mike Bishop?'

'No comment.'

DI Stratman leans in. 'Does the name Fraser Hogan mean anything to you?'

The door to Lauren's office opens. She startles. She's already on edge, and when she sees Fraser standing in the doorway it takes everything she has not to cry out.

He holds up a mug. 'Thought you could use a coffee.'

In Lauren's ear, Stratman repeats his question.

'No comment.'

'You sure about that?' Stratman says, and now Fraser's at her desk, putting down the coffee and leaning down to see what Lauren's watching, and her face floods with heat. *Fraser Hogan*, she hears through her headphones, and he's so close – can he hear it too? Can he read Stratman's lips?

'No comment,' Carrie says.

Fraser rests a hand on Lauren's back. Her hair is swept up in a clip, exposing the skin at the nape of her neck, and as his thumb strokes the base of her skull Lauren freezes. Her terrified face appears, ghostlike, in her laptop screen, and for a sickening moment she catches Fraser's reflection too and thinks he's seen her fear.

He leans forward. 'Isn't that Carrie Finder?'

Lauren breathes out. He's looking at Carrie, not her. Still, she forces her face to relax. Fraser's thumb presses harder, working at the tension either side of her spine. Pressure climbs in Lauren's chest.

'How come she's been brought in?' he asks.

'DI Stratman wasn't happy with the account she gave you.' She stands, because Fraser suddenly seems so much taller than her, so much stronger. He looks rattled, an ugly flush creeping from beneath his collar. He's still staring at Carrie, and Lauren reaches to close the laptop. Her pulse surges, loud and insistent. *Say something, Lauren! He'll know something's up if you don't speak* . . . 'CTU think she's a member of New Dawn.'

'No way.' A vein flickers at the corner of Fraser's left eye. 'She seemed so normal.'

'They walk among us.' Lauren's voice sounds weak.

'I'd love to listen in.' Fraser reaches towards her laptop, but Lauren puts a hand on the lid.

'Sorry. Strict orders from CTU.'

'Oh, come on – who's going to know?'

'It's against regulations.'

'*It's against regulations* . . .' Fraser grins to take the sting out of his mimicry, but there's a hardness beneath it that sends a shiver down Lauren's spine.

She takes a step back. 'Could you take a look at a job that shift have flagged? Currently a GBH with intent, but the victim's taken a turn for the worse and it might be coming our way.'

'Sure.' He doesn't move. Just watches her with such intensity she's convinced he's trying to see inside her head. 'Although . . .' He sighs. 'I didn't want to tell you this until it was sorted, but Foxleigh Manor just called.'

For a second, Lauren's stress levels soar – *can nothing go right with this bloody wedding?* – then she realizes with an almost laughable lurch that there isn't going to *be* a wedding.

It's Not What You Think

She rearranges her face into a plausible mask of concern. 'What's happened now?'

'The couple they double-booked are kicking off. They've got an email chain that shows they made the reservation first. But I'm sorting it,' Fraser adds quickly, as if Lauren cares, as if any of this matters. 'This is precisely why I checked out a back-up venue. I'm going there now to confirm timings.' He presses a kiss to Lauren's forehead, and her fingernails carve crescents in the pads of her palms. 'Don't worry.'

It takes a full minute after he's gone for Lauren to stop shaking. Her mobile rings and she looks at the screen.

Nadeeka Prasanna.

'Hi.' Lauren's voice is wobbly, as though she hasn't used it for a while.

'I had a call from DI Stratman,' Nadeeka says. 'He said I'm getting a new family liaison officer.'

'Yes. I'm sorry. I've been . . .' Lauren hesitates. 'Reallocated.'

'I wanted to check it was all above board. You know – that he was . . . real.' She gives a sheepish laugh.

'He's real.' Lauren feels suddenly overwhelmed by the devastation of discovering who Fraser really is. It must have been like this for Nadeeka, she thinks, when she discovered DI Burton wasn't a police officer; and when Lauren told her Jamie had been working with New Dawn. 'I'm sorry,' she says again. So insignificant, after everything that's happened.

'Not long till your wedding, is it?'

Lauren closes her eyes. The irony of Nadeeka's attempts to change the subject to territory she imagines is more comfortable . . . 'No.' She swallows. 'Not long.'

'If you need any last-minute alterations on your dress . . . I'm not a bad seamstress, as long as you want to be a drone or a library book.' Nadeeka laughs.

'When's the big performance?' Lauren feels more in control now, the anodyne small talk oddly soothing.

'Tomorrow afternoon. Kath's getting there early to bag us seats in the front row. I've got something on at work in the morning.'

A burst of music drowns out Nadeeka's words for a couple of seconds, until someone turns it down. A Christmas carol, Lauren thinks, although she can't place which one. 'Do you usually work on a Saturday?'

'I'm running a recruitment fair at work. Setting up now and we open the doors this afternoon. Back tomorrow morning. The CEO wants to push our family credentials, so we've got music, a magician, even a Santa.'

'Sounds great.' Something hovers at the edge of Lauren's thoughts, unease building slowly but forcefully. On the phone, Nadeeka is calling to someone, her voice muffled as she moves the phone from her ear. *No, the tree can't go there, there's no socket for the fairy lights . . .*

Lauren's thoughts snap into focus. 'Nadeeka—' she starts, but the music has started again and now someone is talking to Nadeeka in insistent, broken English.

'Sorry,' Nadeeka says. 'I have to go.'

'Wait!' Lauren needs more information; needs to confirm what she thinks is right. But Nadeeka has gone, and when Lauren rings back, the call goes unanswered.

Lauren steadies herself on her desk.

It's going to be a fucking bloodbath, Whitty had said.

And now Lauren knows where.

CHAPTER 57

NADEEKA

'Why have we even *got* a Christmas tree?' Nadeeka's colleague Elaine looks up from a tangle of fairy lights. 'Isn't it a bit . . . you know, culturally inappropriate? At least half our staff are Muslim.'

'Instructions from the CEO.' Nadeeka holds up her hands. 'Ours not to reason why . . . Right, I think we're almost there.' The large hall has been cleared to accommodate the tables set around the perimeter, one for each of the 'opportunity paths' they have identified. Nadeeka checks each one off on her list. *Pickers and packers, forklift drivers, returns, inventory, transport, dispatch, quality assurance* . . . 'Who's sorting the outside lights?'

'Valmir Daka.' Elaine names an Albanian man who works on the maintenance team. 'His wife works in the warehouse, so they'll have the kids with them.'

'Great.'

Nadeeka's phone buzzes: a message from Scott. *Are you picking the girls up today?*

She sighs. Why don't men remember things? *No*, she replies, *you're bringing them home after the dress rehearsal.*

She surveys the room. Her mind is cluttered with weeks of emails she's sent to local media, the mayor's office, colleges, Job Centres, community groups. In the centre of the room, rows of chairs face the stage where the glossy recruitment video is already playing. A corporate talking head strolls through the warehouse in a box-fresh fluorescent jacket, his smile unfeasibly white.

Elaine clocks it too and rolls her eyes. 'You'd think we worked at bloody Disneyland.' She stands back to admire the fairy lights, now draped around the Christmas tree.

Nadeeka grins. 'It's a bit full-on for minimum wage jobs, isn't it? Come on, let's have a quick cuppa before people start arriving.' After Nadeeka had pitched the idea of a job fair in a meeting six months ago – *part recruitment, part PR*, she'd said – the idea had snowballed, and there have been times when Nadeeka has wished she'd never raised it. But over the past few weeks it's been good to have something to focus on, and now she feels proud of what they've achieved.

She takes a final look at the room as they leave. Display tables, TV screen, rows of chairs . . . *check*. Everything's done.

They're ready to throw open the doors to the public.

CHAPTER 58

FRASER

You can go anywhere with police ID. It's the ultimate access-all-areas pass, Fraser thinks, as he flashes his warrant card to the security officer and follows the signs to the main hall. A man in overalls is sweeping the floor, and Fraser shows his badge again. 'You'll have to finish that later – I need this area cleared.' He suspects the guy doesn't speak English, but the subtext of *fuck off* is universal, and the man takes his broom and makes a sharp exit.

Fraser surveys the stage. The rows of chairs. He smiles – *this is going to be beautiful* – then he gets to work. He doesn't feel like a police officer any more. He feels like a militant; like a vigilante who knows the truth and puts his neck on the line to make sure others know it too. His nerve-endings are on fire, every muscle tense and ready. He opens his rucksack.

They've made twenty of them. Black plastic discs, no wider than a jam jar lid, containing bleach and citric acid in two crudely separated chambers. A layer of tightly packed nails sits above them. Fraser puts a glue dot on the top of the first, and touches it to the underside of a chair, holding it until it takes. His heart hammers against his chest. He mustn't press the device, not even the slightest bit, because that's the trigger. Quick, clean, silent. As soon as someone sits down, the circuit will close.

Bang.

Fraser pictures it like fireworks; a serious of explosions, a soundtrack of screams. The chaos, the fear.

There will be some innocents in this room, he knows that, but he doesn't dwell on those. Fraser's fellow soldiers had been innocent too. The white girls groomed by 'community elders' up in Yorkshire had been innocent. The little kids at the dance class slaughtered by an immigrant had been innocent.

Once Fraser has planted half the devices under chairs, he walks up the steps on to the stage. It's covered with a thin carpet, and he lifts it and places several black discs where they are most likely to be stepped on. Tomorrow would have been better – more footfall, more impact – but Fraser is adaptable. Today will do.

There's a sound from outside: the heavy front door opening as people start to arrive. Fraser steps carefully off the stage. He swings his rucksack on to his shoulder and leaves the hall.

The caretaker is sweeping the corridor. 'You need other rooms?' He gestures to the series of break-out areas either side of the long hallway. The doors are closed, but the cacophony of sound gives away which ones are in use. Shrill, excited voices; the calm hush of accompanying teachers.

'No,' Fraser says. 'I'm done.' He makes for the exit, stopping to let by a cluster of kids holding hands, their coats buttoned up over silver and gold costumes.

'Thanks!' says a woman with sensible shoes and a harassed expression. She's holding a stuffed donkey.

'No problem. I hope the dress rehearsal goes well.'

'Seven schools, two hundred kids and a load of parents who can't make the real thing . . .' The teacher gives an exaggerated grimace. 'What could possibly go wrong?'

It's Not What You Think

Fraser walks on. And as he leaves the Civic Centre and steps into the pale December light, his smile evaporates. All this could have been avoided by upholding British culture, British values. British traditions. But this multi-faith nativity crap? Fraser's expression hardens. These schools have made their choices.

Now they'll live with the consequences.

CHAPTER 59

LAUREN

She finds Stratman as he's leaving the custody block.

'Carrie Finder's taking a meal break.' He glances around, making sure they're alone. 'How are you holding up?' There's genuine compassion in his eyes and for a second Lauren feels untethered. She rarely feels at breaking point and, when she does, it's Fraser she turns to. Her mother doesn't understand the pressures of her work and nor do her friends. Who will Lauren lean on now?

'I'm okay.'

Stratman holds her gaze. 'Really?'

'Well.' Lauren gives a dry laugh. 'No. But it'll soon be over, right?' By tacit agreement, they start walking towards the CTU office. 'I think I've identified New Dawn's target.'

'As have we.' Stratman holds open a door for her. 'Echelon Warehousing is running a job fair today and tomorrow. A local pressure group has stirred up some trouble in relation to the foreign-born workers they employ. We think New Dawn might—'

'It's a school nativity.' Lauren cuts across him. 'Bishop's

message to Fraser – *all ready for Christmas?* He was talking about the nativity. Nadeeka's daughters are performing in one tomorrow.'

'But New Dawn claim their entire *raison d'être* is the preservation of Christian values – why would they target a nativity?'

'Because it's a multi-faith production. Seven primary schools. Every religion is represented.' Lauren thinks of Nadeeka's wry explanation. *The shepherds are buskers, and the wise men are a rabbi, a Buddhist monk and a Hindu priest.*

Stratman stops walking. 'Okay, now I'm on board. Although we intercepted a message from Fraser's personal phone to Mike Bishop this morning which might conflict with your theory. He told Bishop he was *going early on Christmas*. We're taking that to mean today; we've got explosives dogs at Echelon now.'

There's the briefest of moments when Lauren feels relief at being wrong – *thank God it's not the children!* – before it evaporates. *Scott can't make it*, Nadeeka had told her when Lauren had been admiring the girls' costumes, *but he's going to the dress rehearsal the day before*. 'No.' She turns to face Stratman, her words rapid and urgent. 'They're rehearsing today. There are two hundred kids rehearsing right now.'

'Jesus . . . Where?'

Lauren's about to say she doesn't know, but she realizes she does. *I've booked the Civic Centre as a back-up venue*, Fraser had said after Foxleigh Manor had double-booked their wedding. *Had* the Manor double-booked them? Or had Fraser simply been using their wedding as an excuse to conduct New Dawn business on work time?

'The Civic Centre,' she says.

This is precisely why I checked out a back-up venue, Fraser had said, barely an hour ago. *I'm going there now to confirm timings.*

'And I think Fraser's there too.'

CHAPTER 60

NADEEKA

Nadeeka stands in the car park at Echelon Warehousing, her breath frosting in the cold air. She hadn't had time to grab her coat when they'd been unceremoniously evacuated, and she hugs herself for warmth, freezing fingers clamped beneath her armpits. Around her, Echelon employees loiter in clusters, a few taking the opportunity for a cigarette break. At the far end of the car park are three minibuses.

'I hope they don't give up and go home,' Elaine says, nodding to the buses. Vinyls on the side of each one show where their passengers are from. *Glydale Community College, Open Horizons Project, Northern Pathways Youth Hub.*

Nadeeka watches as two officers emerge from the main building, each with a brown and white spaniel. They're joined by Echelon's security manager, Paul, who looks irritated, even from this distance. 'Looks like they're done.' She crosses the tarmac to speak to them.

'. . . better safe than sorry,' the female officer is saying.

'Can we go back inside?' Nadeeka asks. 'We should have opened the doors half an hour ago.'

'We've checked the premises,' the male officer says. 'No sign of any devices.'

'As I said,' Paul cuts in, defensive, 'no one had access to that room except our own staff. We don't let randoms just wander in.'

The female officer tightens her grip on the dog's lead. 'And as *I* said, we had intelligence suggesting a security breach. I'm sure you'd rather be mildly inconvenienced now than have a bomb go off later.'

Paul blusters, but the officers are already walking away, heading to a police van marked with the words *Dogs – Stay back*.

Nadeeka is about to signal to Elaine that they can get going again when her phone rings. Scott. Again. *For heaven's sake!*

'For the hundredth time,' she answers, before he has a chance to speak, 'you're bringing the girls back to mine after—'

'The Civic Centre's being evacuated.' Scott interrupts her. 'We've only been here five minutes.'

'Evacuated?' The revolving doors at reception are causing a bottleneck as everyone tries to get back in the warm. Nadeeka moves out of the way. 'Is it a fire? Are the girls with you?'

'I don't know. There wasn't an alarm. They're keeping the kids in their school groups so they can call the registers. The parents have been told to go straight to the evacuation point.' A siren sounds with sudden clarity and Nadeeka realizes Scott must have left the building now and be out in the street. 'I cancelled a meeting to come to this shitshow,' he mutters.

Nadeeka stands very still as a thought takes hold. 'Are there dogs?' she says.

'Dogs?'

'Police dogs. Are they taking police dogs into the Civic Centre?'

'Um . . . Yeah. There's a guy here with a spaniel.'

Nadeeka's stomach drops. 'It's a bomb threat.' She starts running towards her car. 'They think someone's planted explosives in the Civic Centre.' She's aware of Elaine calling after her, but she doesn't look back. 'Find the girls,' she tells Scott. 'Keep them with you.'

When she reaches the car, she's shaking so much she drops the keys. She takes a series of deep breaths, reminding herself how relaxed the dog-handlers had been. A precautionary search, that's all. *Better safe than sorry.*

The road leading to the Civic Centre has been closed off, yellow diversion signs sending cars around the outskirts of the town. Nadeeka abandons her car in a side street and runs to a police officer directing traffic.

'I need to get to the Civic Centre.' The words come out staccato, a panicked breath between each one. 'My daughters are there.'

'They'll be at the evacuation zone,' the officer says. 'Northfield Gardens. It's about half a mile that w—'

But Nadeeka's already running. She's trying to call Scott again but it's going to voicemail, and her head is full of nightmarish images she can't shake away. Bombs. Smoke. Screams. The roads are busier now, hordes of people streaming from the town centre. Nadeeka ducks to one side as a mother drags two confused boys along with her, eyes fixed determinedly on the pavement ahead. 'Let's get ice-cream!' she tells her sons, as though that were a totally normal activity for a December afternoon. Someone reaches out to Nadeeka – *the town centre's closed off, there's a bomb threat* – but she shakes them off and keeps running.

She has to get to the girls.

They're all she has left.

CHAPTER 61

FRASER

Fraser has been in tight spots before, but this may well be the tightest. As he'd left the Civic Centre earlier, he'd caught the eye of a police community support officer who'd looked away a beat too fast. When the PCSO had reached for his radio, Fraser had ducked back into the Civic Centre, intending to leave by the rear entrance instead. But the back door had been locked, and, as the building filled up with people, Fraser had begun to get twitchy.

Blowing himself up had not been part of the plan.

He was seconds from brazening it out – walking through the corridors as though he belonged there, past the crowds of children in paper crowns and tinsel halos – when the atmosphere had shifted. A sudden hush. Then a clamour of voices. Someone crying.

When Fraser had heard a police radio, he'd realized he was fucked.

Now he's crouched in a cleaning cupboard on the second floor. The silent streets and the strains of sirens tell him the town centre is in lockdown, and, even now, responders could be in the

Civic Centre. Police officers. Bomb disposal experts. A search team.

Fraser clenches his jaw. He will not go down like this. He will not be hauled unceremoniously from a cupboard like some drugged-up scrote. Fraser is a New Dawn hero, a chapter leader, a revolutionary. If he goes down, he goes down fighting.

He eases the cupboard door open. Just a crack. The corridor is empty. He slides out and stands for a moment, listening. Fraser has a plan, of sorts. From scoping the building – on the pretext of booking it as a back-up wedding venue – he knows there's another floor, closed off to the public. From there, a metal spiral staircase leads to the roof. The buildings in this street are packed closely together; 1960s brutalist boxes with flat roofs and service gantries. If Fraser can get to the roof, he can get away.

A noise comes from somewhere close by and he freezes, one hand on the cupboard door. He's concerned about firearms officers, primed to shoot first and ask questions later. If Carrie has talked, counter-terrorism could know everything and could already have positioned snipers on adjacent roofs.

Another sound. A girl's voice, calling out.

Fraser smiles. A sniper needs a clean shot. No obstructions. No innocent victims in the way. He slips back into the shadows and waits. When the girl runs past, he steps out, fast and controlled. He clamps a hand across her mouth.

'Do exactly as I say,' he murmurs softly. 'Or this will end very badly – for both of us.'

CHAPTER 62

LAUREN

Many years ago, as a uniformed sergeant, Lauren chaired a public meeting at the Civic Centre; an experience akin to being pelted with bread rolls for an hour and a half straight. Complaints about littering, dog mess, and children daring to kick balls against residential walls. Complaints about the police helicopter circling at three in the morning, but also – somewhat paradoxically – complaints about never seeing a copper nowadays.

They're seeing a fair few now, Lauren thinks, as she heads for the outer rendezvous point. People are streaming from the buildings on either side of the Civic Centre, PCSOs directing them beyond the outer cordon to the designated safe zones. It's bitterly cold, and many of the office workers are in shirt sleeves or thin jumpers.

The children are still making their way to the evacuation zone. They walk up the pavement in practised pairs, their costumes sparkly and outlandish under hastily buttoned-up coats. She can hear their excited chatter, too, and, although it's misplaced, she's glad they see this as an adventure and not a nightmare.

It's no adventure for the teachers. One of them – a young woman in a Christmas jumper – is crying, brushing her tears away so the children don't see. Another is urging her charges to hurry. An older teacher – more experienced perhaps – is pointing things out as they march briskly away from the Civic Centre. She has the children spot a fire engine; a police car; an ambulance. *Look for the helpers,* Lauren thinks, and she finds herself doing the same; reminding herself that for every bad cop there are a hundred more good ones. The past sixteen hours have been surreal, but standing here now, amid this organized chaos, the truth feels terrifyingly real. Fraser had been willing to kill innocent children in pursuit of New Dawn's ideology.

Blood rushes to her head.

Look for the helpers.

There are many, many helpers. A large white bomb disposal van is parked near the outer cordon, and armed officers in black baseball caps are dotted in pairs around the evacuation zone. In every direction there are fluorescent jackets, and she feels a flash of pride for all her colleagues putting themselves at risk day in, day out.

Lauren keeps her distance. She listens to the back-and-forth on the radio and pushes her hands into her pockets when she's tempted to chip in. When you've spent years leading a specialist department, it's hard not to get involved.

All the time, her eyes seek out Fraser. He'll be here somewhere, she's sure of it. Where else would he be? She wonders if he's watching from a safe distance or hiding out in the Civic Centre, prepared to go down in a blaze of glory.

It's out there now. His name across the airwaves, albeit couched in a narrative designed to minimize gossip and keep focus on the job in hand. *All units, observations please for Detective Sergeant Fraser Hogan. There is concern for his welfare and officers are asked to report sightings but not engage. Repeat, not engage.*

It's Not What You Think

There has been only one sighting: from a PCSO who saw a man he thinks might have been Fraser, leaving the crime scene in the direction of the town centre.

'I can't see him now,' the PCSO had said unhappily, over the radio. 'He might have gone back inside.'

The police Gold Commander had forbidden anyone to enter the site until the bomb disposal team had arrived, instead positioning officers around the perimeter to report on any movement.

Fraser hasn't been seen again. Is he still in the Civic Centre? Lauren shivers. It is surreal to think of an entire police force out hunting one of their own. Fraser is – was – a good detective. He's received commendations, plaudits from members of the public.

There is concern for his welfare.

The careful words will make people believe Fraser has had a breakdown, Lauren supposes, and isn't it a wild world when that would be the better outcome? Not bad, just mad.

In Northfield Park, the children are clustered in their schools, thirty or so children with three or four teachers apiece. There are other adults there too, hugging the kids and each other, and Lauren realizes they must be parents. She wonders if they were all there for the dress rehearsal, or if they'd seen on social media what was happening and dropped everything to be with their kids.

She speaks to the first teacher she comes to. 'Hi, I'm looking for Elmwood Primary?'

'We're from Chestnut Hill, sorry.' The teacher glances at Lauren's radio. 'Are you police? Do you know what's happening?'

Lauren is about to tell her that everything is under control – with thirty little faces looking up at her, it's the only possible answer to give – but she's interrupted by the radio. She makes an apologetic face and moves away, pressing a finger to her earpiece in explanation.

Then she stands stock-still, taking in what she just heard. Praying for it not to be true.

IEDs found under seats and on the stage.
Improvised explosive devices.

Lauren starts shaking. He really had planned to do it. He really had intended to sacrifice the lives of all these little kids. She looks at them all and her teeth start to chatter as though she's stepped into snow. Thank God they evacuated. If one of those devices had detonated before everyone had made it out—

'Lauren!'

She turns to see Nadeeka running towards her, the heels of her office shoes catching on the damp grass.

'Do you know what's happening? They said on the news there'd been a bomb threat.' As she talks, Nadeeka is checking out each cluster of schoolkids, searching for Elmwood Primary. Her gaze falls on the woman in the Christmas jumper. 'That's Mrs Fairfax! Oh, thank God!' She runs towards the group. 'Maya! Nish!'

Lauren follows, scanning the group for Maya's shimmery costume.

'Everyone stay where you are!' The teacher is struggling to be heard over the chatter. She calls to a man with an Elmwood Primary School lanyard. 'I make it twenty-seven.' Several of the children are dressed as books; Lauren spots *Charlie and the Chocolate Factory* and *The Worst Witch*.

'Nads!' It's Scott, striding towards them, eyes skimming the group to find Maya and Nish.

'Have you seen the girls? Are you okay?' Nadeeka fires questions at him, each louder than the last. 'Where have you *been*?'

'The Old Bill held us all at the end of the road for bloody ages. Fucking fascists. I said I needed to find my kids, and the bloke was like, *everyone's trying to find their kids, sir.*'

'Mum!' Nish comes flying towards Nadeeka.

'Oh, thank God.' Nadeeka holds her tight, and as Nadeeka starts crying, Scott puts his arms around them both. Lauren scans the crowd for Maya's drone costume, but the children are hopping about or running to parents, and it's impossible to keep track of which kid is which.

'Where's Maya?' Nadeeka says.

'Count them again,' the male teacher is saying. 'There should be twenty-eight.'

Lauren snaps around to look at the teachers, who are now huddled together over a clipboard.

'There *were* twenty-eight,' Mrs Fairfax says. 'I counted them out as we left the town hall.' She begins ticking off names on her list, eyes flicking up and down as if she's marking a bingo card. Her hands are shaking.

'Mrs Fairfax!' Nadeeka calls out, breathless. 'I can't see Maya.'

The teacher looks up. Her face says it all, and Lauren's heart plummets. *No, no, no . . .*

'Ms Prasanna.' The teacher's voice catches. 'I'm so sorry. Maya isn't here.'

CHAPTER 63

NADEEKA

Nadeeka stares at Mrs Fairfax. The teacher is still talking, but Nadeeka can't hear her over the roaring in her own ears. *Maya isn't here.*

She drops to her knees so fast she almost topples Nish. 'Where's Maya?' Her hands grip Nish's shoulders. 'Where's your sister?' Her voice breaks on the last word. Nish's bottom lip wobbles.

Scott rounds on the teachers. 'Twenty-eight kids in, twenty-eight out! How could you let this happen?' He rubs a hand over his shaved head. 'Jesus . . . where is she?'

Fear morphs into fury and Nadeeka turns on Scott. 'I told you not to let them out of your sight!'

'We *weren't allowed near them*!' Scott glares at her. 'You have no idea . . . it was absolute chaos, people shouting, running around – getting everyone out of a building that was about to be blown to—'

'A building you left them in!' Nadeeka shakes her head. 'So much for protecting us. Who were you with on Wednesday night? Gabriela?'

'A bloke called Alan, actually.'

It's Not What You Think

Nadeeka blinks.

'That was the plan, anyway, but he wouldn't talk.' Scott rubs the side of his face.

'Did you say *Alan*?' Lauren cuts in sharply. 'Alan who?'

'Don't know his last name.' He jerks his head towards Nadeeka. 'I was doing what *she* wanted. Finding out more about this New Dawn. Someone said this Alan bloke was involved, but he was well jumpy. Wouldn't give anything up.'

'But you were out all night,' Nadeeka says.

'It was late when I got back and I didn't want to wake the girls, so I slept in my car.'

'And last night?'

'Someone said New Dawn would be meeting up at a warehouse out of town.' Scott shakes his head. 'The place was deserted. I reckon he just wanted to stop me asking questions.'

Nadeeka saw enough of Scott's lies when they were married to know he's telling the truth now. 'You could have been killed,' she says, quietly, so Nish doesn't hear.

'Yeah, well.' He rubs his face again. 'What they did to Jamie . . . it's not on, is it?'

'Who gave you this information?' Lauren says sharply.

'I didn't get his name.'

'Don't bullshit me. This isn't a game, it's a matter of national security.' Lauren raises an eyebrow. 'Frankly, it's the least you can do after leaking the story to the press.'

Nadeeka suspects it's a punt, but Scott's sudden pallor says she's bang on the money. *Jesus, Scott . . .* She'd have a go at him, but Lauren's got it covered, and Nish is tugging at her hand. She scoops the little girl on to her hip.

'Maya went for a wee,' Nish whispers.

'Have you any idea what that's done to public confidence?' Lauren is saying. 'There are vulnerable people too frightened to call 999 because the media have told them they can't trust the police!'

Nadeeka looks at Nish. 'When did she go?'

'I'm sorry, all right! It wasn't deliberate. I got talking to someone down the pub and it turned out they were from the paper.'

'It was when we were lining up to leave,' Nish says in a small voice. 'Mrs Fairfax did the register and then we started walking, but Maya was desperate so she went to the loo and she said she'd catch me up but she didn't.' Her lip wobbles again. 'Are we in trouble?'

'No!' Nadeeka kisses her hard on the forehead, but her stomach knots in fear. Maya could still be in the building. Before she can stop it, she pictures a bomb going off. A fireball, a cloud of smoke, a pile of rubble. And under it all: Maya. 'No,' she says again, but she can't stop the sob that makes it a wail.

'I told Miss Key,' Nish says. 'She said she'd go back and get her.'

Mrs Fairfax gets out her phone. 'I'll call Miss Key.'

Out of the corner of her eye, Nadeeka sees Lauren start to walk away. Is she going to look for Maya? Mrs Fairfax tuts and takes the phone from her ear, then tries again, but Nadeeka can't stand here waiting for other people to find her daughter. She hitches Nish higher and starts walking back towards the Civic Centre.

Scott catches up with her in three easy strides. 'I'll take her,' he says.

'I'm not leaving her.'

'You don't have to leave her. I'm coming with you.' He swings Nish into the air and on to his shoulders. 'Hold tight, sweetheart.'

Nadeeka starts running.

CHAPTER 64

LAUREN

Lauren doesn't use her radio. Time is of the essence when circulating details of missing children, but it would be ill-advised to share details of an unaccompanied child when the broadcast could be overheard. Instead, she calls control room.

'Nothing on the system, sorry.' The control room operator dashes Lauren's hopes that someone has already taken Maya to a muster point. 'What's she wearing?'

Lauren describes Maya's shimmery costume, breath catching as she jogs in the opposite direction to the few stragglers still leaving the evacuation zone now. 'Can you check with CCTV? See if she left the Civic Centre?'

If Maya isn't lost in the crowds, she's still inside. Both options turn Lauren cold.

Control room calls back as she nears the inner cordon. 'They've picked up the teacher in the Christmas jumper leading a bunch of kids out of the Civic Centre. Maya Prasanna isn't with them.'

'Then she must still be inside.' Lauren ducks under a line of police tape tied across the street.

'Bomb disposal did a sweep – there's no one there.'

'If she didn't come out, she's still there!' It's an effort to keep her voice calm. 'Ask them to look again.'

A pause. 'Yes, ma'am.'

'What's the status with the IEDs?'

'As soon as the premises have been made safe, we'll let everyone know.'

Lauren ends the call. A hundred metres ahead, not far from the entrance of the Civic Centre, she sees DI Stratman. He's wearing a ballistics vest and talking to two firearms officers with rifles slung across their chest. He frowns as she approaches.

'You shouldn't be here.'

'Nadeeka Prasanna's elder daughter is still in there.' *Please let that be true*, she thinks. Maya would have come out of the toilet to find that her classmates and teachers had already left. Would she have tried to make her way to the evacuation point, or stayed in place? The Civic Centre would have perhaps felt less scary than the noisy chaos of the evacuation.

'She can't be,' Stratman says. 'Bomb disposal—'

'Did a sweep, I know.' Lauren shakes her head impatiently. 'But she's in there. Get them to check again.'

'I will.' His eyes flick towards the Civic Centre. 'But right now we have a developing situation—'

'Yes, a missing child,' Lauren says tautly.

Stratman glances at the firearms officer, who takes the cue and peels away. 'Fraser is on the roof,' Stratman says, when they're alone.

Lauren feels winded. She looks up but a concrete parapet hides the top of the building. A helicopter circles overhead.

'Picked up on thermal. We've got snipers across the street.'

'Snipers?' Lauren's voice is unsteady.

'He's taken a hostage, Lauren.'

Black blurs the edges of her vision and for a moment she thinks she might fall. Is this really happening? Can Fraser really be doing this?

It's Not What You Think

'The hostage negotiator is on his way, but Lauren . . .' Stratman hesitates. 'If firearms get a clean shot . . . they *will* take him down.'

'No!' It comes out before Lauren's even thought it, an urgent, visceral appeal that even now roots itself deeper. 'You can't let them do that.'

'What he's done is evil, Lauren.'

'Let me speak to him. I can make him see sense. Resolve this without anyone getting—'

'Absolutely not.' Stratman shakes his head. Starts walking away.

Lauren grabs his arm. 'I know him better than anyone else. And I'm here. The negotiator's, what, twenty minutes away?' She can tell from the flicker in Stratman's eyes that she's right.

'It's against protocol.'

'Fuck protocol!' Lauren holds Stratman's gaze, imploring him to trust her. 'Please,' she says quietly. 'Just let me try.'

CHAPTER 65

NADEEKA

There's a line of police tape across the street. A uniformed officer is speaking to a brown-skinned woman wearing a red coat with a knotted belt. Beneath the woman's turned-up collar, Nadeeka sees a lanyard the same colour as Lauren's.

She runs up to them. 'I'm looking for my daughter. She was at the rehearsal in the Civic Centre. I think she's still in the building.'

Nadeeka recognizes the police officer, but it's a second before she remembers why. 'Everyone's been evacuated,' he tells her. His name's on his jacket pocket. *PC Dan Harrington.* The guy who wanted to give her a ticket for running a red light. Back when Nadeeka had thought the worst thing that could possibly happen to her was finding Jamie with another woman. It feels like a lifetime ago.

'Please . . . I think she's still there.' Nadeeka turns to the woman. 'I'm so scared. If a bomb goes off and Maya's—'

'The building's been made safe.' The woman pulls on her lanyard and dangles a plastic ID card in front of her. 'I'm Bahnaz.

It's Not What You Think

I work with DCI Caldwell. You're Nadeeka, right?' She lifts the police tape. 'I'll take you to Lauren. If Maya's in the building, we'll find her.' Bahnaz glances at Scott, Nish still riding high on his shoulders. 'Are you Dad?'

Scott nods.

'Okay to wait here?'

Nadeeka gives Nish what she hopes is a reassuring smile. 'I won't be long.' She accompanies Bahnaz down the high street, Nadeeka slightly ahead, trying to hasten the detective's measured strides.

As they approach the Civic Centre, the atmosphere shifts. There's a quiet hum of tension, as if the very air knows something is wrong. There are hi-vis jackets everywhere – police, fire, ambulance – and positioned with what feels like intent. A uniformed officer with red epaulettes speaks into a radio, his eyes trained on the upper levels of the building.

Nadeeka slows. 'What's happening? I thought you said it was over.' Her pulse races as she thinks of Maya. *Why haven't they found her yet?*

'Bomb disposal have neutralized a number of devices found on the ground floor,' Bahnaz says. 'They've confirmed the building is safe to enter.' But her gaze flicks up to the roofline, stark against the sky, and Nadeeka strains to see what's happening up there.

'Then what—'

'They're about to arrest someone. It's all going to be okay.' Bahnaz's tone is the one Nadeeka uses when she's reassuring her girls.

'Do you have children?' she asks Bahnaz.

'Two. Babies, really.' She flashes Nadeeka a small smile. Mother to mother. 'It'll be quieter at the back,' she says, steering them around the side of the building.

There are fewer police officers here, and Nadeeka feels the pressure in her chest ease a little. The building is safe. The police are about to arrest someone – the person who planted the explosives? Any minute now, Maya will be found safe and well.

'Lauren should be around here somewhere,' Bahnaz says.

A memory pierces Nadeeka's thoughts: Maya fizzing with excitement about the nativity, her words tumbling over each other as she told Nadeeka and Jamie about her starring role. 'I get to hide!' Maya's eyes had shone. 'There's a secret door at the back of the stage and when it's my line I appear like *magic*!'

'I think my daughter's hiding,' Nadeeka tells Bahnaz, with a sudden clarity that cuts through her fear. She explains about the secret door. 'I haven't seen it, but Maya said it was at the back of the stage.'

'I'll go and look now.' Bahnaz's gaze falls on a community support officer waiting by a police car. 'If you can stay with—'

'I'm coming with you. I'm coming to find my daughter.' Nadeeka repeats it because she will not be moved on this; will not wait outside while Maya is cowering inside, terrified of what's happening around her.

'It's not safe.'

'You said it was. You said they'd made it safe,' Nadeeka insists. There's a long pause. 'She might not come out if it's someone she doesn't know,' she adds quietly. 'She'll be scared. She'll needs to hear a voice she trusts.'

Their eyes lock. Understanding passes between them.

Bahnaz gives a single, tight nod. 'Okay,' she says. 'Come on, then. But stay close, and don't touch anything.'

And, together, they slip inside.

CHAPTER 66

LAUREN

Lauren steps on to the roof. Wind whips her hair into her mouth and stings her eyes, and her heart punches against her ribcage. Below, tiny people and tiny cars pepper the streets. On the far side of the flat grey roof, Fraser stands on the parapet, his back to an extractor vent. His right arm is tight around a sobbing figure, her tearstained face framed by two plaits.

'Hi, Fraser.' Lauren takes a few steps towards him. Stops. She doesn't know if he's armed. Apart from her rapid heart rate she feels strangely calm, as though her whole life has been building up to this one moment.

Fraser doesn't look round. 'If they shoot me,' he says, 'she'll fall.' A terrified wail comes from the petite figure locked to his side.

'It's okay.' Lauren takes another few steps forwards. 'You're going to be okay.'

'Tell them I want fifteen minutes and a clean route out.' He seems unmoved by the fact that it's Lauren talking to him. The woman he said he loved. The woman he wanted to marry.

'You know I can't do that, Fraser.' She uses his name again, hoping to break through this eerily calm veneer, but he still doesn't look at her.

'If they put down their weapons and give me a clean route out, I won't touch her. Otherwise . . .' He loosens his arm and pushes the girl forward so she's teetering on the edge, and she screams so loud Lauren cries out too, but then Fraser regrips. Gives a short laugh. 'It'll make a hell of a mess,' he says.

The scream becomes a wail. The girl twists her head to look at Lauren. 'Please! Just do what he says!'

She's in her early twenties. Denim dungarees and an Elmwood Primary School lanyard covered with brightly coloured pin badges.

'Are you Miss Key?' Lauren says.

'Y-yes.' She chokes back another sob.

'I need you to just sit tight for a while longer, okay? Just while I talk to Fraser.'

'I don't want to die!'

'You're not going to die.' Lauren walks towards the parapet until she's level with Fraser and Miss Key. The drop to the ground makes her dizzy, and she looks up at the other roofs instead. She can't see the snipers but she knows they're there, their rifles trained on Fraser. She shivers. No sudden movements. She can't afford to make a mistake.

Fraser's jaw is tense, a muscle jumping in his neck. Beside him, Miss Key moans softly, her eyes squeezed shut. The toes of her lime-green sneakers protrude from the parapet like miniature diving boards, twenty metres above the pavement.

'Let her go,' Lauren says softly.

'I can't.'

There's something in his voice – desperation? Fear? Lauren seizes it.

'It must feel like there's no way out. Like you're trapped.' She waits, but he doesn't respond. 'But there's always a way out. You don't have to do this, Fraser. Let Miss Key go, and you and I can walk out together.' She swallows. 'We'll sort it out together.'

It's Not What You Think

Slowly, Fraser turns his head and looks at her, as if he's seeing her for the first time. 'Together,' he says, so quietly it's almost taken by the wind.

'Together,' Lauren repeats. And then she can't say anything at all. She touches the tip of her thumb to the inside of her ring finger, spinning the metal band until she feels the spike of the diamonds against her nail. Grief surges inside her. She swallows hard. Stratman was right – she shouldn't be here.

'We're good together,' Fraser says. 'You and me.'

She nods. Takes another few steps. She's only three or four metres away now. She can make out a badge on Miss Key's dungarees. *Librarians rock.* 'I don't want them to shoot you,' she says in a low voice. She thinks of the explosives taped to the chairs; of the booby-trapped stage.

'If they don't shoot me, they'll lock me up.'

'Maybe, maybe not. You're having some kind of mental health crisis, Fraser. This New Dawn stuff . . . it's not you.'

'It *is* me. This country's being destroyed; we need drastic action to—'

'You've been sucked in. Radicalized.' Lauren takes another step.

'New Dawn is the future.'

'We'll tell the courts you had a breakdown. You never meant to hurt anyone.'

The *whomp whomp whomp* of the helicopter grows louder and Fraser looks up sharply, tightening his grip on Miss Key and making her cry out. Lauren silently curses.

'Let her go,' she says again. 'Please, Fraser. I know you're better than this.'

When he looks at her again, his eyes are shining, although whether it's from tears or the wind, she can't be sure. She steps forward again, and, as she does, Fraser's grip loosens. Slowly, as though she's befriending a wild horse, Lauren reaches towards Miss Key.

It happens in a heartbeat.

Miss Key, grappling for Lauren's hand in desperation; Fraser panicking and snatching her tighter. Lime-green sneakers scuffing at the concrete, and debris falling from the parapet and freewheeling into the sky. Faint screams from the street below. They teeter there, in a moment that is at once slow-motion and terrifyingly brief, their weight shifting, the world tipping.

Then Lauren grabs them.

They fall in a clumsy, breathless heap away from the parapet. Lauren has a fistful of dungaree and a hand on Fraser's belt, and a fat lip slammed on the asphalt roof. Stars flit across her vision.

But the hostage is safe. They are all safe.

Miss Key struggles to her feet and runs. Stratman will be there to catch her at the top of the stairs, Lauren knows, and she pays no more heed to her because now it's just the two of them. Lauren and Fraser, the way it's always been. The way she thought it always would be.

'I never wanted to hurt you,' he says. 'I love you. I'll always love you.'

There's a beat as their eyes lock. Then, with a sharp *click*, Lauren snaps a handcuff over Fraser's wrist. His eyes fly open in disbelief, and before he can gather his senses she uses the metal cuff as a lever, putting him in a wrist lock that has him gritting his teeth in pain. The door to the roof crashes open, boots racing across the roof towards her.

'Suicide by cop,' Lauren says coldly. 'That's what they call it, isn't it?' She twists the cuff and Fraser grimaces. 'New Dawn would have loved that, wouldn't they? You'd have died a hero. A martyr for the cause.' She leans close enough to hiss in his ear. 'I didn't want them to shoot you, because the people you've hurt deserve their day in court. And *you* deserve to go down for a very, very long time.'

Lauren feels a hand on her shoulder. It's Stratman, with what seems like an army of uniformed officers. She gets to her feet and lets them take over, and he helps her up as though she'd been the one held hostage. They walk to the fire escape together, Stratman just close enough to stop her legs from buckling under her.

Lauren doesn't look back.

CHAPTER 67

NADEEKA

The interior of the Civic Centre is as utilitarian as its outside, with stark block walls and harshly lit corridors. In the main auditorium, purple acoustic panels hang on either side of the room and from the ceiling.

Nadeeka follows Bahnaz through the double doors. The chairs, once in neat rows either side of the wide aisle, are scattered haphazardly, some upside down or on their sides. Tied to the backs of several are red tags.

Bahnaz follows her gaze. 'The tags show where the bomb disposal team found devices and disabled them.'

Nadeeka's breath catches. Her children had been in this building. Their father would have been in the audience. They could all have died in the blast, along with dozens of other innocent people.

'Maya!' Nadeeka's voice bounces around the empty hall. 'It's me. Mum. It's safe now – you can come out.'

Silence.

She runs up the steps at the front of the stage. 'Maya!' There are no curtains, only a vast proscenium arch, and she runs her hands over the black paintwork, searching for a door. If only Maya had said where her hiding place was . . .

Fear builds in the pit of Nadeeka's stomach. What if she's wrong? What if Maya isn't hiding, if she got lost in the crowds? What if she's been taken?

'Maya!' She's shouting louder now. She knows she should keep her voice calm – that Maya might not come out if she thinks her mum's cross – but panic is squeezing her throat, forcing out Maya's name in hard, frightened cries. 'If you're hiding, it's time to come out.' She crouches at the back of the stage and runs her fingers along the edges of the wall, the joins between panels, but nothing moves, nothing gives.

'Maya!' Louder again, more panicked. 'It's safe now!'

She won't come out. She'll think it's a trap.

Jamie's voice is so clear it's as though he's in the room. Nadeeka sits back on her heels, suddenly winded. She thinks about him playing hide-and-seek with the girls; pictures Maya's and Nish's faces, flushed with excitement. He was so great with them. Of all the things she had loved about Jamie, she'd loved that the most.

Maya must have been so scared when she came out of the bathroom to find everyone gone. Separated from her sister and her classmates, the building echoing with shouting and heavy boots. If she's still hiding, it's because she's frightened. She won't come out until she can trust she'll be safe. More than anyone, Nadeeka knows how fragile trust is.

It's not a trap, Maya! Nadeeka had shouted, that last time they'd played hide-and-seek, and Jamie had laughed – *now she'll definitely think it's a trap* – and instead he had called out something absurd . . . what had it been?

Must be a weird Golding thing.

Well, now it's a weird Prasanna thing.

Nadeeka gets to her feet. She stands in the middle of the stage

It's Not What You Think

and – feeling at once desperate and ridiculous – she calls out to Maya. 'Olly olly oxen free!'

Nothing.

What had Nadeeka been thinking? Of course Maya wouldn't—

But then . . . a faint *click*.

A sliver of light.

And a panel at the side of the stage pops open.

EIGHTEEN MONTHS LATER

CHAPTER 68

LAUREN

The air in the courtroom is stale and claustrophobic. The public gallery has a brass guard rail tarnished from years of touch, and rows of flip-down seats reminiscent of an old-fashioned cinema. But there is nothing entertaining about today's performance.

Lauren's eyes never leave the dock. It is the first time she has seen Fraser in eighteen months. During the trial, she had kept her eyes trained on the jury as she gave evidence, knowing that if she so much as glanced at Fraser she would have unravelled.

He is almost unrecognizable. If she saw him in the street, she would think he reminded her of someone she once knew. Instinctively she would flash him a smile, then realize he was a stranger to her. Fraser's head is shaved, and he has gained so much muscle the top button of his shirt won't fasten. Lauren realizes with a lurch that he is wearing the pale pink tie she chose for him.

Ten days after Fraser's arrest, Lauren had packed up his

things and taken them to his parents' house. His mother had been quiet and red-eyed, his father angry and incredulous. Both had wanted answers Lauren couldn't – or wouldn't – give them.

'I keep asking if it was my fault,' Fraser's mother had said, and she had so desperately wanted reassurance that Lauren had given her a tight hug and said no, it wasn't her fault. It was no one's fault but Fraser's.

The defence had contested that, of course. They had cited the traumatic scenes Fraser had witnessed in Afghanistan; the pressures of years on a murder squad. They had talked of a broken society, of governmental instability and toxic influences to be found on the internet.

He had been found guilty.

There had never been any question – the evidence had been overwhelming – but still there had been a sudden rush of air, as though everyone in the courtroom had been holding their breath. Fraser's mother had cried, and, when Lauren had looked across, she'd seen that his dad's cheeks were wet too. She had wondered if he felt any of the guilt his wife did, misplaced or not.

They are not here for today's sentencing. Nadeeka has stayed away too, but there are several other parents here who want the closure of seeing justice served on the man who would have let their children die. It has been a long and complex investigation, resulting not only in Fraser's conviction, but in charges for Carrie Finder, Alan Ellis and Chris Morley for Jamie Golding's murder, with associated charges brought against Mike Bishop, Damian and Peter Fletcher, and twelve other members of New Dawn proven to have been actively involved in criminal activity. The investigation into other members of the organization continues.

The clerk calls out – 'Will the defendant please rise?' – and Fraser gets to his feet.

Beside Lauren, Jules Stratman shifts his foot slightly so it's touching hers, a silent acknowledgement that this must be hard for her. That he's there if she needs him. They've been spending time together outside of work. Just the occasional coffee, a comedy show when Jules won a pair of tickets. There is, Lauren knows, something there, but it will be a while before she feels able to let someone into her life again.

'I have read the pre-sentence report,' the judge is saying, 'and considered the reports prepared by your psychiatric team. I take their findings into account in my sentencing, just as I take into account the impact statements provided by the many victims in this far-reaching case.'

Fraser's expression doesn't change. His lips are a thin line, his face angular and hard as he stares at the judge.

'You were a police officer sworn to protect the public, yet you chose instead to betray the very institution you served, pursuing the ideology of what has since become a proscribed organization in the United Kingdom. It is now a criminal offence to support or be affiliated with New Dawn.' The judge pauses. 'Given the nature of your crimes, I find no grounds for leniency. You are hereby sentenced to life imprisonment, with a minimum term of thirty-five years before parole may be considered.'

Lauren closes her eyes as some of the tension she has held for the last eighteen months leaves her body. She knows better than most that banning a movement doesn't make it disappear. But she has confidence in her colleagues, and in society as a whole. Together they can push back against the inevitable rise of the far right. There are enough good apples, she thinks.

No, Lauren isn't scared of New Dawn. But she is scared of Fraser. She sees him in her nightmares; catches sight of him in shopping malls and supermarket aisles. She hears his tread on the stairs when she's lying in bed, and has to breathe her way back down to sanity.

When she opens her eyes again he's looking up at the gallery, searching for someone. For her.

It's Not What You Think

He locks eyes with her and a tingling runs across the back of her neck. She wants to brush it away, but she can't move, *won't* move; won't give him the satisfaction of seeing he's rattled her. His brows draw together a fraction.

'Take him down,' the judge says.

Lauren looks away as two guards escort Fraser out of the courtroom.

Out of her life.

CHAPTER 69

NADEEKA

It is the sort of sunny day that makes people smile at strangers in the street, Nadeeka thinks, as she does just that. The girls skip ahead of her, although Maya looks back every few minutes – a habit she's acquired since that day in the Civic Centre. She is eating an ice-cream and arguing with Nish – who has long since finished her own – about whether strawberry Cornetto is superior to chocolate.

They're heading to the hill above the reservoir where Nadeeka and Jamie had their second date. He had already been there when she'd arrived, with a tartan rug spread across the grass, and a bottle of wine in an ice bucket. *Too much?* he'd said anxiously. *Just perfect*, she'd thought, even when they'd discovered he'd forgotten to bring glasses, and they'd had to take turns swigging from the bottle, like furtive teenagers with vodka swiped from their parents' drinks cabinet.

After Jamie's funeral, Nadeeka had thought long and hard about what to do with his ashes. She had offered them to Jamie's parents, Frank and Penny, who had insisted it was up to Nadeeka where they were scattered.

'He loved you, darling girl,' Penny had said. 'You should do whatever brings you the most peace.'

For a long time, the ashes had stayed in their plastic box on the kitchen windowsill, exactly where Nadeeka had propped her iPad before Jamie had moved in, so they could have long video calls while Nadeeka cooked tea or made packed lunches.

Then Nadeeka had taken the girls to Blackpool, in an off-kilter facsimile of the weekend they had spent there with Jamie, and just as they were leaving the house she had grabbed the plastic box. Later, she had decanted a teaspoon of ashes into a tissue and taken it down to the end of the seafront. As the girls screamed down the helter-skelter, Nadeeka had let the sea take this tiny piece of Jamie.

Since then, she has taken pieces of Jamie everywhere. To places they went together, and places they planned to go. To parks and pub gardens and to the cricket field where he took his first wicket. Penny and Frank have buried a spoonful with their roses, and Nish was most upset when Nadeeka wouldn't let her take a jar into school for show and tell.

'There they are!' Maya says now, waving. They've reached the top of the hill, and Penny and Frank are waiting. The girls give them both hugs and then throw themselves down on the ground, declaring themselves exhausted.

'Mum made us walk all the way!' Nish says.

Maya and Nish had met Frank and Penny at Jamie's funeral, and again a fortnight later, when Penny had called to say they were in the area and would it be okay to pop in for a coffee? She had been vague about her reasons for being nearby, and Nadeeka had suspected there had been none, but it had been so lovely to talk about Jamie with someone who missed him as much as she did. She and Penny had fallen into the habit of messaging, and occasionally videoing, the girls often sticking their heads into shot to say hello. *It's like having a spare granny*, Maya had said one time, and the name had stuck. Spare Granny and Grandad had become a regular fixture in the Prasanna family's life, going some way to ease the grief Nadeeka carried deep inside her.

They don't make speeches. They did, in the beginning, when their pain had been raw and close to the surface. But over the past eighteen months life has grown around them, and what once felt impossible to survive is already more bearable for them all.

Nadeeka takes a pinch of Jamie's ashes. She catches Penny's eye, and they smile, then Nadeeka opens her fingers and lets the breeze take him. She thinks of the restrictions now placed around New Dawn, and how Jamie's actions have resulted in so many convictions. But mostly she thinks of swigging wine from the bottle; of lying on their backs on the tartan rug with her fingers tangled with Jamie's.

The breeze drops, and, for a moment, everything is still. The girls are arguing again – this time about which of them is better at cartwheels – and Penny is rummaging in her bag for snacks.

Nadeeka is lucky, in so many ways. She has her girls, and they have their dad; and although Nadeeka despairs at Scott's continuing steam of girlfriends, he is more involved in Maya and Nish's life now than ever before. There's the ever-dependable Kath, and now Spare Grandparents too, and it might not look like a conventional family, but it works for them.

Nadeeka brushes her hands on her jeans and sits on the grass. She tips her head up to the sun and closes her eyes, and, for the first time in a long while, she feels hopeful for what's ahead.

CHAPTER 70

FRASER

The floor of Fraser's cell is streaked with dirt and grease. He lowers himself until his face grazes the concrete, then he pushes himself back up. He feels the burn across his triceps.

Fifty-four. Fifty-five. Fifty-six.

Slow. Tight. Perfectly controlled.

Fraser works out every day, and the twenty kilos he has gained since being sent down has thickened his neck and broadened his chest. Ex-coppers can be sitting targets in prison, but no one seeks out Fraser. Not unless they're looking for trouble.

Sixty. Sixty-one.

Down the corridor, someone hammers at a cell door, setting off a series of shouts: *Shut the fuck up, you cunt!* and *Who are you calling a cunt?* Elsewhere in the block, televisions and radios compete for attention.

Fraser's pace doesn't alter. The cell is too small to pace and too noisy to think, but the press-ups carve out a kind of silence. A bead of sweat falls from his brow to the filthy floor. Prison can break you, but it can build you, too, and Fraser is using his time wisely. When he's not in the gym, or working out in his cell, he's reading. Learning about the powers of persuasion, about hiding in plain sight. The government can pass laws on meetings – on protests, on action – but no one can police his thoughts.

They think they've broken New Dawn.

Seventy-six. Seventy-seven.

They've only made it stronger.

Made *him* stronger.

Fraser keeps talking. Word-of-mouth. Keeps drip, drip, dripping New Dawn's messages throughout the nick and beyond to the outside world. The prison is full of young, angry men disillusioned with authority, with society. Fraser takes them under his wing and educates them. He helps them see how the housing system favours foreigners over its own; how the courts go hard on British-born offenders and let immigrants go free. He shows them how much money the government sends abroad each year, while the NHS leaves old folk dying in hospital corridors.

Eighty-one. Eighty-two.

The establishment can put in whatever laws it wants; it can't legislate what a man thinks. Not when he's already decided. Not when he already *knows*.

Fraser's arms are trembling now, his chest slick with sweat.

Ninety-eight. Ninety-nine. One hundred.

Done.

The metal bunk creaks as Fraser sits on the edge and wipes his face with a towel. One of the young men Fraser has recruited gets out today. Fraser has furnished him with New Dawn contacts who will help him get back on his feet, cementing the lad's loyalty to the cause. Brick by brick, they are rebuilding. Underground, this time.

A slow, satisfied smile forms on Fraser's lips. No one can stop the sun rising, no matter how hard they try.

The New Dawn is coming.

And, when it does, Fraser and his comrades will step back into the light.

ACKNOWLEDGEMENTS

If you're the sort of person who reads the acknowledgements first, you should probably look away now. I'm not able to talk publicly about the inspiration for *It's Not What You Think* for fear of ruining the book for those who haven't yet read it, but these pages do contain spoilers.

Each of my nine published novels has begun in a different way. Sometimes the setting comes first (as it did in the case of *Hostage*, a locked-room thriller set on a long-haul flight), and sometimes it's a concept (my second novel, *I See You*, is about the dangers of following a predictable commuting routine). Sometimes it's a character; if you've read my *DC Ffion Morgan* series, you'll understand why she was so impossible to ignore.

The books that excite me the most start with a twist. That was the case for *I Let You Go*, my debut and my best-selling book to date. I receive so many messages from readers who love that book, and I have long wished I could write something that would deliver a jaw-dropping moment on a similar scale. But twists are funny beasts. The best ones, in my opinion, arrive naturally and are often very simple: a situation you thought was one thing is in fact another.

When I was a detective, the time I felt most energized was the very beginning of an investigation. Time is of the essence and there is often an overwhelming amount of evidence to gather: forensics to secure, CCTV footage to seize, witnesses to trace. The 'golden hour' is critical. What would happen, I wondered, if all that evidence had already been gathered . . . and destroyed? If the 'golden hour' had been stolen by the very people who committed the crime?

This twist felt too audacious to pull off, and I sat with it for a long time. Could I really do that to a reader? I decided I could. A story began to emerge, and with it, more twists, and before I knew it, I was writing *It's Not What You Think*. Never has a book filled me with more glee, and if you enjoyed reading it half as much as I enjoyed writing it, we will both be very happy.

There are some heavy and potentially triggering themes in this book, and I want to take a moment to acknowledge those here. In New Dawn, I have created a fictional far-right organization, but it is rooted in many similar groups which exist in the UK and further afield. I hope it goes without saying that New Dawn's views are not my own, but for the avoidance of doubt, let me nail my colours to the mast. I believe in a fair, tolerant and inclusive society and I will challenge anything seeking to undermine that.

Corruption exists in any organization in which individuals have a degree of power, and the police service is sadly no exception. But I was a police officer for over a decade, working with some of the most dedicated, honest and compassionate people I have ever met, and I firmly believe there are many more good apples than bad ones. *It's Not What You Think* takes society's fears to extreme levels, and is in no way a reflection of my experiences in the police.

On that note, I could not have written this book without the expertise of four incredible former colleagues. Katy Barrow-Grint, Kay Hannam, Nikki Smith and Tina Wallace have exceptionally demanding jobs, yet still found time to answer all my questions and come up with plausible ways around tricky plot problems. Any procedural errors are mine and generally made for good reasons.

Having access to such an elite 'murder squad' meant I had very little research help from other quarters, but I would like to acknowledge the gentleman I called to ask if body bags could be bought in single units, and do they have serial numbers or are they untraceable? Thank you for not calling the police.

Thank you to my agent, Sheila Crowley, and to Helena Maybery, Camilla Young, Krystyna Kujawinska, Tanja Goossens, and the whole Curtis Brown team for steering my career with such vision and experience.

Thank you to my new publishers, HarperFiction, for your enthusiasm and ambition for this book. Thank you to my editors, Frankie Gray and Belinda Toor; to Vicky Joss and Adam Humphrey in marketing; to Elizabeth Dawson and Felicity Denham in publicity; to Alexandra Sequeira, Alice Brown, and to everyone else who played a part in helping *It's Not What You Think* reach readers.

Which brings me to the most important thank you of all. You. Whether you are new to my work, or have followed me from the beginning, thank you for reading. There are so many demands on our time nowadays, and I never take for granted the decision to commit to reading or listening to a novel. If you enjoyed it, please leave a review or tell someone – tell lots of people! – and I'd love to hear too. You can find me on social media at @ClareMackWrites or join my mailing list via my website, claremackintosh.com.